THE LIGHT CONQUERING

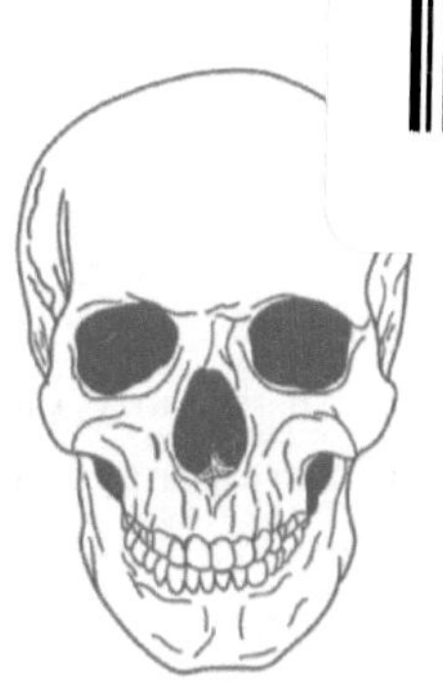

The Death Hunting
Book Three

By Emma Steinbrecher

The Light Conquering
Copyright © 2023 by Emma Steinbrecher

All Rights Reserved.

No part of this book may be reproduced, copied, resold, or distributed in any form, or by any electronic or mechanical means, without permission in writing from the author, except for brief quotations within a review.

This book is a work of fiction.
Names, characters, businesses, organizations, places, events, and incidents are either the product of the author's imagination or used in a fictitious manner. Any resemblance to actual persons, living or dead is entirely coincidental.

ISBN: 979-8-9863115-4-8
Editor: Kenna Karlson
Interior Graphics: Erin Esther (Instagram @erin.esther)
Map Artist: sekcer
Cover Artist: Mousam Banerjee

For Kenna
Because you believed in me and Morana when we didn't
believe in ourselves.

Dear reader,

It is my desire to ensure that everyone who picks up this book feels comfortable in doing so. Because of this, I have provided a list of trigger warnings below.

Trauma
Explicit Sexual Scenes
Death
Graphic Violence
Torture
Alcoholism
Physical Abuse
SA
Negative self-thoughts
Betrayal

As you know, I try to provide a complete list of trigger warnings. If you feel that something is missing, feel free to reach out. It is also helpful if you add trigger warnings in any review you may write.

The Wasteland
Vulcan
Ohriid
Adhara
Ascella
Zora
Named
The Court of Shadow
The Court of Light
Tiranna
Nashira
Debnar
Velas
N
The Fae Realm

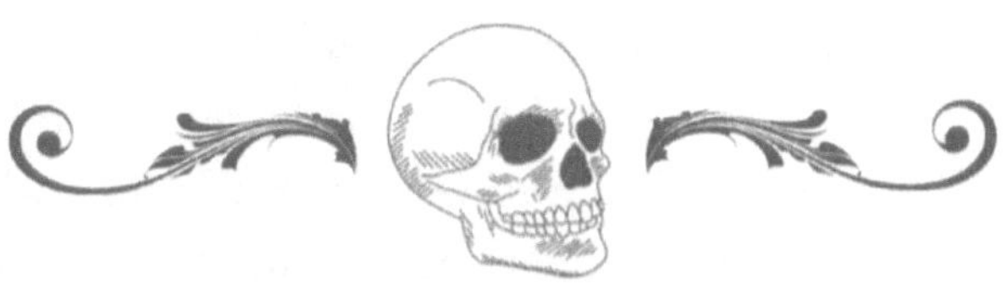

Death

Monsters thrived in the darkness.

But as Death stared at the blood-coated sink, he cloaked himself in mist and magic, hoping his power could keep the darkness from taking him under. Raising a rag to his bare shoulder, he listened to the dripping faucet—keeping time with his count.

One. Two. Three.

He wasn't used to this kind of pain and could usually stitch himself back together easily in the wake of an injury. This wasn't a typical injury, though. While his magic soothed his mind, it couldn't stop the bite of the wound she left.

Preparing himself for the next excruciating bout of pain, he counted again.

One. Two. Three.

The wound burned like acid when he pressed the herb-soaked cloth to his flesh, desperate for some sort of reprieve. That now familiar pain lashed through his shoulder where she had sunk her dagger into his body.

Morana had aimed for his heart, and he wasn't entirely sure she had missed her mark.

He was healing as a mortal, and it infuriated him.

If she believed him to be a monster, then why the hell couldn't he act like one, and why the hell was he still worried about her?

Shadows skittered down his tattooed arms, pain giving way to ripples of pleasure. Death gathered the darkness around the flaming gash and poured his magic into the wound. He gritted his teeth as inky threads wove in and out, working to stitch his shoulder back together.

His shadows stuttered.

No matter how hard he tried to heal himself, they always shrunk back, unable to complete the task.

What the fuck did she do to me?

His power was useless in the wake of whatever she'd done. He had let her in—fully—something he hadn't done since watching his parents die. Consumed by death and darkness, he'd settled into this life until he stood in a quiet room, watching yet another man as he passed away. It would have been like any other passing for him, insignificant and part of his role, but that time, it was more than that. He had taken Morana to the human realm—an attempt to show her the side of himself she longed to see. Morana had been there and grabbed his hand, weaving her magic with his and creating stars in his endless night.

But the stars had a habit of dying.

Just like everything else.

That memory seemed so long ago, and in a way, it was. He hardly remembered the things she'd said—the things that had challenged his experience with death—with himself and who he was destined to be. Still, the memory lingered, finding its way to the forefront of his mind as he held the rag to his wound.

"It's peaceful," Morana breathed, tears still lining her eyes. It was in those tears, in the lingering feeling swirling through his chest, that he remembered the truth—one she seemed to know well.

"Death can be."

"I've seen that," she expressed, and he found himself fighting the urge to pry into her memories. Maybe she could show him what she meant, because this was the first time it had felt like this for him.

"Do you do this often?" she asked, and Matthias stifled his chuckle—his usual attempt to hide the truth. "Do you come to the human realm to give peace to those fading from this world?"

He winced. "Not often enough." Death cleared his throat, working through the swirling emotions. "What kind of god would I be, though, if I could bring comfort, to meet people in their darkest hours and wrap them in something that could heal—if only briefly—and never used that ability?"

He didn't know if she could see through his words or feel the insecurity lying there beneath the surface. What kind of god did she believe him to be? Certainly nothing good.

Death was one with the darkness—nothing more.

Morana looked at him, and in that moment, he felt as if she could see—as if she knew.

He wanted to care more than he did.

"You are good, Matthias." Her hand found his, her thumb brushing over the tattoos inked there before she laced their fingers together. "A good king, a good god, and a beautiful mystery."

And for that moment, Matthias remembered the stars hanging above them—reminded that in even the darkest night, a different kind of light could still exist.

Death pressed the rag against his flesh harder, welcoming the sting. The physical pain wasn't nearly as difficult to tolerate, and it surely helped him forget all else. When he looked in the mirror, his dark gaze stared back until he caught sight of a shadow moving behind him.

"She's gone?"

Willow leaned against the doorframe with her mouth curved downward. Her blue eyes hardened like ice as she stared at Death through the mirror. The woman said nothing more, but the heavy silence that hung between them told her everything she needed to know.

"She's gone." His tone was jagged and rough—cracked and broken like the heart bleeding inside of him.

"Well." The woman tapped a pale finger on her bicep, hair wild and irritation radiating off her.

She was mad at Death—everyone was.

The echoing silence broke with another drip of the faucet—as if the palace was waiting for Matthias to glean what would come next.

One. Two. Three.

Matthias counted the drips like it would steady him, but as he stared at the woman waiting in the doorway, all he could feel was the burning rag on his flesh. The fae woman was wiser than Death himself, and so he didn't know what she had come to say.

"Matthias." Willow had no pity. "Go get her."

He blinked, his brow creasing and his heart pounding a faster rhythm. "In The Wastelands?" he asked.

Willow stepped forward, her dress torn at the hem and dirt streaked across her face. Whatever battle she had fought in the ballroom, she had won. But it wasn't without cost.

Raidan had attacked them, lied to Morana, and convinced her to leave. He'd lost so many from his court— the ballroom all but leveled.

He would give almost anything to watch the major god suffer.

Matthias turned around to meet Willow's icy blue eyes as they cut into him, her wrinkles were highlighted beneath the dim light. It was a motherly warning, and Death would expect nothing less from the woman before him.

"What do you think Raidan wants right now? What did *you* want from Inara?" Willow cocked an eyebrow, her annoyance reaching its peak. "You keep hiding behind shadows and a title, but I know you care for her more than you're letting on, Matthias. And you cannot let Raidan get your blood book." Her eyes flicked to the rag, now bloodied and damp. "Your magic is useless in the wake of whatever she is to you. Don't leave her with a monster. Go get her."

His shoulders tensed, lip peeling back. "And do what, exactly?" Morana wouldn't believe him because he was a monster, too. "Let her kill me?"

He winced, cursing himself for the weakness.

Willow stepped forward, jabbing a finger into his chest—too close to the wound. "Show her the truth."

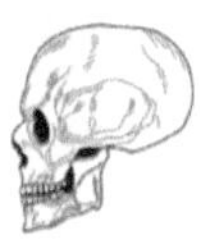

"What did he tell her?"

Matthias had Conan pinned against a wall in the palace of Ascella with shadows his twisting menacingly around them.

Death had gone to the library in Nashira, noting that Jameson, the keeper of his parents' tomb and his blood book had retreated from the ballroom rather rapidly.

After threatening him, ensuring that the fae man was still bound to the library, and telling him to let any visit from Death's fiancée go uninterrupted, Matthias had pried onto the fae's mind.

Jameson had watched the Lord of Ohriid leave the ball. Conan had remained hidden among the crowd and retreated when the attack began. The light fae had followed

Morana, and now that Matthias was in the lord's mind, he knew Conan had seen Raidan speaking to her.

And then the lord fled.

Conan smiled, his breaths coming out in sharp pants, fear shining in his honey-colored eyes. Matthias longed to wipe the smile off his fucking face.

"You're in my mind, Matthias. You know just as much as I do. Or is there something you cannot see?"

Matthias slammed his forearm into the fae's chest, his shadows wrapping around Conan's throat and threatening to cut off the very air he breathed. The fucking fae's mind was like a steel trap. He was *choosing* what Matthias saw.

"You showed up in my court." Matthias's face lingered inches from Conan's, Death's lips peeling back in a snarl. "When you showed up, you called her the Queen of Darkness and asked for an alliance. Don't think I've forgotten." Matthias's head tilted to the side as Conan's smile fell.

Finally.

Matthias pressed on. "How bold of you to ask for an alliance with Death when you sneak around and keep secrets. Probably feeding them to Inara. I should tell her of your betrayal."

Conan gasped for breath, and Matthias eased up slightly—anxious to hear the Court of Light's excuses.

"I can get Sarnai into The Wastelands unseen." Conan lifted his head, the skin of his neck stretched taut over his veins. "She can check on her—make sure she's safe." Matthias blinked. "And I do still want an alliance."

Growling, Death's shadows swelled and whispered dark promises. He didn't understand Conan's offer, especially with part of his mind blocked off—but if he could get into The Wastelands? "Why Sarnai? Why not me?"

Something sparked in the fae lord's gaze. "You think she will want to see you?"

Matthias winced, shoving Conan against the wall to hide his weakness. He grunted, releasing his hold on the lord's body and mind.

The fae was stronger than he looked—blocking Death from the corners of his thoughts and memories. There were only two ways to handle someone like that—kill him or take what he offered. An alliance.

Matthias's heart strained in his chest as he considered his options.

Go get her, Willow had said, and she was right. He still cared for her despite the throbbing wound beneath his clothes. But Conan was right, too. Would Morana want to see him? What lies had Raidan fed her?

If the lord would have fucking stayed to watch and let Death into his mind, then Matthias might have some idea of the lies. Sarnai's help would give him another chance. He would know exactly what Raidan had made her believe—what the major god was up to and possibly what Inara was up to as well.

If Sarnai played nice, he might even see her through the goddess's memories.

"You can get Sarnai into The Wastelands?" Death asked.

Conan gave a half-smile before placing his hands on his knees as he caught his breath. His voice was still raspy from the lack of air.

"I can get you a lot of things, God of Death."

Matthias scanned him, hating the smugness of Conan's expression almost as much as he hated his own weakness.

"Fine," Matthias finally said. "Sarnai will find you in Ohrrid."

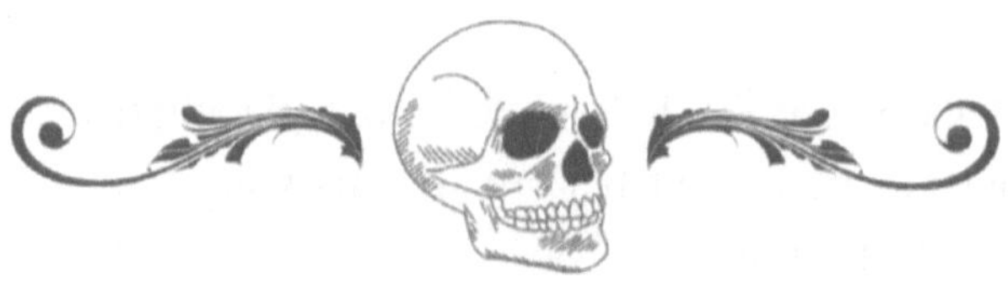

One

The slick sounds of scales sliding across the stone floors of Raidan's dungeon spiked fear in Morana's blood. Fire ignited in her muscles as she pushed forward. Her constant over-exertion over the past weeks made the bitterness rise in her throat—the reminder of who now owned her and the monsters he continued to send her way.

Morana drew on whatever power she could touch as sweat dripped down her spine, drenching her black shirt and staining her soul. Monsters surrounded her in the Court of Shadows, and they continued to lurk in the dark dungeons of Raidan's temple. Morana ground her teeth together. Maybe she was becoming a monster herself.

The way she longed to run her dagger across Raidan's throat for this.

Her mind spun with thoughts of hate and exhaustion when a crack sounded in one of the dungeon cells. At the sound, her fear returned, and she was reminded of the beast prowling through this gods forsaken dungeon in Raidan's palace. It was the same dungeon where the major god had tortured Matthias.

But she couldn't think of Death.

Not if she could help it.

Her head whipped to the side, her heart in her throat as she slowed and backed toward the wall of bone and clay behind her.

Morana's hands trembled. She called the white mist of the power she'd stolen—Raidan's power—as she fought to steady her limbs. The mist floated over the floor until her power was all she could see.

She had only scratched the surface of whatever magic pulsed through her veins. It had been a month of Raidan testing her—shaping her into whatever he wanted her to be. And despite the decision to come here being her own and the pleasure she felt from wielding stolen power, she hated him.

Her anger and bitterness mixed with her fear as she clasped her hand over her mouth. Her control on his magic slipped and causing her fingers to quiver with the emotions stirring in her gut. Morana closed her eyes and slid to the floor, knowing exactly what would come next as the sounds of the basilisk moved closer.

She couldn't run anymore.

Not from the monsters still hunting her, and certainly not from herself.

Blinding pain injected itself in her calf as sharp teeth sank into her flesh—a scream ripping from deep in her throat.

Morana thrashed on the stone, her back burning from the friction of being dragged through her personal hell. She screamed again, pulling her dagger from its sheath at her thigh in a desperate attempt to fight off the creature pulling her deeper into the labyrinth of cells.

Don't look. Don't look.

Squeezing her eyes shut even tighter, Morana bucked, throwing all of her reserves into freeing herself. That struggle against the beast had it halting, and Morana took her chance. She sat up, slashing the weapon blindly until it sank into flesh. She plunged her power through the dagger designed by Matthias's blacksmith—and hoped it would be enough this time—that she was enough this time.

She panted; the burning of her calf ignited as everything slowed around her.

Morana didn't dare open her eyes—not until she felt the powerful jaws around her calf go slack, teeth still buried deep in her skin. She pried the mouth open and ripped her leg free, pushing the shadows over her flesh to stitch the wound. Chills, not from the basilisk bite or the magic mending her, broke out on her damp skin at the sound of a slow clap sounding behind her.

Was her sick fucking performance enough for him?

Once healed and standing, she turned around to face the true predator.

Raidan stood before the cell she was in, his suit stretched across his broad shoulders, silver hair ghosting the black fabric.

Amber eyes shone in the dim light of the faefire. Morana stood stoic, allowing the shadows to whisper across her skin—to soothe her rapidly beating heart.

Fear shot through her when she noticed Raidan's expression.

Cold anger.

"You rely too heavily on the shadows." Raidan's lip peeled back as he stepped closer, crowding her space. His magic rose around them, meeting the lingering white mist Morana had called upon earlier. "And you take too many risks."

Her gray eyes stared at the god, unwavering. The hatred in her gut reignited, her shadows begging to burrow beneath Raidan's skin and rip him apart.

She had once felt the same way about Matthias. After she learned of his betrayal in the ballroom and how he used her, Morana wanted him dead. She'd tried to kill him, and then she'd ran.

Funny how history repeats itself.

If only she had her chance.

"Why do you continue to disappoint me?" He cocked his head to the side. "You are to be my queen, and yet, you are still so weak."

Her teeth ground together, blood dripping down her temple and mixing with the dirt staining her cheek. She could still feel the rough slide of his tongue there—still remember what happened in her apartment within the human realm. She shuddered at the memory. It fed her hatred—kept her skin crawling and her hand close to her weapon.

Morana had willingly followed Raidan—drunk on faerie wine and power. It seemed like the right thing to do, and for a moment, she'd believed in something—maybe not something good, but *something.*

The reality was she had swapped one monster for another, but she didn't think much about it now—at least she tried not to anymore.

During her first week in The Wastelands, the magic that had fueled her settled, and the chaos of the ballroom subsided. When she found herself alone, the pain replaced her anger—eating at her like maggots feasting on rotting flesh.

She could have lingered on the feeling—picked apart every memory with Matthias to find where she'd gone wrong—where she'd been betrayed. She didn't, though. The betrayal had happened, and there was no use in tearing open the wound again and again.

Not when Raidan had his own agenda.

"Answer me." Raidan's booming voice startled her out of her thoughts. She didn't have time to remember his question before the slap landed on her cheek.

Morana didn't touch the stinging flesh, as she knew better than to show weakness in front of the major god.

"Why do you insist on using the shadows?" he asked.

Mist rose, wrapping around her ankles and pulling at the power now within her and running through her veins as if it were her own.

Morana stared into the face of hell; her defiant expression hardened.

Raidan's hand shot out, wrapping around her neck before he shoved her into the wall and lifted her off the ground. Her back slid against clay and bone, burning as his grip tightened, cutting off her access to air.

"Fucking bitch," he snarled.

Morana found his power, now familiar and still growing inside her. If he wanted her to use it, she would.

Calling the mist, she forced it to her neck and willed the magic to push back against his grip. When his hand finally loosened, Morana gasped for air, her lungs filling as she shoved everything she had left into that binding magic Raidan shared with her.

She wrapped the mist around his middle finger and shoved, drawing a snarl from the god when he pulled his dislocated finger back and stepped away from her.

Morana's feet hit the ground, and she spat at him.

"That's fucking bitch queen to you," she said, calling the shadows to her bruised flesh—imagining it unblemished and healing her skin as she walked away.

The courts were still at war, and while she didn't know the status of her engagement, Morana knew there were some things she couldn't abandon. She'd abandoned Death, but she wouldn't let him break her. She wouldn't let Matthias take the strength she had left, and she sure as hell wouldn't let Raidan take it either.

Raidan's power snapped out, halting her steps.

She didn't want to admit the fear that climbed up her throat. While she found she was far more powerful than she'd known, there was only so much left in the tank. After the basilisk, she was still exhausted.

"One more week for the blood book," he growled. "If I don't have it by the time Inara gets here, you're dead."

For a moment, Morana didn't see how that could be such a horrible fate. Maybe death could heal a broken heart.

"I'll get the book," she whispered, loathing the weakness in her voice.

Raidan released her, but she didn't move. He owned her now—whether she liked it or not.

A hand fisted her hair, tugging her backward until she hit the ground. Her mask broke, and the tears leaked out unbidden as she looked up to the major god—the predator.

"I thought you'd be more powerful," he taunted. "Too weak and not enough. Is that the poem you recited to yourself?" Raidan walked forward, crouching down to her level. He trailed his thumb across her scar, wiping a tear from her cheek.

Vomit rose in her throat, her gut twisting painfully at his touch. It took every ounce of strength she had left not to pull away.

"I like weak things," he said. "They don't fight back when you have your way with them."

Before she could respond, Raidan had disappeared.

In his absence, Morana allowed herself ten whole minutes to break—ten minutes of reckless sobbing and slicing sadness.

When her ten minutes were up, she shoved the heady darkness over her body, numbing the pain as she got up and walked herself back to her room.

She needed Matthias's blood book, no matter how painful the idea of entering the Court of Shadows was.

No matter the cost.

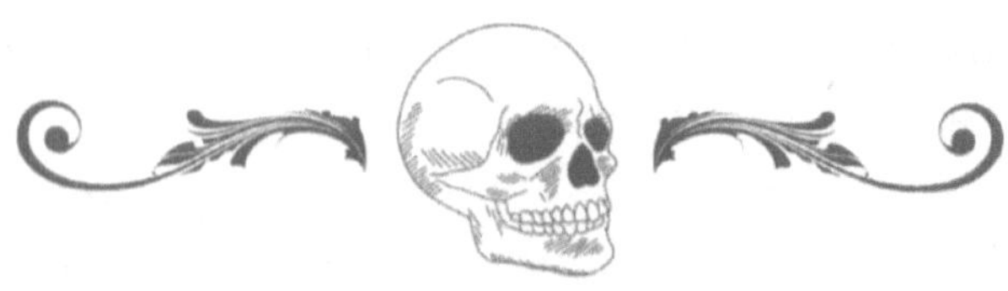

Two

The chill of The Wastelands was bone deep, penetrating, and unrelenting.

Morana sat on the stone floor of her bedroom, staring at the misty light floating in from the singular window.

Everything seemed dim here. Hazy and overwhelming, like the white mist that flooded her body every time she thought of the ballroom. Leaning her head back and closing her eyes, she could see Matthias's eyes, dark and pleading, as he realized what she planned to do.

When it had happened, the bloodlust had been so consuming—the rage so fierce—Morana could only focus on the revenge she longed for. The taste of blood coating her tongue.

It was the reason she leaned into the shadows during Raidan's sick training, the reason she refused to touch the light either. Whatever binding power Raidan had shoved into her lungs the moment his creature attacked her in The Wastelands, she was afraid of it. But only when she wasn't alone.

That fear didn't stop her from learning to control her magic in the quiet hours sitting on the cold floor. The more she practiced, the smaller the fear became.

Using that power fed some sort of beast inside her, the same beast that retaliated when Raidan's arrogance became too much. They were small moments, little acts of defiance during the brutal training she was being put through. If Raidan wanted her power and longed for her to become a monster, a monster she would become, but she would never be *his*.

She hoped his dislocated finger was treating him well.

Morana squeezed her eyes shut and replayed the scene with Matthias for the thousandth time. As she leaned against the worn four-poster bed in her room, she longed to be free from the sting of betrayal, just as she fought the coldness of the Palace of Bones.

If she could feel that betrayal again—relive it in her mind—then she had a chance of reaffirming her decision to leave the Court of Shadows. Even as her hatred for Raidan grew and the crawling across her skin intensified with every passing day, she couldn't regret her choice.   Morana would only go back to another monster—one that lied and manipulated—one she'd trusted.

She ground her teeth together and tried to hold on to that rage surging in her bloodstream. The mist floated around her, thick and swelling like a fresh wound. It stirred in her, calling to the darkest parts of her soul.

She could see the ballroom—bodies and chaos—nothing but blood.

Morana halted.

Her hands were trembling when she opened her eyes and the mist receded, snaking back into her body. With her hand clasped over her mouth, a strained cry broke free from her throat.

She quickly reined it in.

She would not cry, and she would not let him *hear* her.

Over the past month, Raidan had sent her to the dungeons to fight beasts—including himself. She could picture his feral smile and bloodstained teeth as he prowled for her during that first session—the one where he had tested her power. He stood over her as the white mist invaded her lungs, suffocating her from the inside out.

"You are to be queen of The Wastelands," he snarled, "but you will always remember your king."

She could only remember the wicked delight on the monster's face when he stormed out of the dungeons. Rolling to her side, she gasped for breath on the ground, her bruised ribs aching under her tender skin.

And then he left her locked beneath the palace with no access to her magic. She'd spent it all during training and finally found her limit.

After screaming and pounding against a closed metal door, Morana fell into a heap on the floor and allowed sleep to take her.

Upon waking alone, the slick slide of scaled skin rasped against the dusty floors. Morana had sat up, only one word circling in her mind.

Basilisk.

She didn't dare touch the memory further because if Raidan hadn't opened the door when he had, she would have been dead. She had almost looked at the creature.

"I'm disappointed." Raidan had been holding the basilisk back from her and watching her shake on the floor. "I brought you here because you were powerful, but apparently not." He had licked his lips. "No matter. I can help you unlock that power." He had leaned forward, breath fanning over her face and sending a chill up her spine. "I can feel the power running through your veins, Morana." His eyes were almost glowing in the dim light. "And I want to use it."

Morana shook her head against the memory as a vine slithered from the window. It reminded her she was no longer in the dungeon, but in her bedroom within Raidan's temple. He was growing impatient, and she would have to deliver.

The green plant slithered across the floor, moving closer and causing Morana to jolt back. She pressed her spine firmly against the hard wooden base of the bed.
When the vine grew upward, dancing in the misty light of her bedroom, she couldn't help but stare. It was as if the air around the plant had a golden shimmer, one that brought color to her now dim world.

A burgundy flower, dense and dark, bloomed at the tip of the vine, just in front of her face. She could smell earth and taste tea on her tongue.

Sarnai.

Morana reached out to touch one petal with the tip of her finger, marveling at the life in this dead place.

The vine cracked and moved, and her head snapped to the window, realization breaking through her haze as she stood on aching legs. Despite her healing, her calf still throbbed when she chased the retracting vine to the windowsill. Morana shoved the glass window higher, breathing in the desert air.

There was nothing beyond but reminders of death and cracked earth. Yet, in the distance, Morana was certain she saw a shadow moving around the gate surrounding the palace.

The bedroom door opened behind her, and she startled.

"You are to attend dinner." Raidan's voice rumbled from where he stood. The air cooled, burrowing into her veins and shooting through her blood.

"When?" Morana asked, keeping her eyes on the fading light of the desert beyond.

"Now."

She huffed a breath—almost a laugh, but not quite. "I will be down in a minute."

His power gripped her, wrapping around her ankles and tugging with violent force. Morana stumbled, gripping the windowsill to keep her head from splitting on the surface as her knees buckled and cracked against the floor.

Footsteps sounded behind her from the predator still stalking his prey. When Morana turned to face the god, Raidan stared down at her, his head tilted to the side and a goblet in one hand.

Wine, probably.

"You will come to dinner now." He swirled his glass. "We will enter the dining room together."

"I'm not dressed properly," Morana ground out.

Burning amber eyes trailed over her, sending her stomach roiling. "The pants and sweater are fine, but if you would prefer something else, I'd be happy to watch you change. Consider it repayment for my injury."

Bile rose in her throat at the thought of Raidan's predatory gaze watching her undress. He hadn't made advances yet, but he constantly reminds her of his capabilities—and her lack of choice in the matter. His power released her, and Morana stood with her back straight, stepping forward and taking hold of the white magic. She willed it to ghost against his legs, wrap around his now healed finger.

It was only a whisper, but she couldn't hold back her smirk.

She didn't dare do more.

"I'm happy to wear this," she said, forcing a smile.

After taking a sip of wine, Raidan dragged his tongue across red-stained lips before turning to walk out of her room.

Morana followed, knowing the consequences of her disobedience well, and she had already done enough for today. He would only tolerate so much.

The runes on the ceiling lit the hallway as they moved through the palace. The eerie blue light reminded her of Ronan and the temple near Zora. Lux's tomb.

The magic here was different, though. Laced with something ancient and powerful that Morana wasn't quite ready to fight on her own.

Even if she fought it or someone came to help her, where would she go if she escaped?

Home.

No. She couldn't go home, even if she longed for it—for *his* court, despite it all.

He wasn't coming to save her, and she would not give in. They were all monsters—Raidan, Matthias, others too. She had a better chance if she learned to be one also.

When the hallway opened to the dining room, Morana caught sight of the pale fae woman sitting with a cup of tea in her hand. Rose-colored eyes shot in Morana's direction.

Inara smiled, white teeth contrasting against her blood-red lips. Her white hair hung loose over her bare shoulders, olive dress draped around her neck and hanging to her ankles.

"Good to see you," she commented.

Morana silently sat at the head of the table across from Raidan, eyes fixed to the goddess of life.

"The last time I drank tea in your presence, I asked you a question," Inara proceeded. "So." She cocked an eyebrow. "How has Death treated you?" Her mouth pulled up at one corner. "Still kind?"

Morana clenched her teeth, grinding them as her nails dug crescent moons into her palms. "Why are you here?"

Raidan chuckled from the other end of the table, setting his goblet down and taking up his fork. "I invited her," he supplied.

Inara smiled, smug and taunting. "Is Matthias enjoying my blood book?"

Morana's back stiffened, and she pressed her lips together. While Inara's tone remained sickeningly sweet, Morana knew the truth of what her wrath could hold for those she hated. Inara would kidnap, torture—kill.

For a goddess of life, she was certainly fond of pain and suffering.

Morana supposed that made sense considering the pain and suffering she'd endured herself.

Inara leaned forward as if they were having an intimate conversation. "Have *you* enjoyed my blood book?" Her eyes carefully trailed over Morana's expressionless face. She didn't want the goddess to know how her words stung—didn't want her to see the way Death's name still rattled something in her chest. "I'm sure you enjoyed reading about your friend, Axton," Inara continued, leaning back in her chair. "Pity you killed him. He was really quite good at—"

Morana's fist slammed against the table, the white mist blurring her vision.

"Violent," Inara chuckled.

"I like them feral." Raidan brought the fork up to his mouth, eating the meal set out before them.

Morana didn't bother looking at the food—didn't bother eating. "Why are you here, Inara?"

"That's no way to treat a guest."

Morana snarled, punctuating each of her words when she spoke next. "Why are you here?" Her eyes flashed to the pointed ears poking through a curtain of pale white hair. None of the other gods had that. Matthias didn't—Sarnai—none of them.

Not even Raidan.

Something cold overcame the goddess—the musical and taunting tone vanishing from her voice. She was all sharp edges.

"Raidan and I had a deal," she said, slouching back in her chair and scraping her fork against her plate as she cocked an eyebrow. "I wanted power, and he had power. So, I bound Axton to a bargain and woke up an ancient god." She flashed a smile. "Then I became one, myself."

Raidan's laugh cut through the stale air across the table before he wiped his mouth. "Your penchant for bargains seemed to pay off in my favor."

Morana turned back to Inara after pushing her plate away. The more she learned, the more she lost her appetite.

"I forget you know nothing of the fae realm." The sentence sounded like an insult, prodding at the old wound.

Memories flashed in her mind—a warm tub, gentle hands, and the confessions she spoke in Willow's presence. She couldn't entertain the images—not now.

I made my bed, and I intend to sleep in it.

Morana clenched her fists as Inara barreled on. "One of the major gods," she began, "Lady Death. She is the one who put the other major gods to sleep." Inara swirled the tea in her cup, gazing at it. "Her name suits her, I suppose."

Lady Death.

Sarnai had spoken of her.

"Lady Death was meant to put an end to his cruelty, but she never showed."

"Is this a true story?" Morana interrupted.

Sarnai eyed her suspiciously. "It's just legend, older than Matthias. The sleeping gods are true enough, but we have never seen such power, such cruelty."

Morana looked to Raidan.

Certainly cruel.

And Lady Death had put him to sleep—she had shown up despite Sarnai's retelling.

"Who was she?" Morana asked.

"A fool." Inara's voice was sharp again, tinged with hatred.

Morana lifted a brow. "And what do you get out of all this, Inara?"

Raidan cleared his throat before Inara's lips peeled back slowly, revealing straight teeth. "Why," she began, "I get to be queen."

"Of the Court of Life?"

"Of The Wastelands."

Morana's stomach bottomed out as her head whipped to Raidan. The major god sat stoic in his seat; amber eyes boring into Morana's. *Empty promises.* It was the thought that rang in her mind. *Empty promises from an empty god.*

She wouldn't let him see her crumble, so Morana sat up straighter.

Deep down she knew, though. She had always known that there was no power to be earned here. It would be easier to believe she was running toward power instead of running away from her feelings for Matthias—from the betrayal.

"Morana," Raidan's voice cut through the silence. "The blood book," he insisted.

The statement piqued Inara's interest. "She has Matthias's blood book?"

"Not yet," Morana ground out, desperate to wipe the hope from Inara's face.

Raidan's magic touched her ankles beneath the table, tightening painfully in warning.

"Something you will remedy in the next six days." His voice was low and dark, sending chills up her spine.

"Do you know where it is?" Inara asked, excitement burrowed into her words.

Morana's eyes met hers, unfeeling as she spoke. Everyone was lying to her—so she would lie, too.

"No."

She wanted to tell herself that her lie was another one of her acts of defiance—another jab against the major god in the room, but that was a lie, too.

The truth was harsh and haunted her at every turn. It haunted her in the quiet moments when she sat in her room, and it haunted her now.

Morana protected Matthias despite his deception and how he used her in a game she still could not understand.

She was always fucking protecting him.

Morana picked up her fork and forced herself to eat.

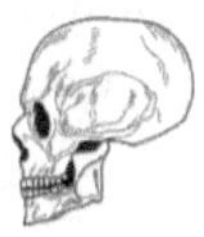

After dinner, Morana walked back to her room and found herself lost in the memories and darkness as she leaned back against the pillows.

"Well, I don't have your blood book." Morana raised a brow. *"I do, however, have access to your mind."*

That you do. *Matthias's voice surrounded her again, but there was no sound running through the tall pines.* You have access to all my secrets without a book. You now know that my parents are buried in Nashira where Garian is lord.

The city includes the largest library in our court and their tomb beneath it. My mother always loved books and hated winter. It only seemed fitting.

He leaned in again, placing a kiss on her temple. You also have the answers to any questions you wish to ask. *His voice was so loud now.* I just don't know if you'll like the truth.

She didn't like the truth.

Nashira was to the south in the Court of Shadows—in Garian's city.

Morana had never been in the library and had never seen the city, but she knew the shadows could take her there. They had taken her to places she hadn't been before.

She kept her eyes pinned at the ceiling above, feeling the rumble of power beneath her skin and questioning if all that magic was worth it. She hadn't asked for it, anyway.

"I've heard about it," she said, thinking back to what Matthias had told her about his parent's tomb. She didn't know if Jameson knew about that, so she played it safe. "I would be eager to explore what the library has to offer."

Jameson gave Matthias a nervous look, to which Matthias nodded his approval. "Ah, you speak of below the libraries, I take it. I tend to that—" He paused, looking for the right word. "Area as well."

Her confidence grew each time she ran from each basilisk Raidan shoved in the dungeon with her. That just left getting past Jameson to retrieve the book, and she was certain she'd be able to do it.

The door opened, but Morana didn't bother to look. She knew he'd come for her—he always did.

When she finally stood up, she walked to the singular wardrobe in the corner of her room and opened it. Her options were few, but Raidan had provided *something* for her. Maybe it was his attempt at fooling her—making her believe he meant what he had said.

"Inara is to be your queen," she said. It wasn't a question, and she didn't turn as the white mist floated across the floor. The fog followed Raidan in the way the shadows trailed behind Death. Death's power fooled the mind, Raidan's power bound the body.

She could feel him standing behind her, his body as cold as his palace.

Too close, she thought as her back stiffened.

Raidan's fingers lifted and analyzed her hair delicately—now longer—and trailing over her shoulder. He inhaled her scent, and Morana squeezed her eyes shut. She wanted to vomit.

"I've tired of her," Raidan spoke, his fingertips leaving the strands. She winced, fighting the tears threatening to leak out. Morana hated when he touched her and had hated it that first moment in her apartment.

Though this time, Matthias wouldn't be storming inside the room. Nobody was coming to save her, and she hated herself for still hoping.

"You've proved more useful than Inara," he started. "Certainly, more powerful." Her skin crawled as he traced the touch over her arm, down to her wrist. "How much power do you have running through these veins?" He wrapped his fingers around her pulse and squeezed. "Why do you hide it from me?" The squeeze turned bruising.

White mist wrapped around her, touching her in all the places Raidan didn't. It pried her mouth open as her eyes stayed pinned on the wardrobe, taking in the harsh carvings depicting death and destruction. A tear streaked down her face as the mist shoved into her lungs, stealing her very breath.

Raidan leaned in, his lips ghosting against her ear. "You can be queen if you wish," he snarled. "But you must continue to prove yourself even more useful, and even more powerful than Inara."

When the mist receded, Morana gasped for air, her tongue dry as sand. Raidan shoved her forward, but she didn't let herself fall, catching herself after one stumbling step.

"Why are pages in Inara's blood book missing?" she asked. "And how did she wake you in the first place? What did you do to give her all that power?"

Raidan smiled as she turned to face him, jutting out her chin in her demand for answers.

"The pages are missing because I didn't want them to know I was coming." His silver hair caught the moonlight streaming in from the window. "And as for your other questions, how do you think I could kidnap Death?"

Her mask slipped, the frown pulling at her lips. "Axton kidnapped him." The Basar had shown her as much.

Raidan tilted his head to the side. "And who do you think was in control?" He licked his lips. "I enjoyed torturing your little death god."

The words cut like a blade through her chest and reminded her of the pain she'd felt seeing Matthias in the dungeon. She knew if she had to see it again, she'd still feel that pain, and that was something that bothered her the most. Morana reached for the mist, tightening the magic around Raidan's finger—she'd dislocate the joint again.

Raidan reared back and gripped his finger. "You still love him," Raidan observed.

Love.

Morana let go, the fog receding as a tear trailed over her cheek. She looked away.

Raidan's uninjured fingers gripped her chin as he forced her to look up into those amber eyes—the eyes of a monster. "Cut the ties." His lip peeled back in disgust. "Love makes you weak, and with everything hanging in the balance for you, you cannot afford to be weak, Morana." His hand shifted, wrapping around her throat as the mist floated higher.

Raidan's hand tightened at her throat before he shoved her to the ground.

"Get me that fucking book."

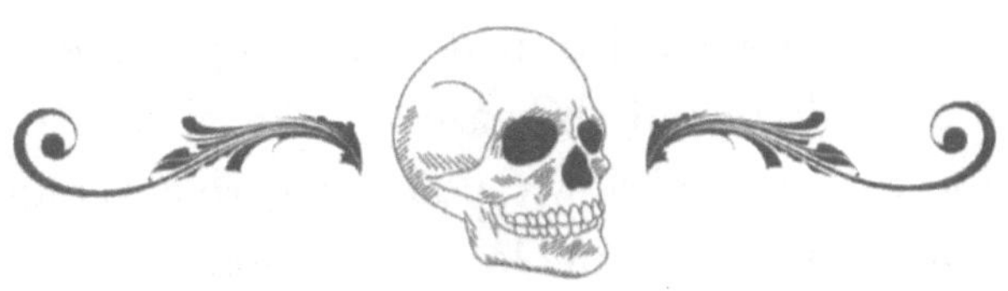

Three

Morana stood with a heavy black cloak draped around her shoulders, shadows swirling in her midst as she looked over the cracked earth of The Wastelands.

She squeezed her eyes shut, her pulse beating wildly. While she knew they could trace her magic in the Court of Light, she didn't know if Raidan could track her movements from The Wastelands. Refraining from using her magic in Matthias's court was a precaution—one she no longer had the luxury of taking.

Morana called on every piece of information she knew about Nashira. She thought of Garian and his wife, her time training in the palace of Ascella. Her shadows brought memories with them. Every flickering image reminded her of the place she had called home, and with each one, the scab over her heart peeled away.

As the darkness swallowed her, Morana fought the surging emotions—the ones that proved Raidan's thoughts to be true.

She still cared for *him.*

Appearing on a spiraling stone staircase encased in a pale tower, Morana frowned. Moonlight streamed through the window, and she gazed at the glittering city beyond. She spun around slowly, noting that whatever tower she had found herself in didn't look like a library.

There were no books.

Her heart sank.

She'd worked so hard to train herself—to get a hold of her power during her time in The Wastelands. Even with the effort in the dungeons and the way she endured Raidan's torture, Morana knew that if she failed, things would get worse. Far worse.

Holding the shadows close and pulling her hood over her head, Morana turned. If this was the library in Nashira, she would need to go down to find the tomb. She had to trust her magic—she had little else.

The descent felt endless, the only sounds being her soft footsteps on stone and the wild beating of her heart. Her hand rested on the dagger strapped to her thigh beneath her cloak. The cool metal of its hilt gave her some comfort as she reached the base of the stairs.

A door carved its way into the ivory stone of the tower—golden and glowing like a beacon in the night.

Morana took a deep, shuddering breath and pushed it open. Beyond it, rows of white, gold, and leather-bound books stretched out before her in the massive room. Candles filled with faefire cast dancing light over the walls. Using the shadows to cloak her in darkness, Morana kept to the wall.

Well, this is clearly a library. Haven't fucked up entirely.

She just needed to find another way to go *down.*

Moving through the stacks, Morana held her power close, fighting the stirring nerves that continued to rattle her bones. She didn't know what she would find here—figured someone would heavily guard the tomb along with the book inside.

Creatures had protected Inara's blood book—one being a malevolent dog she had accidentally killed. Morana still bore the scar of that creature's claws on her shoulder. It may have been her imagination, but that mark began burning beneath her clothes.

Her mind swirled in the same way it did in the dungeons as the burning sensation grew. She could feel every mark—every painful bite from the basilisk she'd endured. The sounds of the library echoed in her mind, and she wasn't entirely sure they weren't all made up.

Her heavy breaths felt almost gasping, and if she'd been in The Wastelands, the cold air would have puffed from her lips—adding to her fear.

Rushing through the aisle, she kept the darkness tight around her. Sweat trailed down her back, and her palms grew slick.

A sound behind her—paper rustling—footsteps.

She looked back, quickening her pace through the tall golden shelves stacked with mysterious tomes.

Morana lost her grip on the shadows as her body slammed against something solid, or rather, *someone* solid.

Steadying herself, she looked up into a familiar face as dread stirred in her gut.

I cannot fail. I cannot fail.

The words repeated in her mind as she tried to come up with some sort of plan—a way to react.

The faefire highlighted the sharp features of Jameson, the one she knew Matthias had guarding the tomb. An uneasy feeling washed over her as she stared into his eyes. The fae man didn't say a word, just looked her over, trying to place her.

When his eyes widened, Morana realized she needed to act. The mist came first, ready to bind. It rose around their feet and wrapped around his legs, keeping him firmly in place.

Deciding, Morana drew her dagger as the slick metal sound filled the room. The fae man was bound by white mist before he could even speak as the tip of her weapon pressed into his throat. Her power and the pressure of her blade forced him to remain still or risk cutting himself.

With Jameson bound, Morana leaned in, pressing her dagger against his skin and snarling. She swallowed the coppery taste of blood and relished in the fear she saw on his face. She would end him, she would—

"Where is the tomb?" she hissed, digging the tip of her dagger into his neck until a thin trail of crimson disappeared beneath his brown, threadbare cloak.

"My queen," he breathed.

Morana smiled at that, the foggy magic feeding her desire for power. It was the most control she'd had since finding herself with Raidan, and that kind of control was dangerous. "Queen of what?" she pressed, carefully running her gaze over the fae.

"The Court of Shadows."

Shadows whispered along her skin as if called on by Jameson's words. Her smile disappeared as sorrow swept through her chest, draining the anger from her body. Before she'd had control of her magic, it had brought bloodlust. The lack of that bloodlust was now both a comfort and a curse.

"The tomb," she whispered—harsh and demanding. "Where is Matthias's blood book?"

"Y-you know about runes?"

The man was stuttering in the way he had the first time they met. There was something behind his eyes, though. This man was no fool.

Morana recalled Ronan's use of runes and blood at the temple near Zora as her eyes flicked to Jameson's neck, his blood already drying. "Will we need blood?" she asked, cocking her head to the side. At the thought, the fog thickened and a feral smile split Morana's face. "We could use yours," she said.

"I am to show you where the tomb is, and I am not to disturb you."

Morana's brows creased, and she snatched the dagger away, drawing her magic back into herself. The shadows rippled along her skin, calming her mind after her use of the mist.

"Who gave you those orders?" she asked.

The fae smiled. "Would it matter?" he questioned. "You are to be queen, after all."

Morana huffed a laugh, realizing Matthias still planned to make her queen. Or at least, he hadn't told his court anything different. She wondered what they thought had happened and what they had seen in the ballroom. But more than that, Morana questioned the truth. Did he still believe she'd want him?

Would it be so bad if he did?

She shook her head, trailing behind Jameson as he turned and moved through the stacks to the back of the library. A wooden door sat undisturbed and out of place—the plain and unfinished material standing out amongst the gilded walls surrounding it.

Jameson glanced back once before nodding toward her dagger. "For the runes," he said.

Morana huffed. "I'm not trusting you with my weapon."

"Then we are locked out." His tone was matter of fact. "I don't have my knife with me, or I would slice my palm myself."

Morana reached forward, grabbed his hand, and dragged her blade across his flesh with precision. The white mist swirled at her feet.

Jameson's eyes were wide, but he shook off his surprise, knelt down and traced the patterns at the base of the door.

Blood coated his fingers as he worked, gold light forming the symbols now on the floor.

The latch opened.

Jameson grunted as he pushed the door open, descending the stairs that followed.

Faefires came to life around them, and Morana fixed her eyes on the man in front of her, stepping carefully and tightening her grip on her blade. She kept her magic close, too, reminding herself that if he turned on her, she could shadow out.

I am to show you where the tomb is, and I am not to disturb you.

Morana didn't know what that meant, didn't like trusting yet another person. It was one more person to betray her and leave her in ruin.

At the base of the stairs, a small room opened up. The large stone structure rose in the center, carved with intricate designs and symbols Morana couldn't identify.

"The tomb," Jameson said, gesturing ahead. "I am to leave you h-here, but you should be able to find the book." His smirk was smug.

Morana's eyes hardened, unmoving as she stared at the fae, trying to understand the uneasy feeling swirling in her stomach whenever he was around. "And you watch over this place?"

"I'm f-forced to. Magic binds me here." He dipped his head. "As punishment."

"Punishment for what?" she asked.

A feral smile pulled at his lips—one she knew well. "For betraying Death's parents."

Anger stirred in her, the white mist rising as Morana reached out with her shadows, prying open the man's mind before making her decision.

The moment she saw his delight—the way he seemed satisfied to have killed the king and queen of shadows, she plunged her weapon into his stomach. His eyes widened in shock, just before he fell dead to the cold floor.

Morana dragged her weapon from his flesh and panted to catch her breath.

The control felt good. No matter how much magic she held, she'd always feel powerless in the presence of gods—but not with the fae. All she'd needed was the memory—the one that told her he'd been a part of Matthias's suffering.

Little mattered apart from that, and she didn't want to read into what it meant.

Once she found herself steadied, she moved to run her fingers along the carvings etched into the stone casket.

Morana shuddered. She could feel Death there, something like his magic embedded in the writing.

She couldn't read it, though.

The only structure in the room was the casket, and bile rose in her throat as Morana thought of ripping away the stone top in search of the blood book. It felt insulting—even after everything Matthias had done to her.

She closed her eyes, breathing deeply to fight off the rising pain. She hated how thoughts of him summoned the feelings—the ones she was trying so hard to ignore.

"Looking for this?"

Morana whipped around, her heart pounding in her chest, fog rising in the room as she beheld the image of Death.

Matthias stood at the base of the stairs; a black book gripped in one tattooed hand. Shadows encircled him, floating over his skin, down his arms, calling to the power that resided within her.

Her emotions ripped the white mist from her body and unleashed Raidan's power. The heady effects of the binding magic had her chest rising and falling rapidly as she zeroed in on Death. A sudden wave of anger, sharp as the bloody dagger strapped to her thigh, washed away any lingering sorrow she had felt.

Her magic lashed out, wrapping around his throat as she lunged. He fell backward, and Morana clamped her hand over his mouth, pinning him to the floor and watching as a wicked smile split the face of Death. She snarled, the tip of her dagger pressing against flesh.

Wouldn't you like to drink of Death, Morana?

The anger tore through her like a wild beast, her vision blurring against the magic rising in the room. "What happens when Death meets his end?" she asked.

The stone embedded in the hilt of her dagger darkened, frosted over like a void. There was nothing in her soul—her heart that recognized her feelings or pain. Morana breathed deeply, relishing in the relief flooding her veins, and the pleasure rising with her anger.

"I'm sure you'd like to find out," Matthias said, his tone steady, but she could see the fear in his dark gaze. There was nothing quite as pleasing as the image of fear on the face of Death, especially with the way Death seemed to betray and lie—a true monster cloaked in shadows. But weren't they all? "So, you killed Jameson," he added. "I should thank you for that."

Legs on either side of his waist, Morana sat up, keeping the tip of her dagger on his neck as she looked down her nose at him. Power fed power, consuming her so fully, it felt like her mind wasn't her own.

Matthias's features softened, the shadows cutting through her magic, coating her arms and cooling her fire.

"Morana," he whispered.

It tugged something inside of her, her brows furrowing. She struggled as she battled her own mind and forced herself to keep the dagger at his throat. Something in his magic called to her own, causing pain to tear through her chest—replacing all else as the mist and her anger dissipated.

Whatever sorrow she had felt before returned. Her heart was bleeding out again, and Morana feared Matthias would see it—see it written on her face. His scent filled her lungs, her shadows now skittering down her arms. The black stone shifted to a deep burgundy.

Too close. That's enough.

She shot up, reeling back with her dagger still held in front of her as if it could cut through whatever emotions were swirling inside her skull.

"I don't suppose you'd give that up freely?" she asked, eyes flicking to the book.

Matthias bent over, picking the tome off the floor before prowling forward. Keeping her dagger in hand, Morana couldn't help the way her body flinched, the tears threatening to spill over.

Feet frozen to the floor, Morana stood as Death moved closer, one tattooed hand running through his dark hair. His movements were slow, but sure, as if he knew she couldn't bear to hurt him.

It was mostly true. She wouldn't hurt him as long as Raidan's magic stayed locked away.

Even so, she missed the numbing anger. It was far better than the reminder of betrayal.

He moved closer—a foot away. Morana took a shuddering breath, and something like pain flashed through his eyes. She tried to reach for the bloodlust—the thing that came to destroy, but she couldn't find it.

Her chest ached instead—the shadows whispering over her flesh.

"I would give up anything freely." He swallowed, and Morana watched the way his throat moved, blinking away the moisture building at the corners of her eyes.

Matthias stared down at her in the darkened tomb, his hand still on the book. "I would give up anything freely," he repeated before continuing. "For you."

Morana's breath hitched, his scent invading her lungs again, reminding her of shadows and nights in the palace spent curled up against him. Now, she was against him in a different way, and the girl in that memory seemed as much of a stranger as Death.

Calling the mist, Morana tugged at the only thing that would help her draw up the wrath she needed to confront Death. The fog circled their feet, but Matthias didn't acknowledge it—didn't look away from her.

Something about his unwillingness to react had her mind mixing. Anger and sorrow woven together.

She desperately wanted him to react. Morana wanted him to fear her or beg for her. To apologize or fight.

Still, she was ashamed that a part of her longed for him to beg for forgiveness.

He had *betrayed* her.

"I'm sure you would." Her tone was sharp as the blade in her hand. "Because you need my power to get your revenge, right? You wanted it so much; you were willing to feed me lie after lie in order to secure it—to make me trust you."

Morana swore he flinched at her accusation, and she clung to the hint of whatever he was feeling like a lifeline.

She needed something from him—anything.

Moving closer, Matthias's proximity began pushing her to the edge. Her magic slipped, sending any wrath tumbling through her fingers.

She would not cry.

"No." He was still whispering, tightening his grip on the book. Matthias closed his eyes.

When he opened them again, meeting Morana's gaze, she said the only thing she could think of. "I hate you." The lie tasted bitter on her tongue.

He nodded. No response.

Morana called Raidan's magic again, tightening her hold on the dagger as the burgundy color darkened.

Wouldn't you like to drink of Death, Morana?

"I could kill you." Everything inside her hardened like ice.

Her cold, gray eyes flicked to his shoulder, covered by the black button-up stretching across his broad chest. She wondered how he had healed after she'd given him the wound. Had it stitched back together easily?

If she couldn't muster up the strength to drag the dagger across his throat now, she at least hoped her previous attempt to end Death had stung.

"And I would be glad for it."

The knife left her hand, clattering onto the stone floors below—the sound echoing through the tomb.

He kept talking, and she was certain she stopped breathing. "If killing me would ease your pain," he continued, "I would give my life up freely, too." He paused, and Morana fought for air as he held the tome out. "Take the book."

Her eyes flicked up to meet his gaze. "Raidan will use it against you." She didn't know why she said it. Maybe it was because she was still protecting him. Maybe she was still deciding what *she* was going to do with his blood book, and deep down, she didn't want Raidan to know she had retrieved it.

Matthias leaned forward, Morana's eyes flicking to his lips on instinct. She could almost feel them on her skin—the way they had trailed over her neck—her chest. Her heart was pounding in her ears, and she couldn't focus with him so near.

Morana grabbed the book, careful not to touch his hand, before she shoved it beneath her cloak. Tears tracked down her cheeks, and her breath shook as she waited for whatever Matthias would say next.

Shadows stretched out to her, calling and begging for access into her mind. She let him in, too weak to lock him out, but still strong enough to refuse allowing him to see the last month. Matthias wouldn't get access to Raidan's empty promises and abuse. Morana fought to keep those parts of her mind concealed. He wouldn't get access to *her.*

With her eyes closed, Morana felt the shadows wrap around her body and mind. She welcomed them, drinking in the familiarity, suspending her hurt and anger for a mere moment.

The shadows gripped her with a force more powerful than Raidan's magic, more powerful than whatever magic flooded her own veins. Though Matthias's voice was a whisper in the dark, Morana heard them. The words were loud and clear as they were spoken into the corners of her inner world.

I love you.

And then he was gone.

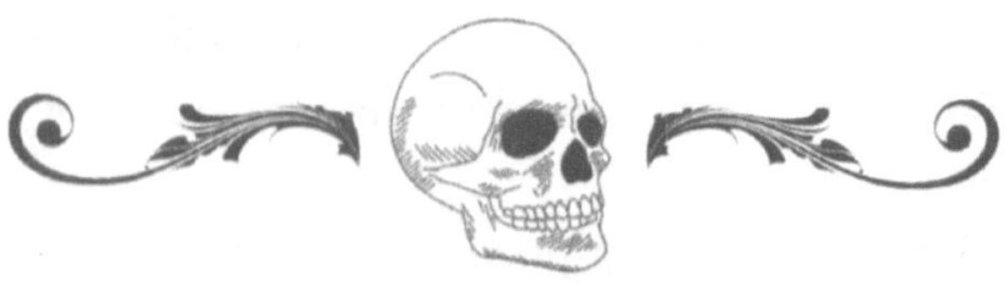

Four

Morana was alone, mouth parted, dagger on the floor, and the silence of the tomb weighing heavier than the book in her hand.

I love you.

The words lingered like the taste of blood—leftover from Raidan's power that had fueled her anger. Anger that was now shattered.

Morana bent down and wrapped her hand around the cool metal hilt of the weapon. Peering at the stone, she took in the deep burgundy color as shadows whispered across her skin, comforting her.

Although she couldn't trust Matthias, something stirred in her gut. It begged her to hide Matthias's secrets from the monster she would return to.

It wasn't as if Raidan's word was any better. The major god had promised her a role in The Wastelands and told her she would be queen. Since then, she had only experienced abuse. While Morana knew she was stronger for it, she also knew that she couldn't trust the god of The Wastelands. He deserved to go back to whatever dark pit he had come out of.

Her fingers trembled against the spine of the blood book. Raidan would be waiting for her—she could feel it in her bones. He would demand the book, and Matthias's secrets along with it.

Did Matthias think she would hand it over? Did he believe she could keep it safe? He gave her access after all, and while she didn't want to believe it, maybe it was an offering—one riddled with the truth of the last words he spoke.

I love you.

Morana wiped the back of her hand across her cheek, smearing the tear that had leaked out. She cursed herself, calling the shadows to take her into Nashira so she could figure out what she would do next.

The gilded city shone like a beacon in the desert when her magic faded. The sand below her boots swirled as she moved between pale buildings bathed in flickering faefire.

Morana pulled the hood over her head—just far enough to conceal her face as she prowled through the streets. For all the feeling inside, she would shove it down for the sake of solving whatever puzzle Matthias had provided for her. Caught between lying vile creatures who justified their actions by being gods, Morana kept moving forward. The gods would use her to serve only themselves, but somehow, she had to believe that she would end up alright.

The shadows whispered around her legs, calming her fears. To her left, a gold sign hung from one of many pale buildings, green succulents lining the small windows at the front. Morana read the words engraved in the metal sign, *Nashira Tavern*.

Lights flickered in the window, and a fae man stumbled through the door, laughing and looking her direction.

Morana tensed, holding her hood in place with one hand, and gripping Matthias's blood book like a lifeline beneath her cloak.

If there was anything to solve, it would be in the book.

She needed to hide it.

Her heart raced as she pushed past the drunk patron, ignoring whatever slurred words he tossed her way as she moved into the open tavern. It reminded her of her old world. Drunk people stumbling in the streets near her apartment. Such a lifetime ago. Funny how she went to feeling out of place in not one world but two. Pulling her cloak closer, she focused on her path.

A carved, stone pillar stood in front of Morana, just past the entrance. Stepping around it, she looked toward the far wall where a red tapestry hung from the ceiling to the floor. Embroidered in shining thread was the image of Garian riding through battle.

Morana's brows rose beneath the hood of her cloak. If Ronan had tapestries of himself hanging around the taverns in his city, she certainly would have heard about it by now.

Shaking her head, Morana found a corner booth carved into the pale stone. She slid in, glancing around the room, her heart still racing. Would others recognize the book if she pulled it out and flipped through it? Would it even open for her?

"Drink?"

Morana looked up, her eyes catching the silver gaze of the fae woman waiting for her order. Pointed ears poked out from the waterfall of black hair. The woman shifted where she stood—impatient with her brow raised.

"Um," Morana trailed her finger over the hilt of her dagger beneath her cloak. "What do you have?"

The woman squinted, adjusting the apron hanging around her waist. "The usual. Alcohol, tea, coffee. It all depends on why you're here."

Morana lowered her hood, her palms slick with sweat. The shadows danced around her ankles, skittering up her body and whispering in her ears, reminding her she could trust no one—not now.

I love you.

She blinked.

Morana's stomach dropped when she saw the fae woman's silver eyes widen in recognition. She had no money, and she hadn't anticipated the fae in Garian's city knowing who she was. Word from the ball could have traveled, and this woman may know more than she let on.

Or maybe Morana was paranoid.

"Nothing, thank you." Her throat was dry as she cleared it.

"Oh," the woman started. "Of course."

The feeling of the fae woman's eyes lingered even after she walked away. Morana let out a shuddering breath and dared to pull out the book as soon as she was alone.

Shadows wrapped around her arms and the tome's cover as if the contents drew her power to it. Without warning, the leather snapped open; the pages flicking wildly before Morana forced the book shut and shoved it back beneath her cloak.

Looking up, she called her magic while stealing a glance at the fae woman, now leaning against the bar and whispering to the man running a white cloth over glass. Those silver eyes lit up, and unease stirred in Morana's gut.

Maybe it was a trap.

Matthias showed up to the library offering the very information Raidan wanted—his memories.

Death could be lingering in the shadows, waiting for his chance to strike. At this point, it wouldn't surprise her. She had felt safe with him before, and all of that had been a lie.

I love you.

Calling on her magic, Morana watched between the woman's fingers, the light crackling and twisting before Morana's shadows swallowed her whole. The darkness threw her back into The Wastelands, back into the monster's nest.

The familiar dripping of the dungeons called out to her first, reminding her that the tavern was long gone. Though, her brows pulled together at the display of the fae woman's power.

The sounds of the palace of bone echoed in her ears as a shiver worked its way down her spine. Memories of fighting for her life surfaced, and she couldn't help the way every cell in her body begged her to run.

She needed a place to hide the book, and with the nearly bare room Raidan had provided her upstairs, she couldn't think of anywhere else aside from the dungeons.

At the very least, Raidan's pet would guard the tome.

Her dagger weighed heavily on her thigh, and Morana took comfort from its presence. Her boot scuffed on the floor, and she halted, head whipping behind her, breath billowing like white smoke from her lips.

It was cold down here, and Morana knew Raidan kept his monsters caged below the palace—more monsters than the basilisk.

The only question now was, had he let them out?

There was no telling.

Shoving herself into an alcove, Morana frantically fingered the stone wall, pressing and prying, begging for a stone to give way. There was no such stone.

White mist gathered at her hands; the same binding power Raidan possessed. Morana wrapped that magic around a larger stone in the wall, pulling it with the force of her power. When it finally crashed to the ground and split open, she looked around again. Flashes of slick flesh sliding across stone floors took over her mind.

"The beast is locked up," she whispered, though she wasn't sure she believed it.

Morana felt the gap, digging dirt out from the hole now etched into the wall. She shoved the book back as far as she could get it, her body tense when she placed half of the stone back in the wall.

When she knew the stone would hold, encasing the book and hiding it well, Morana used the shadows to slip away.

After the darkness cleared, she saw Raidan standing in the center of her bedroom, amber eyes shining with sinister hope.

Bile rose in her throat, her nails digging into her palms. Morana swallowed. If she didn't play this right, he would send her back with his creatures. She wasn't going back.

"Your Majesty," she said.

Raidan's brows rose. "You've yet to call me that, my queen."

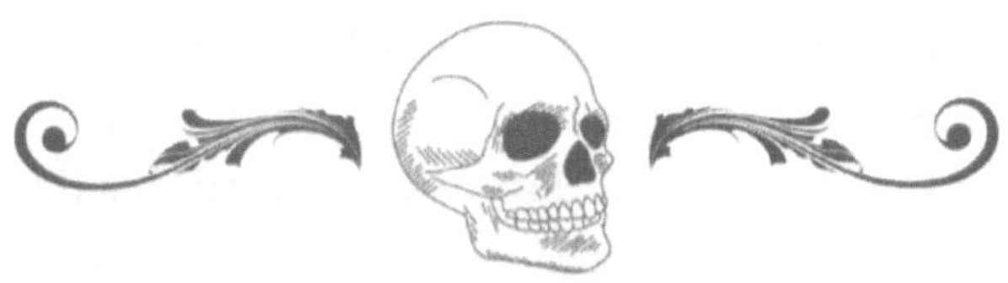

Five

"Did you find it?"

Morana's gut stirred at the savage smile stretching across Raidan's face—the way his eyes lit up in the dim light of her cold bedroom. He knew she had something—she was sure of it. The way his gaze locked onto her had her stomach twisting. She could still feel the crumbling stones beneath her fingers, the ones concealing her new secret.

She blinked, willing her mind to empty her thoughts. There was no way for him to know. He *couldn't* know.

"The book, Morana."

She buried her fear of the god, the twisting pain slashing through her chest at the image of Matthias standing in the tomb. It plagued her mind, but she couldn't let it show. Couldn't think about it with a demon standing before her and looking for an opening.

I love you.

Truth or not, the words held weight, and beneath that weight, she couldn't bring herself to give up his secrets to the monster in the room.

Or maybe deep down, she hoped Matthias had *seen.* When he entered her mind, maybe he had seen what she tried to conceal. Maybe he still cared enough to find her.

"No," she lied. Her tone was ice, matching the palace of bone surrounding them. It was the only word she could force out, unsure of why she was still protecting him.

Or maybe she *did* know and wasn't willing to admit it yet.

I love you.

Morana's skin crawled as Raidan trailed his burning gaze over her body. Something shifted in the air, and his smile fell, lips peeling back to reveal the teeth of a predator.

For a moment, she was certain he would kill her.

Raidan took a step forward, eyes hardening as his jaw clenched. Her mind was spinning and trying to decode what he was thinking. Either Raidan was pissed because he believed she hadn't found the book, or because he believed she had.

The latter was far worse.

"You will get the book," he snarled.

Relief washed over her. Morana's hand fell away from her dagger.

"I was looking for his blood book," she said, trying to convince him that her words were truth. "I think I have an idea, but I'm not sure. It's difficult to find."

"No matter," Raidan said, though the tension hadn't left his jaw. "We will go to Ohriid tonight, anyway. Inara and I will present an official alliance between The Wastelands and the Court of Light." His tongue clicked. "You will be there as well."

"And how will you introduce me?" she asked.

Raidan had promised her power—promised she would be queen. But he promised the same to the Goddess of Life. Inara ruled from the safety of her court, waiting to announce an alliance, while Morana ran errands and fought Raidan's ridiculous pet in the dungeons.

If there was anything she had learned during her time in the fae realm, it was that a god's word was worth nothing.

Raidan scoffed. "Brave to ask such a question."

Anger swelled in her chest—the kind that called the white mist to twist around her ankles. Her fear took a backseat as she looked up, sticking out her chin in defiance.

"You made a promise." Her power wrapped around her, rippling over her skin and feeding the deep pleasure that came with its presence.

Raidan's face twisted into something sinister as he took another step forward. He lifted his hand, dragging his thumb along her jaw, trailing it over her flesh until he dragged her lip lower with the pad of his finger.

"A promise I intend to keep," he whispered. A smile pulled at his mouth. "After you retrieve what I want. I told you that your position in this realm wholly depends on what you're willing to give me." When his gaze dipped lower, Morana shuddered. "I will present you as a consort—a whore until I decide you hold more value than that."

He released her, his smile slipping. "And I need one more thing from you, *Queen of Darkness*." The title sounded like an insult as it left his lips.

Morana hated herself for it—couldn't stand any leftover weakness but forced herself to take a step back. Her jaw tensed as she worked to put distance between herself in the monster.

He *was* a monster.

I love you.

The thought was unwelcome as she stood there, refusing to speak.

"Inara insists that the lord over Ohriid has betrayed her." Raidan cleared his throat. "Now, it's no business of mine. There are plenty of traitors in both courts, but you will be there for a secondary purpose."

She cocked a brow. "Conan?"

Raidan's head tilted to the side. "You know him?"

"I've met him," she confessed. "I don't *know* him."

Morana had met the fox following Axton's death. The lord had spewed information about suspicious creatures, betrayals, Inara's purpose in arriving to the palace of Ascella.

"You are to keep tabs on him tonight." Raidan's tongue rolled along his cheek. "You are to kill Conan and anyone who gets in your way." His head flicked to her wardrobe. "There's a gown for you in there. Wear that."

With wide eyes, Morana nodded. She longed to reach for her dagger and use it on the major god, but she knew his power would overtake her. Running her finger first along the scars on her cheek and then the tattoo behind her ear, Morana felt the stinging memory of the lives she'd already taken.

There were other scars now, ones her skin didn't speak of, including the death she'd caused tonight and the one she'd nearly caused.

If killing me would ease your pain, I would give my life up freely, too.

Raidan spun to leave, but paused at the door. His hand hovered over the knob. "And Morana?" he said.

"Yes?"

"Your loyalty," he began. "Your loyalty is to be rewarded." The door creaked open as the light from the hallway filtered in. She swore it highlighted her own betrayal. "But if you fail," he continued, "Death will not be around to comfort *you.*"

Clearing her throat, Morana nodded. "Of course." Her hand drifted from her tattoo to the dagger, as if she could seek comfort from the weapon instead. She knew the blade would do nothing. She wasn't ready to challenge the major god's power.

"Good."

The door to her bedroom closed. Raidan's footsteps faded as Morana let out a slow breath.

She untied her cloak and draped it over the bed, walking to the wardrobe to find the dress Raidan had picked for her.

While the major god had promised her power—a position—all of that seemed to hang in the balance. It was contingent on her ability to perform—to find the blood book for him.

And she had.

Still, as she stood in the silence, prying the doors to her wardrobe open, she couldn't help but hear Matthias's voice in her head. Three words slowly seeped through the cracks and threatened to take her under.

I love you.

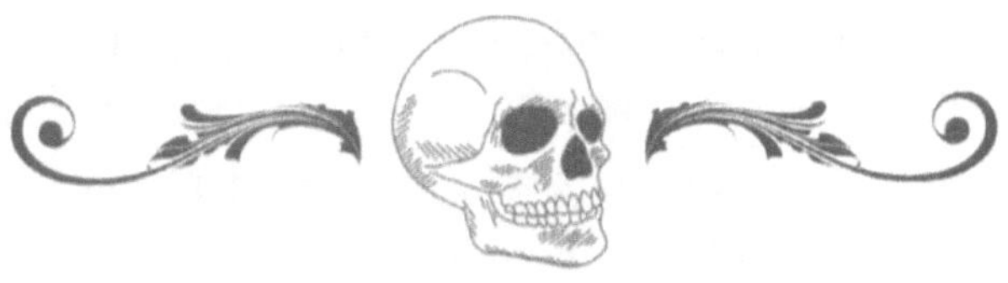

Six

"Morana," he placed his hands on her knees. His touch burned her with a desire she could hardly contain. "You just took a life. Some wounds run deeper than the flesh." Something softened in his features. "Now tell me, what other scars have you earned?" He moved his hand up, placing it on the left side of her chest. "The ones that reside here."

The memory faded as Morana thought about the scars Matthias spoke of. She'd killed Jameson, thought of Raidan's death frequently enough, and had almost killed Matthias for the second time.

Almost.

Those scars marring her heart—the ones he spoke of—were numb now. Calloused as she walked with her back straight, Raidan just a step ahead and leading her through Ohriid's palace halls.

She relished the relief that came with the numbness of scars. Hardened like her, as she felt nothing for Jameson, and nothing for the lord she would kill tonight. Or maybe she felt something but refused to acknowledge it.

Either way, she was confident in her ability to do the job. If she were to be stuck in The Wastelands, she'd have to prove herself—just like Raidan asked.

Her heels clicked on the gray stone floor, white mist drifting over the spots where she stepped. It was as if the magic had a mind of its own and was asking her to pay attention. While she felt more in control, the power lingered still—appearing as if it were a part of her instead of taken, just like the shadows. Raidan slowed to walk next to her, tucking her arm beneath his as he leaned in.

"You remember what you are to do, yes?" he asked, his hot breath scalding the skin beneath her ear. Morana hated when he did that. The god took every chance to invade her personal space and touch her. She wanted to scrub it off, remove every trace of him that had ever lingered on her skin.

Again, she was thankful for the numbness. If she didn't feel it entirely, she could keep going. She had to. Detaching herself from her body, she took a steadying breath and hoped that she would please the god next to her. It was her only chance at survival.

"Of course," she said.

The palace walls were not dark and gilded like the palace of Ascella, nor were they sparkling like glass as the walls and windows in Inara's court. Here, they appeared to be stone—dark gray and cold like the winter lingering outside the castle doors.

There was beauty there, though. It seemed to be hidden beneath the layers of dust coating the long table against the wall. Something felt unbalanced in the city—something felt *wrong*.

Conan had once begged her to come to Ohriid and see what was happening for herself, though she wasn't sure why the lord hadn't sought Matthias. Or maybe he had. Matthias had been imprisoned in Raidan's palace at the time.

The fox, Conan, had claimed that Inara was up to something—detailing the creatures crossing the border, and Morana supposed it made sense—his betrayal. Inara believed Conan to be a traitor, and Inara already knew him as such. It was possible he deserved the fate she would bestow upon him.

Guarding her mind against what she would be forced to do, Morana felt as if she were floating through the castle. The palace was set against a backdrop of snowy mountains and tucked within the city that reminded her of Vulcan.

Or at least it reminded her of what she remembered of Hames's city.

Hames, the lord of the northern city in Matthias's court, hadn't liked her to begin with, and maybe he'd seen through what Matthias was doing. It could have been a warning, and now she was left to regret the time she hadn't talked to him.

"I want to remind you," Raidan's voice interrupted her thoughts of the Court of Shadows. A small smirk formed on his lips. "Loyalty is to be rewarded, and for now, you belong to me."

His grip on her arm turned possessive, and Morana's mask slipped briefly, bile rising in her throat.

She had received too many warnings from the god. Each time he reminded her of her place and worth, she longed to run and leave Raidan and his empty promises behind. He was constantly dangling power in front of her, but Morana wasn't naïve anymore. It was all to ensure her submission.

Maybe she would run. If only she knew where to go once she left.

It seemed she'd always be hunted.

Morana blinked, bringing her fingers up to trail over the scar on her cheek. The skin there was raised and numb, all damaged nerves—just like her heart.

She had earned those scars. Earned them with sweat soaked skin and trembling hands—earned every ounce of numbness she now carried. She would need them to remind her why she would play this little game of submission even though she internally screamed in protest.

They paused in front of the double doors, sounds of celebration rising from within.

Raidan straightened the lapels of his jacket, smoothing the black fabric until the wrinkles faded.

"Once our introductions are over," he began, "you are to find the lord and do what is necessary. Kill anyone who sees you and show them no mercy. Once it's complete, return to me. I have plans for our evening together."

Morana nodded, clenching her jaw against the mist swelling around them.

The heavy, wooden doors swung open, a breeze billowing the skirt of her low-cut, burgundy dress. Raidan squeezed her arm once—just shy of too painful.

When the doors closed behind them, the fae in the room turned to look, eyes wide as the crowd parted, making room for them to approach the dais where Inara perched. Her rose-colored eyes hardened like ice.

"Welcome," Inara began. Her gaze trailed over Morana's dress, and she scoffed when she took in the low dip of the neckline.

Morana kept her expression blank, eyes dead like the lord she would murder.

"I see you brought a *friend*," Inara started, attention flicking to Raidan.

He placed a cool hand on her back possessively while he licked his lips. "A friend, indeed."

Morana fought the way her body wanted to stiffen; the way Raidan's low voice sent fear through her blood. Each time he spoke, it brought back the memories of all he had done—all she had endured.

Her power rose, and with it, it brought the taste of blood to her mouth and ignited rage in her chest. She wanted to kill him, possibly add him to the list of those she would end.

If he knew what she was thinking, he didn't say anything. Raidan simply leaned in, inhaling deeply, with his nose buried in her hair. "More than a friend," he whispered, "if you kill the lord."

Inara nodded toward the chair next to her throne and Raidan took a seat, dragging Morana down until she sat on his lap.

She wanted to vomit. His touch was way too possessive—too comfortable. Maybe her pain in the presence of Matthias wasn't so bad after all.

"I am pleased to announce," Inara began, "that the Court of Light has secured an alliance with The Wastelands to the north."

Hushed whispers erupted through the ballroom. The fae still focused on the gods in the room.

Morana caught a glimpse of auburn hair through the crowd, her eyes meeting with the honeyed gaze of the fox. She focused on him, keeping her attention there as her hand itched to grasp the dagger beneath her skirts. It helped keep her mind off the hardness now digging into her thigh— the proof of what all those unwelcomed touches were doing to Raidan.

"Enough." Inara's voice rang through the space, settling the questions being asked of the crowd. "It is an honor to be aligned with a major god," she spoke. "Raidan has provided a very important asset to our court—creatures created by the major gods themselves. These have all helped in our efforts to unseat Matthias in the Court of Shadows." She tapped a manicured finger against the arm of the dais. Morana looked away from it, gluing her gaze to the fox once again.

Conan's features were sharp—angry as he glared at the goddess.

"That, there," Raidan whispered, nodding in Conan's direction. "That expression is exactly why you will *obey.*" The last word had her gut churning, but Morana didn't flinch. "I should remind you," he started, his arm wrapping around her to place a heavy hand on her thigh. Inara was prattling in the background about the creatures and Zora—something about getting the city back from the Court of Shadows.

"You will do as I say," Raidan hissed in her ear. "If I say jump, you *will* jump." His touch rose higher, and Morana swallowed. "If I ask you to run, you *will* run." Morana shifted uncomfortably, fighting the urge to shove him off, as well as the mist rising at her ankles. "And if I ask you to part your legs for this crowd," his hand tightened around her inner thigh, and she bit the inside of her cheek. "You will do it."

His mouth, smelling of rancid wine, was almost to the corner of her own now. "Are you hiding things from me, Morana?"

The air felt as if it had been knocked out of her lungs. "No, your Majesty," she said, turning her head slightly.

"Should I find you are," Raidan whispered, "I want to remind you that you will die a whore."

Morana swallowed, tuning into Inara's announcement.

"As I mentioned, Raidan rules The Wastelands—a major god awoken and aligned with the Court of Light. As you know, Zora was attacked, but with Raidan's help, we acquired enough power to win our city back."

Morana watched Conan disappear and reappear through the crowd, padding away quietly in the middle of the speech. She could no longer hear Inara—no longer cared.

She needed to follow him.

When the cheers erupted around the room, Raidan released her, and she quickly shifted through the crowd. Finally released from Raidan's scrutiny and distrust, Morana followed the fox's trail as Conan disappeared through the heavy set of double doors. His eyes flicked over his shoulder once before he slipped away, and Morana knew this was her chance.

Without Raidan constantly questioning her loyalty, it was much easier to breathe—especially since her loyalty should be in question. She had a book hidden in his dungeon.

Morana tried to hang back, keeping herself far enough away that Conan wouldn't know she was after him. When she got to the hallway, she called the shadows. The familiar darkness rippled over her skin to conceal her movements.

Leaning down, Morana pulled off her heels to help silence her steps as best as she could manage. The cold stone floors of the palace soothed a bit of her nerves as they touched the pads of her feet, allowing her to focus on her breathing.

Morana cursed in her mind as she took in the almost bare walls. There weren't many decorations or tapestries hanging on the sad, gray walls to help her. It would be harder to navigate with no clear markings to note where she was. Wooden accents and sconces filled with faefire were the only decorations, and unfortunately, they all looked the same.

There was less life in Ohriid than in the Court of Shadows—a different kind of darkness than the one she kept around her when she found herself at the base of an old stairwell. It looked as if servants used it.

With her heart pounding in her chest, Morana's fingers ghosted the dagger at her thigh. She could feel the shadows twisting around her, the rest of the power in her blood stirring. A sense of euphoria overcame her as she could already taste his blood.

At the top of the stairs, Conan turned left, his footsteps sure and hurried. He was silent in his movement, glancing over his shoulder every few minutes to ensure he wasn't being followed. Little did he know, the predator had just become prey.

Morana stood silently in the hall, her shoes in one hand and dagger in the other, as she watched the fox slip behind a small wooden door. When the door closed with a gentle click, her mind swirled with a plan.

She supposed she'd settle on entering the room, binding Conan where he stood, and plunging her weapon into him. Her fingers twitched on the dagger at the thought.

But before she could carry out her plan, a scuffing sound to her left caught her attention. The wide eyes of a servant locked with hers.

The red hair and freckles reminded her of Cain as a frown pulled at her mouth.

You are to kill Conan and anyone who gets in your way.

Morana could see it then, the servant's plan to turn and run. His desire to get away and alert the palace was something she couldn't risk.

Before his frozen state of shock thawed, Morana called the mist, hoping it would give her the strength to do what she was about to.

She pressed a cool finger to her lips, a smile splitting her face. If she was going to kill an innocent, she had to commit.

She lunged, dagger slicing cleanly across the man's throat until he dropped to the ground, the crimson staining the gray stone.

There was no time to feel guilty about what she had done. This wouldn't be the first death she dealt tonight—not if she completed Raidan's task. And Morana desperately needed to complete Raidan's task.

She turned away from the scene and pressed her forehead on the wooden door, calming her trembling hands. When she called on the mist, it filled her lungs and helped ease the sting of regret.

She let the power rise, using it to numb her emotions and still the shaking hands at her sides. One hand still gripped the dagger, the blood of her first kill dripping down its length to soak the floor.

Looking back at the body once, Morana then turned and opened the door to the mysterious room beyond.

When she stood at the threshold of the massive study, she halted—losing her grip on her magic completely.

"Queen of Darkness." Conan's voice skittered across the carpeted floors, but Morana's eyes glued only to Death, his dark gaze boring into her own as her jaw clenched.

"Are you here to kill us?" Matthias asked, one brow cocked as the shadows trailed over his skin.

I love you.

Morana clicked her tongue, tilting her head upward. Her grip tightened on her dagger as her heart pounded wildly in her chest. She took another deep breath before offering her answer.

"Something like that."

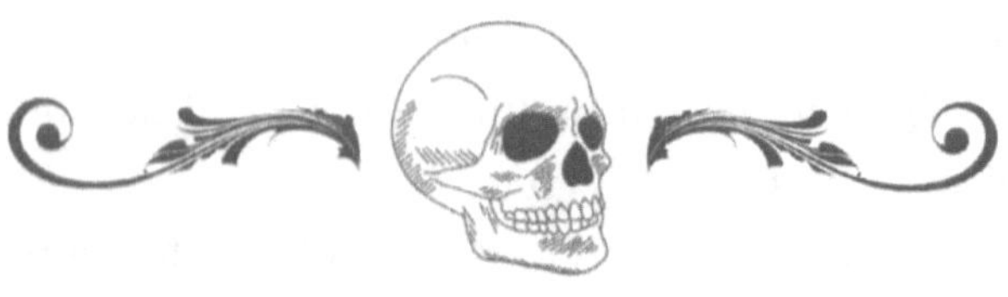

Seven

Morana's eyes flicked to Conan, her dagger still dripping blood from her last kill. She needed to do this, needed to do *something* that would keep Raidan from finding out about the book. He was looking for her to betray him, and if Morana couldn't kill Conan, Raidan would begin asking questions. It would put her in danger, with no place to run.

She needed to get it over with and kill the lord.

One corner of Conan's mouth pulled up into a devious smirk. He turned slightly, cocking a brow in her direction. "And if we ask nicely, will you spare us?"

Matthias's gaze held firm, burning her skin from where he stood. She could feel his eyes in the same way she had felt his fingers ghost over her flesh. The crawling sensation she felt when Raidan looked at her was gone, replaced with a different feeling under the fixed gaze of someone she'd once felt so close to.

The only thing she hated about the heat of Matthias's glare was the emotion it brought with it—pain, sorrow, *longing.*

The last one was something she couldn't afford.

Morana recalled the words spoken in the tomb, hardened her heart against them, and steeled her spine as Death tracked the shift in her body language.

"Not likely," Matthias spoke, his voice sending goosebumps over her skin. There was an intensity to his expression—one that kept Morana pinned to her spot, just like the servant she had murdered in the hall.

Matthias turned, stepping around Conan without breaking eye contact. His dark hair fell across his forehead, tattooed hands clenching at his sides. There was a coldness in his eyes, one that sucked the breath from her lungs. It reminded her that the darkness descended in the night, when the temperatures dropped and secrets came out.

Matthias had secrets. She'd learned them at the ball, but something about the way he looked at her spoke of the time that had passed since then. What had Death gone through? What did he believe?

When he was standing a foot away, Morana noticed the rapid beating of her heart as the shadows twisted around the two of them. The inky darkness swallowed Conan's image, and soon the shadows encased them in their own world. Once more, Morana stood before Death, her chin tilted up in defiance.

"Did you read it?" he asked.

Keeping her face expressionless, she edged her own power into the darkness filling the room. Her jaw clenched, teeth grinding against the force of the pain she was feeling. If she could focus on that—maybe she could make it through this interaction.

She was here to kill Conan, *not* deal with her emotions regarding Matthias, and she'd already hesitated too much.

"No," she responded.

Matthias hummed once, taking another step forward. His full lips pressed into a thin line, contemplating her words. The disappointment flickered across his features. There must be something in the book he wanted her to find.

But why?

Reading the book would give her power over him and answer why he was here—what he was doing, and what he felt. She would have access to his thoughts completely, even when he wasn't in the room. Why would the god of death want her to have access to his vulnerabilities after she stabbed him—and was planning to again?

She should have read it sooner, gone after it long before Raidan demanded it. Maybe then she would have whatever answers she sought.

"Did you give it to him?" Matthias asked, his voice low and laced with anger.

He was questioning her, and she wanted to let him. He could suffer, too.

Morana didn't answer.

Deep down, she knew why she was keeping Death's book hidden. She knew why she wouldn't give it up to the major god, but none of that mattered.

Morana wanted him to be angry with her. It would help her hide the way his words had taunted her since the moment she left the library.

I love you.

Still, despite the way she hardened herself toward him, it felt as if he could see right through her. The way he looked at her felt like he knew the depths of her soul. It was too vulnerable, so she leaned into his icy silence and offered it back, glancing through the parting shadows towards the bookshelves built into the walls behind Conan. Maybe one of the books stuffed onto the shelves could teach her how to escape Death.

Matthias's brows rose, and the shadows dissipated, and Morana watched as Conan trailed a slender finger across the wooden desk. Morana watched as Conan trailed a slender finger across the wooden desk.

She was here to kill him for his betrayal—nothing more.

"You betrayed Inara," she said, ignoring Matthias completely. It wasn't a question. Morana knew as much, especially since she walked into the room with the lord and Death meeting in secret within Inara's court. Though she didn't know the reasons why, Conan's angry expression during Inara's speech said enough.

She wondered how many secrets still existed between her and Matthias. The numbness moved to a cold rage, one frozen like the space between them. Had he been working with Conan the entire time? Was there another game at play?

Another reason to read the book.

Conan scoffed, folding his arms across his chest. "Inara is not exactly noble either," he supplied. "She's made deals with a major god in pursuit of power. I'm still trying to figure out exactly how she woke him up. Which reminds me," His eyes lingered, questions dancing in his honeyed gaze. "How *is* Raidan?"

Morana swore she felt Matthias stiffen as she kept her attention glued to the fox, his thin nose crinkling in disgust.

"Has he forced himself on you yet?"

"That's enough," Matthias interrupted, his tone laced with the darkness sharp enough to crack ice.

Morana couldn't help the way it pulled her attention to him—to the way his expression flashed pain at the idea of her with Raidan.

"Well," Conan stepped forward. "If you're going to kill me, now is your chance. Though I don't believe you will. You hate Raidan just as much as we do."

Faefire chased some of the shadows in the room, flickering in the sconces lining the wall and highlighting the lord's sharp features.

His mouth spread into a slow smile. "Or—" Conan continued.

"Or?" she asked. Her eyes hardened against the swirl of emotions in her chest and the thoughts racing through her mind.

"Or maybe you don't hate him, and you're going to kill us, anyway. I suggest you don't, though."

Morana bit her cheek, aware of the dripping dagger at her side. She should move—should work to end him, but he was right about one thing. She hated Raidan. "What could I possibly gain from keeping you alive?" she asked.

She had waited too long, lingering in their presence without acting. Anxiety took hold of her, mixing with the pain she was suppressing as she stood with Matthias next to her, his words echoing in her mind.

"You could gain a free trip to visit The Oracle. I'll be with you, looking for answers as well." Conan ran a hand through his auburn hair, hanging loose around his shoulders. "It would be a chance to visit with your mother."

Her breath lodged in her throat. Morana couldn't help the way her gray eyes flicked to Matthias, gauging his reaction in the dimly lit study. The god didn't flinch, simply held her gaze and waited for her answer.

"You would take me with you?" she asked. There was doubt—a large amount of it, but she was being given a chance to run. And while Matthias had betrayed her, he certainly hadn't laid a hand on her the way Raidan had.

Everyone in the damn realm had burned her, and she knew Conan could be no better if he was sneaking around and plotting against Inara.

Raidan had sent her to kill Conan, knowing of the betrayal that Morana now knew to be true. There wasn't a singular person she could trust amongst the gods and the fae. At the very least, if she had Matthias's blood book when she went with them, she would have access to his thoughts—even more than she'd had when she was in his mind.

At least she would know his motives and his lies. There were also the questions buried deep within her—ones she hadn't had time to think on since her departure from the Court of Shadows. Her mother was surrounded by the same magic and within the same realm—hidden with The Oracle.

If she chose this—if she ran from Raidan, there would be no returning. He would kill her. But trading the monster of the mist for the monster of shadows seemed like her only option. She'd find her mother, ask her questions, and protect herself with Matthias's thoughts and memories laid bare through his book.

And if she could find a way to blame her departure on Matthias—maybe then she'd secure herself an out. She could go back to Raidan if she chose—stronger and willing to take his promises for herself.

Use them, Morana. Use them like they used you.

Matthias put his hands in his pockets, turning until he stood in front of her again, blocking her view of the fox. Her hand squeezed her weapon, ready to attack.

"We are going to The Oracle tomorrow morning--early," Matthias started. "You're welcome to come with us."

"Raidan sent me to kill Conan," she asserted. "What will I do when Raidan finds out that he's running free?" She swallowed then, revealing the truth. She needed to find a way for someone else to take the fall of her failure. It would give her the time she needed to protect herself from the major god until she was strong enough to fight him herself. "You don't know what he will do to me if I fail."

Matthias's gaze darkened briefly, anger rippling off him before it dissipated. "I'm a death god, Morana. I'm fully capable of faking the man's demise." His nostrils flared as he looked down at her. Those dark eyes ripped through her as if he saw it all. Her plan to protect herself from everyone in the damn realm, including Death, was so obvious to him. It was as if she'd spoken it aloud. "You can return to the ball, claim you were successful, and lie to the bastard. Go back to The Wastelands and read my book, for fuck's sake." His eyes were blazing. "Then I can come for you."

"And why would I want you to do that?"

His head tilted to the side. "Morana." He inhaled deeply, his annoyance making the cut of his jaw sharper, his shoulders tensing.

Matthias took another step forward. He was close enough to touch as his voice lowered, shadows twisting until darkness surrounded them again and embedded itself in his voice. "You can't possibly want to stay with him," he continued.

"Maybe I do." She didn't, but Death wasn't a good option either.

Matthias was still angry. She could see the power surrounding him—the frustration. "There's a reason you kept me locked out of that part of your mind," he growled. "I won't ask you what he's done, but I'm going to beg you." His brow furrowed, clearly uncomfortable with the thought of begging her for anything. "Come with me."

There was nowhere safe in this fucking realm. But safety was a small price to pay for answers.

"I'll come with you," she said.

Matthias's eyes lit with hope—a tiny flicker. "Good," he said, the corner of his mouth tugging upward just briefly. "Good girl." His head flicked to the door, missing the blazing fire in her eyes. "Now get back to the ball. We will take care of the rest."

Morana swallowed, composing herself. She tried to keep her tone cold. "Why should I trust you?" she asked. She shouldn't—didn't. Not anymore. But there was still a small, stupid part of her that wanted to hear what he had to say.

Matthias stepped closer still; his expression stripped bare as pain shone in his eyes. He observed her with steady breaths—taking a moment to let her in. The vulnerability shocked her and caused her to suck in a sharp breath. "Because," he said, "I meant what I told you." He paused, studying her reaction. "In the tomb, I meant every word, and I only wish I would have told you sooner."

Morana nodded once as the mask returned, the coldness returning to his gaze. Those pretty lies cracked open the scars on her heart, and she wondered if she were really using him at all.

Those words he had spoken had haunted her since the moment he'd pushed them into her mind, running like a record she couldn't escape from.

He couldn't fool her again, though. He had given her his blood book and given her access to his inner world.

When she returned to Raidan's temple, she could read Death's book and figure out his true intentions. If Matthias was to betray her, he couldn't hide it for long.

If he was lying, he wouldn't win again.

"Okay," she said before turning and leaving Conan with Death—very much alive.

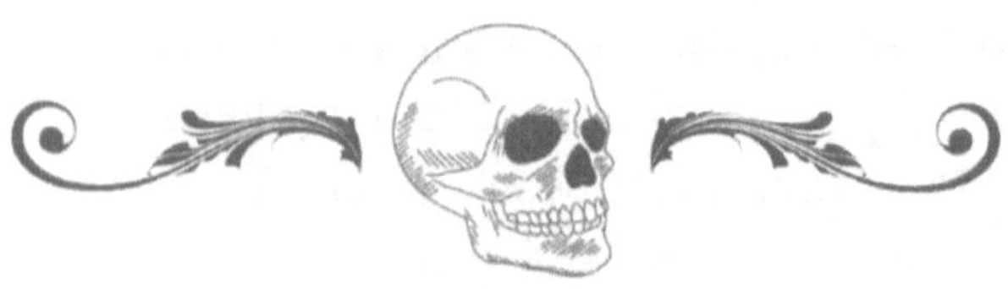

Eight

When Morana entered the ballroom, it was like she had never left. Raidan stood next to the throne where Inara perched, sipping faerie wine and laughing at whatever the god had said.

Morana pulled the skirts of her dress tighter, concealing the bloodied dagger beneath them. If she was thankful for one thing, it was that there was blood on her weapon to prove her story true—for now.

Morana walked through the crowd; eyes cold as she moved to stand at the base of the dais.

"Morana." Raidan smiled, flashing his teeth when he saw her. "Please," he said, gesturing at his side.

Moving to stand next to the god, Morana walked up the staircase, her hands steady and her face betraying nothing. At least this time, Raidan hadn't forced her to sit on his lap.

Matthias said he would fake Conan's death, but Morana couldn't shake the doubt that lingered in the back of her mind. She needed to get his book again, to make sure he carried out his side of the deal.

She needed to leave.

Raidan's arm hung heavy around her shoulders as he leaned in, breathing deeply and burying his face in her hair. She stiffened as his grip tightened around her. "You smell like blood," he whispered, his tone pleased.

Morana cleared her throat, desperately trying to ease her way out of his grasp. Raidan was bad enough on his own, but being drunk on fae wine and his own ego, he would be far worse. He didn't let her go, magic wrapping around her in a thin fog, holding her to him.

"I completed my task," she said, eyes fixed forward as Conan's words spun a web in her mind. *Has he forced himself on you, yet?* "When can I leave?" she ground out.

Raidan ran a thumb over her shoulder, sending her gut stirring uncomfortably. "Whenever you choose." He leaned in closer, lips ghosting over her neck. Morana halted, her mind shutting down to cope with what was happening. She wanted to run. "There are rewards for your loyalty," he whispered. "Many rewards."

Morana closed her eyes, focusing on the binding magic until she felt herself grasp t and shove his power away. "Wonderful," she said. Morana stepped forward, striding down the stairs and moving further away from the god.

Inara's voice sounded behind her, low enough to be directed toward Raidan, but loud enough for Morana to hear. "Pity about your whore," she spoke. "Seems as if she's constantly trying to leave. Not very faithful. Not fit to stand beside you."

Morana didn't look back, her eyes locking on a spot toward the back of the room, a dark alcove where she could call the shadows—disappear.

Movement caught her eye from the large double doors she had entered upon her arrival.

She heard the rushing sound of wings, followed by a chorus of screams and the sound of light crackling behind her. Morana turned, watching as two enormous creatures poured into the room all leathery wings and fire—*dragons.*

Morana's eyes widened, her heart hammering in her chest as she turned to sprint away from the chaos.

She pulled off her shoes in frustration for the second time and pushed through the crowd. Even magic couldn't make heels easy to escape death in.

A large, scaled dragon descended in front of her, blocking her retreat. The creatures weren't as big as she'd imagined, small enough to fit in the massive ballroom, but large enough to send fear shooting up her spine.

It brought back memories of the harpies Raidan had used in the ballroom at Ascella. Though these creatures seemed far more magnificent—something Callum, the fauna god, would covet.

Morana reeled back, looking into the blazing red eyes of the monster as its hot breath blew over her face. The creature's head tilted to the side, regarding her carefully before it turned, sharp teeth digging into the flesh of someone from the Court of Light.

Rather than waste time, Morana moved toward the alcove behind the dragon, calling the shadows to cover her until she was nearly gone.

Before she could vanish, the shadows around her swelled and parted until Matthias stood next to her, concealed by their combined magic.

"What are you doing here?" she shouted, trying to talk above the noise of death and destruction.

Matthias looked down at her, hair damp, and eyes lighted. A smile stretched across his face. "Staging a man's death, of course."

Morana's eyes widened. "With dragons?" She was practically screeching. This isn't what she agreed to. Raidan would know.

Not to be trusted.

"A gift from Callum," he supplied, looking at the chaos around the room. "There's been a change in plans," he said. "It's time for us to go." A warm, tattooed hand wrapped around her bicep, gentle and familiar. "I'd like for us to grab the book first, though."

Morana didn't have time to think. She simply nodded and let the shadows conceal them further.

"Where to?" Matthias asked, leaning down, his lips just inches from her ear. "Where have you hidden my book, Morana?"

Her eyes dragged over to his hand, still wrapped around her arm. The dark rumble of his voice sent shivers down her spine, and she silently cursed herself for the way her body sparked at the sound. She couldn't give in to those feelings—couldn't forgive him for his betrayal, so Morana turned to look up into the face of Death, and she vowed to prod at his wounds. Raidan had locked Matthias in the dungeons, too. The major god had tortured Death. Now she had his blood book hidden in a cell that would certainly serve as a reminder of his weakness. Hopefully, it would also overshadow the weakness she felt at her body's response to his voice—his proximity. "The dungeons," she spoke, a smile of her own crossing her features. "In Raidan's temple."

Matthias's grip tightened subtly, the only sign of his discomfort. "Interesting choice," he mused before the darkness swallowed them whole.

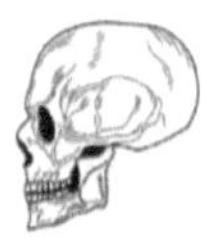

"Explain to me, Morana," Matthias began, "why you hid my book in a fucking torture chamber." His voice held a sharp edge, one that cut through the air and echoed around them, pleasing Morana as her fingers dug at the stone.

The smug satisfaction fueled her. Matthias had used her to start a war. She wouldn't feel sorry for returning the favor—or for trying to dig up his wounds in the way he had dug up her own.

For a god hidden in darkness, Matthias sure knew how to shine a light on her flaws—her weakness—and with her vulnerability at relying on him so fully, she needed to level the playing field.

The stone broke away, revealing the crevice she had created. "You don't really have a right to speak on that right now." She yanked the book when it caught on a jagged piece of rock, pulling it out of its enclosure. "Maybe I wanted to see you crawl after the book and find it in a spot that would be painful for you." Morana turned, the dark dungeon dripping around them. She focused on him instead of all the fear crawling down her spine—the memories of what Raidan had put her through. "Maybe I'm paying you back for what you did to me. You still betrayed me, Matthias."

His name sounded like a curse.

But if he remembered being trapped and tortured beneath the temple, too—he didn't allow it to derail him. He held firm, intensity rolling off of him and stony eyes fixed to her.

Her own gray eyes were blazing as anger mixed with hurt in her chest. It was far better than the ridiculous shiver she felt at his voice in the alcove. White mist rose at her feet, called by her heightened emotions. "You betrayed me," she repeated. "Used me to start a war."

He stepped closer, his scent filling her lungs. "You stabbed me." He didn't flinch. "And you didn't read it," he said, tone steady.

Morana grimaced, but the sound of slick skin sliding caught her attention and they both turned to look through the tunnels. Fear spiked in her blood, draining all the other emotions away. "No," she whispered.

"What is it?" Matthias asked, shadows dancing across his skin.

"A basilisk," she answered. "We need to leave." Morana turned as the sound moved closer. "Now!"

The darkness swelled as magic wrapped around them, preparing to send them out of the dungeons.

Morana squeezed her eyes shut, fighting the temptation to look for the monster—one of many, she was certain.

Before they could retreat, sharp pain slashed through her as the serpent lunged, digging its teeth into her leg. It dragged her away, and she lost her grip on Matthias's blood book.

Morana screamed; her eyes still closed while her back scraped along the stone. It burned just like it had the last time, but her mind was whirling—making it difficult to concentrate.

When she'd done this before, she had been ready. This time, the creature had taken her by surprise.

"Morana!" She could hear Matthias's shout from behind her, muffled through the haze of her increasing panic.

She couldn't think straight with the burning of teeth in her leg. She needed to draw on her training, the time she had spent in this very place fighting the same creatures.

Reaching for the shadows on instinct, Morana grasped at the already bloodied weapon still strapped to her thigh. She couldn't get a good grip, the force of the beast jostling her as she tried to heal her calf.

Morana called on the binding magic, wrapping it around the basilisk until its movements slowed. She gritted her teeth, but doing so took so much of her power that she could feel the magic draining away.

Finding her dagger and dragging it from the sheath, Morana squeezed her eyes shut. She lashed out and dug the metal into the now cracking flesh of the serpent. Still refusing to look at its body as it slackened, she pried her leg free, and turned to open her eyes, finding Death waiting for her.

Matthias appeared in a fog of shadows just behind the creature. He kept his eyes locked to hers, refusing to look at the overgrown snake as his grip squeezed the blood book in his hand.

"You've gotten better."

Her calf was already healing, itching as she stitched back together with her magic.

"Of course," she said, her tone hard. She needed to get out of the palace of bone to avoid his condescension or pity. Still, the look on his face caused her to slip up and confess. "Raidan only throws me in this dungeon every other day." It was more information than she meant to give him.

Matthias reached out, handing her the book again and wrapping them in darkness to bring them back to the Court of Shadows.

"Don't worry," she said, before the shadows whisked them away. "He won't miss the creature. He has plenty."

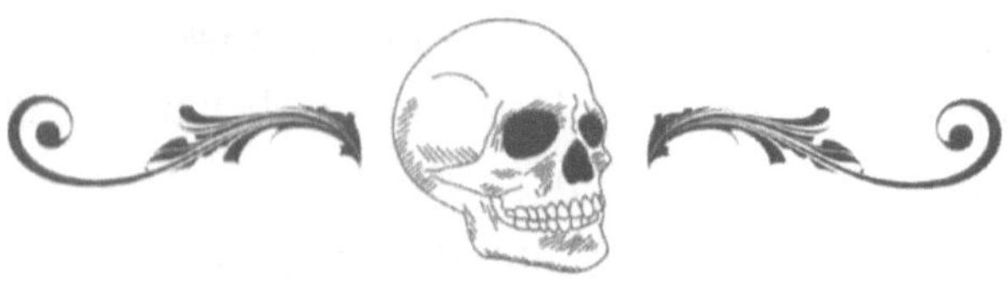

Nine

A steaming cup of tea sat on the table near the fireplace, along with a glass vase of fresh flowers. Dark walls, gilded accents, and memories that felt like daggers were next to greet her.

Morana gripped the leather book in her hand and turned to see Matthias leaning against the doorframe, locked in contemplation. Darkness oozed from him, his jaw working as if he wanted to say something. Faelights from the hall flickered with the fading shadows, and Morana took a deep breath, the tension in her shoulders loosening slightly now that they were out of the chaos.

Still, she didn't know how to proceed after her confession, and now that her mind was catching up with her body, she realized what she'd done.

She'd escaped Raidan, neglected to kill the fae Raidan wanted dead, ran off with Death, and found herself back in his clutches.

He could lie to her at any moment, and she wouldn't know because the book was still closed between her fingers.

Matthias breathed deeply, the line of his jaw sharpening with his anger. "He throws you in the dungeons," he said, breaking the silence just like his stare fought to break through her defenses.

While Morana could feel the desperate desire to crumble beneath those words, she wouldn't. He couldn't see her mind spinning or the hurt buried beneath the surface. Instead, she would show him strength—anger.

"I'm stronger for it," she asserted, keeping her tone steady.

Matthias nodded once, considering. "And that's why you returned to my court? You felt strong enough to kill me?" His eyes narrowed. "Or is it something else? Maybe you just wanted to escape him. Or maybe you've thought about what I said."

She blinked as the air seemed more difficult to swallow. What was he getting at?

I love you.

It could still be a lie.

He could be lying about his feelings, resulting in the pitiful attempt to ask why she'd come with him so easily. Whatever his reasoning, Matthias wanted her to believe he loved her. Regardless of what she felt, she wouldn't admit to anything more than cold indifference.

"Actually," she said, brushing a strand of hair away from her face. "I recall Death begging me on his knees to return."

One brow rose as Matthias pushed off the doorframe and prowled closer to her. "I have been on my knees for you before," he said, and her stomach dipped as she glanced away. "I was not on my knees this time, but I'd be happy to show you what that looks like."

At his nearness, Morana's memories spiraled. She could see moments with him in the quiet of the night and feel the way her body settled in his presence. All of those memories dug at the wound in her heart, prying it open and reminding her of what he'd done. So much of it had to have been fake, and the thought stirred rage in her gut.

He fucking used me like everyone else.

Morana lifted her chin. She would not be weak. "I would have you beg," she said. "You will beg for my forgiveness, Matthias."

"And why would I want your forgiveness?" He was so near now that she had to glance up to see his expression clearly.

A fucking liar.

"If you loved me, you would want my forgiveness. You'd already be on the floor."

His voice dropped to a whisper, eyes flicking between her own as she held on to anger. "I would," he whispered, a small smirk forming on his lips. That smile infuriated her.

"So, you lied."

Matthias leaned forward, his breath fanning out over her face as his lips hovered inches away. He was testing her to see how close he could get. His scent lingered, filling her lungs with darkness and desire—and hatred. He wouldn't get close—not again.

"I did not lie to you, Morana."

Morana held the book tighter, moving it between them as if the truth of his memories would protect her from whatever he was doing.

"Then prove it," she challenged. Stepping back, she dropped her gaze to the floor, insisting he show up—do what he promised for once in his unnaturally long life. "Beg," she commanded.

The dark laugh that left his lips had her mask slipping and left her grappling for control. Maybe she should stop goading him—read the book like he asked and run.

"You would have me beg you for forgiveness?" he asked, crowding her space again and pressing his thumb gently beneath her chin. His eyes were a kaleidoscope of emotion—annoyance, vulnerability, desire. They each flashed until only one thing remained—*want.* "Would that prove that my feelings were true?"

Morana ground her teeth together. She should really just read the book. "It would be a start."

"My memories laid bare aren't enough?" He breathed; lips now close enough to kiss.

She felt the heat of his body then, the way he pressed in—pushed every button she had. "Maybe they won't be," she confessed.

If they weren't enough—

She refused to think of it.

"Very well." The smug smirk returned as he took a step back. With eyes blazing, the god of Death lowered himself to the floor.

Morana looked down, her heart pounding rapidly in her chest as took in his mussed hair, the dirt coating his clothes from the dungeons.

It reminded her of her own exhaustion, but she couldn't rest until he was gone.

"Is this what you wanted?" he asked. "Because my confessions remain. If you should choose to run your blade across my neck, I would allow it. If you believe me so vile, then have your way with me, my Queen."

Morana wished she could give in to his pretty words. *Pretty lies.*

"It's still not enough," she nearly whispered, watching his shoulders lower in disappointment.

He quickly recovered, replacing the sorrow on his face with something far more heated. "Shall I use my tongue to beg without words, then?"

Hot desire pooled at her core, and Morana realized what he was trying to do. Regardless of the way he'd hurt her, she still wanted him, and he was trying to uncover that secret for himself.

By the look on his face, he still wanted her, too. *Good.*

She could use that.

"The only thing I long to do with your tongue is cut it out." To her surprise, Matthias smiled up at her as his fingers brushed her thigh. She sucked in a sharp breath and cursed the way her body betrayed her.

Morana didn't miss the way he paused. Even as they grappled for dominance, he still waited for her to retaliate before skimming those fingers up to the weapon at her thigh.

His touch burned, igniting sparks across her skin before he quickly snatched the dagger from its sheath.
She reached for it, but he was too quick, moving his hand away before returning it between them and offering her the hilt.

"Go ahead," he whispered, and Morana stared down at the weapon in shock. "If that's what you really want."

Fuck him.

Tears threatened to spill over. She was so very close to revealing the truth that had haunted her quiet nights in The Wastelands.

As she watched Matthias, she realized he would let her do it. He trusted her far more than she trusted him, and that thought scared her.
Morana grabbed the dagger in her free hand, clutching his blood book to her chest as she turned away, quickly wiping the tear that had leaked out.

"You should go," she said.

She could feel him rise behind her—feel the disappointment. "I should," he answered before clearing his throat. "I need to check on what is happening in Ohriid," When she turned back, the tears wiped away, Matthias took another step away with his hands in his pockets. "Then I'll be back to take you with me to The Oracle."

The question slipped out before she could think better of it. "Is it safe?" she asked, the words implying far more than she intended.

She still cared for him.

Love. Raidan had said.

Matthias's eyes met hers, one corner of his mouth turning up before shadows began twisting up his arms. So, he'd gotten enough of an answer, she supposed.

Cocky bastard.

"Does it matter?" he asked.

She knew what he wanted her to say, but she wouldn't give him the satisfaction. Death would not hold that power over her again.

As his smile turned cold, Morana watched the shadows swallow him, carrying Death away from Ascella's palace.

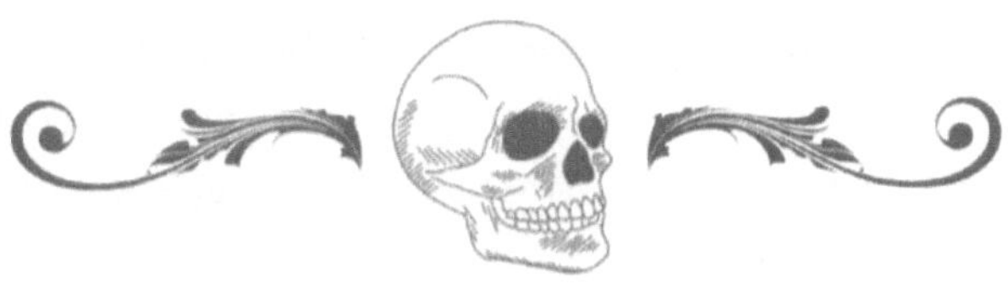

Ten

With the fire crackling in the hearth and Matthias's departure, the exhaustion took hold of her.

Morana moved around to the chair, leaning her head back against the cushion and staring at the steaming cup as she brought his book to her lap.

The cup sat undisturbed. She longed to drink but didn't know his motives, and so she sat questioning the contents of the tea laid out for her. Such a change from her time in the court previously.

"It's not poisoned."

Morana sat up, reaching for her blade again on reflex. It was the only protection she had when her magic became too drained, and after the events of the night, she felt drained in every way possible.

Sarnai stood at the door; umber eyes lined with emotion. Her black hair descended over one shoulder; her brown skin glowing—as if the magic she possessed longed to be seen.

"Sarnai," Morana whispered.

"I can't stay," she said, "But I'll be back. I just needed you to know you could drink the tea."

Morana stared at the goddess, remembering the slithering vines on the floor of the palace of bone—the shadow by the gate.

She wondered what the flora goddess had been up to. Sarnai had access to different realms and access to both courts since she cared for the plants. Was she also allowed in The Wastelands? Morana had seen nothing but desert and dry ground there. It was hard to believe any life could exist beyond the border.

"Sarnai," she repeated.

Sarnai shook her head. "I have to go," she insisted before a wan smile appeared on her full lips. "But I'm glad to have you back." Sarnai nodded toward the book. "Read it," she said, and then she was gone.

Morana blinked before taking the cup of tea and drinking deeply as she opened the book in her lap.

It would take far more than Death on his knees for her to trust him again. She had to know the truth now because, with every passing moment in his presence, she felt an odd stirring deep in her soul.

The feeling was dangerous—more powerful than the magic pumping through her veins. He'd very nearly gotten her to give up her emotions. She had to keep them locked away until she knew what the book contained because the knowledge of her feelings—the things Raidan knew she harbored in her chest—all of that gave *him* the power to break her.

And if he were to break her again—

As the pages turned, Morana inhaled the scent of old parchment and magic—the power that bound Matthias's memories to the tome.

She had no clue where to start, so she flipped toward the end, hoping to glean whatever information she could from Matthias's meeting with Conan.

If his desire was to hand her over—to kill her or something else—she was certain she would find it in his memory of their meeting just hours ago.

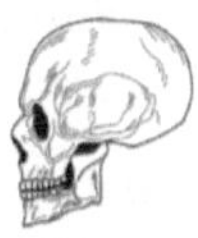

Death stared at the lord in front of him, the man's oddly colored eyes lit with a fire.

He hated relying so heavily on the lord—throwing too much of himself into Conan's hands, but it was a necessary evil. He'd proven faithful—giving Sarnai access into The Wastelands, and for that, Matthias was grateful. Morana had locked him from her memories in the tomb, but Sarnai hadn't been so closed off.

The goddess had seen things—things that made his blood boil. If Morana had been the stars—the light that pulled him out of the darkness—he couldn't bear to watch that light wink out one by one.

Even so, Sarnai hadn't seen enough. She'd lingered on the outskirts of the palace, gleaning as much as she could—hearing the way the major god spoke to her—used her—lied.

He still didn't know what happened in the dungeons, and Morana didn't want him to know.

Death's gaze snapped back to the lord. For what it was worth, Conan really hated Inara. It was a mutual feeling—one that bound them together—one that sparked an alliance.

"She wants power, but so does he," Conan said. He had snuck away from Inara's announcement to meet in the study. "I'm surprised Inara and Raidan haven't killed each other already."

His lip turned up at the corner as Matthias played out their deaths in great detail. If he had his way, Raidan would die at his own hands—punishment for the way he spoke to Morana at the dinner table—for the things Sarnai had shown him.

"I'm sure it will come to that after the war." Matthias cleared his throat. "Can you get Sarnai more access in the Wastelands? Lingering outside of the palace isn't enough."

"I can't get her in the temple," Conan said. "She can't use the shadows like you."

"Then get me inside."

"Matthias."

The look of annoyance on the lord's face sparked rage in his blood—the same anger that had been boiling since the moment Death had sought him out.

"I want inside Raidan's palace," he growled, stepping forward. "I need to know what happens in the dungeons."

Conan straightened. "I can't give you that, and you fucking know it."

Death's dark gaze cut through the air, taking in the harsh angles of the lord's face, the serious etched into his forehead as his brows furrowed.

"Why not?" His patience was wearing thin.

"You know why." For what it was worth, Conan didn't back down. "These things are delicate. One misstep, and I will lose access entirely. Raidan could ward his temple against me—against you."

Grunting in submission, Matthias pushed his sleeves up his forearms. The lord was right. If he lost access to the palace, and she needed him—there'd be no hope then. Not that there was hope now. She'd still wanted to kill him.

As much as he hated to admit it, Conan was a valuable asset, and he needed to be reasonable. It would be so easy to allow his emotions to rule him, but he couldn't. This was a business meeting—an alliance—and there was more to discuss.

"I'm headed to speak with The Oracle in the morning," Matthias said. "For Cain."

"The seer?" Conan questioned.

Matthias tensed. For as faithful as Conan had been, there was still a sliver of distrust. If he would betray his own queen, there was no telling what the lord would do. He already had the upper hand.

"We don't know that for sure," Matthias said.

Conan's eyes rolled as he folded his arms across his chest. "Oh, please."

Matthias ground his teeth, the arrogance causing frustration to rise within. His shadows swirled, moving over his flesh and sending pleasure down his spine. They were calming—keeping him in check. "We don't," Matthias ground out. "It's what I'm trying to figure out in the first place, but I'm certain you need to visit The Oracle, too. Your own questions regarding your court."

"Of course," Conan answered, shifting uncomfortably. "The Oracle may ask for his return," Conan warned. "If she believes he is a seer like herself, she may want him back. Of course, she'd offer you a bargain, but I wouldn't advise getting roped into one with the old woman."

Matthias thought back to the scribe working in his libraries. If The Oracle wanted him back, she wouldn't get him. She'd had her time with the boy, and he'd proved less than useful for her—sold like cattle by Inara's court. Cain had wanted out by whatever means necessary, and The Oracle had let him go—his gifts too weak for whatever she needed.

"I don't think she cares for him," Matthias answered. It was true enough. "Inara sold him to her once, and he wasn't useful. The woman's reclusive, anyway."

Matthias fought the image that flashed in his mind— the image of a woman who looked so similar to the one he loved.

He closed his eyes briefly, trying to keep himself from falling into the trap that was sorrow. The scar to the left of his heart stung—a reminder of her hatred for him.

That was the worst part.

"And what of Morana's mother?" Conan asked.

Death didn't expect the way her name would pierce through his chest—making the scar feel as if it were ripping apart. The ache returned—the feeling of loss at her absence. But also anger for her not coming to him and making this decision to leave without him.

"What of her?" Matthias asked, keeping his voice level and even. He wouldn't betray his emotions to the lord. While Conan had shown loyalty so far, there was no telling where that loyalty stopped.

"Did you know?" Conan asked, his voice lowering despite their privacy in the study. "Did you know the woman was her mother?"

There was no point in lying to him. Raidan would have her and the world believe something else, but whatever lies the major god had told her, whatever story he'd spun—

Fuck.

None of it mattered—the truth didn't matter.

Still, Matthias couldn't help the way he longed to say it—to voice the reality.

"Not at the time," he admitted. "Later, though. I figured it out later." Death's dark eyes cut away, the power rippling over his skin in an attempt to calm him. "I found out far too late."

Conan hummed before speaking. "She's here, you know—in the palace."

Time seemed to stop—his heart beating a frantic rhythm.

"And if I'm correct," Conan spoke, a smug smirk forming on his lips, "She should be here any moment. Followed me in the hallway. I think she's supposed to kill me."

Something hit the ground beyond the door to the study, causing the shadows to wrap tightly around Matthias's shoulders. He could sense it—the Death beyond the door. And just the same, he sensed her magic there too—the very shade of darkness that called out to him.

She was here, and he knew it before she'd even set foot in the room.

The door opened, and Matthias's eyes tracked to the blood dripping from the dagger in her hand—a fresh kill.

Impressive.

"Queen of Darkness." Conan's voice traveled along the stone floors, his smirk lingering.

Her eyes fixed to Death—gray like storm clouds waiting to unleash themselves on the scorched earth. Her anger and sadness swirled in the shade, reminding him that he hurt her—even if he hadn't meant to—even if she thought wrong about what he'd been planning, he'd still hurt her, and for that, Death would never forgive himself.

He longed to rip the sorrow from her soul—take it away and break apart anything that threatened to steal her peace.

Staring at the beautiful woman, a picture of strength and death, Matthias cocked an eyebrow before speaking—trying to calm his beating heart. "Are you here to kill us?" he asked, reminded of the weapon she held—the same one she had shoved into his shoulder. The wound still hadn't healed, and if he were being honest, he didn't want it to.

She licked her lips, raising her chin and taking one steadying breath before offering her answer.

"Something like that."

Morana fingered the page, unable to keep going as tears streamed down her face, her mind working to keep up with what she read.

He hadn't known half of what she assumed he had. It seemed that gods were more like mortals than they appeared.

Along with that, there were the little slices of emotion written in Matthias's blood book. As she turned the parchment, glimpses of what he felt for her assaulted her established truth. She even saw what had been in his mind when she entered the room to assassinate Conan.

That and the fact that she'd read his memory—watched the interaction through his own eyes. Something about that felt far more intimate than she was ready for. Maybe before—maybe when she hadn't thought Death had used her. But now?

Morana pulled her knees closer to her chest, bending the pages. She wiped her tear-stained cheeks as she realized what Raidan had done and who he really was.

While she didn't fully trust Matthias, yet, she had to accept the reality that she'd been wrong about at least this—following lie after lie.

And her time in the Wastelands only confirmed Raidan's nature.

The flowers in the vase next to her shifted—living and breathing in the way they reached out to her. Sarnai couldn't have gone far. The goddess had been with her in the Wastelands, watching from afar. There was still the question of what Matthias knew—what he'd seen through Sarnai, and why he was so adamant about knowing what happened in the dungeons.

It was a part of her experience she'd locked him out of, and a part Sarnai hadn't been able to see.

Still, Sarnai had been there.

She smiled, and a hallow laugh escaped at the irony of it all. While her trust had been shattered and her emotions still swirled around in a confusing storm within her chest, a part of her warmed at the thought of where she was.

Home.

Morana leaned back, taking a long drag from the tea—now cool on the small table next to her. She set the cup down and gave in to the exhaustion.

Darkness lingered beyond the walls of her room, and she found it to be a comfort. The darkness wasn't what people claimed it to be—and maybe Death wasn't either.

Maybe she had been wrong to believe him a liar.

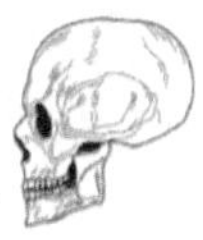

Shadows flickered in the corner, slowly fading to reveal Matthias's tall frame. Morana sat up and moved her fingers to her cheek. She knew he could see the tear stains there—the exhaustion.

His eyes widening as they met hers, glancing over her ragged appearance.

At least she'd gotten a few hours rest.

He strode forward, darkness traveling in his wake.

"What happened?" he asked. "Why are you crying?" He knelt beside the chair, eyes searching. She could see the way his fists tightened, as if he wanted to touch her, but knew she wouldn't accept it.

Not yet.

Matthias glanced down at the book in her lap, and Morana suddenly felt stripped bare. There had been no time to process what she'd read—sift through it. And if she were honest with herself, they were mere breadcrumbs—not answers.

Nothing had changed, but at least she knew the betrayal didn't run as deep as she'd thought.

Even so, one couldn't be sure.

Uncurling her body, she gripped the spine of the leather book and snapped it shut, standing and straightening in front of Matthias.

"Is it time to go?" she asked.

There was a pause. Death's shadows ghosting around her legs, reaching out to her in her sorrow. She couldn't read his expression and didn't know if she wanted to. Morana set the book on the side table, determined to come back for it when they returned.

"You'll need something warmer." Matthias said. "Some boots." He cleared his throat. Something had clearly unsettled him—melted the ice in his tone and softened him. "I had clothes set out on the bed for you."

Morana turned, glancing at the thick pants and sweater, the cloak, and the boots laid out for her to wear.

She turned back to Death, brows furrowed.

"Where are we going exactly?"

He didn't respond, simply nodded toward the outfit before turning and walking toward the door.

"I'll wait in the hall." Matthias didn't look back, and she debated following his request. She longed to crack open his book again instead—read exactly what was in his mind.

Was he thinking of the memories they shared? Or of the way he'd mapped out every inch of her body with his tongue? Or had he given up on her entirely?

Somehow the words she'd read and the feelings her room dragged from her chest had sparked hope.

But hope was dangerous, so she stood and stared at him, waiting for what he would say next.

Matthias grunted, the shadows still twisting along his skin. "Come out when you've changed," he said, and then he was gone.

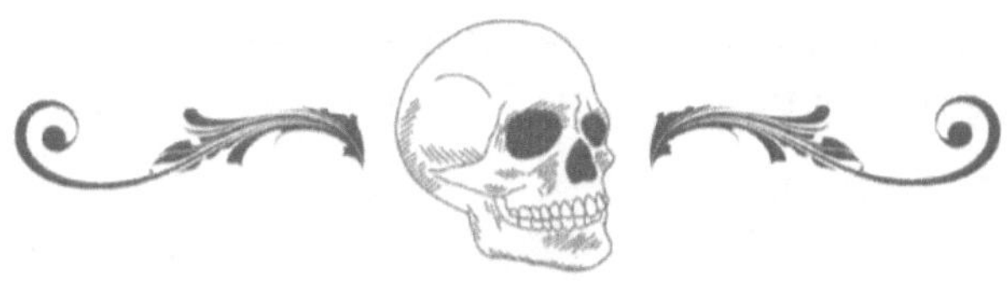

Eleven

A cold breeze whipped through the trees, shrieking on its way out of the forest they landed in.

Morana pulled the cloak tighter around her shoulders as she surveyed the snow-dusted ground shaded beneath the canopy. Gray clouds stretched overhead, mirroring her mood.

"Where are we?" she asked, that same wind lowering to a whisper as it lifted stray strands of her hair when she turned to see Matthias.

His features hardened, jaw clenched tight, as he stared at an invisible path through the trees. When his eyes finally met Morana's, he spoke. "The human realm." He paused. "Appalachia. Stay with me, and if you hear your name called out in the forest, *don't* respond."

Morana followed Matthias out of the trees until they emerged at the base of a winding dirt road, her boots crunching over the thin layer of snow and fallen leaves. The tall trees of the mountains framed the worn, gray buildings on either side.

Her voice dropped to a whisper, as if speaking would disturb the residence. Whether anyone was alive in the abandoned-looking town, she didn't know. "Do people live here?" she asked.

"Not anymore," he answered, climbing up the dirt road.

Morana nodded before trekking up the steep mountain behind him with her breath casting a white mist in front of her face. She could feel Raidan's power stirring in her blood at the reminder of the magic she held. Her nerves were on edge, and she had a difficult time not grasping for the power like a tether.

Abandoned or not, she didn't dare use that magic here—not in any way that would be apparent.

"You read anything interesting?" Matthias finally asked, breaking the silence.

Morana's chest tightened as she thought back to the entry in the blood book. It wasn't much, but his feelings were apparent, as were Raidan's lies. Matthias hadn't known who was with The Oracle, but she still didn't know how to respond—what to feel. "Things have not changed," she said, though she wasn't certain that was the truth.

Matthias glanced back over his shoulder with an amused expression. "At least you're not holding a knife to my throat."

She blinked, feeling the weight of her dagger against her thigh as cold indifference hardened her expression. It would be too easy to give in to his teasing and slip back toward whatever they had had prior to the events of the ball.

The mist rose around her ankles, copper coating her tongue as she gave herself permission to drag that power from the pit of her stomach. Morana used it like a barrier—something to keep her anger boiling—a way to keep her distance.

Being on an abandoned mountain, alone with Death, set her on edge. Her power was all she had.

"I could fix that."

Matthias chuckled, hardly acknowledging the threat as she fought to keep up. The dirt hardened beneath her boots and made her feet feel heavy with every step.

After the basilisk in the dungeon, her muscles burned, but her magic was returning. She could tell by the way she had to fight to keep the fog and shadows from twirling around her skin. The light was there, too—but Morana hadn't touched it—and it didn't beg for release.

She thought back to what she'd read with a clear mind. At some point, Matthias knew who the woman was. Maybe not in the beginning, but eventually he'd learned of her identity, and he still hadn't told her then.

Raidan had lied, but so had Death.

"When did you know?" she asked, a lump forming in her throat. "When did you know it was her?"

Matthias slowed until he was walking next to her, his dark eyes sliding in her direction. "The day I found out, I nearly told you," he confessed. "It was right before the ball."

Morana nodded, remembering that night—the way he stumbled over his words.

Their time at the dock—

She shook her head; the doubt returning. He'd confessed his feelings for her, knelt at her feet, yet still—she couldn't believe him with so many questions lingering in the air. "And why didn't you tell me?"

Matthias looked pensive, lost in memories and thought before he responded. "I didn't know how to say it. What it meant, Morana—it was a clue about your magic. I didn't want you to believe that when I asked you to marry me, it was only for your power. I see now that keeping it hidden made it appear that way."

She cleared her throat as her heart squeezed in her chest. Every part of her wanted to believe him. She'd lost everything coming to this realm, and when he spoke with vulnerability in his voice, she couldn't help the way she leaned in—ready to listen. But all of that could still be a lie.

She needed to change the subject. "Where's Conan?"

Matthias chuckled, the smokey sound making her skin warm despite the cold. "Eager to get rid of me?" One corner of his mouth turned up, his breath still visible in the winter air.

"No." Morana pinned her eyes to the ground, watching her steps carefully. "I just—"

"He's coming," Matthias answered, cutting her off. "He should be here soon." Clearing his throat, Matthias kept his gaze forward. "Conan would make a fantastic spy. I'm sure he has his reasons for seeing The Oracle. The man wants to know how Inara did it—is hoping the knowledge will help us get rid of Raidan and find a rightful heir for the Court of Light.”

Silence stretched between them as different emotions fought for dominance in her body. Morana listened to the sound of the wind, now lowering to a quiet whisper as they continued their trek uphill.

She was about to see her mother.

It was possible that the woman wouldn’t recognize her and that she wouldn’t recognize her mother, either. Morana didn’t know how to feel about it. For so long, she’d been numb. Maybe she’d be angry or feel resentment. Or maybe she would still feel nothing at all.

“Morana, talk to me.” Matthias’s voice cut through her thoughts, bringing her back to the other issue at hand. Even though Matthias hadn’t known until later, he still hid the information. Still asked her to marry him immediately after. He was right. It *did* seem like he wanted her for her power, the same as Raidan.

“You used me,” she whispered. “Maybe not completely, but you used me.”

He had known *something* in the beginning, being told that Morana was the answer. It was the entire reason he found her in the human realm. She didn’t know why she was bringing it up—maybe she just wanted to hear him say something different.

Maybe she needed a distraction from what they were about to do.

“I know you won’t believe me.” His voice sounded resigned, and she didn’t dare look at his expression for fear of finding the same coolness returning. "I—it wasn't intentional."

It wasn't intentional.

"Elivira practically admitted it. Said this was all bigger than myself while we were in Namid." And Morana had foolishly fallen for it, thinking she could actually help the fae—the gods.

But that thought had come when she had believed the people around her had truly cared for her. And now that it was all in question, she wanted to hear him admit it. She wanted him to say that she wasn't a pawn in his political game, and Morana was willing to toss out accusations until he denied it.

"It was all political." Deep down, she knew there was more to it than that—after reading the entry in the blood book, Morana knew he had feelings for her, but still—

Matthias stopped, moving to stand in front of her. Her legs burned from climbing uphill, her heart bleeding out in her chest and begging him to give her a different answer—to tell her she was wrong.

Matthias shook his head, stepping closer and crowding her space. "No," he said. "It wasn't all political."

Morana kept her eyes on his—unwavering. "I don't trust you," she confessed, vulnerability making her voice waver. One part of her wanted to, especially as the words left his lips.

It wasn't all political.

"And you trust Raidan?"

It was a fair question, but still made her wince. Did he judge her for leaving?

"That's not fair."

"Isn't it?" he asked, frustration shining in his eyes. "You're *here*." He was so close she could feel the heat from his body, a stark contrast to the cold that surrounded them. "You jumped at the chance to leave, and you clearly had something to hide when I entered your mind in the tomb. Memories you didn't want me to access."

She lifted her chin in defiance. He could see right through everything she was hiding, even as she cut him off from access to her memories.

The wounds were too fresh, and she couldn't let him in again—not yet.

"One prison to the next and back again." Her words cut like shards of glass as the wind picked up around them, snow twisting with it on the mountain.

Matthias looked as if she struck him. Questions, worry, and sadness crossed his face before they disappeared so quickly, she thought she'd made it up.

Her anger and sadness swirled in the shade, reminding him that he hurt her—even if he hadn't meant to—even if she thought wrong about what he'd been planning, he'd still hurt her, and for that, Death would never forgive himself.

Matthias stared at her, the intensity of his gaze scalding her skin. "You don't mean that," he said, inching closer. Morana felt his breath on her face, his shadows calling out to her and begging her to answer—to take it back.

For a moment, she was lost in his presence, eyes fixed on the lips she had kissed before. She longed to relive those memories, to find herself elsewhere, a place where the god stood in front of her with clear intentions.

For that moment, she *wanted* to take it back. Her breathing grew labored as she held his onyx gaze, keeping her expression hardened against whatever feelings were rising in the pit of her stomach. She felt as if he could see her—see the truth written there. She *wanted* to trust him again.

Light cracked from behind one of the trees as Conan appeared, playing with his magic and weaving it through his long fingers.

The fox prowled forward; one corner of his mouth turned up at the sight of them. Morana noted that the fae always had this air of smug superiority and suspicion. Something she both admired and hated. "Am I interrupting?" he asked. "And before you answer, I would like to say that The Queen of Darkness interrupted me and Matthias first." The light between his fingers winked out, and he lowered his hand. "And when *she* did it, she was, in fact, out to kill me."

Morana didn't laugh, but kept her focus locked on the lord in an effort to turn away from whatever was happening before he showed up. She could feel Death's eyes lingering on her skin, begging her to turn back, finish the conversation they had started.

Looking at Matthias, Conan cleared his throat uncomfortably. His smile fell as he looked up the snow-dusted hill and winced. "Well," he began, "let's see what the old hag has to say."

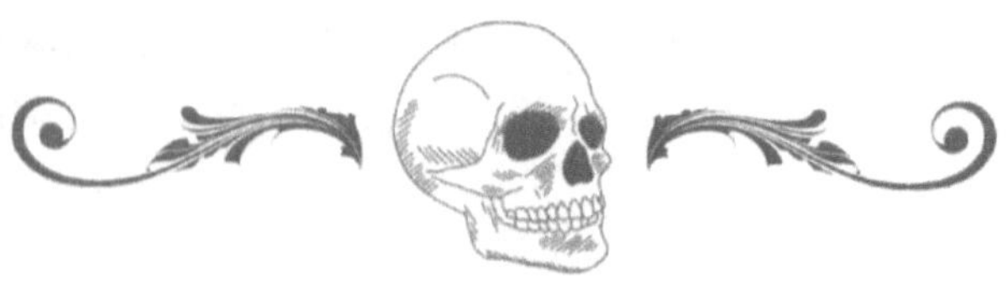

Twelve

They walked in silence, quickly rising higher above the valley below. Morana let the forest's quiet carry her uncomfortable conversation with Matthias away. The increasing chill in the air as they ascended was enough to keep her mind focused on the task at hand.

She stared at Conan, watching the lord step over the logs on the forest floor. They'd departed from the trail fifteen minutes ago, and there was no telling where they were headed.

The amount of trust it took to follow unsettled her. Morana recalled the hesitancy in Matthias's thoughts regarding their initial meeting, and the way he'd begged Conan for access to the Wastelands—for access to her.

Conan had provided a way for Sarnai to get there undetected, and he was now heading to the Wastelands for information regarding his court. It was information that could prove useful—something she should be aware of.

Morana sidled up to the lord, trying to get away from the quiet and her swirling feelings.

Conan had a reason for seeing The Oracle that didn't involve Matthias at all. The lord was smart—cunning—and he had secrets and capabilities that Matthias had been interested in. He wasn't to be trifled with.

"What are you attempting to learn from the *old hag*?" Morana allowed light to enter her eyes, hoping it would soften her questioning. "You must have some reason for seeing her."

Conan looked her over, and despite his assessment, his shoulders remained relaxed as he pulled on a branch to help him over the small clump of roots on the steep hill.

She grunted as she followed his lead, looking back once to check on Matthias who was listening behind them. Not that her questioning needed to be private. He probably already knew Conan's reasoning.

"I have some questions regarding my court," Conan offered, his expression turning serious. "My power."

"Something about the light?" she pressed, hoping he would feed her more information.

"Curious little thing," Conan said, cocking a brow in her direction. His voice lowered as Matthias lingered behind them, now out of earshot. "What makes you think you're privy to my innermost thoughts and concerns, hm?" He leaned in ever so slightly. "Maybe I don't want to tell you why I'm going to see the woman."

Morana turned away from him, calling the shadows now that they were hidden among the trees. Her magic taunted him, slowly circling until she directed the darkness to his mind.

Conan promptly shut her out, well equipped to block the intrusion, but not before she felt it—felt the immense power of light running through his veins.

It called out to her, sparking her own magic in her chest.

Her eyes widened, and she stopped her ascent, causing Conan to turn around, lips pressed into a thin line. He didn't say anything as Matthias caught up, briefly stepping in front of her. The tension in Death's shoulders increased as he stood to block her from Conan, his brow furrowed and magic swirling around the god.

"Problem?" Matthias asked.

Conan's jaw ticked as he stood with his arms folded across his chest. "Not at all," he answered.

With her heart racing, Morana focused on the wind through the trees, the gentle flakes of snow falling from sleepy limbs above. She couldn't get the feeling out of her bones—the light he held inside.

"Perfect," Matthias said. "Let's keep going." He prowled up the hill, irritation clear in the heaviness of each step.

Morana lingered, waiting for the distance to stretch far enough between Conan and Matthias that she could speak privately. They walked together up the mountain, her mind still trying to piece together the lord's intentions.

"What interesting secrets you're hiding," she said.

Conan's expression didn't change—relaxed and unbothered, regardless of his true feelings. "Keep your prying to yourself, Queen of Darkness. Death's been in my mind, same as you. He found nothing amiss."

"Did you block him out, too?" she questioned. "And can he sense the light?" Moran's gaze worked to see through the fox, but it was no use. "He can't sense it can he?"

"You're much more familiar with it, I suppose." Conan's jaw worked. "I don't know what he knows, but I know that Death keeps to the shadows. He's lived most of his existence in darkness, caring very little for the Court of Light. That is," he narrowed his foxlike eyes, "until you came along."

Morana's brow furrowed.

"Maybe you've inspired him to act—seek something good."

Morana scoffed. "I highly doubt that. He's merely using me for a war he already wanted."

Conan lifted a brow, his eyes sliding in her direction briefly. There was knowledge written there—a sense of knowing that seemed to follow him. "If you're sure," he spoke, but there was a mocking element to his tone. "That, or you finally gave him a reason to fight—to care."

His casual manner disappeared, and Conan's voice snapped through the trees. "Just a reminder," he said, "keep your findings to yourself."

Hearing the tightness in his tone, Morana dropped the subject. "Of course," she said.

Her legs burned as they walked to the top of the mountain in silence, the light dusting of snow swirling with the wind. They didn't speak any more, and Morana had time to let her thoughts wander, her mind turning back to the truth of what she was about to do.

It was likely that her mother would be there when they arrived, and after so much time away, she found herself more resigned than she'd expected. Even so, she wondered if seeing her mother would drag up those old feelings—unearth them from the grave they'd been buried in for so long.

The dirt road narrowed, leading to a worn fence barely propped up by a wall of snow. A crow perched on one of the posts, as if waiting for their arrival. The bird ruffled its feathers, sending a shiver of foreign magic down her spine. Somehow, she was certain The Oracle had been informed about her approaching guests.

Morana's eyes caught the old house, worn with age and peeling white paint. The building looked gray and ominous where it sat on the mountain.

Matthias opened the wooden gate, stepping aside for Conan and Morana to enter before they all made their way to the porch.

Morana flinched when the screen door snapped open, a gust of winter wind swirling in the air, beckoning them inside, though nobody stood at the entrance.

"Our invitation," Conan said with a smirk before entering.

Matthias gestured her forward, and Morana couldn't fight the nerves swirling in her stomach. The dusty hallway they entered was nearly empty and overrun with cobwebs. Each step that they took caused the old floorboards to creak beneath them. If The Oracle didn't know they were here, she did now.

A shadow caught Morana's eye as it shifted at the top of the stairs. When the woman came into view, Morana could feel her heart rate pick up. Her palms grew slick as she stared at the face of The Oracle.

She could feel the magic, sense it in her blood. Whatever the woman held within her was powerful, stirring up Morana's own power in its presence.

Shadows cascaded down Morana's arms, meeting the white mist gathering at her feet. She could feel the light crackling in her chest, her breathing quick as if her entire being anticipated—*something*.

The tall woman moved slowly; harsh wrinkles gathered at the corners of her eyes. A hand dappled with age spots slid gently down the railing until The Oracle finally made it to the bottom of the steps with a light scuff on the hardwood.

Morana looked up into the woman's face, centuries of wisdom etched into her skin.

"Queen of Darkness," she said as a smile cracked to reveal crooked teeth.

The shadows answered her words, floating around Morana until pleasure rippled along her skin.

Matthias's eyes were on Morana, gauging her every reaction as his own shadows whispered in the room.

The Oracle turned her head slowly to Matthias, that smile still stretching across her face.

"Second time you've been in my house, god of Death," she said. "The payment will be steep."

"Name your price, Baserah."

Morana got the vision of Matthias—the one that creeped up on her when she least expected. It reminded her he was both god and king, and despite the tension still between them, she liked it.

"The boy," the woman suggested just as Conan predicted, and Morana watched Matthias flinch. It was barely there—well hidden beneath his harsh expression. He was protective of Cain, and something about that warmed her chest even as it tightened at the request.

Morana reached out to Matthias, her shadows asking for access to his innermost thoughts, and without question, he let her in.

You wouldn't, she said.

He didn't respond.

"My scribe?" Matthias finally asked aloud.

Matthias, don't.

Morana didn't like the way she was begging, but the sharp pain in her heart at the idea of bringing Cain back here was unrelenting. Regardless of all that happened—the Court of Shadows had become home. Cain was just a boy— one that had already suffered at the hands of Inara and the ancient woman before them.

Morana was staring at him now, begging him to listen as she practically shouted into his innermost thoughts. *Matthias, you—*

Relax, he said.

The silence stretched on. "Something else, then," Baserah suggested. "An object from the Hall of Relics, perhaps."

"What do you have in mind?"

"Something pretty." Her head tilted to the side, and Morana thought she heard a creaking sound at the motion. It was as if the woman were so old, her bones needed to snap and settle with every movement. Baserah's dark eyes fogged until they were completely white.

Morana watched as the woman's features shifted. The wrinkles disappeared, aged skin tightening until the woman standing before her had completely changed.

Young, beautiful—

Frightening.

"I think I can do that."

Baserah turned, gesturing for them to follow her up the old steps as Matthias led them, Conan trailing behind Morana. The fox was eerily quiet after the comments made in the woods.

Losing some distance, Morana glanced back at him, wondering.

She stretched the shadows out, running them over his mind, requesting, and to her surprise, she found access, though limited.

What are you looking for here, Conan? she asked easily enough, turning to keep her eyes fixed forward.

I want to know how he gave Inara all that power, Conan answered. *Maybe then we could take it back and find the rightful god or goddess of life.*

When they reached the top of the stairs, Baserah led them into an empty room with worn wooden floors that matched the rest of the house. Light filtered in from the window, casting the chilly room in a blue tinted glow.

The door slammed behind them, and Morana jolted, glancing back once before watching The Oracle sit in the middle of the floor.

"Please," she said. "Sit down."

Matthias grabbed Morana's bicep, gently guiding her to sit next to him—his touch warm on her skin—comforting and protective. For the first time since she'd seen him, she found herself leaning into it. He may be a liar, but he had reason enough to keep her alive.

Conan sat on her other side. His sharp features hardened into an impenetrable mask.

"You have questions about the war, Death," Baserah mused.

Morana couldn't look away from the white eyes, noticing a thin trail of gold lining the bottom, like tears threatening to run free.

"I have no answers for you," she said. "But you have, however, found the answer for yourself."

Those white eyes held Morana in place as her shadows swelled, bringing comfort with them.

She couldn't look away from Baserah—couldn't look away as one of those golden tears spilled down her pale face.

Morana blinked as the words washed over her. With them, she could feel the hint of anger bubbling beneath the surface.

The answer. Nothing more.

Though doubt lingered at the edges of her mind—a reminder of Matthias's thoughts laid bare in the blood book.

"You brought the answer here," she said, smiling. Her teeth still crooked despite the change in her appearance.

Morana could feel her anger rising. Matthias hadn't come to hear the same useless excuse. Even then, she didn't like the idea of being used.

"The answer?" Morana's tone cut like a blade. "You mean the way to start a war?"

That golden tear dripped off her chin, staining the floors below as the woman tilted her head. "The way to win it."

Morana scoffed, finally glancing away.

"How are your new powers suiting you, Queen of Darkness?"

Her head whipped back to Baserah, that same anger swelling at the title—the reference to what Raidan had placed inside her—the ownership he had over her.

The Oracle brought to light the unanswered questions Morana grappled with. Why did she have this power? How was she to win a war? What did the title mean?

"You mean Raidan's power?" she seethed. "The power force fed to me through the Veeden." Morana's mouth twisted in disgust, that white mist rising as if called by the woman's very presence. "It's fine."

"That power," the woman began, her smile fading, her voice deathly serious. "That power is your own, Queen of Darkness. It is the power that all the major gods hold."

Conan was looking at her, mouth parted, eyes wide, and mask broken.

Morana didn't dare breathe as she allowed herself to look to Matthias. Shock hid in his dark eyes, reminding her that even the gods had questions—apparently, that included herself.

The door behind them opened, and a cloaked figure entered the room. *A woman.*

She circled around where they sat on the floor to stand behind the oracle, slowly lowering her hood to reveal a face so familiar, Morana thought she was hallucinating.

"Queen of Darkness," The Oracle spoke. "Meet Lady Death." There was a pause—another beat of silence as the blood rushed out of Morana's face.

"Your mother."

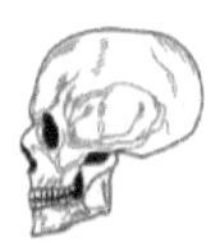

Breathe.

His voice was in her mind.

She didn't remember The Oracle leaving the room—didn't remember her mother sitting to take the

woman's place—didn't register anything happening around her.

There was only his voice—his shadows reaching out to comfort—to soothe.

Morana, breathe.

Did you know? She wasn't looking at him—merely staring at the familiar face in front of her. Looking at the woman who ran and left her family in shambles.

I didn't know. Matthias's hand moved to rest on her knee, and she didn't pull away—welcoming the touch despite it all. *I swear to you, Morana. I didn't know.*

The way he said it—she wanted to believe him.

"This may be a shock to you," her mother began. "I understand you may be confused."

Matthias's grip tightened on her leg—just briefly. "I think we should take a break." His tone was dark—a warning.

Morana turned to look at him. She felt as if she were in a haze, as if none of this were real, and she would wake up at any moment from the awful nightmare surrounding her.

Watching Death, she tuned out the conversation—ignored the words exchanged between Matthias and *Lady Death*, her mother.

Morana didn't stop looking at Death as her mother walked out of the room, Conan following in her wake to ask his questions, no doubt.

"Morana." His voice cut through the heavy roaring in her ears, drawing her back to herself.

"You didn't know?" she asked again.

Matthias placed a hand on the side of her face, fingers threading through her hair—his touch gentle. "I didn't know," he whispered.

She nodded, closing her eyes and leaning into the touch. Maybe she shouldn't be taking comfort from Death, but *damn* she wanted it.

Taking a deep breath, Morana sat on the floor until the thoughts quieted. Those thoughts of her obligation, her responsibility, and the fact that there was more to her life than avoiding Death and his lies—or truths, maybe.

If she was a god—a major god—then she couldn't run off like the woman who'd done exactly that to her own family.

With those thoughts came the fear of failure.

Matthias sat with her until the fear faded, finding its place hidden somewhere in her mind. Her body steadied as he watched her, gently brushing her hair back behind one ear. Matthias grabbed her hand and threaded his fingers through hers.

The warmth of his flesh drew her back to the present.

She couldn't wallow about the lies she'd been told. If she were honest, the lies had been her constant companion since she set foot in the fae realm. To her surprise, the fae were not responsible. It was the gods who would bend their word and manipulate the truth to serve their purposes.

"We can leave," Matthias said. "We do not have to stay here if you're uncomfortable."

"I'm not—"

"You've suffered enough. It wasn't my intention to take you from Raidan and throw you into this." The regret flashed in his eyes—barely there before it was gone and replaced by the confident and steady presence of a king—a god. Just like her. "We can leave."

"No." Morana stood as she straightened her clothes. At some point, she would have to deal with the truth of what her life had become and where she had come from.

She refused to run from her problems—refused to be like the woman waiting somewhere in the godforsaken house at the top of this snowy mountain.

There was no more room for feeling sorry for herself—just the responsibility of taking control of her emotions and using them to move forward.

"I want to see her," she said.

Matthias stood in front of her, unsure and intense. He carefully watched her as if he were looking for the crack in her expression or the thing that would alert him to some truth she was hiding.

There was nothing to hide. When the shock faded, Morana realized what she needed to do.

Maybe The Oracle wasn't crazy at all. Maybe she could be the answer—even if she didn't know how to be that, yet. And then there was the reality that her responsibility extended beyond Matthias's court. She wasn't *his* answer.

Raidan had kept her tortured and broken. If she were a major god herself, Morana could be her own answer.

Her chest cracked open at the way Matthias stepped forward, his gentle touch trailing along her jaw. Those feelings she had buried were still there, waiting to resurface—waiting to forgive.

For the first time since seeing him, Morana saw the possibility of that forgiveness as well as the twisted reality of Raidan's words. Maybe he knew what she was and filled her head with falsehoods fueled by a hunger for whatever power The Oracle seemed to believe belonged to her.

"If you're sure," Matthias said.

"I'm sure. I need to understand who she is—who I am." Morana cleared her throat, nerves coursing through her body. "If I'm truly here to be the answer, I need to know."

Matthias nodded, turning to exit the empty room.

Dust floated through the air as Morana thought of all the ways she could crumble in the following moments. She wouldn't, though.

"Morana." Her mother walked in first, Matthias on her heels with a harsh expression and shadows swirling in his midst.

"That's far enough." Matthias's hand reached out, stopping her mother before he moved to stand between them. "Say your peace," he spoke—his voice a command. "Then we are leaving."

Morana's mother nodded.

"So," Morana began. "Lady Death?"

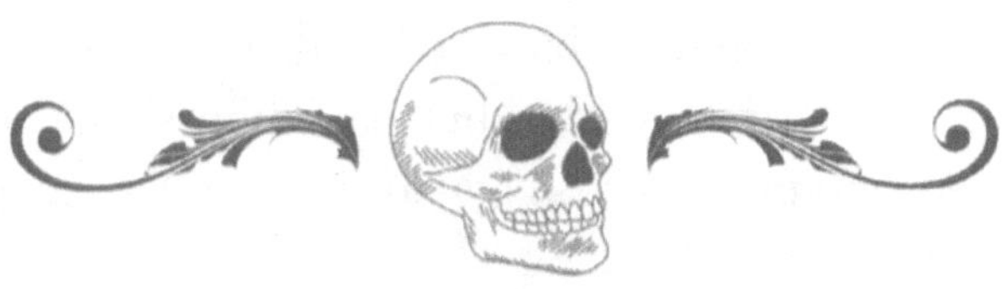

Thirteen

Morana sat on the dusty floors of The Oracle's house, her eyes fixed to her mother, and her mind clinging to Death.

She had allowed him into her mind—letting his steady presence help her find some sort of courage. She desperately needed it to face, not only her mother, but the reality of who she was and what she was learning.

Even so, she still kept careful control of what Matthias could see. There were still parts of herself she didn't want him gaining access to. Not yet.

Her mother took a cup of tea from the floor, delicate hands lifting the saucer along with it. She appeared cold and unaffected—utterly detached.

Maybe all the gods behaved that way. Morana had certainly found her fair share of indifference since her time in the dungeons with Raidan. Matthias had shown the same cool mask, too.

No.

This was not the same. If it were an attribute common to all gods, Morana wouldn't feel the sting of her mother's absence creeping up on her. Her mother wouldn't have shown her love to begin with. And she had—for a time. Morana also wouldn't have offered her emotions to Matthias. She certainly wouldn't have him sitting next to her—angry and protective—ready to rip Lady Death apart.

He was a god, too.

Setting the cup down, Morana's mother looked up with cool gray eyes. Her black cloak still hung loose around her thin shoulders; hood lowered to reveal her face. Her cheeks were hollow, but aside from her slim appearance, she looked good.

"There were prophecies about me," her mother began. "Prophecies about what I would do, you know. Prophecies about how Raidan would be ended, and how I was to be the one to stop him."

Morana kept quiet, thankful when she felt Matthias's fingers skim her knee gently—the softest touch of encouragement—support. It was making her greedy. She'd been so set on keeping him locked out, but in this moment, for whatever reason, she needed him, and he was willing and ready.

The cup clattered when Lady Death set it down, wincing. The icy mask thawed, and Morana saw a new emotion there. Something raw and painful.

"I failed," her mother admitted.

Morana blinked, shoving the questions she had—the personal ones that didn't matter—outside of her brain. "How did you fail?"

"I was meant to kill him."

Morana nodded once, understanding entirely. Her mother had failed her duty as a major god—nothing more. "And that's where you failed. Your responsibility to this realm." Her hurt swelled, seeping out of her pores and unable to be contained. While she'd thought she'd gotten over her mother's absence, Morana realized that wasn't entirely true.

She longed for her to care—to admit that she failed as a mother.

An apology. That's all Morana wanted. And if she got that, she'd walk away, never thinking of the woman again.

Matthias's hands threaded through hers as he read those thoughts. Morana allowed it, gripping Death like a lifeline. Her mother's eyes flicked briefly to their intertwined fingers, and then away again.

"I couldn't fathom killing another major god—the task requiring immense control of my power." Her mother winced. "So, I bound him instead." Lady Death cleared her throat, her finger skimming the rim of the cup. "Centuries after I'd bound Raidan, I'd built a life for myself in the mortal realm—a life I wasn't willing to sacrifice when I finally learned of his return."

"Bullshit." Morana stood up, towering over the woman seated on the floor. From this angle, her mother looked small—helpless. As power whipped through the room, Morana lost hold on to her rage.

"You sacrificed everything," she seethed. "You abandoned that life entirely and look where we are now."

Lady Death stood up to meet her, white mist floating over the wooden floors beneath them. The rage and pain in her eyes glowed. "Not by choice." The words cut through the air, coated in bitterness. "I didn't stay away by choice, Morana. And you'd be selfish to think so."

Matthias was standing between them in an instance, shadows swirling in his midst as his breath became heavy. "Watch your words," he warned, "or they will be your last."

Lady Death's nostrils flared. The pain left her expression—once again replaced with indifference as she composed herself—closing herself off once more.

"You're coming to realize our fate is not entirely up to us," she began, staring directly at Morana. "I had no choice but to come back. Baserah called me, thought I could do something to fix my mistake."

Morana felt the sweat trailing down her spine, heard the muffled voices coming from downstairs. "And how did you plan on doing that?"

"Just as my fate wasn't my own, yours isn't either, Morana. Your fate is not your own. You have responsibilities—obligations."

"My fate is mine to choose." Morana tried to steady herself. "As for obligations, my only obligations are to myself and those I care for." Morana fought the urge to look to Matthias—to think about his court and the fae within—the ones she still longed to protect. "I would choose to protect those I care about. I would not run as you did—but I assure you, *Mother,* it would be my choice."

Morana inched closer, that same anger bubbling over. "You, on the other hand, didn't care enough to make a similar decision. You *ran* from those you claimed to love."

A slow smile split Lady Death's face. "I guess I'm very good at running." She glared at Morana, any ounce of love for her daughter completely missing as if it had never truly been there to begin with. "Like mother, like daughter."

Matthias was on her in an instant, arm pinning Lady Death to the wall as shadows darkened the room like an oncoming storm. "I spoke of my warning," he growled. "And I'm very good at keeping my promises when it pertains to death."

Morana stared at him in shock, watching as Death fought to defend her against her mother's barbs.

She couldn't be bothered by Lady Death's callousness. She'd lived long enough without the woman's presence; it would not make a difference now.

As Morana walked toward her mother and Matthias, she steeled her spine. Her mother was right. She had run from a lot—her old life in the human realm—Matthias as soon as she caught wind of his deceit.

Even so, Matthias had once offered her a way out—and she hadn't taken it. She'd agreed to marry him instead. And while she wasn't certain of her place within his realm, she knew she couldn't abandon the others if things were really as bad as they seemed.

One thing had become abundantly clear—Raidan needed to die, and Morana was more than willing to deal him that fate.

Maybe she wasn't as much like her mother as she thought.

"Enough, Matthias."

He released her with some hesitancy.

"Explain exactly what happened," Morana demanded. "Then we are leaving."

Her mother felt at her throat in an attempt to ease the ache of Matthias's wrath.

"The magic binds," she began, voice raw. "And with the right rune magic, and a specific relic, it can bind well. I bound him to sleep, and then I made a life for myself in the human realm. Met your father and had you. It was only a matter of time before I'd be called back here." For what it was worth, Lady Death had the decency to look guilty. "Once I'd learned of his return—"

"You did what you do best." This time, it was Morana's words that carried the insult. "You ran again." Morana's stare cut into the woman so familiar and yet a stranger. "You bound Raidan, came to the human realm, realized your mistake, and then you ran again."

"I did," Lady Death agreed. "I didn't kill Raidan. I failed as a mother. I *failed.*"

The mask disappeared again, revealing the broken woman before her. A god—still broken and vulnerable.

Morana straightened, unfazed by the woman's pain this time. There was nothing she wanted more than to see Raidan ripped apart from the inside out—nothing she wanted more than to deal death to the vile monster. She wouldn't fail like her mother did.

"So," Morana began. "How does one kill a major god?"

If she was going to be the answer, then it would be on her own terms. She certainly had no qualms about murdering Raidan—especially not for the others in the Court of Shadows.

A small smirk pulled at the corner of Lady Death's mouth. "The same way you kill anything. Equal power."

She'd seen Raidan's power firsthand and knew the amount he had. There was no way she could defeat him on her own if that was the case. Her power was nothing compared to a major god. The reality was that while her mother sat before her, a major god herself, Morana was still half mortal.

Her brows furrowed. "We will need a powerful relic."

Lady Death stepped forward, and Matthias angled his body between them, defensive.

"I don't think you understand, Morana." Lady Death's gray eyes were cold—serious and scolding.

How dare this woman believe she had a right to speak in such a way? She'd given up her right to reprimand the moment she walked away from her family.

"Of course. I don't fucking understand," Morana spat, folding her arms over her chest after releasing Matthias's hand. "What do you expect me to do? I may have some of your power, but I'm still mostly mortal. So, I ask, why are you here, *Mother*?"

"You have no idea what you are," she said. "None at all."

Morana raised a brow in challenge, begging her to continue. "And what am I, exactly?"

Silence stretched on before Matthias finally broke in.

He was staring at Morana—that dark gaze burning.

"You have equal power," he breathed as he took a step back—in awe of her. Matthias blinked a few times, letting that realization marinate. "You're a major god, Morana."

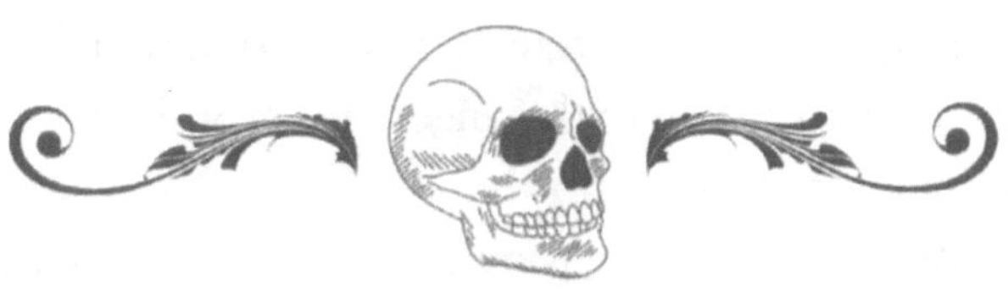

Fourteen

Maybe gods were made from people who had nothing—those who had been betrayed and battered. The ones who didn't respond with grace or kindness. Maybe gods were made from the people who had been betrayed a thousand times and then finally found they had the power to do something about it.

Maybe the gods were evil, and Morana was becoming one of them.

White mist surrounded her when she returned to the palace in Ascella. The smoke rose as if it was acknowledging her ownership of the magic—the magic of all the major gods.

You brought the answer here.

What was she to do? Kill Raidan? Raidan had an entire army of creatures he controlled. He had power and ancient magic. He had the entire Court of Light supporting him in a war against fae and monsters.

Six months ago, Morana had been a *mortal*—a failure and a runner hiding away in a new city with no goals or dreams.

And now she was supposed to be a god.

It was so easy to pretend as she stood in front of her mother. Easy to give in to the anger and promise retribution for the major god to the north.

But now that they were back, she had time to think about all the ways she could fail—just like her mother.

Like mother, like daughter.

"Do you want to talk about it?" Matthias asked from the doorway to her room.

She hadn't even noticed his presence—too consumed with her own thoughts and the frantic heartbeat in her chest.

"Do I want to talk about it?" She halted her pacing, staring at Death filling the door frame. "Why would I want to talk about this with you? Why would I want to *be* this?"

Morana clenched her fists, her breathing rapid as her emotions spilled over.

"This is why I'm the answer?" she asked, venom leaking from her lips. "Why you wanted me here? I'm the answer because I'm this all-powerful god that had no idea who the fuck she was." Morana stepped closer. "You saw an opportunity to use and manipulate me to start a war. Well, you got that. You wanted to train me, and you started to. Is this why, Matthias?" She couldn't stop, not while she was unleashing all of this on him. "You wanted to use me to start a war and then teach me to be a weapon."

"*No.*"

He crowded her space—larger than life as the shadows twisted around him—his nostrils flaring. It was the image she'd seen in the house when he pinned her mother against the wall. "You think I knew all of this and used you?" he asked. "After everything—after how I defended you against that vile woman who abandoned you."

"You have no right to talk about her."

Matthias prowled closer, so close she had to step back, and even then, he didn't cease.

"I don't have a *right* to speak about those who harmed you." His body was nearly shaking as Morana felt the wall of her room hit her back. "I was about to make you my *wife*, Morana. And I still would, if you'd let me."

Lifting her chin, she glared up at him, refusing to be intimidated by his presence. She was a major god, after all.

"You wanted my power. Nothing more."

His fist hit the wood behind her, body tense. "Bullshit!".

She didn't stop—wouldn't. "You just knew I was too stupid to realize what was happening. Too broken to see past a little attention." Morana threw her hands up. "You *knew* that. You were in my head, Matthias. You're always in my head!"

"I'm not in your head now." Matthias leaned down; his breath hot on her neck as his lips got dangerously close to her ear. Despite her better judgment, her body hummed at his nearness. "And if you would realize that I gave you that damn book so you could be in mine, then maybe you would understand that everything you just said, all of that was a lie.”

She didn't move from her place on the wall, didn't speak as his nose gently brushed up her neck. His chest pressed further into her until she could feel his warmth everywhere. His scent wrapped around her, and she inhaled deeply as their shadows began mixing—dancing around them as if they had their own grievances to air out.

 “If only you'd realize how much of myself I've already given to you,” he breathed against her ear and she shivered. “I've been thinking about you since the moment I watched you order that ridiculous coffee in the coffee shop. You were in my head then, and I want you in my head now. I want you to know every part of me, and I wish you would just read the fucking book, Morana.”

She swallowed, squeezing her eyes shut against the warmth in her chest. She needed to fight the feeling—fight it until she knew she could trust him. As it stood, she wasn't there yet—but she was willing to hear what he had to say.

“Why?” she whispered.

“Because,” he began, stepping away from her until she could see his face clearly. “Then you would understand this deep desire to know you—all of you. As you are. I know you are scared to care about other people because of how others abandoned and betrayed you. I know that you're strong, because not once have you given up. You're beautiful, adaptable. I've heard the stories Cain tells about you—watched the way you respond to Ronan.” Morana could feel the furious beating of her heart as he leaned in, his lips hovering over hers. She could feel the ghost of his kiss, haunted by the softness and fury. And fuck if she didn't want to close the gap. "And if you read the book, you might understand that because of who I am. You haven't had time to show me who you are when your life isn't falling apart, and I hate myself for being the reason that's happening to you. I hate myself for only knowing death and darkness."

"The reason that it's happening to me?" She swallowed.

"I would have *never* brought you here if I had known the suffering you would have to endure. I would have *never* let you anywhere near Inara if I knew she would have tortured you the way she did."

Morana pushed back, trying to increase the distance, but the wall at her back wouldn't allow it.

"I would rather feel your dagger." Matthias reached for the weapon, his fingers trailing up her thigh and toying with the hilt as the heat in her body grew. "I would have rather felt your dagger sink into my flesh again than watch you lose your chance at happiness because of me."

Her hand touched his, and Matthias sucked in a sharp breath. The warmth of his flesh seeped into her skin, warming her body from the outside in.

It was the confession that eroded the wall she'd built between them. His confession that seemed so real—so genuine.

The tears burned like acid. The truth. It was more than Death had offered her before. She had been in his mind, heard his voice in her own head, and still he had told her more in the last few minutes than she had ever gleaned from being that close to him.

"I'm a major god," she whispered as he placed his hand on her cheek, his fingers twinning in her hair.

"You are whatever you want to be." His voice was low—face close.

Morana leaned forward. She rested her forehead against his—relishing in his touch, closing her eyes, and breathing before the reality came creeping back in.

It wasn't long before it did.

"I am going to have to kill Raidan," she admitted. It was the idea that scared her—a task so large she wasn't sure if she'd be able to do it.

Matthias shook his head slowly. "You do not," he answered. "You once offered to carry my sorrows, and I am here offering to carry this. If you want to run—disappear into the human realm, I will make sure that it happens. I will deal with Raidan."

"I've spent a lot of time running, Matthias. I think it's time to try something else."

When she opened her eyes, he was still there, his forehead on hers and his eyes open and searching.

Heat washed over her—her stomach twisting as she looked at him. Her mind traced back to the way his fingers had intertwined with hers. He had held her steady when faced with her mother. Death had been there from the beginning, and she had been a fool to run off. Drunk on power and the fear of betrayal, Morana had run off with Raidan at the soonest opportunity.

His lips parted, and his thumb gently traced her jawline, sending shivers down her spine.

"I think you should go," she whispered.

Matthias groaned as if in pain, hesitating before he pulled away. The heat was gone when he looked at her again—the moment passed. "Of course," he answered.

She needed time to sit with her thoughts and scrub the wild mountain air off her skin.

"I'll read the book," she finally said, hoping he heard all the things she wasn't ready to say. "I will read it, and maybe you can come back later." Morana cleared her throat. "You could stay with me."

"Always, Morana." A small smile stretched across his face. "Always."

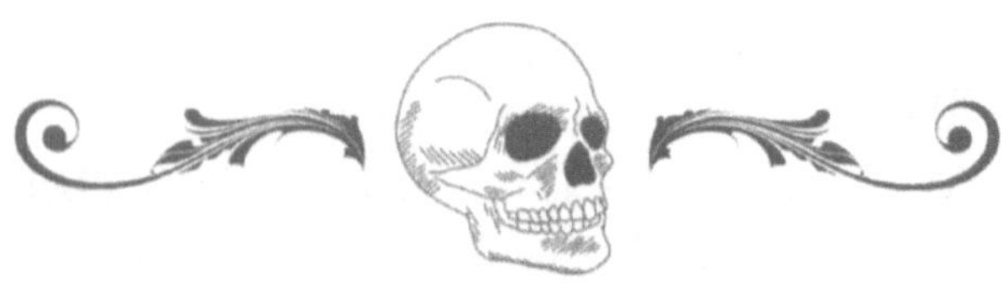

Fifteen

Morana pulled her knees to her chest, resting her chin there as the water sloshed around her.

The night had been long, the hours slowly creeping toward morning. Her time in the human realm had lasted only a couple hours. If she had to guess, it was just past midnight.

Closing her eyes, she breathed deeply and tried to hold herself together. *You could stay with me,* she had asked, and she hadn't regretted the request. Every ounce of emotion was leaking from her and reminding her of the feelings she had for Death—the feelings that no power could burry.

His confessions ran circles around her mind.

She had been wrong.

The door clicked open, and Morana turned slowly to watch as a familiar fae woman entered the room.

Willow held a fresh towel in her hands, refusing to make eye contact as she placed it on the bathroom counter.

"Hi," Morana squeaked, still holding her knees to her chest.

"You stupid, *foolish* girl."

Morana winced as Willow spun, her blue eyes sharp as weapons. That gaze peeled back every layer of calloused skin Morana kept around her heart—they always had.

"You would honestly believe that *vile* god over Matthias after *everything*." The fae woman prowled to the tub, pointing her finger in Morana's direction as she bit back tears. "Don't you dare cry."

Clenching her hands tight enough to carve crescents into her palms, Morana fought to obey. Willow was right—and the longer she sat in the silence alone with the hot water cooling around her, Morana had realized her mistake.

Axton's betrayal had made her a flight risk.

No.

She had been one since the very beginning.

"I'm sorry," Morana whispered.

Willow's eyes caught fire, shifting in the dim lights of the bathroom. "You don't get to be sorry," she spat. "And it's not me who requires your apology."

Willow moved to sit on the chair next to the tub. She pulled the comb from her apron and gathered Morana's hair before detangling the strands.

The tears burned at the back of her throat, but Morana didn't let them fall.

Despite the woman's anger and frustration, Willow was surprisingly gentle—the mother Morana didn't have. She couldn't tell if it was a good time to bring up what had happened, who she had seen. It didn't seem to matter, because Willow brought it up for her.

"Your mother is Lady Death." It wasn't a question.

"So, it seems."

The scent of jasmine invaded Morana's lungs as Willow worked the soap into her hair, helping to clean the dirt and grime from her body.

"I have no advice to give you," the fae woman said. Morana could hear the hint of disappointment in her words—as if she had hoped to have *something* to give—even in her anger.

"I don't expect to be given advice," Morana responded. It seemed like the right answer as Willow hummed her approval. "This is something I will need to figure out myself. I think I've hidden long enough." Morana trailed her fingers over the water, watching the ripples on the surface. "My father took advantage of me," she said. "He was broken and hurting, and so he wanted me to match." Her lip pulled up in a small, forced smile. "Maybe I've been afraid of giving any pieces of myself because those pieces have been used in the past." She cleared her throat. "Raidan, though." Morana turned to look at Willow. "I've seen evil and lies. If I kill him, I would be doing the right thing. Nobody is taking advantage of me here."

"We're not?" Willow cocked an eyebrow. "You seemed to believe that pretty fervently before."

"Matthias offered to help me leave—run. He said he would handle it."

Willow sighed, sitting back in the wooden chair. "That boy would."

"He won't," Morana answered. "It's time I stop running." She set her eyes on the fae woman, catching the pointed tips of her ears before meeting her gaze—no longer sharp with malice. "It's time I stop running from my feelings, my power—all of it."

Willow reached out, running her thumb along Morana's cheek. The warm pad of her finger soothed something in Morana's chest. Willow had every right to hate her, and while the woman loathed her choices, there was still a softness to her touch—one that said she cared.

"Glad to have you back, Queen of Darkness."

Morana closed her eyes, smiling. "I'm glad to be home."

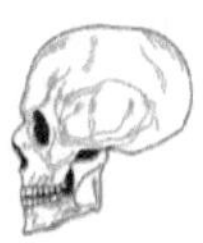

Death glanced at her, desperately trying to hide his nervous thoughts.

He hoped if he introduced her to the court and brought her through his city, she would see the beauty of the fae realm and begin to trust him—see the truth.

With her arrival, and the magic she showed, it was only a matter of time before the Court of Light came to collect. Inara only cared for power, and he would be damned if the goddess of life found an opportunity to exploit the girl further.

Matthias knew her behavior well—the way she built armor around herself to protect her—pretending she didn't feel deeply.

He had done the same for centuries after his parents' death. After so long in the darkness, he'd become callous and cold—the embodiment of the darkness.

He couldn't subject her to the same fate.

"Well," she began, "you know I'm human. I know very little about this."

He smirked, watching the way her brows furrowed, the crease forming. It was the same frustrated line that appeared when he had brought her to the land of the gods for the first time.

"So," she tried again as her voice cracked. She was nervous. "What do I need to know about the fae realm, Your Highness?"

His face fell, the title piercing through his thoughts. She was still putting on a front, but she had cared. She cared when he told her he didn't want to touch her again, and gods, he'd wanted to. But the truth was, she didn't belong to Death.

He couldn't touch the human girl, not when she had another man waiting on her—a man she wanted. But in that moment, encased in her mind, he liked pretending that maybe she saw something in him—that she wasn't afraid.

"So," he said. "Now you're willing to be respectful."

Morana scoffed, quickening her pace and folding her arms over her chest.

The morning was foggy, cobbled streets uneven and calm. A fae woman working in her garden turned toward them—the muted sunlight highlighting her surprise at their approach.

Morana's face fell.

"You said I had to wear the dress." Her brows furrowed again, and for a moment, Death thought he might do anything to keep the irritated expression on her there. If only it kept her talking to him.

"I suggested it," he responded, pausing and fixing his gaze to Morana. Death chewed on his cheek, trying to hide his amusement. She was easily riled.

Morana swatted him; her fist colliding with his chest as she began hurling insults.

"You arrogant, self-centered, callous, belligerent, domineering—"

Matthias raised a brow. "Are you done?" he interrupted, but she continued.

"Obstinate, tactless, and sullen son of a bitch!"

He'd been called worse.

When she shoved him again, he stumbled back a step, watching the fire in her eyes. The thing that was burning and wanting to lash out. The amusement disappeared when Death realized another truth—the girl had been stripped of her freedom at some point and was fighting to gain it back.

Another sentiment he knew well.

"Is this payback for breakfast?" she asked.

Breakfast.

He hadn't meant to act the way he did, but after what had happened between them—knowing he couldn't touch her—

Death took a deep breath and shoved his hands in his pockets. "So, you admit you were being petty?"

Morana's eyes flicked to the fae woman behind him, widening when she realized what she had done.

"Don't call me names." Her voice was lower as her gaze flicked back to his—eyes like storms.

He almost chuckled at the statement.

Ridiculous, intriguing, beautiful, passionate, hurt.

Certainly off-limits.

Matthias ran a hand down his face. "Right," he said, turning to look at the fae woman, who was, in fact, shocked. He smiled to ease her worries, and she bowed, muttering something to herself before retreating indoors.

"You're walking around with me; you should wear a dress and be willing to learn." It was the truth—it would also keep suspicions down about why he had brought a mortal into the fae realm.

The Oracle had mentioned an answer, and at first, he had wanted to see what power she held—to watch her crack the code. As far as he knew, she was a mortal who held the shadows—shadows that called to his own, even now.

It was the last sentiment that held his attention, the way his magic mingled with hers—the way it made him feel.

She stiffened. "I am willing to learn."

Death flexed his hands at his sides, that same stirring in his chest reminding him of how similar they were.

"I want to learn," she admitted. "And then maybe I want to go home."

Something in his chest twisted at that, though he knew he had no right. "You can go home." He stepped forward, hardening his gaze. "I want you to understand, Morana. I am trying to help you. You can shift realms." He gestured to her. "You can enter minds as easily as I can once you learn to wield that power."

Worry etched into his brow. "I don't trust Inara," he said. "What began as curiosity has changed for me. She wants something from you, and I'm not sure what it is." If The Oracle had told Inara the same thing, there was no telling what the woman would do. She had killed Death's parents, and while he knew very little of the strange human girl standing in front of him, the idea of Inara getting to her—

"She's taken Axton to get to you. You have to be able to protect yourself."

Morana's eyes turned searching. "You almost sound like a noble king, eager to protect your people." Her eyes narrowed. "Does the fae realm have some incredible power to change you from an asshole to a caring teacher, longing to help me figure out what's going on in my blood?"

He laughed then, the sound echoing in the street.

"Are you hungry?" he asked. "We need to eat before we go to the palace. It's nearly noon."

Morana jolted when the door clicked open, revealing Matthias's tall figure looming in the darkness as his shadows curled around him.

There was a vulnerability on his face—one that spoke of how nervous he was entering her room in the middle of the night. She could see it in the way he avoided her gaze, in the way his hand rubbed the back of his neck, his black T-shirt stretched tight around his biceps. Morana traced the crows inked there with her gaze and moved her attention to the stray strand of dark hair falling across his forehead.

Home, she had told Willow.

She had meant it.

Closing the book gently, Morana turned, setting the tome on the nightstand next to her bed.

"You asked me to stay," Matthias said, his voice raspy as his eyes met hers.

Morana allowed a small smile to split her face as she looked away. "I did." Her voice was low—a soft encouragement.

Despite herself, she'd softened toward him after watching the way he handled her mother—after reading his thoughts and finding no ill intent. She could give him a chance—at least.

Morana was certain of two things. Matthias hadn't known what Raidan claimed he had known—not in the way she thought he did. He hadn't known all the details regarding who her mother was and wasn't.

The second thing she was certain of, is that Matthias cared for her—truly.

Closing her eyes, she leaned back against the headboard, listening to Death's footsteps as he moved nearer.

She was a god.

Morana breathed deeply, reminded of the way her mother had peeled back the hood of her cloak, revealing her identity. Her throat tightened at the memory.

Being a god meant she had more power than she thought—more than she had explored. It had to. She couldn't keep running. Her life wasn't the only one at risk here, and while she spent most of her existence trying to survive, survival wasn't a good enough excuse.

Raidan's abuse. Her mother's lies. The deception. The uncertainty.

All of it swirled in her mind and gave way to the fear seated somewhere in her heart, tucked away where she could keep it hidden. It was that same fear that drove her to the running, the self-loathing, the wallowing in her circumstances. That fear allowed her to believe she could treat others poorly—because she deserved to.

None of that was the truth—not in this place where so many lives were at stake.

For the first time, Morana let her new title marinate. They called her the Queen of Darkness. A queen should be concerned with more than their own misfortune. She had been given the power to change the fate of this realm— save it from the evil of the major god to the north.

That was motivation enough. It was enough to *try*.

Still, the expectation of what she could accomplish was like one who robbed graves. It was the expectation of what she could accomplish that would dig up the dead pieces of her soul, the ones she longed to keep buried.

With her fear unearthed despite her desire to play hero, Morana finally opened her eyes, patting the bed next to her.

"You can sit," she said, watching Matthias move to the other side of the bed, propping himself up on the pillows there.

He was stiff—uncomfortable in her presence, and something about that made her pause. His discomfort picked at the scab over her heart—the one from the wound she had created.

"Willow called me foolish," she said, wringing her hands in her lap.

She could hear the smile in Matthias's voice, even as she kept her gaze fixed downward. "Don't take it to heart."

"She also told me I wasn't allowed to cry." Morana smiled to herself, remembering the harshness in Willow's tone—more of a mother than that stranger in The Oracle's house.

Matthias shifted. "Perhaps she's become too comfortable with her position. I will need to speak—"

"No." Morana finally looked at him, cutting him off. "No," she repeated.

"No?" he cocked an eyebrow.

Morana's chest tightened. Her vulnerability out in the open. "Willow is more of a mother than I've ever had. I would like her to speak freely—no matter how difficult the truth is to hear."

Matthias nodded, staring at the wall on the opposite side of the room.

Staring at the same spot, Morana wondered what he saw there. Was this place as much of a home to him as it was to her? Or maybe it was a prison. Taking in the gold trim decorating the room—bringing her a sense of comfort—Morana realized just how much she longed to be here. Did he want her here, too?

"My real mother—" She cleared her throat. "She's truly Lady Death." It wasn't a question.

Matthias lifted his hand, placing it on the mattress between them before smoothing down the fabric. There was still so much distance between them, but she could tell by the way he glanced at that tattooed limb, he was thinking about closing it.

She was, too.

"So, it seems," he said. When his dark gaze finally met hers again, Morana felt the lump forming in her throat—the words she longed to say—the apologies she longed to give.

Would they ever be enough?

Before she could speak, Matthias interrupted her thoughts. "How are you?" he asked.

A breathy laugh left her lips. That wasn't where she expected the conversation to go, but it was a nice distraction, regardless.

"I'm a god," she admitted. "For so long, I felt utterly useless in this realm—worried that I was some defenseless and messy burden your court had taken on." Morana smiled. "Elivira and Hames let me know as much." She pulled her knees up to her chest, resting her chin on them and fixing her gaze to the golden thread embroidered on the dark comforter. She traced the floral designs with her fingers. They reminded her of Sarnai. *More reminders of home,* she thought. "And now," she began, "I'm being told that I have everything within me to do far more than I ever thought possible."

"God or not," Matthias interrupted, "you've always had it in you, Morana."

When she shoved him again, he stumbled back a step, watching the fire in her eyes. The thing that was burning to lash out. The amusement disappeared when Death realized the truth—the girl had been stripped of her freedom at some point and was fighting to gain it back.

Another sentiment he knew well.

"I read some of the book."

Matthias frowned, clearing his throat again. "And?"

"And I'm sorry. I am used to betrayal. Maybe I'm so used to it that the betrayal has become a comfort." Morana hesitated as she looked at the space between them.

She risked scooting closer, watching the way Matthias stiffened and then relaxed. "I'm also comfortable being used. It was easier to believe what Raidan was saying. Harder to believe I had any merit in your eyes aside from the curious power running through my veins."

"You don't owe me an apology," Matthias said.

"Don't enable me." Morana grinned at him before reaching out to trace the moth tattooed on the back of his hand. For what it was worth, he didn't pull away.

"I'm sorry, too," he said. "I should have told you about your mother." She could feel his gaze on her then, burning and insistent. "About my feelings."

"And what feelings are those?" she asked, meeting his dark eyes as warmth washed over her body.

"The ones I admitted to you mind-to-mind in my mother's tomb." Matthias searched for the answers in his gaze. What he was looking for, she didn't know. "You deserve to hear it out loud, though." Morana couldn't help the way her chest cracked open, that warmth spilling everywhere. "I love you."

Silence stretched between them, still like the night beyond the windows in her room. Morana held his stare as he waited for an answer—the one she had known from the start.

"I mentioned something to Willow earlier," she said.

Matthias's face fell infinitesimally, and she had to keep herself from chuckling.

"I told her I was happy to be home." Morana gently turned his hand over, lacing her fingers through his.

"Is that all?" he asked, and she could hear the layers beneath his question.

"That's all," she answered. "I'm still thinking through the rest."

Matthias grunted, resting his head on the headboard as she traced the lines of his face. Somehow Raidan had known before she had.

"I care for you, Matthias." She shifted closer, feeling the gentle press of his arm against hers. "It's why I ran—why it hurt. Only people you love can hurt you like that."

Matthias sat up and held her gaze. "And is that how you feel?" he asked.

Morana nodded, and that motion seemed to give him permission as Matthias reached up to thread his fingers through her hair, his palm pressing to her cheek. He moved closer, lips inches from her own as his breath fanned out over her face. With lips parted, Morana felt the warmth wash over her body.

"You stubborn woman," he whispered, shaking his head as one corner of his mouth turned up. "Absolutely infuriating."

There was no malice in his tone, and he didn't say anything more, simply leaned in and pressed his lips against hers. For the first time since she'd returned, she welcomed the touch—all of it.

Morana matched his motions, heat spiraling through her as his touch sent sparks across her flesh. His hand skimmed the skin beneath her shirt, gripping her waist and causing a gasp to exit her lips.

When the deep rumbling sound pulled from Matthias's chest, Morana moved, resting her knees on either side of his waist and tracing his lips with her tongue.

His mouth parted, hungry and wanting as his shadows appeared in the room, dancing across her skin and sending ripples of pleasure down her spine.

Running her hands through his hair, Morana gripped the strands at the back of his head and tugged gently, angling his mouth so she could go deeper. Her mind quieted, leaving only the thoughts of his fingers skimming her breast beneath her shirt, and the whispered truth of his emotions.

And for the first time since the ball, she thought she could believe them.

His hands worked their way down to wrap around her hips, pulling her tightly to him until all she could think about was *friction*.

Morana ground herself against him, feeling the hardness of him beneath her—the way his tongue sought to claim her mouth.

A soft moan left her lips, and she ground herself again—feeling the pleasure rise in her belly, her body longing for release.

"Matthias," she whispered against his mouth, and he hummed his approval—fingers pulling at the waistband of her sleep shorts.

She could feel the grin at his mouth—feel the soft puff of air against her skin when he chuckled—dark and seeking. "You told me to beg for your forgiveness," he whispered.

Morana ground herself against him again, her mind dizzy. "And I'd do it again."

His fingers dipped beneath her waistband, skimming lower—lower until she was panting. "How would you have me beg?" His tone was taunting. "If you were to ask me again."

Morana's grip tightened on his hair and Matthias groaned, lifting his hips to meet her grinding movements. She could feel all of him against her, ripples of pleasure shooting through her body with every slide of her against him.

"Tell me," he insisted, his other hand rising to cup her breast as his thumb ghosted over her nipple. "How would you have me beg your forgiveness?"

Morana's back arched, her body seeking more of his touch. Matthias's lips trailed down her neck, hot as they left a fire in their wake. When she felt his teeth slide against her skin, her body felt as if it would combust.

"Whatever you're doing seems to be just fine." The next grind of her body had her body climbing—release within reach.

"Shall I make you come?" he asked.

His words had her moving faster, pressing herself harder against him.

Morana lowered her hands, skimming her fingers down his chest in a way that had him shivering, his breath shuddering when she finally dipped below his waistband, fingers gently brushing against the tip of his hardened length.

"*Fuck,*" he whispered against her neck.

Morana moved her hand lower, grasping him and sliding her fingers against his flesh. Matthias's head fell back against the headboard—lost in pleasure.

Before she knew it, he'd taken control again, flipping them over until he hovered over her, lips hungrily pressing against her collarbones. "Should I stop?" he asked.

Morana pressed her body upward, anxiously seeking more contact. "Don't stop," she breathed.

When he sat up, his dark gaze peering into hers, Matthias smiled. The shadows twisted around him as he lowered himself, his fingers pulling at the hem of her shorts until she was bare beneath him.

With one firm hand, he separated her thighs, his tongue meeting her and causing her to cry out.

Matthias didn't relent, sliding—sucking—plunging a finger inside her until she gasped. Her release plowing through her.

When she'd come down, he moved up her body again, gently kissing the corner of her mouth, her jawline. He moved next to her, pulling the sheets around him and tucking her under his arm as she rested her head on his chest.

Morana listened to the steady beating of his heart, her body relaxing against him as the silence stretched between them.

Her mind lingered on his thoughts—the things she'd read in his book—the hints at his past and what he believed of himself.

She knew she could read the book again and find any information she wanted. Yet, with her head on his chest and his breathing steady, she longed to hear some of those memories leave his lips.

Longed to take some of the pain of his past in the way he'd longed to take hers.

"What exactly happened to your parents, Matthias?" she whispered.

"You've asked me this before, you know." Matthias ran his fingers through her hair, and her body melted against his. "I recall a very similar conversation coming up at least two other times."

"And still," Morana said, "you haven't given me the entire story. What happened to them?"

"Inara's rise to power was—" he paused for a moment. "It was unconventional." Matthias took a deep breath before continuing. "I won't bore you with the details of spies and court politics of the past. My parents knew there was something wrong and chose to attack after the coronation. I was twenty, and it was my first taste of battle." Matthias's fingers continued to run through her hair, his heart still a steady drum in her ear. "Battle is a different kind of death—one I struggled with." He scoffed. "Some Death god, I suppose." Morana pressed closer, wrapping her arm around his torso. "During the attack on the palace, I noticed my father was missing from the battle. When I finally made it to the throne room, Lux was dead and bleeding on the ground, and Inara was in the process of running her blade through my parents."

Death stared at the ceiling, cold and unfeeling as he recounted the story—as if centuries passing buried the pain until it became nothing but an old coffin—rotting beneath the surface of the earth.

"I was still cloaked in the shadows," he continued. "My father had been teaching me how to use them to numb emotions and sensations, but I couldn't bear to numb my parent's minds in their death. I sent them memories—as many warm memories as I could think of. I didn't want numbness to overtake them, but joy."

Morana could feel her throat tighten as she looked at him—the pain now etched into his features. It was clear he hadn't spoken of this much, and for someone who had lived so many years, this surprised her most. She supposed grief hung around as long as it wanted.

"What I didn't realize then," he continued, "is that all of those memories I cast into their minds would become tainted for me—laced with the sorrow of their deaths." Matthias stared at the wall, his grip on her tightening. "I was a coward, then. I ran—called a retreat—ended the war my parents were starting."

"And now you're finishing it."

His dark eyes met hers. "And now we're finishing it," he said. "I refuse to let you do this alone, Morana." Matthias's gaze returned to the ceiling, a sigh exiting his lips. "I have so thoroughly destroyed your life," he admitted. "The least I can do is help you find it again."

Morana leaned up, watching the pained expression on his face—the one that said he truly believed what he was saying.

He smiled at her—devastating and beautiful.

"We will find happiness, Morana."

She gripped him tighter. "Is that a promise?"

"More than a promise," he whispered before placing a gentle kiss to her forehead. "It's a truth."

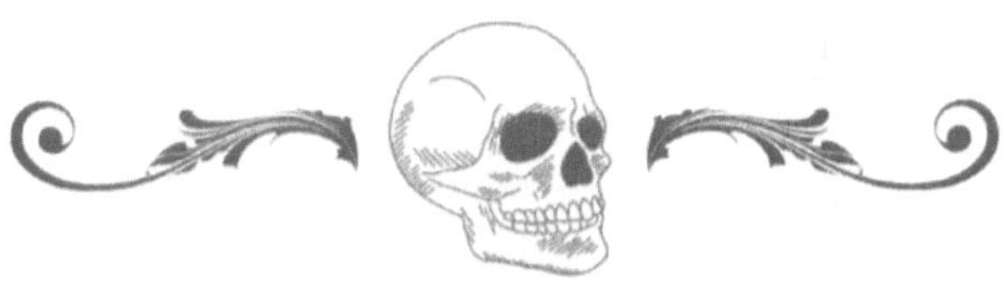

Sixteen

Three weeks.

It had been three weeks in the palace of Ascella with no signs of Raidan or the Court of Light. And unfortunately, there weren't many signs of Matthias either.

She'd seen very little of him since that first night—questioning what had gone wrong—if anything had gone wrong at all.

Allowing herself to read his memories after what they'd done, she knew that he'd enjoyed it—more than she truly needed to know.

While she skimmed the moments of the past, she realized how hopelessly wrong she'd been. But Morana refused to touch the memories beyond that—however tempting.

It was the start of vulnerability between them, and Morana vowed she would give him a chance to continue the trend—or shy away from it.

Though he hadn't been completely absent, returning from Zora and crossing paths occasionally. He kept a respectful distance every time, and for some reason, the distance had the nerves swirling around in her gut—allowing doubt to creep back in during the hours she spent alone in her room.

The doubt taunted her—hanging in the air around her like a ghost—a constant presence she didn't want or need. So, Morana distracted herself.

She spent her days bothering Willow and Kit in the kitchens, growing tired of Cain's company in the library, and swapping it for the company of his twin, instead.

If Cain had known all that had happened, and she expected he had, he said nothing. It was both a blessing and a curse—a reminder of what was to come.

Her time would end. Eventually, she would have to act on the promises she made—the fate she'd chosen.

Morana stood in the kitchen, watching Willow whisk whatever concoction the fae woman had created in the last thirty minutes. She had a gift, and Morana was anxious to benefit from it.

"You're eyeing this whisk like it's going to save you."

"It *is* going to save me." Morana cocked an eyebrow, elbows leaning on the counter across from Willow.

Willow chuckled. "It could taste terrible—like dirty dishwater."

Morana eyed the smooth chocolate coating the bottom of the bowl. "All the more reason for you to give it up. Leave some extra on the whisk."

"She becomes a god and suddenly feels she has the right to make demands of me." Willow gave the chocolate batter one last pass through and handed the whisk over.

Morana didn't miss the way she dragged it across the top, picking up more batter intentionally.

The first lick proved everything she'd hoped for. "*You* must be the god, Willow." Morana practically moaned.

"Am I interrupting?"

Morana jolted on her stool, standing and spinning around at the sound of Matthias's voice. He stood at the far end of the kitchen, his shadows swirling around him, slowly fading as he stepped forward.

Her heart pounded in her chest—that doubt slowly creeping back to the surface and reminding her of the chasm between them.

"Maybe," Morana answered, attempting to keep her tone cool and collected.

A small smile pulled at the corner of his mouth; eyes dark as they held Morana's gaze. "Sounded like it," he said. "Quite the pleasurable experience, I take it?"

Morana turned to see Willow humming by the sink, ignoring the two of them—though not quite. She knew better.

Morana cleared her throat, her stomach twisting at the insinuation—at the memories of his head between her legs. Then the doubt shot out again, spinning a web around her mind and trapping her in confusion. "Right," she said, desperately trying to stop the way her body buzzed before turning her eyes back at Matthias. Did he know what he was doing? What he *wasn't* doing? "Did you need something?"

A knowing smile appeared on his lips, voice low and laced with wicked delight. "You."

Morana heard Willow snort a laugh behind her and fought the urge to turn around and glare. "You'll have to be more specific," she said, turning away from Willow.

Shadows stretched out to her, requesting access into her mind, and in her need for clarity, she let him in.

Would you really like me to relay exactly what I want with you in front of poor Willow? Some of it is harmless—preparation for what's to come. But other things—

Morana's lips parted, her body buzzing with whatever *things* he meant.

Matthias cocked a brow, clearing his throat and gathering himself before speaking. "The lords are coming tomorrow to discuss the war. I've tried to—" He ran a hand through his hair, mussing the strands as if he were uncomfortable—unsure of how she would react to what he would say next. "I've tried to give you some time—rest, I mean. The freedom to think about something other than war and court politics. If you had some distance from all of this, I thought maybe your decisions would be easier to make."

"What decisions?" Her eyes narrowed.

"About how you would like to use your power, and what you would like to do with the problem that needs solving."

"Raidan," she said. There was no sense in beating around the issue. Raidan needed to die, and she had promised to have a hand in dealing that fate. Her opinions had not changed.

"Yes." Matthias nodded once, eyes searching as he waited for her response.

"I'm still committed to fulfilling my promise," she said, her tone steady. "Though I'm not sure where to begin."

"I would like you to meet me in the training room in an hour." His lip curled up again in satisfaction. "If you're certain, then we need to explore whatever magic you have—start training again. But this time, with a different purpose."

"Will Garian be there?" she asked, nerves knotting in her stomach. She didn't know how the lords would react to her return—if they knew she had returned at all. Maybe they still viewed her as a traitor.

The thought reminded her of all the questions she still had—the details they hadn't discussed in Matthias's absence. While she felt more comfortable in his presence—with the memories she'd read, she still didn't know what to expect from the others.

There were things they needed to discuss.

"No," Matthias answered. "Not this time."

Morana lifted the whisk to her lips, licking off another section of batter. She wouldn't have time to eat whatever cake the batter became.

"Alright," she said before tossing the whisk into the sink. "The training room, then."

Matthias's dark eyes fixed themselves to the sink, avoiding her gaze. He nodded again and exited the room, his shadows trailing behind him.

"You know," Willow began. "You can't come in here to taste all the batter without working."

Morana turned to see Willow pouring the mixture into a pan, one corner of her mouth turning up. "Okay."

"You're on dish duty."

Morana made her way to the sink, picking up a wet cloth and some soap. It gave her time to think—time to address the worries she'd kept at bay for the past few weeks. Raidan and Inara hadn't come after her. He had to have known. Raidan wasn't stupid—she knew that for certain.

Dread found its way into the pit of her belly, reminding her that while she was home, nothing was solved. Matthias may have been giving her time to rest, but he had still been distant for the past three weeks. After what had happened between them, she had a right to feel annoyed.

And even more, Raidan wouldn't stay away for long. The god was demanding—brutal.

It was only a matter of time until he came looking for what he believed belonged to him—and Morana hoped by the time he did, she'd be ready.

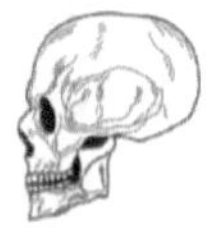

Standing in the empty training room, Morana ran her hands down her thighs, smoothing her training pants. Her palms were sweaty, nerves coursing through her at the thought of training again—using her magic.

With Raidan, each training session had held harsh memories. Images of his palm hitting her cheek, his hot breath ghosting over her skin flashed through her mind.

Swallowing, Morana forced herself to settle. She couldn't let the memories distract her from the battles to come. The training room didn't look like the dungeon, and she was certain Matthias didn't keep basilisks hidden in the palace.

Then again, with the creatures Callum was providing, she couldn't know for sure.

Morana allowed her shadows to calm her as they crawled up her skin. She felt Raidan's—*no*—her magic pull in her chest. The white mist coated the floor as she allowed it to rise in the training room.

It felt good to touch her magic, to call on it as she stood alone. Something about that power settled her spirit—reminding her she wasn't helpless.

Even so, the light sparked in her chest, and she refused to touch it. The power was unfamiliar—harder to harness. Every time she felt the tug of it, fear crawled up her spine, reminding her how that magic felt lashing across her bare back.

She also wasn't sure how Matthias planned to use the light—how he planned to help her wield it. She didn't know if he would ask her to use it at all.

"Oh, good." Matthias's voice sounded before he appeared in front of her, shadows caressing his skin. "You're already practicing."

The crooked smile he wore sent a wave of heat through her. It had happened in the kitchen—the first reminder of what they had had before—before Raidan and the lies. A reminder of what they'd done that first night in the palace.

"What is the plan?" she asked. "Are you going to make me drive a knife through my hand again?" Morana cocked a brow, letting her shadows mix with his.

Matthias's eyes glittered in the dim light. "What a gross exaggeration, Queen of Darkness." His gaze flicked to the hand at her side, his own limb flexing as if he longed to touch her, and for a moment, Morana's thoughts lingered on what it would feel like to have his fingers tracing over her skin, warm and reassuring.

She blinked.

"Shall we begin?" he asked.

Morana let the shadows swell, willing her mind to do her bidding. She moved through the darkness until she appeared a few feet behind him.

Matthias turned as Morana tilted her head to the side, a smug smirk finally pulling at her lips. "Of course," she said. "What's the goal?"

"First to get a dagger pointed at their throat loses."

Morana's hand flexed near the dagger strapped to her thigh. She could feel the tug of the weapon calling for her power, and the longing in her soul begging her to use it.

"Are you sure you trust me with a dagger at your throat, Matthias? You have been missing for the past three weeks."

"I wanted you to clear your head."

"And I wanted *you.*" Morana stood firm, waiting for a response.

Matthias pushed the long sleeves of his shirt up his forearms, revealing the crows inked on his skin. The tattoos seemed to dance in the dim light as his shadows moved over them.

"I apologize if I've made you angry. Do what you must." Taking a step forward, Matthias bowed slightly as he spoke. "It would be a privilege to die with your dagger across my throat." His dark eyes peered up at her, a stray dark strand of hair hanging over his forehead. Morana sucked in a breath. "An honor to be murdered by the Queen of Darkness."

And with that, he was gone.

Morana growled at his departure, the blood rushing through her body so quickly she could hear the sound in her ears. Her heart rate spiked as she peered through the shadows, desperate to find where he went.

If he was toying with her—drawing out a game to mimic his absence over the past few weeks, he was doing a damn good job of it. Frustration released itself, but she didn't give in to the emotion. Instead, she used it to fuel her actions—used it to find him.,

Gripping her dagger, she called on the darkness, searching the shadows for Death, wondering if she could find him with her magic. When she came up with nothing,

Morana let out a breath and changed tactics by searching for his mind. If she could sense him, she may be able to sense what he would do next.

When she found him, he blocked her out. The darkness surrounded her and despite the nerves now coursing through her blood, Morana held that power close.

Right when Matthias appeared behind her, she moved, her magic spitting her out at the corner of the room, cloaked in darkness and hidden from his sight.

Morana watched as he stumbled forward, knife in hand. Matthias laughed, turning to search the space around him.

"Nicely done." Matthias turned, and Morana couldn't help the smile that broke across her face—not that he could see it. "What other tricks do you have up your sleeve, Morana?"

Just as she drew on her magic, Matthias appeared before her, a firm grip on her wrist as he pressed forward, crowding her space and keeping her present.

His teeth shone as he smiled, proud of his accomplishment. Fire wrapped around her wrist where he touched her, igniting the thrill of the chase as they stood in the corner surrounded by darkness. Morana's eyes flicked to that point of contact, then back to the hand still gripping his weapon at his side.

She let his magic move around them, keeping them encased in blackness. Pulling on the binding magic, Morana carefully bent it to her will, readying herself to strike.

"Well," Morana breathed. "Aren't you going to bring the knife to my throat?"

He cocked his head to the side, his expression devastatingly handsome. "As you wish," he said.

Before Matthias got the chance, Morana lashed out, pulling him with her magic until he fell back onto the floor. His shadows stuttered as he looked up at her, propping himself up on his elbows.

Morana held him there with her binding magic, keeping him pinned in place. Her eyes glittering as she watched him try to get up.

He thought he'd bested her—thought he knew better. But Matthias wasn't the only god in the room.

Not anymore.

"That won't work," she said. "Unless you're hiding something from me." Morana stepped forward, pressing a boot to his chest. It was unnecessary in the wake of the white mist, but she did it anyway. Just toying with him.

Smiling, she tightened her grip on the dagger.

"If I didn't know any better," Matthias began, "I'd think you were trying to seduce me, Morana."

She took her boot off his chest. "Is that what you'd want?" she asked.

She didn't miss the way his eyes darkened or the way her own breath caught in her throat. The memory of his skin on hers was too much.

He smiled. "I think you know the answer to that."

Releasing him from her power, Morana watched as Matthias stood up and walked in the other direction.

She chuckled at his retreat, her body still buzzing with the tension pulled taut between them. She suspected this training session wouldn't be particularly useful. Especially with the game they seemed to be playing.

It had been a long three weeks alone, and something about the way he played off her taunts—the glint in his eye—it all pushed the doubts out of her mind.

He'd said he was giving her space—time to think—and if she were honest, she was grateful.

Shadows grew around her, and Matthias appeared behind her in an instant. He grabbed her wrist and moved them across the training room until he pinned her against the far wall. His breath fanned over her face as he stood in front of her, leaning in.

He spoke low. "Just a reminder," he said. "Never let your guard down."

"Why?" she asked. Her voice sounded breathless. She chuckled then. "What kind of reward are you expecting?"

Matthias cocked an eyebrow. "A dagger to your throat," he responded. "I'm expecting to win."

She felt the metal tip gently press where her pulse fluttered at the base of her neck and fought the urge to reel back, lifting her chin as she stared into his eyes. "Violent."

"A death god?" Matthias tilted his head to the side. His nearness was as intoxicating as the shadows. "Never," he finished.

As silence stretched between them, something in the air shifted—a crackling tension that sent lighting through her veins. Morana's lips parted as she watched him, feeling his body press closer to her.

Matthias left the dagger at her throat as his eyes flicked to her mouth—hungry for whatever she had to offer.

Heat washed over her, a sign of the coming storm.

The dagger dropped away, and Morana nearly closed the space before the doors to the training room flew open and startled them both.

They broke apart, her cheeks pink as she cleared her throat and watched Ronan stride into the room.

He looked more severe—serious. It was nothing like the Ronan she remembered, and fear gripped her at the thought that he had hardened—possibly toward her.

She hadn't had time to consider what the lords were told—hadn't bothered to ask for fear of the response.

For the past few weeks, Morana had considered herself at home, relaxing in the peace of the palace in Ascella—allowing herself to get comfortable with Matthias again. Attempting to stop wallowing and prepare for what was to come.

She hadn't seen Sarnai since the first night—hadn't seen Elivira at all. Garian hadn't come to train her, and Hames was nowhere to be found. A million questions flashed through her mind as she surveyed Ronan's determined expression. All harsh angles with his neatly tucked-back blond hair and sword at his hip.

She had tried to *kill* Matthias.

Morana stiffened, cheeks still flushed after whatever she and Matthias had just done. Squaring her shoulders, she faced the lord to take whatever he would throw at her.

Ronan still hadn't looked at them, speaking as soon as the doors closed behind him. "I figured I would come early for the war council tomorrow. I wanted to—"

His eyes met hers, and he froze.

Morana fought the urge to run—the urge to use her magic to pull her as far away from the training room as possible.

She stood suspended in the moment—awaiting his response as Ronan took her in.

Matthias sidled up next to her, threading his fingers through hers. Ronan caught the touch, his eyes softening as his lips turned up at the corners.

The relief was palpable.

"Morana, darling," Ronan began. "Welcome home."

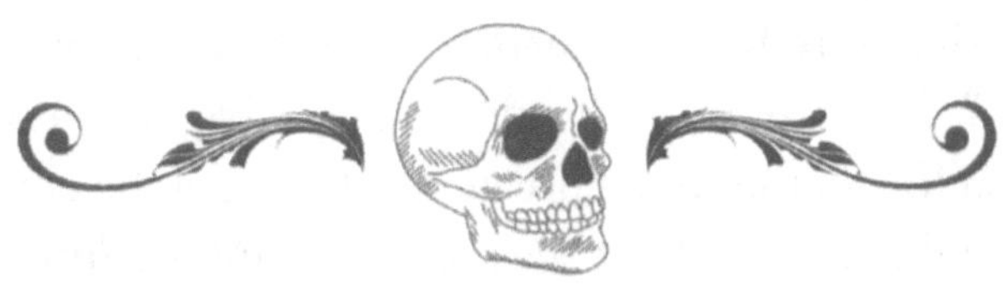

Seventeen

Ronan smelled like the sea. The salt clung to his skin after his time in his own city, and Morana took comfort from the scent as his arms held her in an embrace she hadn't expected.

Matthias cleared his throat from behind them.

"I am not done, Matthias, and I ask that you do not clear your throat so rudely as I welcome my favorite dance partner back to the palace." Ronan squeezed tighter before releasing her.

Morana stepped back, hardly looking at Ronan as her chest tightened.

Home.

She had spent so much of her life running—surviving, that she hadn't stopped to think about what home could look like for her. It certainly couldn't be found in the human realm.

It certainly wasn't with Raidan, either.

"What were you saying before, Ronan?" Matthias asked, his expression unreadable. "What was it you hoped to accomplish by coming early?"

"Oh, trust me," Ronan began. "I never do that." His smile fell before he continued. "As for my arrival into your court—" He wrung his hands out, looking nervous, and Morana fought the smile threatening to pull at the corner of her mouth. "I wanted to check on the weapons. Stopped by Ore Else to see how they were coming along."

Matthias's brows climbed higher as Morana's eyes narrowed.

Being away from Ascella after the ball had left her in the dark regarding what was happening. Consumed by the heaviness of what occurred in the Wastelands, Morana thought little about what was going on between the lord and Reese.

"Visiting a friend?" Morana teased, as she gave him an assessing look.

Ronan scowled. "I was checking on the weapons," he asserted, and Morana fought the desire to laugh at such a ridiculous statement.

He clearly had feelings for the woman. There was no other reason for Ronan to appear so nervous when Reese's name was brought up.

"Right."

"And how *are* the weapons?" Matthias asked. Morana's gaze slid to the amused expression Matthias tried to repress.

"Very well," Ronan answered. "I apologize for interrupting your training session, I suppose."

"You suppose," Matthias scoffed, but Ronan didn't acknowledge it.

"I will see myself to my rooms, and have the staff bring me a few bottles of wine." Ronan turned on his heel, exiting as quickly as he arrived, leaving Matthias and Morana standing. Alone again.

"I was afraid—" she didn't finish the sentence, still staring at the closed doors of the training room.

"Afraid he would have harmed you since you stabbed me the last you saw him?"

Morana winced, fighting the uncomfortable feeling twisting in her stomach. "Something like that, yes," she admitted.

"No reason to fear," Matthias said. "Ronan is quite fond of the nude painting you worked tirelessly to create. He could never hate his favorite artist."

Morana chuckled, turning to meet dark eyes as the shadows danced over Matthias's skin. "Of course," she said.

After a moment, Matthias's face fell. "Though I'm afraid," he began, "when the other lords arrive, it may take some convincing."

Morana chewed on her cheek, gnawing at the flesh like the discomfort continuing to gnaw at her gut. "Less forgiving?" she asked.

"You *did* try to kill me."

Morana nodded as Matthias kept his eyes pinned to her, watching for what she assumed was any emotion that shone through her mask. He would see it—he always did.

There was truth to what he said almost a lifetime ago. The shadows truly knew no secrets. Especially between Death and the Queen of Darkness.

"Why did you disappear these past weeks? Was it something I did?"

"No," Matthias quickly responded. "No, Morana. I meant what I told you. I wanted you to have time to decide what you would do." His brow furrowed. "Without my influence, of course."

"Well, I'm still here," she admitted.

He smiled then. "You are." Matthias's eyes lingered, burning everywhere they touched. "We should keep training," he grunted as his expression fell. "Less playing around. We need to find out the extent of what your powers can do."

"Keep grunting like that, and I will assume you've been taking lessons on teaching from Garian," Morana teased, her eyes lighted. The mention of Garian's name had her shoulders tensing, though she tried to hide it.

If Matthias was right, if the other lords would be more difficult to win over, Morana didn't know what the meeting would hold for tomorrow.

All she knew was that she would be a part of it—a god ready to strike down a monster.

And Raidan deserved it.

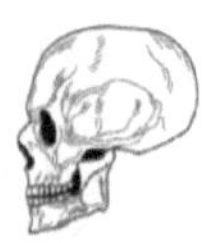

Sweating and exhausted, Morana found herself running through the same drill for what felt like the thousandth time.

While most of her training with Garian had consisted of defense, learning to wield a weapon and her magic to defend against the Court of Light—against creatures—her training, now, seemed to take a different approach.

Matthias crafted creatures out of shadow, manipulating her mind until the beasts seemed real enough to attack.

And attack, she did.

Morana panted as she waited for the next one to appear, her sword clenched firmly in her hand. Matthias had her get rid of the dagger and reminded her it wasn't the only weapon she had at her disposal. She needed to get comfortable with something larger, especially with the war going on.

"Go again?" he asked.

The stinging in her lungs and the burning in her thighs told her she should stop and quit while she was ahead. But Morana had spent her entire life running from her problems. If she was going to be a god, if this was what was to be had for her, then she had no choice but to continue.

The longer she trained, the more she pictured Raidan in her mind. It was almost as if she could feel the sting of his hand against her cheek, the feel of his magic wrapped around her throat. It fueled her.

The Wastelands were a dead land—one filled with sorrow and the numbing sadness of betrayal. What she wouldn't give to take control of that place—those memories.

Morana nodded, wiping her brow with her free hand as shadows gathered across the room. She lunged, reminding herself that if she didn't move now, her muscles would surely protest against what she was asking them to do.

Raising her sword, Morana grunted as she made to shove it through the mist. Before she could get any further, the darkness parted, and Cain stood within the shadows—waiting.

The sword ripped through the mat on the floor as she sent it away from the scribe. Morana let out a hissing breath and dragged the weapon from the torn padding below.

"Are you crazy?" She prowled forward, tossing her sword away from them and letting it clatter on the floor. "I could have *killed* you, Cain." Her heart was pounding in her chest, the tightness taking over and caging the organ in. She could have ended the scribe in the middle of her training session. She couldn't have forgiven herself.

"I'm glad to see you care about me so much. What with my insults regarding your reading ability."

"This isn't funny." Morana wiped the sweat from her brow as Matthias moved to stand beside her.

"Can I ask what you're doing here?" Matthias spoke, his features tight and his shoulders tense. Morana's eyes slid away from him, back to the red-headed boy standing in his robes.

His irises were lighter—almost white as Morana tried to make sense of what she was seeing. As quickly as it had happened, they returned to their normal color, and Cain wiped his eyes.

"She's afraid," he said.

"Afraid of what?" Morana asked, frustration still churning in her chest. "I'll admit I'm afraid of many things in this godforsaken realm. You're going to have to be specific." That irritation bubbled as the image of Cain broken and bleeding on the floor flashed in her mind. She couldn't bear the thought—couldn't stand the idea of killing the kid the way she would have.

"You came all this way from the library to tell me this? Almost get yourself killed?"

Cain's features hardened as he looked at her—gone was the image of the scribe, replaced by something far older—wiser. "You're still afraid of your power, Morana. If you don't get comfortable using the mist and the light, there's no way you'll survive this war."

"What do you mean?" Matthias asked, taking a step forward.

"Exactly what I said." Cain's eyes still pinned hers. "You need to stop having her attack shadows. She needs to use her other magic."

Matthias eyed him carefully, and Morana was certain Death would retaliate. Cain wasn't a lord—he wasn't part of the court in the same way Ronan and the others were. There was no way a king who had rescued the boy from The Oracle would allow him to speak out of turn—to give advice he knew nothing about.

Matthias's eyes flicked to the boy's hand and back up. "Quite right," he said, his brows creasing. Matthias nodded in acceptance. "Noted. We will begin as soon as possible."

Morana's head whipped between the two as she tried to hide her confusion.

It wasn't until she glanced at the spot Matthias had looked at before it dawned on her. Looking at his hand, she noticed the gold smeared there just before Cain exited the room.

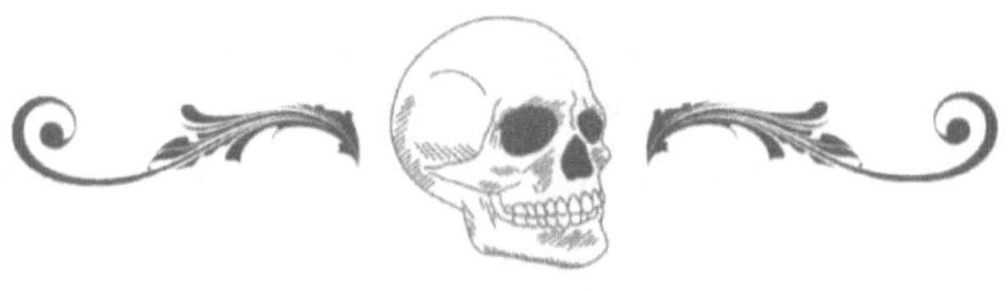

Eighteen

"Would you like to drink of Death, Morana?"

Raidan's voice had her opening her eyes, finding herself in The Wastelands. The dried, cracked earth surrounded her, scorched like the sun had leeched the life from the deepest parts of the soil.

Morana wiped a hair away from her face, turning as the wind whipped around her, bringing with it the scent of blood and magic.

She had been here before; stood on this same ground with her finger swirling in Garian's blood. This time, there were no dead bodies—only bones littered on the ground.

"There you are."

Morana turned around to find a silver-haired demon standing atop the cracked soil. Raidan's smile stretched across his face; nefarious promises woven into the expression.

"Here I am," Morana spoke. She was vaguely aware that she was dreaming, able to piece together the scene enough to give her courage.

"Where did you go, Queen of Darkness?"

"I'm not sure what you mean," Morana responded. "I just told you I'm here—in The Wastelands." She knew he could see through what she was saying—knew what he was really asking, too.

Raidan wanted to know where she had run off to after the chaos of Ohriid. He wanted to find her—not in her dream, but in the flesh. The thought sent a shiver down her spine, fear gripping her tightly and twisting her stomach until it was in knots. Of course, she didn't let it show.

"Where are you?" he asked again, taking a step forward and grabbing her face with his hand, forcing her to look up into amber eyes. "I would like to think you were stolen from me, but I find that difficult to believe."

"Yeah," she said through gritted teeth. "And what makes you think that?" Morana could feel the anger welling up in her chest, ready to explode.

"Why, Morana," Raidan tsked, "I am in your head."

Morana paled as Raidan took a step back, the wicked smile still playing on his lips.

She had been visited before in her dreams—her mind open to Inara before she knew how to close it off. And now, through her weakness, Raidan had made his way here, too. She fought to push him out, but it was useless.

"Not so easy, is it?" he taunted.

Morana could see them then, the Veeden gathering around her. It was like an entire army of the creatures coming for her as the mist rose.

"Tell me where you are," Raidan demanded, watching with feral delight as his threat of the Veeden inched closer.

She wouldn't—she couldn't.

Raidan couldn't know she had gone back to Ascella. And while Morana and Matthias weren't what they were, her return to the Court of Shadows was the first glimpse of home she had had since the ball.

Raidan was destruction—torture. She couldn't go back—not now.

"No," she whispered.

"You forget that your power is my own," he growled. *"Let the Veeden take you."*

White mist seeped between the cracks in the ground, growing and consuming everything in its path as the Veeden pressed in. Morana fought to move but was held still as Raidan watched his plan unfold.

She grunted, trying to fight against his restraints as panic took over. Without thought, she called the shadows, hoping they would soothe away the fear thrashing in her chest. Sweat beaded on her brow as the Veeden came closer. She could smell the scent of soil wrapping around her as one creature ran a long nail down her arm, scratching on its descent.

Morana fell to her knees, hands digging into the earth as the mist swallowed her up. A scream ripped from her throat as she fought for the mist within her. She grabbed hold of it, bending it to her will, forcing the creatures away *while calling on the shadows—hoping the darkness would consume her.*

"Morana!"

Morana opened her eyes, Matthias's panicked face being the first to greet her. His hands were on her shoulders, shaking.

Looking around the room, that's when she saw them. Veeden, everywhere. They were inching closer, the floor in her room coated in the white mist. She could still feel that power like a thread in her chest, the same as the shadows skittering down her arms.

Morana was panting, sweat rolling down her temple as she acted on instinct. That binding magic was within the Veeden. It must be possible to control them, since Raidan, a major god, created them. She possessed the same power as him, anyway.

Morana let her power take over, forcing the Veeden to stop moving and sending the darkness over them, her shadows carrying them off with the wind. Where they were deposited, she didn't know.

"What was that?" she asked, looking to Matthias.

"I don't know." His voice was low as he kneeled next to her on the bed, rocking back on his heels. Matthias ran a tattooed hand through his dark hair, his chest rising and falling rapidly. "I don't know," he repeated.

The dream came back to her in pieces, slowly building until it became a clear picture of what had happened. "Raidan was in my mind," she said, and

Matthias's face hardened. "The way he spoke—" Her brow furrowed. "It sounded like he didn't know who I was—what I was, I mean. He certainly knows who."

"What you are?"

"A major god," she answered. "At the very least, he doesn't know that I know what I am." Morana held Matthias's gaze, letting the truth wash over her. "He's looking for me, of that I'm certain."

"He won't get to you," Matthias promised, face severe.

Looking around the room, Morana could see the picture of the destruction that came into the palace. The Veeden had truly been there, though now gone. Or maybe it was all in her head like Raidan had been. "Did you see—"

"The Veeden," he finished. "Yeah, they were here. It was like you called them yourself. They appeared from the shadows and crowded into your room."

Morana nodded, staring at the window, watching the stars as if they held the answers.

Then a smile pulled at her lips—spreading slowly at first. "Maybe I did," she said, looking back to Matthias.

"Maybe you did what?"

"Maybe I called them here." Her smile fell, her face taking on a more serious expression. "If The Oracle was right, if I am a major god, that means I hold the same power as Raidan—I hold it as my *own*."

Matthias's dark eyes stared at her, trying to follow.

"It means that if Raidan can control The Veeden, then maybe I can, too."

"I'm not entirely sure I want to test that," Matthias said. "It's dangerous."

"This is all dangerous. Do you think Callum could get us one? A Veeden, I mean."

For a moment, hope bloomed in her chest. While Callum had given Matthias an army of creatures to support the Court of Shadows, Raidan had an army of creatures of his own.

But if those creatures could turn on him—

"It's entirely possible. It would be unlikely that he couldn't, actually." Matthias's brow creased in concern, though he didn't seem unwilling. He handled her training, after all.

Morana nodded once, throwing off her blankets and moving to pull a sweatshirt over her head. Her leggings were damp from sweat, T-shirt as well, but she didn't bother changing.

"Where are you going?" he asked, rising from the bed to follow behind her.

Morana turned around, noting the panicked expression on his face. "Relax, I'm not going after creatures tonight," she said. "I am, however, going to get something to eat."

"Allow me to join you."

"For protection?" she asked, cocking a brow in challenge.

It was the first she would spend time with him since that first night, and she wasn't entirely sure of how to act—what to expect.

"For company," he clarified, and the nerves spiked in her blood.

Morana moved to the hall, making her way down to the kitchens. Thoughts spiraled in her mind, all the things she had heard from Raidan, what she had experienced with the Veeden. She needed to make sense of it all.

"Maybe a bit of protection, too." Matthias's deep voice cut through her thoughts, and she glanced back at him briefly, wondering how long he had been in her room for—why he'd come in to begin with.

"You said the Veeden came in with the shadows. They weren't in the rest of the palace?" she asked when Matthias caught up to walk beside her. "Did others see them?"

"No, they just appeared in your room. I watched them arrive."

Morana swallowed, keeping her eyes fixed to the dark floors. "And you were in my room because—"

"I—" Matthias rubbed the back of his neck, a nervous gesture. He wore a black T-shirt that showed the tattoos inked on his arm, shifting with the movement.

Morana stopped and turned to face him. "Why were you in my room?"

His brow furrowed; dark eyes boring into her own. "I wanted to check on you—after today. After Cain—"

"He's an Oracle," she said. "I saw the tear, Matthias. He saw something."

"He did."

Morana looked at him then, noting the familiar cut of his jaw, the full lips she had kissed time and time again. Her mind flashed to the training room, the unfinished business of whatever was brewing between them again.

"What did he see?" she questioned, drawing her thoughts to refocus. "And don't bother lying. I'm not foolish enough to believe you didn't check.

"If you can't accept your power, Morana." Matthias's eyes softened, one hand coming up to tuck a strand of hair behind her ear. "If you can't accept who you are, we have no way of winning."

His touch lingered for a moment, Morana's cheeks heating before he cleared his throat and pulled away.

"I've been able to use my powers just fine, and in case you've forgotten, I've accepted who I am and I'm doing what's necessary to help win this war."

"But you shy away from the light, and there's still fear regarding the other magic." Matthias shifted where he stood. "You fight to keep it under control. I've seen you do it."

As they stood in the dark hallway, the truth of her power stripped bare, Morana took a steadying breath. She hadn't touched the light much—didn't want to—couldn't.

The light was too much to handle—reminded her of Inara. Raidan's power was no better, but Matthias was right. She had no choice in the matter. His power was consuming—it demanded to be seen. And it wasn't his power to begin with, anyway.

The light, on the other hand—

It didn't linger when her emotions rose. It sat dormant in her chest until she chose to use it.

So, she hadn't.

It was the one thing about her trauma in the fae realm that she could control. She didn't have to face the memories with Inara if she didn't want to, though she couldn't say the same for Raidan.

Morana bit the side of her cheek, uncertain. She didn't know if she wanted to give up that control. "Then I suppose we should keep training," she offered.

Matthias's gaze lingered briefly, and she wondered if he saw her fear before he turned to lead her to the kitchen.

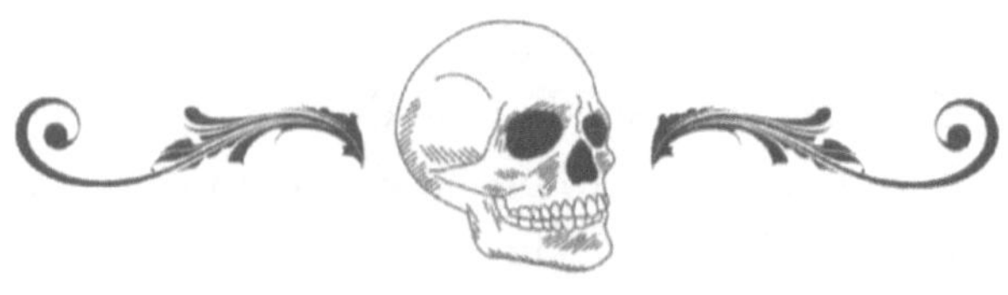

Nineteen

Morana leaned over the counter; her elbows propped on the wooden surface as she stared at Matthias standing on the other side in the middle of the kitchen.

Night still hung in the air, undisturbed, as if Morana hadn't called on dozens of feral creatures from The Wastelands only an hour ago.

"I never got to eat whatever cake Willow made earlier." Morana tilted her head where it rested on her fists. "A shame, really. And I wholeheartedly blame you, Matthias."

Matthias chuckled, his eyes shining in the faefires as the corner of his mouth turned up, causing Morana's heart to skip in her chest. "I will have to remedy that. You had the batter, though."

With her features deadpanning, Morana pushed off the counter and stood up straight. "That doesn't count, Matthias."

The smile on his face held firm, but something darkened in his gaze. "It sure sounded like it did." Matthias's deep voice lowered, and Morana found her body responding. It was as if they were back in that place—back in the training room.

"Based on the sound you made," he continued, letting the sentence drop off, though his meaning was fully understood.

Morana looked away, her stomach fluttering. It wasn't just sex anymore. It hadn't been for a while, but now with that knowledge, she couldn't help the way her cheeks turned pink, the flush working up her neck. This interaction was unfamiliar territory, and there were still so many things unanswered between them.

"We haven't discussed the meeting that will take place tomorrow." Her eyes cast downward as she picked out the wooden countertop, the splintered wood speaking of years—centuries—of use. This was the smaller kitchen, the more intimate one Willow used for her meals. The others working in the palace didn't come here often, and Morana was glad of it. "Who will be there?" she finally asked.

Hardened features and harsh lines overtook Matthias's face. "All the lords," he answered.

Morana held his gaze, fighting the lump forming in her throat. "And what do they know? Are they under the same impressions as your court?" Whatever those impressions may be.

"Aside from your attempt at killing me? They don't know much." Matthias cleared his throat. "They know you are here, though—in the palace."

Morana nodded once, accepting his answer, though she wasn't certain how they would behave. The other lords weren't Ronan. Ronan was the least of her worries, and yet she had still feared him when he walked into the training room.

"And what is to be the expectation, Matthias?" she asked. "I left after we announced our—" Morana fought for the word. "Engagement," she finished. "How are we handling that?"

Matthias blew out a breath, leaning over the counter on the opposite side. "There are a lot of political details. Moves that I made afterward and—"

"And if you expect me to help, which I fully plan on doing, I'm going to need to know what those political details are and what you expect of me." She knew he had kept her in the dark, not for nefarious reasons. His blood book proved that, but Matthias had kept the details of court politics away from her. In the beginning, it made sense. Morana was merely a mortal with curious powers. Now, however, she was a god, expected to show up not only for the Court of Shadows, but for the Court of Light, too. Her time of rest was over. She'd made her decision and needed to be a part of the conversation.

"We couldn't exactly hide that you tried to kill me from the rest of the court," Matthias began. "You joined Raidan, and then paraded around Ohriid, standing by his side with Inara. Things are," Matthias paused, running a hand down his face. "They're complicated. We haven't announced anything in particular, but there are more individuals closer to the lords—people in positions of power. We discussed with them."

"But the court was left in the dark," she deduced. "What did you tell the people in power?"

Wincing, Matthias grabbed an apple from the bowl in front of him and began tossing it in the air—a distraction. "The court was in the dark, yes." He swallowed, eyeing the fruit as it rose and fell back down, landing in his hand with a gentle slap. "It was presented to those in power in the Court of Shadows that our engagement was never called off."

She bristled. "So what?" Morana licked her lips, confusion and frustration taking hold of her. "We are still engaged, and these important people believe I was just—" She didn't finish the sentence, letting the question hang in the air, hoping for an answer from his own lips.

Matthias set the apple down, standing to his full height when he turned to her. The way he was looking at her reminded Morana that he was, in fact, a god and a king—making decisions she hoped to learn how to make eventually. If they were to still be engaged, that was.

I love you.

It was all so very complicated.

"Spying," he finally offered, and Morana flinched. "Those who are important to the court assume you were sent into The Wastelands intentionally—as a spy."

Lovely.

"We are engaged, still."

Her heart beat a heavy rhythm in her chest. While he'd confessed his feelings, and she'd read them over the past weeks, it wasn't the best way to find out.

"And I am expected to behave as such tomorrow." Morana's brow furrowed. It had been her choice to help kill Raidan, her choice to use her power as a god and do what was right.

She hadn't considered the possibility of still becoming queen in Matthias's court.

"You are not *expected* to do anything, Morana." Matthias strode around the counter to stand in front of her, expression severe. "You chose to help, and with that, the plan would be to win over the Court of Light, get rid of Inara, and get rid of Raidan, too. Nothing more."

"Nothing more?" She couldn't help the way those words stung. After what he'd confessed, and what they'd done her first night back, she couldn't handle the feeling of rejection sweeping through her.

Did he still want her as queen? Did she still want him the way she had?

"We are still engaged?" she questioned.

"We don't have to be."

She could hear the sound of roaring in her ears. "We don't have to be," she repeated.

Matthias lifted a hand, gently skimming his thumb along her jawline, his expression softening. "I would like to be," he admitted. "I would still have you as my queen, Morana. I thought I had made that apparent."

Morana brought a hand up to his, running her fingers along the moth tattooed there. In the time she'd spent back in Matthias's court, she'd realized the truth. Even if she wanted to return to the human realm—a normal life—she wouldn't fit. Nothing about her old life would make sense anymore—not with what she knew.

And if she were honest, she wanted the offer he was making—wanted it desperately.

"And so, I will need to win over your court as well—in preparation to become queen." Morana cleared her throat. "By your side."

The relief that washed over Matthias was almost visible. A smile stretched across his face. He kept his voice low—quiet like the night surrounding them and dark like the shadows he ruled. "You will have no problem winning over my court," he whispered.

"Yes," she said, sarcasm oozing in her tone. "I will win them with my charming personality. I am exactly the queen they're looking for."

"You are charming," Matthias supplied as he stepped closer. "In your own way." The light in his eyes betrayed the humor behind the words.

She huffed a laugh, allowing for more distance between them as she folded her arms across her chest and looked to the floor. "What a wonderful compliment."

Matthias moved slowly, testing the waters with every inch forward until he had her back pinned against the counter.

The languid movements sent fire through her blood, ripping the breath from her lungs. The way he looked at her—the way he leaned down to gently kiss her jaw, her cheek—all of it sent sparks flickering across her skin.

"I still fell in love with you," he confessed. Morana's heart raced in her chest. It was the first they had spoken of their feelings since that night a few weeks ago—the first they had acknowledged whatever remained between them, and she didn't know how she wanted to respond—the kind of vulnerability she could trust him with.

He kissed her neck once, sending shivers down her spine, and Morana tilted her head to give him more access. "More and more," he continued, "when I hear you talk about my court like you are fit to rule it."

"Rule it?" she whispered. Her mind jumbled when his palm ran up her torso, lifting the hem of her T-shirt with it. With her breath caught in her throat, Morana leaned into the touch, allowing the buzzing sensation to overtake her. She wanted more of his touch—more of his presence.

"I think you should," Matthias said as his lips ran down her neck, over her shoulder. "Rule my court, that is." He kissed her again. "With me."

There was something in the last two words, some question he had laid out to her—more of a confession than anything he'd said thus far. Matthias pulled back, searching her gaze for whatever answer he hoped to find. "My feelings have not changed, Morana. I meant that."

She nodded, desperately trying to decide what she could offer him—what she could give him in return. She settled on the bare minimum. "I'm willing to do what needs done." Morana cleared her throat. "I'm willing to fight this war with you, and to marry you, Matthias."

She swore she could see him flinch, and guilt twisted in her gut. The way she'd presented it was as if her feelings were a mere duty to him and his court. That wasn't the truth, and even as she ran away from those feelings during her time in The Wastelands, the truth still sat buried beneath the surface.

Morana didn't want him to question, and she didn't want to run—not anymore.

"I love you," she confessed, her voice low. "While I'm willing to marry you and win this war, my feelings have also not changed. I still want it all."

Relief. All she could see on his face was relief before his hands found her face, caging her in as Matthias pressed a bruising kiss to her lips—a claiming.

Her mind emptied, and she was caught in the sensation of his hands on her. He lifted her until she sat atop the counter, his fingers playing at the waistband of her leggings while he trailed kisses down her torso.

When Matthias tugged at the fabric, looking up with a question in his gaze, Morana nodded.

Pulling her leggings down, Matthias's eyes darkened as his fingers ghosted over her sensitized flesh, causing her to fight for breath. She lifted her hips until he could drag the fabric down to her ankles, slowly freeing her from it.

Matthias kissed the inside of her knee before making his way back up. "My Queen," he whispered, almost reverently. "Queen of Darkness."

Shadows danced over her skin, and Morana offered her own magic, allowing it to mix with his while his lips rose higher—higher still.

She wove her fingers through his hair as he kissed the apex of her thighs, tilted her head back as his tongue moved over her.

And then she was lost to him—allowing Death to take her on the counter before moving them to his own room—one she hadn't seen in what felt like ages.

Something about it was different—scarier.

But Morana refused to run—she refused to hold back as they both went over the edge.

She was done running.

Gods didn't run.

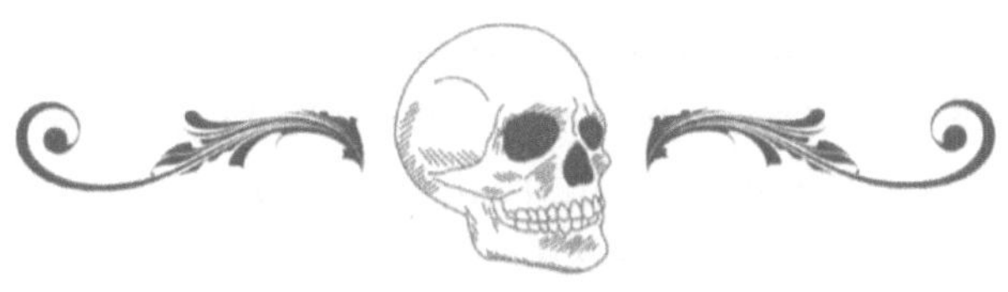

Twenty

"Do you think this is a good idea?" Morana asked. "Attending this meeting—I mean."

Matthias stood in the hall just outside his room, his shoulder leaned against the wall and his arms folded across his chest. He looked like a king. Black button-down, hair considerably less mussed than it was last night, with his head between her thighs and his mouth on hers.

Morana pushed the images away, the way they tugged at her heart—reminding her of the sweet things he had said, the way she had given up everything to him. Instead, her stomach twisted at the thought of attending the meeting with Matthias's court. Ronan was the least of her worries. It was the other lords that concerned her. Garian, Elivira—*Hames.*

Discussing things last night gave her a solid place to get her footing. She knew what would be expected of her— knew the goal of the court. The only thing she felt lost about was the strategy. God or not, Morana had no plan for going after Inara—no answer to how to kill Raidan. And even more worrisome, a nagging fear that rose whenever she thought of winning the courts over.

It was the right choice, though—becoming queen. But Morana would have more to think about and consider. Maybe Cain had been right. She should have spent more time learning about war—especially a fae war—in the library. It would have served her well.

Morana's brows pinched together, her worry etching its way onto her skin. She didn't have the faintest idea of how to win people over—had never worried about being likable—only surviving.

A bitch queen, Sarnai had once called her. It wasn't exactly a charming title.

Matthias's features looked severe in the glowing faefires. "It would be a poor decision on my part to have you sit out of the meeting."

Morana ran a nervous hand down the burgundy dress, smoothing the luxurious fabric to calm herself. "Yes, but—" Her brows furrowed even further. "There's plenty I don't know—things I may not accomplish. Winning their favor, for one." The vulnerability slipped out easily enough. He had seen all of her—accepted her.

"Morana." Matthias pushed off the wall, stepping closer to her. His dark eyes bore into her own, and for a moment, she could see something in them that had her chest tightening. He believed in her—for whatever reason. "You are a god," he continued. "You have every right to be here, to make decisions." He reached up, tucking a strand of hair behind her ear. The touch warmed her from within.

"You won't run, you will fight, and you will do it well." Matthias placed a gentle kiss on her lips, one that told her what he said was true—at least to him. She wanted to believe it.

"And you will win the courts over just as you've won me. You do not have to be likable—you have to be a good ruler."

Morana nodded, blinking back the tears that threatened to escape before the shadows whispered across her skin. Matthias plunged them into darkness until they were standing before a table, familiar eyes staring at her—taking her in.

Sarnai stood up abruptly, her chair sliding against the stone floors of the war room. Tattered maps hung on the walls, both courts depicted in great detail—elevation, bodies of water—everything they would need to see to decide where to move an army.

Morana was out of her element.

Her eyes flicked to the goddess, wondering what she was feeling—how she would react. Would she turn her away? Would she *want* her here?

Their initial interaction had been awkward and filled with unspoken words. Sarnai had left quickly, and she hadn't returned.

"You're here," she whispered, wrapping toned arms around Morana's shoulders and breathing her in. Morana did the same, fighting the emotion welling in her throat. "Welcome home, Morana."

Welcome home. They all knew.

The scent of roses and black tea filled Morana's nostrils before she pulled back, taking in the lavish black dress draped over Sarnai's lithe body. Gold highlighter dusted her cheekbones, her brown skin glowing as it always did, the tips of her fingers painted with shades of earth's soil.

Morana had nearly forgotten how beautiful the flora goddess was—nearly.

Looking at the others around the room, Morana noted the hardened expressions.

None of them softened.

Garian sat rigid in his seat. It was as if he expected to spring across the round table at the center—expected to save Matthias from whatever ill will Morana had boiling in her blood.

It made her stomach churn.

Elivira's expression remained unreadable. It was when she looked at the disgust on Hames face that Morana knew her first task would be to win the favor of the lords— never mind the two courts.

Clearing her throat, Morana took the seat Matthias had pulled out for her, running her hands down the skirts of her dress.

Matthias's expression was tight, and she didn't know if he had suspected how they would behave. A little tension was to be expected because of their soon-to-be queen—the one who had betrayed them all for fear of being betrayed first.

Willow was right. She was a fool.

"We need to talk about Ohriid," Matthias began, resting his elbows on the table and lacing his fingers together. Morana saw the shadows swirling in the air around him, a reminder of his status in the court.

It didn't make her feel any better about the harsh gazes of those she had considered friends.

The door slammed, and they all turned to watch Ronan saunter into the room. The bun at the base of his skull looked messily put together, and he wore that same hardened expression she had seen when he first arrived.

"You're late," Matthias said.

"Apologies, my King." Ronan threw himself in the chair next to Morana, a wild smile now on his face.

"Welcome to the war room, darling. Happy to have you here."

Hames scoffed, folding his arms across his broad chest, his chair creaking when he leaned back.

Matthias's dark stare whipped to Hames, his tone scolding. "You will offer nothing but respect," he warned. "I hope you understand."

"Ohriid," Ronan interrupted. "You wanted to discuss Ohriid."

"Yes," Matthias said. "We don't exactly have their support."

"Because Conan is dead?" Elivira supplied. The question was rhetorical.

"Conan isn't dead," Morana chimed in, her voice soft. She didn't want to back down from a challenge. Before, she would have held her head higher, acted the part. She needed to channel that side of herself, though she now found it difficult. Especially when she longed for their approval so fiercely.

New territory.

"Excuse me," Elivira's voice cut through the stunned silence. "Conan is *alive*?"

"We faked his death," Matthias offered. "It was fake."

"I'm sorry," Garian interrupted, still sitting rigid in his chair. Morana didn't miss the way his eyes briefly slid to her, moving away just as quickly. "Conan's death was what?"

"It's complicated," Matthias grimaced, but his tone held steady—authority still woven in his voice.

"I'm sure it is," Elivira said, leaning back in her chair. Her brown eyes widened as she crossed her arms, demanding an answer. "Explain."

Matthias cleared his throat. "We were getting her out," he answered, and Morana stiffened.

Silence stretched across the room, allowing the panic to fester in Morana's gut. She wanted to vomit.

There was no way the lords sitting around the table believed her to be a spy. They knew the truth of what had occurred—watched it with their own eyes.

"Perfect," Elivira spat, her voice sharp as a blade. "This is the plan, Matthias? How are we expected to win a war without the support of the fae? How are we expected to garner support when our queen has vacillated between sides? When she appears hot-headed, unpredictable, and untrustworthy."

Morana jolted, blinking as the words hit their mark. Matthias's shadows reached out to her, and she let him into her mind.

I know what you're thinking, he said.

Of course, you do. You're in my head. She paused before continuing. *She's right.*

And even if she were, he began, *what's wrong with a hot-headed and unpredictable queen?*

Everything. Even mind-to-mind, she knew her voice had been quiet.

You're wrong, he finally spoke. *I believe they are strengths. If you were to learn how to use the traits in your favor.*

"Which brings me to the next piece of information worth sharing," Matthias continued, penetrating the silence as if it hadn't bothered him at all. He didn't acknowledge Elivira's slight. "We visited The Oracle."

"That hag," Hames muttered.

"What information did she give you this time, Matthias?" Garian chimed in. "Actual answers, I hope."

Morana looked to Matthias then, feeling the heaviness of his words before he even said them.

"Morana is a major god."

More silence.

Morana sat up straighter, willing herself to calm. Her eyes were blazing as she waited for a response.

It came in the form of Elivira's laugh—forced and tight. Not quite a mockery, but more disbelieving than anything.

"Lady Death is my mother," Morana admitted, and the lords stared at her, measuring her against what they knew of her as a mortal. The strange human with unfathomable amounts of power she couldn't control. A woman living in the mortal realm, oblivious to all that existed outside of her world.

"Well," Elivira said, raising a brow in Morana's direction. "What does this mean for the war, then?" she asked, and somehow Morana could see past the layers in her question.

"It means we are going to win." Morana licked her lips, holding her hands steady beneath the table.

She didn't miss the way one corner of Elivira's mouth turned up. "And we will accomplish this how, Queen of Darkness?"

Morana could feel the shadows swirling at her feet, and something about their presence, the caress of that power, made her brave. Matthias's magic moved to join her—a soft encouragement. "We will win over Ohriid, charm the rest of the court, kill Inara, and *I* will kill Raidan."

There was a pause, and Morana wasn't sure her words struck the right chords. She wondered if they could see the fervent determination in her voice. Or even read the hidden message—the one that spoke of what Raidan had done to her while she was in The Wastelands.

When she saw the slow smile spread across Elivira's face—saw the small crack in Garian's own expression, the approval in his eyes. She sat up straighter.

"And so, we will," Ronan sounded from her right.

Sarnai tapped a finger on the table as her own expression shone with pride. "We will," she asserted.

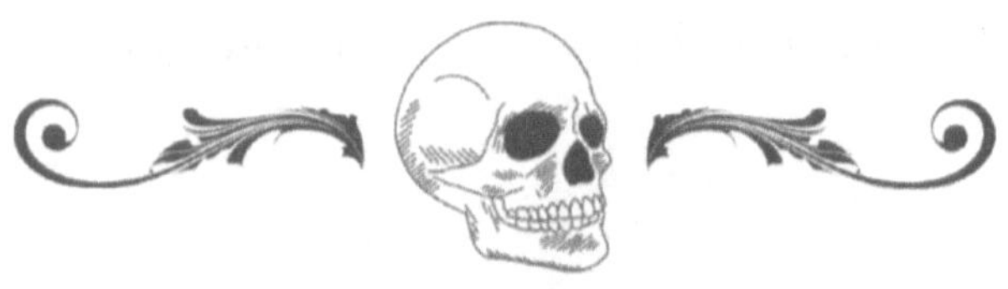

Twenty-One

They would return to Ohriid the following week.

Even after the lengthy discussion in the war room, Morana still didn't feel prepared to win over Conan's city. Elivira seemed pleased with her performance, but Hames still despised her. Garian seemed more indifferent with each passing moment.

If she couldn't win over the lords in Matthias's court, the place she called home, how could she ever expect to win over an entire city in a court she had barely set foot in?

"What are you thinking about?" Matthias asked, walking her down the corridor to her room.

Morana's brow furrowed, worry blooming in her chest. "She's right, Matthias."

He stopped, gently grabbing her arm until she faced him fully. "Who?" he questioned.

Morana swallowed the lump in her throat, holding back tears.

"Elivira," she whispered, gaze lingering on the obsidian floor below.

"Elivira believes in you," he said. His finger came up beneath her chin, forcing her to look at him.

"How would you know?" Her voice was louder, and Morana quickly scanned the hall for other servants, finding none. "Her dissatisfaction was clear, and she was right to feel it. I have no redeemable qualities. I never even asked what was happening on account of our engagement. Not until weeks after I returned." Despite her best efforts, Morana's voice still echoed through the halls, the tears threatening to spill over. "And now I'm expected to show up in Ohriid after I appeared with Raidan? Explanations be damned. The fae will draw their own conclusions, and I'm somehow supposed to garner support from them all."

Matthias's voice was soft, his features softer as he tucked a strand of hair behind her ear. "Is this because you're scared of winning them over?"

"It's because I don't believe I can!"

Her words echoed long after she said them, and Morana stood before Death, her chest pounding—her heart bare.

Without muttering a word, Death pulled her in, kissing the top of her head as she sobbed into his shirt.

She hadn't thought twice about confessing her worries to him—hadn't pretended—hadn't even wanted to. Walking through the palace, Morana had given up her fear freely to Death. There were no more masks between them, and it settled her.

When her tears dried up, she breathed deeply, reminding herself of who she was—what she was.

"I meant what I said." Matthias interrupted her thoughts. "You see every single part of yourself as weakness, Morana." While his thumb gently traced her jawline—moving slowly, his tone held a certain edge to it—one that demanded to be acknowledged. "You need to accept it all—the darkness, the power. Cain was right. You're afraid of yourself."

Morana cleared her throat, holding his gaze. "Hot-headed and unpredictable." She echoed Elivira's words.

Matthias didn't shy away or deny it. "So, what if you are?" The authority in his voice gave her pause. He pressed forward, testing her. "You are many things," he asserted. "Exactly the kind of queen that could kill a god."

His words sunk deeply into her bones, carving themselves there until she felt she believed them herself. It was coming—a war of fae and gods.

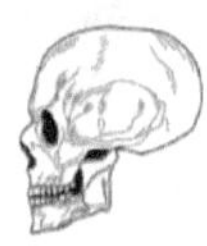

Morana sat near the fire, legs curled up on the chair as she flipped through Matthias's blood book. She quickly shoved it behind her when Sarnai walked into the room carrying a cup of tea.

"I'd knock," she said, "But I figured we had been past that before. We could be past it again."

Morana chuckled, looking down as she ran her fingers over the ends of her hair, longer than the last time she sat in this chair across from the goddess.

Sarnai's emerald dress flowed gracefully over her lithe form, typical to what the flora goddess usually wore.

"Matthias made a request," she said when she handed Morana the tea.

Once the scent hit her, she knew what it was immediately, thinking of her time in the kitchen with Death.

Morana took a sip of the contraceptive tea. "Thank you," she whispered.

Nodding once, Sarnai threw herself in the second chair, draping her legs over the arm as her umber eyes looked up at the ceiling. "How are you?" she asked.

A soft smile tugged at Morana's lips. "Good." For the first time, she meant it. While the worry hadn't disappeared fully, she felt more settled than she ever had—at least as long as she could remember.

Sarnai looked at her then—assessing. Once the goddess determined she wasn't lying, her full lips pulled up at the corners, white teeth flashing. "Turns out you are more powerful than me," she said.

Morana chuckled, taking another sip of tea. "I wouldn't say that."

"Of course you wouldn't. You care about my ego too much."

Silence stretched between them, lingering like the night outside Morana's bedroom window. Stars flickered in the sky above, the glass firmly closed to keep out the cold of the winter in Ascella.

"I want you to go into the city with me," Sarnai interrupted. "If you are to be queen, it's time you pick out your own dresses."

"Right," Morana said. "I would like that." She smiled at the goddess before cocking an eyebrow. "No more painting classes, though."

Sarnai looked offended, spinning to sit properly in the chair. "But your talent was so incredible the last time!" Her eyes glowed with mischief. "I was really looking forward to seeing Garian's dick this go around. Have you seen how beautiful his wife is? He doesn't speak on it much, but I'm certain his co—"

"Please stop," Morana interrupted, clutching her stomach as the laugh was ripped from her lips. "Actually," she began, "Maybe we should go. I'd be happy to give my interpretation of whatever Callum is working with. Since you seem to enjoy his presence so thoroughly."

"Oh, gross." The look of disgust twisting Sarnai's features had Morana laughing all over again. She was thankful that the time apart—the events that had occurred since the last she saw the goddess hadn't divided them in the way it divided her from the other lords.

As their laughter died down, they sat in companionable silence, the fire crackling in the hearth.

Sarnai lifted a hand, fingers stained the color of red soil as she formed a flower in her hand. It resembled a flower Morana had seen before—seen in The Wastelands.

Eyes narrowing, Morana watched as the plant disappeared, absorbed into the flora goddess's palm.

"You were there," she whispered, and Sarnai looked up, her expression betraying nothing. "In The Wastelands. You were there."

The goddess had the decency to look uncomfortable. "I couldn't go in," Sarnai confessed, her jaw tightening. "Raidan's magic is powerful—he had wards, and Conan could only get me so far."

Conan.

She hadn't seen the lord since they left The Oracle, but still, she remembered the interaction from Matthias's book. Conan had ensured access for Sarnai—access Matthias wanted and couldn't have.

"But you still came?" The statement sounded like a question.

Sarnai's eyes softened as she leaned forward a fraction. "Morana," she spoke. "I saw what was happening as best I could from the outside."

"And you showed Matthias. Morana's back stiffened; her attention fixed to the goddess. Sarnai had never spoken so seriously with her before. "And what did you see?" she asked.

"Enough," Sarnai answered, avoiding the statement about Death. "I saw enough." Sarnai sat back, running a finger over her lips as she appeared deep in thought. "We are going to fucking kill that bastard," she finally spoke.

Morana nodded, her eyes fixed to the fire in the hearth, watching the flames dance where they burned. "You're right," she said, though it sounded like a promise. "We are."

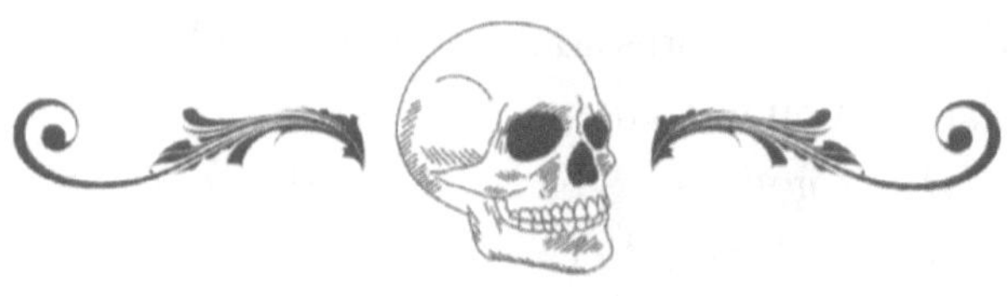

Twenty-Two

"What was it you saw?" Morana stood leaning against a shelf in the library, arms folded and eyes fierce as she stared at the scribe working.

Cain looked up, taking in the shadows still twisting in the air. The hollows beneath his eyes had sunken to a deep purple, and Morana's heart tugged at the thought of what he must be experiencing—seeing. If it was true, if he had the same power as The Oracle, there's no telling what horrors his visions might have.

"Morana," he said, nodding once and turning back to his work. His pen scratched against the parchment—the only sound in the nearly empty library.

Shadows licked down her arms, transporting her until her palms rested against the wooden surface of the table.

"Cain." Her tone was laced with authority as she leaned toward the scribe now opposite her. "What did you see? What have you been seeing?"

The scribe threw the pen down, eyes peering up at her—somehow wiser than they once were. "I've seen many things," he spoke low. "A war is coming. Seems to be a good time for an oracle."

"You are, then?" Morana asked, hands still placed firmly on the wooden surface of the table, as if it would give her the support she needed. "An oracle?"

"It appears so." Cain leaned back, giving up on his writing completely, and the corner of Morana's mouth lifted—just slightly.

"Okay," she began, moving to take the seat across from him. "Let's talk about it."

A crease formed on Cain's brow—his eyes cast down toward the parchment. "My power is inconsistent," he confessed. "It's new, and I don't fully understand it—or trust it."

"And how long have you had the visions?" Morana tapped a finger on the table, her features softening. It couldn't be easy—especially with how young Cain was.

He sighed. "It's been a little while. A month maybe? I've shared most of them with Kit, though I'm not sure that was the best idea. It had her worried. The visions started the night Matthias brought you back from Ohriid."

Morana leaned forward, tucking a strand of hair behind her ear. "I'm not here to make you uncomfortable," she said. "I'm just trying to understand."

"You've changed." A small smile broke across the fae boy's face, his freckles scrunching with the expression. "And here I was, thinking you were just coming in here to distract me—or heckle me. I can never be sure which it is."

"Oh, I am most certainly here to do that as well. However, I would like to know more about this power," she confessed. "So long as you'll let me ask questions."

"Have I ever prevented you from asking questions?"

Morana huffed a laugh, leaning back in her chair. "You've tried." A beat of silence stretched between them before she broke it. "Have you been wrong?"

Cain's face turned severe, his expression tightening. "Not yet."

"And what is it you've seen?"

He looked at her then, and Morana felt the sharp pain of truth before it even exited his lips. A darkness overtook his features, and she wished she could carry the burden for him. "If you do not accept who you are—what you are—then we will lose. You need to know that you're worthy and what you're worthy of."

"You hinted at as much," she said, tilting her head back to look at the dark ceiling, a chandelier hanging overhead with dozens of faefires. "That still doesn't help me know what to do."

"Look," he started, and Morana could hear the subtle humor in his voice. "I'm new to this. I could hardly tell you exactly what to expect. All I know is that if you can't seem to handle all the power flowing through your veins, then Raidan will kill you." He swallowed. "Maybe even Inara."

That caught her attention. Looking back at Cain, Morana saw the seriousness in his expression—the intensity.

"And how much of this did Matthias know?"

Morana didn't want to believe that he'd been keeping secrets. He'd seemed so open. Morana had his blood book—his memories, and maybe it was because he believed she'd continue reading it. But she had promised herself she wouldn't keep going back to the book. She wanted him to communicate with her.

"Matthias knew the moment he saw me enter the training room with you. He came to me afterword." Cain's eyes narrowed. "Why?"

"He knows details of these visions?" Her palms were slick with sweat, frustration beating an increasing rhythm in her chest.

Cain hesitated, and that moment of uncertainty had her feeling a different emotion—*anger*.

The mist worked around the floor of the library, called with the force of her wrath.

"Cain," she growled.

"Matthias knows of the visions—all of them." His words seemed like a confession.

"Wonderful," Morana gritted out.

She couldn't linger here—couldn't have Cain reading into the emotions now swirling in her chest. He'd seen too much, anyway. It wasn't his place.

The only problem now was how to handle the situation with Matthias. Before the war meeting, he'd seen so set on including her in every part of his world—the war, but the reality that he had omitted information made her stomach churn.

It made her feel used.

"That settles it," she said, fighting off the uncomfortable emotions. "I will need to do as you say."

Cain winced, and Morana took the hint that there was more.

"You saw something else, too?" she asked.

"One of the lords," he answered. "I can't tell you which one, but he was standing at the bank of a river, watching a woman wash her clothes in the water."

"What does that even mean?"

Cain shrugged, picking up his pen and placing it back on the paper. "I haven't figured it out yet."

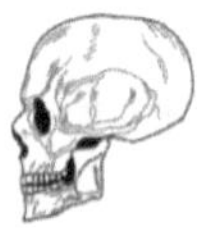

"Again."

Matthias's voice rang out through the training room as Morana groaned, dragging herself from the floor.

She'd wanted to confront Matthias after speaking with Cain, but instead, she brought it up hesitantly. He hadn't told her much other than he knew Cain was an oracle and had visions about the war.

He said he knew as much as Morana if she'd talked to him already—but that wasn't true.

Matthias immediately suggested extra training, and she'd dropped it. The feelings still lingered, though. The seeds of distrust planted once more.

Morana stared ahead, watching as another shadow creature—crafted by Matthias's magic—moved toward her. This one shaped so similar to the wolf creature she'd slain in Lux's tomb.

Morana launched, her sword arching down in a quick motion as she slashed through the darkness. It quickly reformed, lunging at her again.

"I know you're tired," Matthias shouted. She could barely hear it over the beating of her own heart. "But you won't kill it with the sword alone, Morana. You need to use your magic—all of it."

She rolled her eyes, moving toward the beast again.

"Morana!" Matthias yelled. "Use more fucking magic!"

Brow furrowed with anger bubbling in her chest, Morana pushed her power down the weapon, the gem in the sword's hilt brightening. The stone glowed a deep burgundy as her shadows rippled over her skin. The light crackled in her chest as fog rose around them.

It was all-consuming—the power.

Morana lunged forward again, driving the sword through the belly of the beast—the shadows breaking apart on contact as her head spun. She could hear her pulse in her ears and feel the sweat on her brow, slowly dripping down her temple.

Panting, Morana turned to look at Matthias, a pleased smirk on his face.

"Why did you lie to me?" she asked between deep breaths.

"What?" The bastard had the audacity to look confused.

"You *lied* to me," she spat, "about Cain's visions."

Shadows twisted around him, his own irritation rising. Those emotions were no match for the anger she now felt. It was betrayal all over again.

"I don't know what you're talking about." The tone he used said otherwise.

"Bullshit," Morana growled. "Cain told you the details of his visions and you kept it from me." Advancing on Death, she gripped her sword tighter.

"What did Cain see?" she demanded. "And why the fuck didn't you tell me Matthias?"

Letting the anger take her, the mist rose. It was far better than the hurt lying beneath the surface.

"I had reasons," he said, folding his arms across his chest. *Stubborn.*

Morana crowded his space, eyes blazing as she peered into the face of Death. "No reasons are good enough to lie to me by omission, Matthias. You expect me to be queen? Then treat me as such." He didn't move, and in her anger, she shoved at his chest. "You fucking bastard!" she yelled. "After everything, you would *lie?*"

He was breathing heavily, anger swirling in the air around them both. "You don't understand."

"I'm trying to!" Her voice echoed through the training room—rising like the tide.

"He watched you die," Matthias said, the scowl on his face holding steady. "He watched you die a thousand deaths and forgive me, Morana, if I didn't believe that to be useful information for you to have. You already doubt your abilities."

She stood there, her sword lowered, eyes wide. "You should have told me."

"Maybe," he said, stepping forward. "But forgive me for refusing to relay the graphic depictions of you dying at the hand of our enemies." His eyes flicked between hers, voice low. "What is the darkness without the stars?"

"What?" she asked.

"The darkness." Matthias shook his head. "It's all I've known. I've become so comfortable with death and shadows—with the dark things in this realm. Then you got here, and for some reason, you poked holes in that." Matthias's thumb dragged across her bottom lip, sending hot sparks across her skin. "You brought the stars with you, Morana. You brought hope that this realm could be set right." He shook his head again. "Why would I want to talk about those stars winking out?"

Morana sucked in a sharp breath, their shadows mixing around them until those shadows swallowed them whole.

His lips crashed into hers, and Morana dropped the sword, kicking it further away on the mat before tangling her fingers in Matthias's dark strands.

He groaned, his hand gently grabbing the side of her neck as he pressed in further.

All too soon, Matthias pulled away.

"I'm sorry," he breathed, still close. "I'm sorry you thought I kept you in the dark."

"Isn't that what you do?" she teased. "You are the King of Shadows, after all."

Matthias chuckled, pressing one more chaste kiss to her mouth before he walked toward the long table stretched out at the end of the training room.

"Take a break," he tossed over his shoulder, taking a long drink of water as Morana picked up her sword. She moved and placed the weapon on the rack, swapping it for her dagger.

Though her muscles ached and her stomach felt hollow, she felt prepared. Maybe not for Ohriid—for the political game she would play—but she felt stronger in combat and was pleased to know that she'd taken Cain's advice seriously.

Whether his visions came to pass or not didn't matter. Regardless of the outcome of the war, Morana needed to know she could tap into all of her power without questioning it.

It was as good for her as it was for the court.

Queen of Darkness.

Morana halted, slowly turning to look around the room, her heart still pounding from exertion. "Did you hear that?" she said, though she wasn't certain Matthias had heard her.

She could have sworn the whisper came from somewhere in the room, but they were both alone. No sounds echoed across the floor—nothing moved save for Matthias turning to face her.

"What?" Matthias asked. He sat on the edge of the table, sweat dripping down his temple.

"Nothing," Morana responded.

She gripped the hilt of her dagger, watching the gem as she began calling on her power—feeding it into the weapon until the stone showed that familiar deep burgundy color.

"It was black," Matthias interrupted from where he sat. "When you tried to kill me at our engagement celebration, that stone was black." His mouth quirked up at the corner when he said the word *engagement*, and Morana chuckled.

"Not the gift you were expecting?" she teased. "Black like my soul." Morana sheathed the blade at her thigh. The weapon had become a comfort over the past few months. After what had happened with the Veeden—after everything that had occurred in the fae realm, she couldn't stand to be parted from it.

The blade was as much a part of her as her magic.

"I don't believe that," Matthias finally answered.

Grabbing a cup, Morana filled it with water from the jug on the table and took a long drink. The cold liquid soothed her burning throat. When she finished, she set the empty cup down, moving to stand between Matthias's legs.

"Reese said it'll reflect whatever is inside me," she said. "I don't know which color to believe then. Fancy mood ring, I suppose."

"Whatever is inside you?" he asked, a wicked glint to his eye. Matthias trailed the pad of his thumb along her jaw, over her lips as they parted for him, that one touch making her stomach curl. "Shall we see what color it when I'm *inside* you?"

"An interesting experiment," she whispered, taking a step closer.

Queen of Darkness.

Morana's brows furrowed, that same whisper sounding closer this time.

"What is it?" Matthias asked.

Morana looked over her shoulder, taking in the empty training room, the dark mats on the floor, the faefires flickering in sconces along the wall. "Whispering," she answered, her voice low. "I keep hearing something—"

She stepped away, moving to the center of the room, feeling Matthias's power swell behind her. It was as if her shadows called to his, drawn up by his own darkness. Matthias's shoes hit the floor.

Spinning around the room, Morana noted they were the only ones still there—just as she thought. Even so, dread burrowed beneath her skin—as if she knew something was amiss.

Raidan had tried to find her in her dreams—she'd be foolish to think nothing of the whispering.

"Queen of Darkness."

The voice sounded moments before a fae man appeared in front of her. He held a sword in one hand and had a feral smile plastered to his face. The shadows twisted around him when he looked at her—and she knew what he had come for—her life.

Morana fought the burning in her body as she moved quickly away, avoiding the man's blade by a mere inch.

That dread that had burrowed beneath her skin intensified. He had come for her—she was certain.

Matthias was there in an instant, shadows pulsing around him. His face hardened, a sword appearing in his grip as if he'd used the shadows to retrieve it.

Morana watched as Matthias growled, moving his sword with precise movements. The fae man drew his own weapon quicker than she'd foreseen.

Metal clashed together as Matthias wielded the sword, his shadows twisting around him. The fae must have been powerful, his own shadows thrown in the mix—though more blue than black.

Something about Matthias's struggle told Morana all she needed to know. This man was from the Court of Shadows, and he was stronger than the average fae—the perfect weapon—the perfect assassin.

She reached out with her own shadows, searching for the mind of the fae man.

Morana had watched Matthias kill in the throne room before. She could still hear the screams. And the fact that the fae man hadn't been, told her everything she needed to know.

Something was wrong—very wrong.

As she fought to find his mind amongst the darkness, she came up empty, reaching for the mist next.

"Queen of Darkness." A new voice sounded behind her, feminine.

The woman wrapped an arm around Morana's neck, catching her by surprise.

Light crackled over her, and Morana tensed, remembering the way she'd been beaten—the scars that should have existed along her back. It was the one type of power that still felt chaotic and unpredictable—the power she could avoid if she truly wanted.

Fear rose in her throat as the panic took over. She reached for her dagger, struggling against the woman now holding her in place.

Feeling for her mind, Morana fought to feed the shadows into her thoughts—rip the assassin apart from the inside out.

Still, she came up empty.

"I've always wondered what sounds the Queen of Darkness would make when she died." The woman's lips were at Morana's ear, hot breath trailing over her skin as she grappled with the fear of the light. It was the one power that reminded her of Inara's whipping—Axton's betrayal.

When her hand tightened around the dagger, Morana moved. She allowed the shadows to twist over her skin until she faced the woman before her, fae ears pointed and short black hair swaying in the faefire light.

The woman held a dagger of her own, and Morana briefly registered the sounds of sparing behind her.

She couldn't look away, though. No matter how much she wanted to. If she glanced back at Matthias, this woman would certainly lunge.

Matthias was a god—he could certainly handle the fae man in the room.

So, why the fuck isn't it over yet?

"Who are you?" Morana questioned, gathering her power, letting it swell beneath her skin until it was all she could feel.

If she needed to, she would lose herself to the magic—lose every scrap of emotion in order to protect herself and her court.

Raidan couldn't have her—not like this.

"Inara sent me," the woman answered, and Morana's brow furrowed. "And she sent *him*." The woman's head nodded to where Matthias was still fighting with the intruder. "Your future court doesn't support you, Queen of Darkness. There are traitors in your wake."

Morana laughed, flashing a feral smile of her own. "Sure," she said, pushing her power through her weapon, hesitating if only to hear what more information this fae woman would confess.

Inara had sent these fae—not Raidan. That was something she still needed to piece together. It was unexpected.

"You can't truly believe you will win this war," she spat, taking a step forward. Light lashed out from her. It crackled through the air, and Morana twisted away from it, desperately fighting the twisting of her gut that came with the display of power.

"What makes you say that?" Morana asked.

"Because," she said. "Raidan is still looking for you. You're *his,* and he won't stop finding ways to get to you until you return to him."

Ah, there it is.

"But Inara sent you?" she questioned; her head tilted to the side.

The woman cocked an eyebrow. "Raidan wants to find you, but Inara wants you dead."

At that last statement, Morana lost control of her emotions—her power.

She let herself give in despite the fear and drew the light from her core.

The anger ripped from her chest as that light burst around her, searing the woman until she lit up in flames. A scream ripped through Morana's throat when she turned to see Matthias pinning the fae man to the wall, his eyes wild—smile wilder.

She walked forward, her power twisting around her. With the influx of magic, she hardly remembered who she was. Instead of a mortal, she was a god, and she would demand retribution.

Moving to stand beside Matthias, she noted the strain of the fae man's neck. Noted the way Matthias's dark eyes flicked to hers, widening when he saw whatever expression sat on her face.

She didn't care, though.

"Let him go," Morana said, and without question, Matthias did.

There, on the man's arm, sat a rune—glowing blue like the symbols in Raidan's temple. And when she fought to reach out with the shadows to attack the fae man's mind, she found herself blocked again. That rune must have had something to do with it.

Ancient magic.

The light, then.

It took her seconds to reach out, grab the man by the throat and igniting his flesh, burning him from the inside out.

Morana felt nothing—knew nothing aside from the taste of blood in her mouth, and the mist rising around her—the very mist that helped her hold the man in place as she killed him.

When her power settled, her mind slowly returning to her, she looked over at Matthias, standing there with his brows raised.

She could see the look on his face—read his expression easily enough, and Morana had the sense to feel uncomfortable.

Her magic was still too powerful when left unrestrained. She needed to train more.

"Well," he said, "That's one way to tackle fear."

Morana let out a breath, looking down at the dagger still in her hand, the weapon she hadn't even had to use.

When she glanced at the stone resting in the hilt, she noticed the marbled pattern now etched there.

A deep burgundy—with darkness streaked right through it.

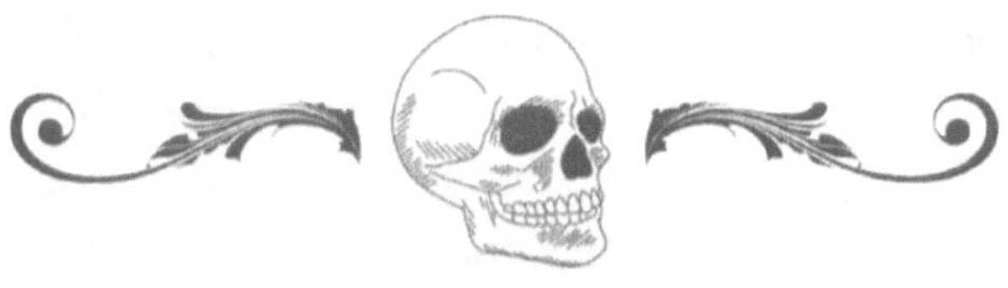

Twenty-Three

Snow settled over Ascella as Morana sat near the window. She used one hand to sip the tea Sarnai left for her and the other to dig the tip of her dagger into the sill. Light pouring into her room, reflecting against the stone seated at the hilt.

Burgundy.

Black.

Burgundy.

Reese had mentioned something about the stone when her power fed through it, and Morana had now noted two colors. That night of the ball, the gem had been pitch-black—dark like the night.

She's afraid.

You see every single part of yourself as weakness, Morana.

You need to accept it all—the darkness, the power. Cain was right. You're afraid of yourself.

Morana's stomach churned with the force of her emotion. She'd killed two people—no hands trembling—no qualms. The only thing she remembered from the training room was the immense pleasure of her power coursing through her veins. It had felt good to rip them apart with the light—to unleash the last of her magic that she had within her control.

But somehow, watching the gem spin on the sill, she couldn't help but wonder who she was becoming—a major god—cruel and calculating. Would she end up like Raidan? Would the power consume her and take away the last of her humanity?

Maybe it had been better when she thought she was mortal. As a mortal, she'd done damage enough to those around her. Now she could rip them apart from the inside out—light their bodies aflame and keep them from running. She could use the shadows to make it far worse for them, too.

Morana squeezed her eyes shut, her firm grip digging her blade further into the wood of the windowsill. She should feel something—she *did* feel something, just not for those she'd killed.

"Keep that up, and you're going to dig a hole in my palace."

Morana didn't turn, feeling his presence as the shadows licked up her arms. For the first time in the last month, she wanted to hide from him. If she were to be a monster, how would he ever accept her? Sure, a hot-headed bitch queen was one thing, but an all-powerful god with no remorse?

Matthias stood closely behind her, leaning down to brush a kiss against her neck. His lips sent a chill down her spine as she breathed in the scent of tobacco and darkness.

"I'm afraid I've already torn things up. First the mats in the training room, now this." It was the most she could offer him. The statement had layers she was unwilling to peel back. He'd have to do it for himself.

Pulling the dagger from the wood, Morana leaned back into him as Matthias trailed tattooed hands down her arms—palms warm.

She relished the touch—knowing how fleeting it could be. Morana had left him once before, and now it could be his turn to leave her. He could reject her for what she was becoming.

"We leave for Ohrrid tomorrow," he whispered, his hands moving higher to her shoulders.

She could feel the nerves spike at his words. There was still no telling how their time in Ohrrid would go, and she certainly wouldn't be accepted if she lost control. It would be Morana's first task to win them over, and by what Matthias said, Conan would be coming with them.

At least Conan had wanted her in his court before. He was on her side—or so she thought. Maybe his presence would be the last-ditch effort to get them to trust her.

It might work.

"I know," she said as Matthias trailed one hand up higher, gently running his fingers over the pulse at the base of her neck. "What are you doing?" she asked, her eyelids fluttering.

"Distracting my queen," he whispered, his hand moving to wrap around her throat. "You were remarkable yesterday."

"Yeah?" she asked, voice breathless.

She didn't feel remarkable. She felt like one of the monsters she was running from.

"Absolutely stunning."

Morana chuckled, but the guilt cut like a knife—cooling the fire.

"I didn't feel anything when I killed them," she confessed. "I felt nothing."

"Is that what has you digging holes in my palace?" Matthias's lips trailed slowly down her neck, sending ripples of pleasure down her spine. "Are you feeling guilty?"

I'm feeling terrified. It was a thought kept only to herself.

"Let me in that mind of yours, Queen of Darkness. Let me carry your burdens."

Morana gasped when the shadows caressed her skin, gently prodding.

She let him in to see her fears.

"You're scared you're becoming like Raidan?" he questioned. The low rumble of his voice vibrated against her shoulder. "Because you killed a few assassins."

"I lost control." Her voice was a whisper.

"You think I'm not hardened against death, Morana? Do you see me behaving as Inara—as Raidan?"

His hands stroked down her arms in a soothing motion.

"No," she admitted.

"You're not like them." The ferocity in his voice had her almost believing it. "You're here—sacrificing yourself for my people."

"But is it enough?" she asked.

"It is."

Matthias backed away and Morana stood from her chair, facing him, as he pulled her closer. Her lips parted as she stared up at him, his dark eyes burning with desire.

It was as if his gaze were burning right through her. Even when she wanted to hide, he could still see it all.

"My queen," he whispered, one hand rising to grip the side of her face as his lips brushed over hers—gentle at first—seeking. Matthias deepened the kiss, swallowing her moan as his fingers threaded through her hair, tugging at the roots.

When he pressed in, she moved backward. The backs of her knees hit the bed. Morana allowed herself to lower, sitting and looking up at Death as if she were worshiping his very existence. He could have run, but he was here, her fears shared openly.

Maybe she would take him up on his distraction. "What do you want?" she asked, though she knew full-well.

Matthias's dark laugh had her licking her lips, anxiously awaiting his response.

"You," he said, running the pad of his thumb over her mouth to part her lips. He tugged gently, and she gave in to desire, flicking her tongue out over his skin, pulling his finger into her mouth.

Her eyes were wide as she stared up at him innocently.

Matthias groaned, gently pushing her back until she was on the bed, his body between her legs. He rolled his hips once, pressing his length to her in a way that made her head spin.

She thought back to their time in the training room—the two fae that had attacked them—attacked her.

Whatever their purpose, they'd been sent to prove a point. Even in the palace she called home, she was not safe—always to be hunted.

While they would be in Ohriid tomorrow, there were still concerns over whether she could win the courts over—and if fae in her own court were betraying her—

"Stop thinking," Matthias whispered against her neck. "I don't even need to enter your mind to know what you're worried about. Your thoughts are so loud."

"I was thinking about the assassins," she confessed, unable to help the way her body arched into him when he trailed his mouth lower. He used his teeth to pull at the hem of her shirt and expose her breast. His mouth closed over her hardened peak, and she gasped, the thoughts fleeing her mind.

"I said I was here to distract you," he said. "Am I not doing a good enough job?"

He pulled at her shirt, and she let him, removing it and discarding the article on the floor. Morana closed her eyes, feeling the way he trailed kisses down her stomach—lower.

"There's so much to think about," she answered, though her voice sounded breathless. "The war, Inara," she let out a harsh breath as he unbuttoned her pants, peeling them off her body until she was bare before him. "*Raidan,*" she said.

Matthias halted, moving up until his gaze held hers. His tone hardened. "He's not worth your thoughts."

"I know," she said, eyes flicking between Death's. She trailed a finger over his cheek, tracing his features until Matthias closed his eyes, leaning into the touch.

"You're right," she said.

"Mhmm." Matthias nodded—his eyes still closed as he rolled his hips once more, teasing. "I usually am."

"Shut up." Morana reached for the hem of his shirt and peeled it off. He rolled his hips again, sending pure heat to her core. "Let's forget them," she breathed. "You're right. I need a distraction." When she smiled at him, he matched her with a grin of his own. "Ohriid can wait until tomorrow."

Matthias chuckled before pressing his mouth to hers, his kiss relentless as the thoughts—the worries fled her mind.

She allowed herself to get lost in his touch, his presence, and when Matthias pushed himself into her, Morana couldn't help but let the rest of the world fade away.

He punctuated his thrusts by trailing kisses over her neck, her shoulders, her collarbone.

"Don't stop," she whispered, the pleasure winding tighter with each motion.

Matthias moaned when she nipped at his lips, trying to capture them with her teeth.

"Don't stop," she said again—breathless.

Matthias reached down, stroking her until her release crashed through her.

His motions slowed as she came down with harsh breaths.

Matthias slid out of her, his eyes taking in her body. "Turn around," he said, his tone commanding.

Morana obeyed, lying on her stomach as he pulled her hips toward him, running a palm up her spine when he entered her again.

Her eyes squeezed shut at the fullness, her body buzzing with need again as he moved faster.

Matthias trailed soft kisses up her spine and over her shoulder. She moaned, pressing her hands against the headboard to push back into him. She rocked, listening to his breathing—the rumbling sound reverberating through his body.

"Fuck," he whispered, nipping at her skin.

"Harder," she said, and Matthias obliged. She could feel herself climbing again, lifting herself to feel him deeper.

"Fuck, Morana." Matthias's hand found her shoulder as he held himself steady, pushing her gently into the mattress.

The loud moan left her lips as she pushed further back. "More," she whispered.

Matthias's breath shuddered, his motions erratic as he came, taking her along with him.

As they curled up on the mattress, staring at the ceiling above, Matthias drew her closer.

"I love you," he whispered, kissing her temple gently. "You're going to win them over," he said, his voice assured. "And we are going to win the war."

She wanted to believe him—wanted to have the same assured confidence in her abilities—but as her distraction vanished, she was left with the painful thought that maybe Cain's visions would come to pass.

Maybe she wouldn't make it out.

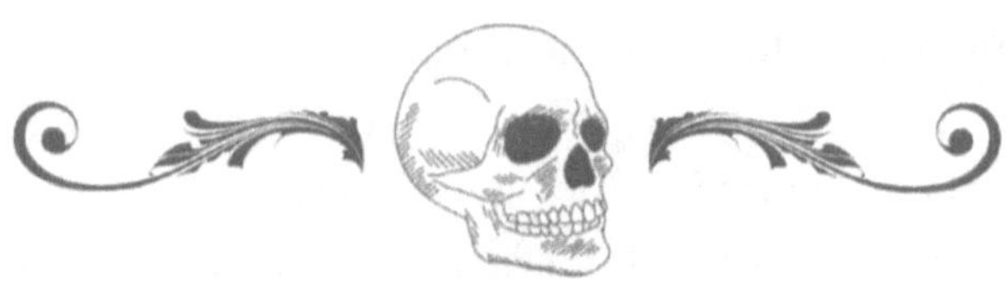

Twenty-Four

When they crossed the border on horseback, Morana felt the shift in the deepest parts of her soul. Returning to the Court of Light had her stomach twisting with memories of how Raidan used her when Inara announced her alliance with The Wastelands.

If only she knew how untrustworthy the major god was. He wanted power—cared for little else.

In that moment, Morana had been consumed by her magic—same as she'd been the other day, but worse. The heightened emotions from the betrayal had her losing control and feeling nothing for those she would hurt.

It was the reason the assassins in the training room scared her so much. How far could her power push her? Was there anything she wouldn't do?

"So many thoughts, darling. What is going on in that head of yours?" Ronan rode up beside her, a wide smile stretching across his face as his blue eyes looked her over.

His presence with them was a comfort—the one lord she didn't have to win over again.

Morana chuckled, eyes flicking toward Matthias riding just ahead of them. His shoulders still rigid from crossing over the border. He'd hardly mentioned what happened in the training room, but the way his eyes flicked back to her every few minutes became more apparent since their arrival in the court. He wasn't telling her something.

Again.

"Matthias said something similar last night." Her hands gripped the reins tighter as she urged her horse onward, trying to keep pace with Death.

Ronan's gaze turned wicked—his smile devious. "I'm sure he didn't say it exactly like that. He probably punctuated each word with his tongue."

A flush worked its way up her neck as Morana cleared her throat. She glanced down at her hands, suddenly distracted by the horse's trimmed mane.

"I'm glad to see your attempts at murdering Matthias didn't harm your relationship too much." Ronan's gaze shifted away from her as he watched Matthias intently. His smile fell as he lost himself to his own thoughts.

"I was thinking," she said, finally answering his question, "about my time in The Wastelands. I was thinking about the threat Inara and Raidan sent to the palace—how one of the assassins happened to be from the Court of Shadows, and I was also thinking about how I am to win Ohriid's support after all I've done."

Ronan's eyes slid to her briefly before glancing away. Silence stretched between them—weighted and heavy.

She didn't know how much he would be willing to offer her. Ronan wasn't one for serious discussions—but he had told her once that he would be there for her. And he hadn't abandoned her on account of her decisions and mistakes.

Maybe he didn't want to discuss her worries, and she would accept that. But she needed to practice being open about her thoughts—her feelings. And out of all the lords, Ronan was the safest bet.

Clearing his throat, Ronan kept his gaze averted, as if he weren't used to the seriousness of their conversation. "You'll make a fine queen, Morana."

Morana's mouth hung open as she watched him, searching for any doubt etched into the lines of his face.

She found none.

Maybe if he knew how much of a monster she could be, or the fear of losing control of her magic—her empathy.

"I can't think of a better fit for Matthias," he said, voice steady.

"What makes you say that?" she asked.

He finally looked at her, sincerity in the way his features softened. "You're thinking about a court you didn't know about a year ago. You've been thrown into this world—abused. After secrets and lies—Elivira's insults." Morana flinched at the mention of Elivira's harsh words during their last war meeting. "You still found a way to see that you've been given power, whether you wanted it or not, and now you're riding a horse into an enemy's court, pondering how you'll win over a city. And for whom? Because it's not for yourself. Not entirely."

Morana let the compliment wash over her, her cheeks pink as she pulled her cloak tighter around her body to keep out the chill.

Snow fell slowly from the sky, powdering the forest floor, and decorating the ground.

Looking up, Morana gazed through the bare branches, seeing the thick gray clouds stretching for miles. She'd never been a fan of winter—the cold, but somehow here, it didn't seem as terrible. Not with the company surrounding her.

"Is Ronan tormenting you?" Matthias asked, drawing her attention away from the sky to where he now rode next to them, dodging trees, his horse stepping over roots and snow dusted logs.

"We were just discussing how Morana will need to adjust her newest painting," Ronan began. "When she paints you, there will need to be some subtle differences. Nothing you're unaware of." Ronan held the reins in one hand, riding casually through the forest with his cloak hanging over his shoulders. "She will have to adjust the size—make it considerably smaller."

Matthias laughed, his voice echoing through the trees, and Morana chuckled under her breath. Clearly, Ronan was still obsessed with her drunken art.

"Nothing you haven't seen, Ronan. You know full well how much of a liar you are."

Morana laughed as Matthias grinned in her direction. It was so different from the dark god she had first met. It was as if this smile—the one that was so easy and carefree—had been reserved for her. "I didn't realize you two had been so intimate," she said, and Matthias rolled his eyes.

"I," Matthias said pointedly, "would never mix business with pleasure. Ronan, on the other hand, has no boundaries. He'll sleep with anyone—even if it's a conflict of interest."

"I promise," Ronan vowed, "there was no *conflict.* Not a one."

Their laughter died on the winter wind, picking up the further they moved through the trees. They would need to set up camp for a night, and Morana didn't look forward to sleeping in the weather that had now come over them.

"Conan is coming?" she asked Matthias as Ronan moved to ride ahead.

"He will be there," Matthias answered. "He went ahead of us, though most of those in the palace believe he's still dead."

"I don't know if sparing his life will give me enough credit with those in Ohriid," she confessed. "They sent me to assassinate him, and I nearly did."

That same discomfort wound its way around her heart, squeezing until she could hardly breathe. She would have killed him if she'd lost control. Thankfully, the servant she'd slain in the hallway hadn't triggered the same amount of bloodlust as her unbridled emotions.

But that thought didn't settle her either. She'd hardly thought of the fae.

"Conan supports our court." Matthias looked to her, dark eyes blazing. "He supports *you*. It's the entire reason he had come to find you while I was in The Wastelands." Matthias's brow furrowed. "You need to make an appearance in Ohriid, attempt to win them on your own, but at the end of the day, Conan is still alive, and he's still lord there."

"So, he wants us to win the support before it puts him at risk?" she asked.

"His name does mean fox," Matthias supplied.

Morana smiled, allowing the motion of the horse to calm her nerves, desperately dreading the moment they would stop in the forest—make camp.

"So, it does," she spoke softly. "So, it does."

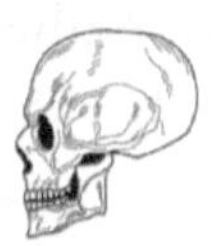

The sun set below the horizon, bringing with it a bitter chill that seeped into Morana's bones.

Their fire had died down, and Matthias expressed the danger of leaving it lit through the night. Creatures from The Wastelands—fae. There were too many risks, and after the assassination attempt in the training room, Morana was inclined to believe him.

"Well," Ronan said, breaking the silence. His boot scuffed across the snow coated dirt—the space they'd cleared for the night. "I don't suppose you guys want a third?"

Morana choked on the bread half sticking out of her mouth as Matthias's brows drew together. "Excuse me?" she finally said.

"It's cold. I'm suggesting I join you two in your tent."

"We brought plenty of blankets," Matthias answered. "I'm sure you'll be fine, Ronan. You're a fae lord and warrior."

Ronan shouldered Morana gently from where he sat next to her, smiling. "You could convince him," he whispered. "Death would never say no to his queen."

"I'm not interested in finding out that my painting was terribly inaccurate," Morana supplied, her tone laced with humor.

She watched the steady stream of smoke float upward from the leftover embers. Watched as it twisted higher into the darkened sky, snaking through the sleeping limbs above.

"Because it's bigger, right?" Ronan waggled his eyebrows when she looked back at him, and Matthias huffed, standing and offering his hand to Morana.

"Let's go," he said. "Before he convinces you that he's a lost puppy in need of shelter and warmth."

"You wouldn't leave me out in the cold to die?" Ronan asked, and Matthias gave him a flat look—one that said he most certainly would.

"Sorry," Morana shrugged. "I guess you'll only have thoughts of Reese to keep you warm tonight."

Ronan's face fell, his jaw ticking in frustration. "We haven't," he muttered.

"Excuse me, what?" Morana said.

"I haven't," he admitted. "With Reese."

"Yet you're out here making passes at myself and your king." Morana offered him a soft smile, noting how differently he behaved when it came to the blacksmith. "She cares for you," Morana said. "It's only a matter of time."

Patting Ronan's shoulder, Morana let Matthias lead her into the tent.

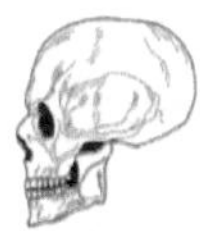

The winter chill was bone deep as Morana listened to the creaking limbs stretching and swaying outside their tent. Every howl of the wind haunted her as she lay awake, her eyes fixed to the tent above. Her mind filled with all the ways the meeting with Conan's counselors could go horribly wrong.

Matthias shifted until he faced her, tracing a finger down her arm until he grasped her hand, lacing his fingers through her own and resting them on her stomach.

Staring at the moth tattooed there, Morana sighed. "Ronan told me I would make a good queen," she whispered into the darkness.

"I've been saying that." Matthias's dark chuckle rumbled next to her, warming her just slightly.

"You have," she said, a smile breaking across her face. "I am sleeping with you, though."

Turning her head to face him, Morana watched as his features turned more severe, his brows pulling lower and his mouth turning downward.

"I thought it was more than merely sleeping together," Matthias said.

Looking down at where their hands intertwined, Morana began tracing the moth inked there, memorizing every mark on his skin. Her lip turned up at the corner. "Who knows?" she spoke. "I might just be using you for your body." Her smile widened. "Especially with how cold it is."

Matthias chuckled again and moved closer, adjusting the thick blankets covering them. She shifted, allowing her body to mold into his once she moved to her side.

"So," he whispered before placing a kiss on her neck, just below her ear. "You're not using me for my title, then?"

"Of course not."

The wind whipped against the tent, and Morana tucked herself even closer, feeling the warmth of Matthias's chest against her back. She wasn't sure how Ronan was doing in his own tent alone. Maybe he hadn't been merely joking earlier.

Matthias shifted, his arm pulling her tightly to him. "We never talked properly about what happened in the training room," he said.

Morana's mind drifted to the man Matthias had fought—the power he held. "Who was he?" she asked. "Was he from your court?"

"He was," Matthias answered, and she could feel his discomfort. "But there are light fae in the Court of Shadows." His thumb stroked her stomach over her thick sweater. "Cain, for example. Whoever he was, he could have been living in her court—aligned with Inara from the beginning."

"I don't know why anyone would do that." Morana's brow creased as she adjusted the makeshift pillow beneath her head.

Matthias shrugged. "People flock to things that are powerful."

"Is that why you're with me?" She meant for it to sound like a joke, but something in the way she said it betrayed her emotions. Though she had read Matthias' blood book and believed what he said, she still yearned for reassurance.

"You know that's not true," his voice was low— nearly a whisper.

Morana cleared her throat, allowing herself to speak freely. "Raidan wanted me for my power," she began. "It was the only thing he talked about. It was the reason he constantly pushed me in training—locking me in the dungeon." Morana's chest tightened at the memories. She could still feel the sting of Raidan's hand hitting her flesh, feel the way his breath ghosted over her, making her skin crawl. "Sorry," she said. "I haven't talked much about my time there."

"I still like listening to you talk about it. It's important," he confessed.

She licked her lips. "Why?"

A silly question—one loaded with all the worries plaguing her during the night.

Matthias placed another kiss on her neck—another as he breathed her in. Her cheeks flushed despite the cold.

"Trust," he answered.

"And do you trust me?"

He chuckled again. This time with his lips so close to her ear, she could feel the sound everywhere. "I let you hold a dagger to my throat," he supplied.

She laughed at that. He had fought her in the training room—welcomed her choice to kill him should she choose it. When Morana found Matthias in Ohriid with Conan, she could have killed him then, too.

"I told you about my parents," he said, interrupting her thoughts. "The entire story."

The wind seemed to die down, replaced by a steady quiet. "You did," she whispered.

Matthias kissed her shoulder then. The touch sent shivers down her spine. "I gave you my blood book." The truth of that struck her. She still had access to any secrets he was keeping. "Ronan is right," he finally said. "You're going to be a fine queen." She locked her fingers with his, taking strength from the way he gently squeezed her hand. "Believe that you will be, Morana."

"I'm trying," she answered, and somehow, in the cold winter night, Morana felt warmth wash over her. Warmth and the hope that what he and Ronan had said would be true. She would be queen of the Court of Shadows, and she hoped she would be a damn good one.

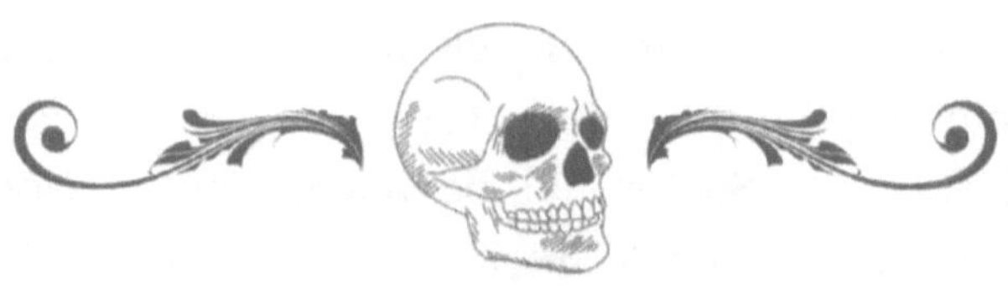

Twenty-Five

The stone floors of the palace dragged memories from the depths of her mind. Morana kept her eyes forward as Acacias, the counselor who had received them, led Morana and Matthias as Ronan trailed behind them.

The welcome wasn't exactly warm. Acacias hadn't been cruel, but the brief flicker of disgust that crossed his face when he looked at Morana told her everything she needed to know. It was in the way his lip curled, just slightly. He didn't want her here—didn't believe in her.

She took a deep breath, her boots keeping time with those around her as she followed, desperately trying to believe everything Ronan had told her. His encouragement kept her moving—kept her hopeful.

"We will meet first," Acacias said, keeping his pace quick and his eyes forward. "The counselors are all here since our city has no lord. Inara has aligned with The Wastelands, and we still have creatures breaking through the borders."

Morana's eyes slid to Matthias, but he didn't look at her, merely kept his expression blank and fixed his stare on Acacias's graying hair.

"And after?" Morana asked, lifting her chin. While the nerves still unsettled her, she promised herself she would be brave—wear the mask she was so used to. This one, however, wasn't of someone hardened or cold or jaded—it was the mask of a queen.

At least, that's what she told herself.

Acacias stopped, turning to face them with his brown eyes sharp, the wrinkles lining his eyes more prominent in the dim lights. He looked down at her, that familiar snarl on his face. "After the meeting, we will decide if you should stay or go."

The counselor turned abruptly and moved through the hall again, but Morana didn't back down. Instead, she kept her shoulders square and her expression determined.

When she looked at Matthias again, the tension in his shoulders had tightened, and his dark eyes had turned murderous. Ronan, despite his typical casual charm, had a similar expression—turned warrior in the presence of the fae man.

Morana's shadows stretched out toward Matthias, entering his mind easily. *He's so kindhearted.*

While she meant it as a joke, that tension Death carried didn't ease. She could feel his magic around her, in her own mind, before he spoke. *I would never take away your chance to prove yourself,* he said. *But the way he looked at you—*

There was a pause, and Morana used the lull to sneak one more glance, noting how serious Death had become.

Say the word, Matthias said. *Say it, and I'll kill him.*

A ghost of a smile snuck its way onto her lips as they entered a large room at the end of the hall, the round wooden table set for six individuals. Two fae were seated, one man and one woman, their expressions severe.

They didn't stand as Acacias moved to his chair, gesturing for their guests to sit down. Morana debated for a moment, trying to choose her next move wisely. This felt more like a game of chess than anything. If she remained standing, would it show her strength and move them toward her side, or would it display her insolence and push them away?

Hot-headed and unpredictable.

While Matthias and Ronan took their seats, Morana remained standing. Even though they were guests in this foreign court, she knew she was making her first impression as a queen. It needed to be a strong one.

"We are here," she began, "Because—"

"We know why you are here, Queen of Darkness." Acacias glared at her—his brown eyes boring into her as she tried to keep herself from deflating. "Now, please," he said. "Sit."

She refused, her mind a wild storm of thoughts, plays she could make in whatever game this was. Politics— she had been reading about fae politics, but all of that information seemed fleeting in the presence of the Court of Light counselors.

The information in the books didn't feel real. Advice of the past.

This, however, this would decide their fate.

Morana felt the fog rise at her feet, a reminder of who she was—what she was.

"It is my understanding," she began, tone tight, "That we have not yet been welcomed into your court. That fate is to be determined after this meeting." Morana's gray eyes were blazing, her tone steady. "As I was saying—"

The woman, bronze skin and hair braided back, scoffed, folding her arms across her chest as she leaned back in her chair.

Morana's anger rose, welling inside her as she clenched her fists. "Conan is alive." The woman's smile instantly fell, and Acacias shifted uncomfortably.

The confident assurance the counselor had before disappeared, just slightly, and Morana took that as a good sign.

Matthias tapped a finger on the table, casually leaning back in his chair as the shadows twisted over his skin. He wore a smug smirk, one that held a lethal promise.

Acacias's gaze flicked to Ronan, who was also sitting casually, giving Morana the space to prove herself. "It is our understanding," Acacias began, "that you killed him." One thick brow quirked up at the accusation.

"It is a poor understanding." Morana's tone cut through the air as the feral smile pulled at her lips. "I suggest you get to know your audience before casting blame and treating them so coldly in your court." She stepped forward, her cloak still hanging from her shoulders as she placed her hands on the table between Matthias and Ronan, leaning in slightly. "Then again, maybe you should understand your own court first, too."

"What do you mean, exactly?" Acacias asked.

"Conan came to me a while ago—in Ascella. I met him in a tavern where he spoke of the creatures that plague your border." Morana licked her lips, her confidence building the longer their conversation played out. "He *asked* me to come here. It's no secret Inara's rise to power came with some—controversy."

"Your point," Acacias gritted out.

For what it was worth, the fae man flanking the counselor's other side—the one who hadn't said anything— looked relaxed. His dark eyes kept pinned to Morana as he sat completely still, waiting for—something.

"My *point*," she said, "is that Conan cares about this court and his city. He made risky decisions to learn what was going on. Those creatures from the border, they live in The Wastelands—and now, Inara has aligned herself with a major god—woken from a supposed slumber and is set on taking over the Court of Shadows."

"And I suppose you're here to stop that?" the woman asked, one brow rising.

They didn't trust her—nor did they believe she was fit to rule. Morana could tell by their questioning, but she didn't let it keep her from the truth of her plans.

"I'm here to kill Raidan," she said. "And we need your support to do it."

Silence stretched on, and Morana fought the doubt that slowly wound around her, making her stomach churn uncomfortably. She fought to keep her breath steady as she awaited their response.

They had no reason to believe she could do it, and if she were being honest, she wasn't sure of herself either.

Ronan's words be damned.

"Mere weeks ago, you paraded through this very palace as his whore," Acacias finally said. "Right after your announced engagement to the King of Shadows—and right after your attempted assassination on Matthias."

Matthias's chuckle echoed through the room, carrying the same darkness he held just beneath his skin. His power twisted, shadows almost dancing in the dim lights. Morana felt the shiver work down her spine, the small spike of fear in her blood at the realization of who he was to these people. Matthias was more than Death—more than a man who had lost his parents. He was a king.

"Acacias," he said, his voice low. "I suggest you listen to *my wife*. It's unlike you to make enemies of the gods."

Morana's stomach dropped at the title. *Wife.* She wasn't his wife yet—they hadn't necessarily discussed when that would happen. His use of the word took her by surprise.

She fought the urge to look toward Matthias, trying to maintain her careful mask—to play the game the way

Matthias wanted to play. Morana wouldn't correct him, but she did stretch out with her magic, finding his mind open to her and waiting.

Wife? Her question sounded too loud, even in her head.

You wish to contradict it. Morana briefly caught sight of the dimple forming in Matthias's cheek, the subtle way he glanced down at his hands, trying to keep his amusement to himself.

No. Morana watched Acacias carefully as the fae's brows furrowed. Ronan's soft chuckle sounded next to her, and she knew the lord would know the essence of the private conversation happening in the room.

We can discuss semantics after you put this asshole in his place.

Morana fought the urge to smile.

"What do you mean, exactly?" Acacias asked.

As if summoned by the question, the door behind them clicked open, and the fox snuck into the room. Conan was so silent they hardly realized he had entered until his smooth voice echoed across the table. "He means," Conan interrupted, long before anyone looked in his direction. "Morana is married to Death, and she's a major god, set on repaying Raidan for his wrongdoings."

The three counselors stood up immediately, bowing before the lord of Ohriid.

Morana smiled as honey-colored eyes met hers. She lowered her head in an acknowledgment of his status here—and her respect.

"Morana, dear," he said, white teeth flashing. "It's so nice to see you again."

"Conan," she greeted, holding a smile of her own.

"I'd like to offer you a warm welcome to my city." Conan moved on long legs, stepping closer to the table. "Stay as long as you like," he said. "I consider everyone who has come for me with a dagger and spared my life a dear friend."

Morana kept her discomfort concealed, reminding herself that, though a fox, Conan was aligned with the Court of Shadows. He betrayed Inara and wanted Raidan dead—same as the rest of them.

"Please," the lord said, gesturing to the chair. "Have a seat."

Morana locked eyes with Acacias and held his stare in challenge as she lowered herself into the chair at the table—ready to discuss the realities of the war to be won.

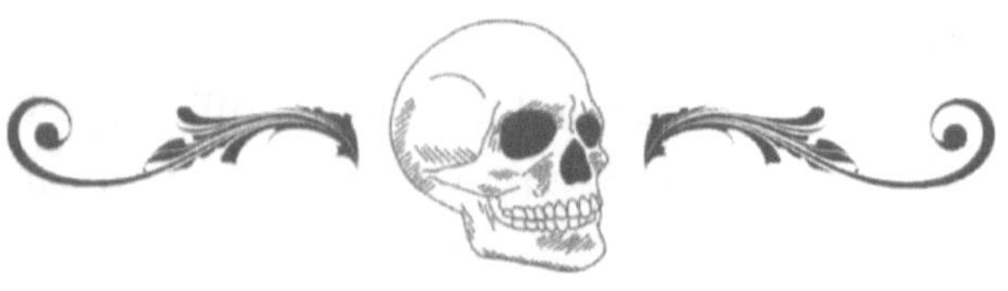

Twenty-Six

"Wine?" Conan asked as a petite woman entered the room, carrying a tray that held multiple goblets.

Morana sat back in her chair, her eyes lighted as she registered the shocked faces around her. And while she felt more assured after the way she had handled the initial start of the meeting; it didn't mean they were in the clear yet.

"Sure," Morana answered as the goblets were passed around. She sniffed the drink once before taking a sip. The sickly-sweet taste reminded her of how the faerie wine affected her, and she set it down.

"King of Shadows, Queen of Darkness," Conan began as he nodded to each of them, "Ronan."

Ronan laughed low before taking a long drag of wine. "Lord of Adhara might be more appropriate, or shall I suggest a name that emphasizes my good looks?"

"Lord Ronan." Conan rose a brow before his honeyed eyes turned to the counselors at the table. "Acacias," he said, gesturing to the counselor who sat with his tail between his legs. "Theon and Aris. These are my counselors, as you know. I apologize for their cold welcome. Though I must admit, it was very entertaining."

Matthias huffed a laugh, leaning forward in his chair. "Well," he began, "I suppose we should start with the obvious." Matthias took a drink of wine, and Morana watched the cup touch his lips, staring as his throat worked when he swallowed. She refocused on the meeting when he began talking.

Conan nodded, turning to his counselors. It was strange to see the fox turn lord as he commanded the room. "Morana is correct," he supplied. "Inara's rule was brought about when she made a bargain with the major god to the north." He swirled a ringed finger around the rim of his goblet, keeping his tone firm and authoritative. "Inara believes she will win a title, but from Morana's time in The Wastelands getting close to Raidan, we know that isn't the case. The major god seeks power and destruction."

"Her time in The Wastelands?" Theon questioned, looking at Morana.

Morana stared at him, recalling what Matthias had allowed others to believe about their engagement in his own court. She decided to play on that. "As a spy," she offered, noting Conan's raised brow.

Her shadows reached out to the lord so she could speak to Conan in private. *I dare you to question me. Keep in mind, I've come to know the power running through your own veins.*

Conan smiled, taking a sip of wine to hide the expression. *And what power might that be?*

It's not the power of a lord, she said. *Whatever did you learn with The Oracle?*

Acacias sat rigid in his chair, his expression tight as his eyes trailed over Morana, taking in the woman at the table. She didn't shift or move, but merely allowed him to determine her worth for himself. Smiling when his eyes finally met hers.

"An alliance," Conan interrupted, "with the Court of Shadows would afford us the Queen of Darkness and her protection." His eyes hardened as he spoke. "It would be what is best for Ohriid and her people."

"So, we align with her out of self-preservation?" Acacias scoffed, his lip peeling back in disgust.

"We align with her," Conan responded, "because we care about our fucking city, Acacias."

"And what is it you plan to do, *Queen of Darkness?*" the counselor asked.

Matthias's lip turned up at the corner as he swirled the wine in his cup, shadows twisting around him. "She once asked me what it would take to kill a god," he spoke. "You provide us with the forces we need, and we will worry about killing Raidan."

"And how can we believe she could achieve something like that?" Acacias asked. Morana could see the disbelief in the way his cold gaze stayed fixed to her, determining that despite her display of knowledge and power, she wasn't worth much. It was difficult to not slip back into old habits, to believe that the counselor was right.

Instead, Morana straightened, keeping her head held high when Matthias entered her mind.

Well, he said. *Time to show him something spectacular, my queen.*

A smile slashed across her face when she stood up, calling on the shadows as they swirled over her skin, slowly darkening the room.

"So, she's from the Court of Shadows," Aris said, watching Morana intently with her hazel eyes.

Morana glanced at her, cocking her head to the side and allowing the white mist to trail across the stone floor until it reached the counselor's ankles. Pinning her in place. When the room was plunged into darkness, all three counselors were pinned to their chairs. Morana called on the light, fighting the urge to shy away from it as it cracked through the air like lighting.

She struggled to remain in control, her power swelling as the taste of copper coated her tongue. Morana breathed deeply; her emotions quieting in the wake of her magic.

When Morana felt the lords struggle against their chairs, it fed a feral part of her. She kept going, trailing the shadows over their skin, longing to enter their minds—have them suffer for judging her—doubting her.

Is this enough for you, Acacias, she spoke—feeling his own fear.

Morana.

Her name echoed in her mind, drawing her back to the present. She felt guilt stirring in her gut—the uncomfortable and unwelcome fear that she couldn't handle the magic she held.

Morana drew back, calling the power to herself and letting Matthias's voice ground her.

Acacias sat still in his seat, blinking up at her where she stood.

"So?" Morana questioned, turning toward Conan.

Conan chuckled, taking a drink of wine before his eyes looked up, glittering in the faefire light. "Of course, my dear," he said. "We accept."

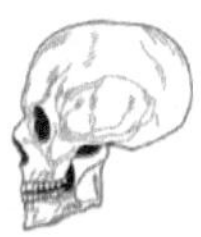

"Spectacular."

Conan stood at the door to the room Matthias and Morana would stay in, his auburn hair tied back at the base of his neck. Morana hadn't seen the lord since The Oracle—had been given little information regarding his whereabouts and what the man was doing.

None of that mattered, though. He had set her up well in the meeting, secured the support of his counselors despite their hesitance. After Morana displayed her power, she tried not to question if the support was merely fear based.

"You think?" she asked, moving to the small table set with a silver tray filled with various pastries and snacks. She picked up a piece of flaky bread filled with jam and took a bite before turning to face the lord.

"Absolutely." Conan ran his ringed fingers over his chin, regarding them. "I see you've made up." His eyes flicked to Matthias. "Wife?"

"Soon," Matthias's deep voice rumbled, and Morana felt the air leave her lungs. They were discussing the future she thought she wouldn't have—not after what she had done—how she had betrayed him. Even so, after Matthias's decision to use that title in the meeting, they needed to discuss logistics.

"Ah, so I've lied to my counselors on your behalf," Conan said, striding over to the tray and taking a piece of cheese for himself. "I will leave you to it, but please," he said, "I ask that you join me for breakfast in the morning. Tomorrow, we will gather our forces and announce our alliance with the Court of Shadows." He prowled back to the door on silent feet, glancing over his shoulders. "Your magic is being tracked after Morana's display. In the evening, you will have the opportunity to return home. Our alliance will be announced."

"Of course," Matthias said before sitting on the end of the bed, his hands resting behind him as he looked to Morana, eyes darkening with promises. "We need to get Ronan back tomorrow. He's terrible unsupervised."

Death didn't remove his gaze, and she bit her lip, watching Conan nod once before responding. "I'm no stranger to rumors, Matthias. Good evening."

As soon as Conan left the room, Matthias stood up. His tall form coated in shadows before he walked toward

Morana, moving them both to the other end of the room, pinning her against the door as he turned the lock.

Morana's breathing turned shallow at the sound of that click, the promise that they were alone for the evening. Matthias pressed his body to hers, his mouth parted and his eyes hungry.

Arching her back, she gasped, feeling his hardened length press against her. She urged him on until Matthias pressed a soft kiss to her lips, deepening it as his hand moved up to tangle in her hair.

He broke away for a moment, muttering, "You are magnificent."

Morana smiled against his mouth as he kissed her again.

"Impeccable," he whispered, moving his lips to trail down her neck.

Her body wound tightly as her skin ignited under his touch. She gripped his waist, trying to drag him closer.

When Matthias chuckled, his mouth at her collarbone, Morana felt the rumble of that sound vibrate beneath her skin, and she clenched her thighs together.

"Morana," he said, voice low—genuine. "Would you do me the honor of becoming my queen?"

"After the war?" she questioned, her voice a bit breathless.

Matthias withdrew to look into her eyes, his expression intense. "Before," he insisted. "As soon as possible." He kissed her once more, rougher. "Right now," he said, and Morana felt her stomach twisting, the desire buzzing over her skin. "I don't really care; I just want you by my side. Ruling."

Morana let out a breathy chuckle, leaning her head back to rest against the door as Matthias resumed his earlier endeavor. She groaned softly when his tongue flicked out over her skin, and he sucked.

"Do we host a ball where I get to attempt another murder?" she asked, the humor barely audible beyond her harsh breathing.

Matthias laughed, his hand tightening in her hair and pulling as he nipped at her bottom lip. Morana lost herself to the sensation of him, her shadows twisting down her arms, increasing her pleasure.

"We host a wedding, and then a prompt coronation," Matthias answered.

"When?" she asked.

"When we return."

Morana ran her fingers through his soft strands of dark hair as he moved his mouth lower, pulling her shirt down to brush his lips against the swell of her breast.

Matthias chuckled again, his hot breath fanning out over her skin and driving her mad. "Yes," he whispered. "As soon as we get back."

Morana raised a brow, tugging at the roots of his hair until he looked up at her. "Well," she said, her voice laced with something darker—taunting. "You'll have to ask nicely."

Smiling, Matthias licked his lip, slowly lowering to the ground until he was on his knees. He looked up at her, fingers trailing over the waistband of her pants. "And how would you have me do that?" he asked. The depth of his voice almost had her lose her nerve, give up the taunting and beg him instead.

"On your knees is a start," she said, tilting her hips forward.

By the dark smile that appeared on Death's face, Morana knew exactly what would come next—what he would consume.

Matthias's fingers tucked beneath her waistband, tugging her pants down gently. "Anything for my queen," he said.

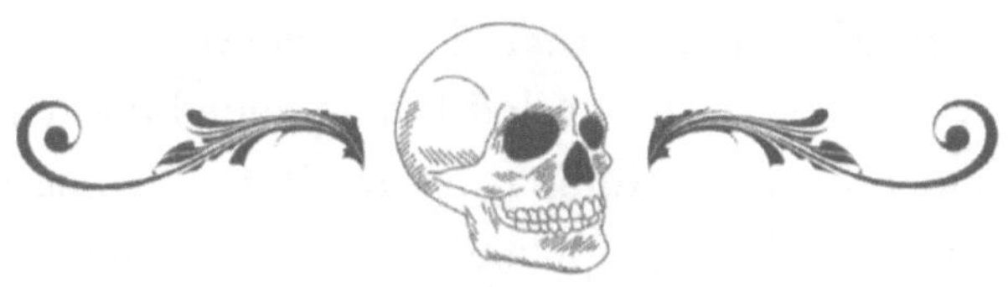

Twenty-Seven

The cold water hit her skin as a knock sounded outside of the bathing chamber. Morana looked up in the mirror to see Matthias leaning against the doorframe with his arms stretched above his head.

His eyes met hers, and she remembered all the dark promises he had whispered in her ear the night prior, her cheeks flushing at the memory. And by Matthias's smug smirk, he seemed to remember those dark promises, too.

He walked forward, his black button-up smooth and rolled at the sleeves, his tattoos visible—the same tattoos Morana had traced—licked.

"Are you ready?" he asked, eyes tracing over the black dress flowing to the stone floors of the palace of Ohriid. Morana fingered the high slit, turning to face Death.

"For breakfast?" she asked.

"For our return to Ascella." Matthias reached up, trailing the pad of his thumb along her bottom lip before pulling it away from her teeth gently. Heat washed over her at the touch—at the hungry look returning to his eyes.

"Of course." And after their meeting with Conan's counselors, Morana was beginning to believe it.

A somewhat disheveled Ronan joined them as they walked to breakfast. Morana raised a brow, taking in the wrinkled white button-up, and his blonde hair hanging loosely around his shoulders.

"Up late?" she asked.

Ronan's gaze hardened, his jaw tight. "Not what you think," he said.

With her brow furrowing, Morana looked him over again, noting the tension through his shoulders.

"Are you alright?" she asked, placing a hand on his forearm to stop him.

"I spoke with Acacias." Ronan's eyes flicked to Matthias, who still stood stoic in the hall. "He is in full support. Not that he couldn't be considering Conan's involvement." Ronan took a step forward, worry shining in his eyes. "Morana," he said. "There have been whispers of Raidan securing an army of—" Ronan winced. "Creatures."

"We knew that," Morana stated, her heart pounding in her chest.

"No," he supplied. "You don't understand," Ronan wiped a hand down his face, the stress painted there. "You are a major god, and Acacias believes you can control these creatures—take their minds for yourself."

"He wants me to steal Raidan's power with—with what?" she said, her heart still increasing in speed. "With my magic."

"Morana," Matthias stepped forward and placed a tattooed hand on her shoulder. "Morana, Acacias may have a point."

He gave her a pointed look, one that spoke of the night before—the Veeden called to her room and surrounding her.

She'd done exactly what they were talking about, but still, the fear wrapped around her heart. If she lost control of her power—especially with an entire army of Veeden and other magical creatures—there was no telling the damage she could do.

She'd nearly lost control in their meeting, and Matthias *knew* that.

Morana laughed a harsh sound. "You're kidding. As if killing Raidan isn't enough of a task, he wants me to command an entire army of creatures during battle?"

"You did it once," Matthias asserted. "You already summoned the Veeden once."

Morana's head whipped between them. "And I'm not even sure how I did that." The panic sounded in her voice—though she didn't want it too, it did. "Then there's the matter of my control."

Matthias's hand rose to cup her cheek, stroking once. "It'll be okay," he said. "Let's just get breakfast."

Morana's mind swirled, twisting with the expectations of what she could do—the part she would play in the war. While her hatred for Raidan consumed her and allowed her to hope for the god's death, controlling an entire army when she was still training terrified her. She was still learning to use all the power pumping through her blood. That fear of failure crept back in again, burrowing deeply beneath her skin.

If Acacias had such expectations, holding their support may be difficult. While Conan remained on their side, he was still a lord going against the court his city was under. He could be turned in. He could be betrayed.

She wouldn't allow it.

As they walked into the dining room, she couldn't fight the fears swirling like a wild storm. She could kill them all and feel nothing while she did it.

"You made it." The fox himself sat at the end of the long table, drinking wine from a goblet as his honeyed eyes glittered in the faefire.

"We did," Morana answered, shoving her fear down.

Matthias and Ronan flanked either side of her, following her lead as she sat at the table.

She supposed it was a good thing—intentional—both men taking a clear stance on what they believed Morana's role would be. They sat back, trusted her, allowed her to decide.

The thought eroded some of that doubt—if only a little.

"Thank you for your hospitality," Morana said, dragging her own sip of wine from the goblet set out for her.

A servant came around, revealing the contents of one of the trays. Potatoes, eggs, and different pastries, similar to the ones left in her room, filled the table.

Morana's stomach growled as she waited for Conan to help himself. As soon as he did, she began piling her plate with the food offered to them.

It was nothing compared to Willow's cooking, but still, she was starving—as if her power ate up more of her energy in recent days.

"Thank *you*," Conan said, taking a bite.

Matthias sat back, watching the interaction with predatory focus. His shadows twisted in the air and reminded the lord exactly who he was—even if he was allowing Morana to take the lead.

Morana thought back to her first encounter with the lord, the tavern, the sadness, the feelings of doubt that existed then. They were far worse before. She had felt weak—ridiculous. Conan had called her by the title then, referenced the whispers.

"Queen of Darkness," she mused. Morana looked up at Conan, gray eyes swirling with questions. "Where did the title come from?" she asked. "You called me that in the tavern," she added. "Where did you hear it first?"

Conan gestured to Matthias, his tone matter of fact. "King of Shadows," he said before turning his focus to her. "Queen of Darkness."

"We were not engaged at the time," she said honestly. Matthias wasn't even in the court—kidnapped by Raidan and tortured in his dungeon.

"I had been watching you," Conan answered before taking another sip of wine.

"And the whispers of the name?" she asked. "You said others knew about it. Others *did* know about it. Who was responsible for that?" Morana cocked a brow, pushing her food around her plate.

Conan smiled slowly, the kind of smile that preceded a confession. "A wonderful question, my dear."

"A true fox," Ronan muttered before shoveling more food into his mouth.

They ate in comfortable silence, Matthias resting his hand on her leg beneath the table, playing with the slit that rose up her thigh.

The door opened, a guard plowing into the room and crossing it in three strides as he stood before Conan. Behind him, Acacias entered, his expression tense.

"My lord," he began. "The Veeden. They're crossing the border."

Acacias's eyes settled on Morana, and fear crawled up her spine, a reminder of what Ronan confessed in the hall.

While she didn't think the counselor had called the creatures, they had been crossing the border for a while. She saw the look in his brown eyes—the one that said he had expectations for her ability.

It was a test.

Morana stood, tying her hair back with a leather chord. "We will change," she said, "and then we will join you."

Without thinking, she shadowed out of the room, quickly donning the same clothes she wore in training, her boots, her cloak.

Her movements were jerky and forced, fear bleeding from her like a wound. She couldn't keep it contained—not for long.

"Are you alright?" Matthias asked, expression tight.

Morana looked at him with that fear in her eyes. She couldn't give into it, but she wanted him to know it was there—that it existed.

Morana ran her fingers over the scars on her face, remembering the sentiment behind leaving those wounds there. They were there to remind her of who she was—human before anything else. Her status as a god didn't change that, but still—if she lost control, there was no telling what would happen.

They could lose the alliance—the war—but none of that mattered. She cast the fears aside.

"I have to be," she said.

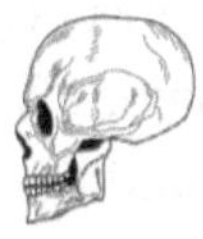

The wind cut through her cloak as Morana kept her hand tightly wrapped around the hilt of her dagger. Her boots crunched in the snow as they walked along the top of the wall, stretching along the edge of the Court of Light.

Beyond them, The Wastelands sat stretched out, cracked earth free of snow. It was like falling into a different realm. Amidst all the death waiting ahead, Morana glimpsed through the white mist. Within it, the lithe creatures prowled forward, their intoxicating song rising from the fog.

She looked around, taking stock of the army Ohriid had stationed on the wall—the men that they would now loan to the Court of Shadows—her court.

"What is it you usually do?" Matthias asked. His own sword was sheathed at his waist, making him look more warrior than king.

Beside him, Ronan stood ready, his sword already drawn, the humor absent from his gaze.

"We fire at them," Acacias answered.

"Arrows," Conan added, his brow creased as he took in the image before him. "Occasionally using the light to lash out against them. But they've never come in these numbers before."

Morana didn't miss the way Acacias's eyes slid in her direction, and her stomach churned with the fear that she wouldn't be able to do anything of value.

If this were to be unsuccessful, they would all die—by Veeden, or by the major god in their midst. And the worst part was that she wouldn't care if she killed them—not when her power took over. For now, she cared—cared immensely.

"Do you lose any soldiers to their song?" she asked, recalling the intoxicating lure of the Veeden. Like sirens of the land, they called out to their prey and begged them to come closer. Then, the Veeden would consume.

"With this many," Conan mused, "It's only a matter of time, but we usually can handle them from the wall. The distance helps."

Morana took a breath as Ronan came to stand in front of her, placing his hands on her shoulders. "Try," he said as she attempted to hide the doubt in her eyes—the window into her true feelings. In the presence of a court they were trying to win, her doubt wouldn't serve her. "Morana, you have to try."

She nodded, closing her eyes as she drew on Raidan's power.

No.

Her power.

If the major gods created these creatures, and she *was* a major god, then she should be able to control them. She should be able to ward them back—send them into the desolate land of The Wastelands to protect Ohriid.

In order to do that though—with these numbers—she would need every ounce of power flooding her veins, and that hadn't boded well in the past. She could taste the copper already, remembering the way she'd swirled her finger in Garian's blood during that first dream with Raidan.

Cain was right. She would need to embrace all of her power to be successful, but she would still need to maintain any scrap of control she could manage. Had he seen this? Did he know this would happen when they left for Ohriid?

She didn't know if he had control of his sight yet. Maybe the visions simply came when they chose to.

Morana felt for the mist, testing and allowing it to stretch out from her. It cascaded down the wall, rolling like a cloud of dust overtaking the earth until it reached the creatures walking slowly toward the city—hellbent on taking over. She felt for something—*anything* that resembled a fae or human—something she could bind. The Veeden weren't human though—difficult like the basilisk.

Even so, that binding magic would only halt them—it couldn't force them back. And if she left with them bound, would the magic hold?

When Morana opened her eyes, she saw nothing. The white mist disappeared, mixing with the already rising fog and slipping through her grasp.

As the creatures advanced, sounds started drawing her attention away from her task.

Soldiers loaded their bows, shooting sharp arrows toward the creatures. The wave felled a small amount, but not before their song lured a fae man over the edge. Morana watched as his eyes glazed over when he climbed the lip of the wall and let himself fall to his death. The Veeden were on him in an instant, hidden by the magic that concealed the way they devoured and consumed.

She was *failing*.

Morana remembered the way it felt to have the tongue of a Veeden shoved down her throat. Her mouth went dry as the shouting rose around her, but she couldn't focus on it. They wanted her to do something—they were relying on her—some mortal turned god and ripped from the human realm.

That was their saving grace.

A god with power too intense to be used.

Matthias stood at the wall, focused, as his shadows twisted out before him. When the Veeden began climbing the massive stone structure, all Morana could hear was metal and flesh, the cries of dying soldiers.

They crested the ledge, pouring onto the walkway. Eyes glazed, swords drawn, the entire scene played out in slow motion—the noise rising around them.

All she could hear were the cries of those dying and the whip of the wind mixing with metal.

"There's never been this many," Conan shouted, his sword cutting through the neck of one of the creatures.

"You have to *try*." Acacias's voice slithered across her skin from where he now stood behind her. Morana's skin prickled at his nearness, her fear rising in her throat.

She closed her eyes again, trying desperately to use her magic to stop their advance. Yet, every time she made contact, that power slipped through her grip and left her desperate for a new solution.

It was her fear of losing control that held her back—she knew it to be true, but still, she couldn't combat it.

"Use it like the shadows," Matthias shouted. "Find their minds, and will them elsewhere."

Morana didn't know what he was talking about, knowing that the white mist didn't work in the same way as her shadows. Raidan could control the Veeden, but he had taken part in creating them, and she had not.

In her room, she'd only drawn them to her with the mist. She'd used the shadows to banish them.

Morana felt the tears prick her eyes, the fear of failure consuming her almost as much as her fear of her magic.

They were right. She had to try.

She called on the mist again, weaving her shadows into it, combining the power and reaching out. It was then that she felt it—the mind of one of the creatures. The feeling was familiar—akin to what she experienced after waking in Ascella with the Veeden surrounding her.

She let her power pour from her, magic moving across the landscape and latching on to each of them.

Morana grunted, gripping the stone wall as her power took over. She shoved it into the Veeden in the same way the creature had shoved its magic into her. With everything she had, she stood panting on the wall, forcing them to listen—to *obey*.

When she opened her eyes, Morana watched the retreat, watched as the creatures moved back into the hellscape they came from.

She added the light, letting it crack as it reached forward, connecting with a creature.

With all of her power working as one, Morana shoved the fiery magic into the monster, burning it from the inside out.

It felt good—intoxicating.

She couldn't stop. Listening to the sounds of metal around her, Morana reached out, incinerating the creatures where they stood. It was a heady sort of power she couldn't escape.

The wind whipped at her hair, chilling her bones like the cold and calloused heart beating in her chest.

Inhaling the scent of blood, she released herself, felling monsters and creatures before they could do any more harm.

Morana.

Matthias's voice sounded in her mind again, and she halted. Her eyes squeezed shut and her hands gripping the wall, Morana leaned into the sound of his voice.

"Morana," he said. His chest was against her back as Matthias drew close to her, and for a moment, she feared his nearness—what she would do to him.

"Morana, open your eyes."

When she did, she saw The Wastelands stretching out beyond the border—black smoke rising from the ashes of her destruction.

Morana stood panting, turning to see Acacias's brown eyes widened in shock.

The remnant of the darkness still surrounded her, eclipsing the sun as the mist floated over the stone they stood on.

"You did it," Acacias whispered in amazement. "You truly are a god."

Morana turned back, looking out at the dry, cracked earth and pulling her cloak tighter around her shoulders. Her blood was boiling, and she almost wanted to throw the garment off.

"Apparently so," she whispered. "Apparently so."

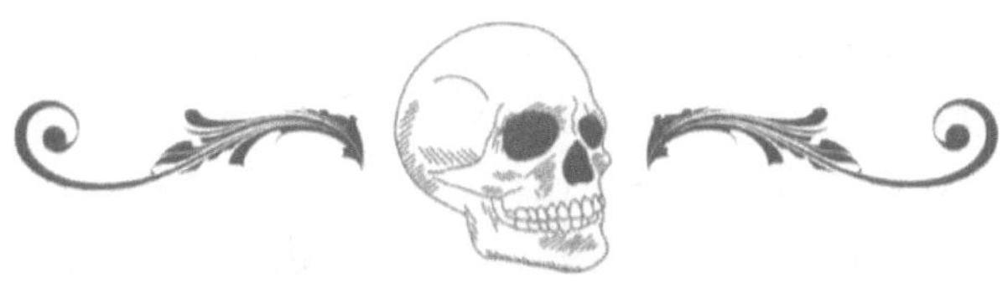

Twenty-Eight

"Again."

Garian watched with Matthias at his side as Morana fought to mix her magic, weaving together the light and dark—life and death.

The small lizard scuttled across the stone floor, scales shining silver—another gift from Callum.

"Don't let it touch you," Garian reminded her. "They're poisonous, deadly things. The last one got too close."

"I get it," she ground out, twisting the white mist into the cocktail, stretching it out across the floor until the mist pinned the thing in place. Shadows overtook its mind, and light engulfed its tiny body, burning it from the inside out.

She watched its little body set aflame, eyes glowing with wicked delight as her power sent ripples of pleasure down her spine. Her mind was spiraling—a feral smile on her face as she let the creature burn longer than she should have. It would get rid of the poison Garian spoke of—every trace if she kept it burning.

Morana's brow furrowed, the white mist floating over the floor. Both Matthias and Garian watched her use her magic after exhausting her with the sword. Matthias had asked the lord for help when they returned from Ohriid. While Morana didn't know where the lord stood, he certainly didn't let those feelings cloud what he set to accomplish.

With all the power in her veins, now able to be used as one, Morana was anxious to see just how far she could go.

Stop.

Matthias's voice entered her mind, and her magic retracted as she took panting breaths. When she looked at him, the pain etched itself into her features. Every single time she'd done this, she'd needed Death to draw her back.

Why couldn't she fucking do it on her own?

Morana blinked, her mind returning to the present along with her humanity.

"Well," Matthias said, brow furrowed. "I have another task for you, I suppose." He wasn't smiling as he moved to the doors of the training room.

Morana caught her breath from exertion as she watched two palace guards dragging a woman into the room. The chains around the fae woman's wrists—the dirty rags she wore told her everything she needed to know about the woman's position in the court—a prisoner.

The mist swirled against the stone floor, no longer as intoxicating as it once was, but Morana still seemed to taste blood at the thought of ending a life.

Matthias wanted her to kill the woman, of that she was certain. The Queen of Darkness would gladly oblige.

"Her punishment," Matthias said, facing Morana as the woman struggled against the iron around her wrists. The metal clanked together, the woman grunting and struggling to get free.

"For?" Morana asked, raising a brow. Sweat dripped down her back, soaking the black t-shirt she wore.

She'd still needed Matthias against Callum's creature. Could she really handle taking the life of one of the fae?

When she looked back at the woman, silver eyes met hers, the woman's long black hair calling on a distant memory.

The feeling of the fae woman's eyes lingered even after she walked away. Morana let out a shuddering breath and dared to pull out the book as soon as she was alone.

Shadows wrapped around her arms and the tome's cover as if the contents drew her power to it. Without warning, the leather snapped open; the pages flicking wildly before Morana forced the book shut and shoved it back beneath her cloak.

Looking up, she called her magic while stealing a glance at the fae woman, now leaning against the bar and whispering to the man running a white cloth over glass. Those silver eyes lit up, and unease stirred in Morana's gut.

"I know this woman," Morana confessed, looking frantically between Matthias and Garian. "She was in Nashira."

Garian stood in the corner, stoic and waiting as Morana's chest tightened. "Inara sent her," Garian supplied. "To kill you, me, anyone she could get her hands on. Much like the assassins in the palace."

Morana's stare hardened, her magic swelling beyond her control. Despite everything, the lords in Matthias's court still felt like family—like home. Morana had seen this woman *before.* It meant that Inara had been trying to kill her for longer than she'd anticipated, and she wondered if Raidan knew about it.

The other assassin had admitted that Raidan wanted Morana very much *alive.* Probably due to the lack of control she had over her magic.

That same magic rose within her as she lost herself again, plunging the room into complete darkness, the copper taste intensifying.

Morana searched for the woman's mind, opening the fae's mental barriers with ease. She saw Garian arrive at the tavern shortly following her own departure. Saw herbs slipped into his drink, the way his nose crinkled as he brought it close to his mouth.

She'd tried to poison him, finding herself imprisoned instead.

Memories flashed in Morana's mind. They were memories of Garian whittling inside a cave—thinking of his son. She saw Garian's wife at their engagement celebration—

the smile on her face as she looked to her husband. Garian training her—joking with her—talking about his family and his life. The tapestry hanging on the wall of the tavern indicating his position and the love his people had for him.

Then an unwelcome memory.

Morana watched The Wastelands stretch out before her, saw silver hair and amber eyes. She felt Garian's blood coating her finger and the way she'd slain those around her.

It was a memory that spoke to her fears—what she could do if she couldn't get a grip on her magic.

Her power pulsed in the room; those fears forgotten as she stepped forward. Wind whipped around her, and she could feel the heady desire to seek death—deal it to whomever got in her way. On instinct, Morana prowled toward the fae with her dagger in hand, the stone at the hilt plunged into pure blackness. The mist held the woman to the ground, her eyes glaring up in defiance.

Something in that stare fed into her desire to destroy. All Morana felt was pure rage.

She used the shadows, wrapping them around the woman's mind to make her stand as Morana shoved the hilt of her dagger into the fae's hand.

Smiling, Morana cocked an eyebrow. "You get one chance to fight back," she said, knowing full well how useless that chance would be. "One chance to save yourself."

The woman growled; yellowed teeth sharp as she lunged forward like a wild animal.

The blade bit at Morana's arm, dragging across her flesh to form a shallow cut. Before more damage could be done, the light plunged into the woman, igniting her body in the darkness before Morana allowed the shadows to consume her entirely—intensifying the pain.

The light winked out—conquered by the darkness.

She couldn't stop. Morana was truly a queen, darkness surrounding them as the shadows spun. The woman was gone, her chains melted on the floor.

Morana.

His voice was in her mind again, and she grunted, trying to ward him off.

Morana, stop. Come back to me.

She turned on him. The shadows parted to reveal Death, standing in his own darkness—a scowl on his face.

Morana.

She hesitated, her magic dwindling as fear crept up her throat.

Morana screamed when her magic slithered back to her. The loss of that heady power was painful. When she looked up at Matthias and Garian, she touched the small trickle of blood running down her arm. She pushed the shadows into the wound—nothing else. She didn't trust herself with anything else.

She pushed the shadows into the wound, healing just enough to repair the damage, but not enough to get rid of the scar.

It didn't feel right—not when she'd taken the life so easily—but it was all she had. Hope that she would eventually gain control on her own.

The door to the training room opened as Morana picked up her dagger, Elivira striding in wearing an elaborate dress, her hair braided down her back.

"Ronan informed me we now have Ohriid," she said. "And you two are set to wed by the end of this week." The lord's expression was fierce, her tone determined. "How did you do it?" she asked Morana, who now stood with blood painted on her boots.

Wiping the blade on her pants, Morana feigned disinterest, using Elivira's own words against her and hoping they'd bite. "How?" she asked, keeping her eyes to the dagger. "As a hot-headed and unpredictable bitch queen." Morana looked up then, sheathing the weapon at her side. "That's how."

To her surprise, there was a moment where Elivira processed her words, her shoulders softening, and a slow smile spreading across her lips. "Lovely," she said.

Morana didn't read much into it.

"There she is," Elivira said, folding her arms across her chest. "Our bitch queen."

Morana couldn't help the huffed laugh that escaped just as Sarnai entered the room with her skirts flowing around her toned legs.

Matthias ran a hand down his face. "An entire audience," he muttered. "Did I call a meeting I forgot about?"

Sarnai scowled at him, straightening her dress. "Of course not," she said. "I'm not here to *work*."

Morana rolled her eyes, earning her own scowl from the flora goddess.

"I suggest you change your attitude. I recall asking you to town prior to your trip to Ohriid," she began, pointing an accusatory finger in Morana's direction. "You said yes, and then you scurried off to another court."

Morana glanced at her nails in mock disinterest. "Sorry about that," she said, her jaw ticking as the threat of a smile loomed.

She'd spent her time in Ohriid battling monsters, counselors, and herself. It wasn't exactly leisure. Sarnai's offer sounded far more appealing.

Sarnai turned to Matthias, set in whatever decision the goddess had made. "I'm kidnapping your fiancé tonight," she announced.

A wide grin broke out across Morana's face. "Perfect," she said. "I could use a break."

Matthias grunted. "No painting classes," he uttered. "Please."

"Something far more fun, Matthias. An early wedding present, if you will." Sarnai pulled the long strands of her hair over one shoulder, turning her nose up at the god of Death.

Morana felt the anticipation rising in her chest. Putting a halt to all the training and politics would be a breath of fresh air. After Ohriid, she wouldn't turn down an offer for a break. It would be a moment of reprieve, one where she wouldn't worry about being consumed by her power or needing Matthias to draw her back to herself.

She could feel like herself again.

Sarnai clapped her soil-coated hands together. "A wonderful idea!" she beamed. "I'll need to find Reese."

Groaning, Matthias turned his attention to Garian, and Morana tried not to laugh at his distress. "Do not," he began, pointing a finger at the lord. "And I repeat, do *not* tell Ronan about this. I don't need a celebration."

"Of course," Garian said. "The court had only been waiting centuries for you to get married. We would certainly pass up the opportunity to parade you around Ascella."

The lord's jaw ticked—the smallest hint of a smile.

"Don't," Matthias warned.

Garian didn't move, merely pressed his lips together before answering.

"No promises."

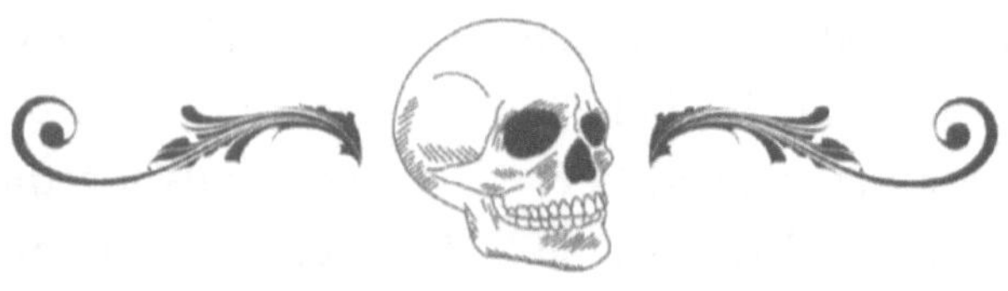

Twenty-Nine

A soft dusting of snow decorated the cobbled streets of Ascella, illuminated by the gentle glow of streetlamps. Night had descended on the city, and Morana had a bachelorette party to attend. *Her* bachelorette party.

She fought the smile forming on her lips as she walked behind Sarnai, her boots crunching gently with every step. Deciding against a dress, Morana had donned a pair of jeans, boots, and an old sweater. It felt human.

No gods.

No monsters.

Nothing but the excitement of the new life she would have if they won.

Unable to let the fae realm go completely, Morana gripped the cloak tightly around her body, the hood shielding her face from the cold.

"Where are we going, exactly?" she asked, fighting to keep up with the goddess's long stride.

"A bar," Sarnai responded as she lowered her cloak and turned back. Her umber eyes shone with mischief, and

Morana knew there was more to that answer than Sarnai was letting on.

Morana flushed, her mind stirring with ideas of what kind of bar the goddess might take her to.

"It's not—" Morana's brow furrowed when Sarnai walked away.

Rushing to catch up, Morana caught Sarnai's arm, gripping her gently and forcing the goddess to turn to her. "Will there be naked men?" she whispered.

Sarnai tipped her head back as she laughed, snow decorating her dark hair. She finally regained control of herself. "No, there won't be naked men, Morana. Though I'm not sure why you're blushing, considering the tea I deliver to your rooms each morning." Sarnai's eyes slid down the cobbled street, past the stone buildings. Below them was a larger street, bustling with fae laughing in the faefire. "I hope you like singing."

Morana groaned while Sarnai continued to push forward through the increasingly busy street. When they made their way to a more crowded section, Morana noticed the stares and subtle whispers. She kept her head held high as fae parted upon their arrival, giving them access to a wooden door which Sarnai promptly pulled open.

Sound poured from the bar, and if Morana were being honest—it was completely unpleasant. The fae woman standing on stage cackled with delight as she spun a circle. When she stopped to face the front, Morana caught a glimpse of who had been singing as she pulled her hood down.

The laugh pulled from deep in Morana's stomach, punctuated by Sarnai's own laughing.

On the stage in front of them stood Willow, smiling and singing at the top of her lungs for a bar filled with citizens of the Court of Shadows.

Looking around, Morana noted Reese and Elivira sitting in the front, sipping some form of alcohol from thick mugs and grinning.

When they both turned back, noting Morana's arrival, Reese stood, moving to wrap Morana in a warm hug. She smelled of soot and cinnamon, mixed with something like the open ocean.

"You're late to your own party," Reese said before giggling—clearly deep in her cup already. "We started drinking without you. I hope you don't mind?"

Morana's eyes flicked to Elivira's, and while the lord's smile was tight, it didn't hold her usual disgust or disapproval. Something about that settled her, if only a little.

Spending the day training and reading up on war strategies, Morana found herself lost in fighting for something. Instead of running away from the past—her trauma, she was running toward the future—the opportunity to become a queen that would be spoken of for centuries to come. Hot-headed and unpredictable, but also very in line with the characteristics of the fae before her. It was something she had learned in her time reading.

"Good to see you," Morana said, nodding toward the lord. Elivira bowed her head—just slightly—in response.

"Queen of Darkness," she said, her voice smooth—steady.

Morana's insides twisted, something warm washing over her like a summer tide. She held Elivira's brown gaze, her body frozen as she recognized something new in her eyes—approval.

"Thank you," Morana whispered just before Sarnai shoved her forward, and Reese shoved a drink in her hand.

"Willow's almost done," Sarnai cackled. "I'd like to see our queen on the stage singing her heart out."

Morana released a breathy laugh. "You won't like it once you hear it," she admitted. "It's terrible."

"A terrible singer seems relatable," Elivira commented. "Just the right way to win over your people."

Taking a drink of ale, Morana found herself lost in the music and laughter—the home she had built for herself. Nearly a year prior, Morana never thought she would have one. She looked at the fae who brought her here. Not only did she have a home, but she had a family. One she would do anything to keep safe.

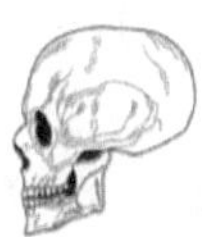

"Morana!" Sarnai shouted over the music before shoving a silver-eyed fae man toward her. "Keep Tomas busy," she said before disappearing into the crowd.

The tall fae man stood before her, pointed ears decorated with gold rings, a smile wide and bright as he looked down at her. "The queen," he said before bowing his head. "An honor to celebrate with you."

Morana chuckled, taking a long drag of the drink in her hand before discarding it in a nearby bin.

She gently grabbed Reese's arm, leaning in to whisper in her ear. The blacksmith was already busy staring at the fae man she had been dancing with. "Do you think this is appropriate?" Morana asked. "I mean—for a future queen?"

Reese chuckled. "Elivira's right. It makes you more relatable." Her voice dropped even lower, barely audible over the sound of music floating through the bar. "It'll tone down your god status. Besides," she grinned. "He seems nice enough."

"The court doesn't know about the god status," Morana laughed, moving toward Tomas, who offered her a hand, already dancing.

She let go, finding a rhythm that matched his as he smiled down at her. *Nice enough.*

He certainly looked pretty, but maybe it was the alcohol running through her blood that clouded her judgement.

Sarnai reappeared; her face ashen as she hurried back toward the group. The goddess's umber eyes flicked to the door where Morana noticed the red curly hair and freckles. Cain walked into the bar. The fae had an intense look on his face, and Morana's breath hitched.

Something's wrong.

The bar quieted, music ceasing as they all turned to look at Cain, and when the crowd parted, Morana understood why.

Her shadows were already twisting over her skin, begging her fears to calm as she watched a golden tear escape his eyes—wholly white and lost in a vision.

The entire room seemed to hold its breath.

"They're coming," Cain whispered, and Morana stepped forward, her shadows swelling. She suddenly regretted the amount of alcohol she'd consumed—losing herself in the night—in fun.

"Who?" she asked, gripping his shoulders as she tried to find a hint of the scribe beneath The Oracle standing in front of her. "Who?" she shouted, shaking him.

His eyes still held that ominous white glow, golden tears tracking down his cheeks. Cain held his head straight and forward, his tone sounding like someone else entirely—*something* else.

"They're coming now."

When Morana turned, Elivira's features had hardened, her warm eyes turning cold as the winter snow coating the streets of Ascella.

Without another word, the shadows darkened the room, parting the world until a disheveled Matthias strode forward. The top button of his shirt undone; his hair mussed as if he'd tugged at the strands relentlessly.

As he walked through the room, Morana watched the slow bow of the other fae, the way they acknowledged his status. It was hard not to, with his power still lingering around them after his prompt arrival.

She hoped one day, she would garner the same response from the court—that they would see her as queen. Whatever was happening—this might be her chance to prove that she deserved just that.

Garian appeared behind him, dressed in battle leathers and looking more prepared for war than anything. He carried a sword at his hip, along with the expression of a warrior.

"They're here," Garian informed, his tone dark.

"Who?" Morana asked again, her heart rate picking up with every second that ticked on. Cain still stood by the door, deep gold tears running down his face.

"Inara and Raidan," Matthias answered.

She felt like she was falling, hearing the names leave Matthias's lips, sending her stomach plummeting into the dark abyss below. Morana fought to catch her breath as reality came crashing into her. Until now, it had been easy to shove down her time with Raidan and to view the war as some ominous thing off in the distance—something she planned for but never took part in.

Training in the Court of Shadows provided a sense of safety, but her magic, though more controlled than before, still overwhelmed her without Matthias nearby.

And now, the war demanded attention—bringing itself to their doorstep—to her home.

The fear had her back in Raidan's dungeons, pain threatening to take her under.

"Here," Sarnai said, handing her a vial. "Drink this." Morana trusted her, tipping her head back and swallowing the herbal concoction in one go. "For the alcohol," Sarnai finally supplied.

Morana fought for composure, quickly shadowing herself back to the palace. She changed into her own fighting leathers, the ones Matthias had gifted her earlier in the week. She sheathed her sword and dagger, tying her hair back, as she watched Matthias come into the room.

Gone was the appearance of a king—a god. Matthias had become a soldier—a warrior.

She'd seen glimpses of this side of him before in Lux's tomb—sparing in the training room with Ronan. She'd seen it with Raidan and Conan—her mother.

Shaking her head, Morana brought herself back to the present. Raidan and Inara were here—in Ascella. And regardless of what they had planned, they would need to fight.

"Is Cain alright?" Morana asked as Matthias checked her over, testing the sharpness of her sword—the adequacy of the leathers she wore. He knelt down, tightening the strap around her thigh that secured her most coveted weapon.

"I've never seen him like that," Morana confessed, "lost in a vision. Whatever he saw—it was still happening when we left."

"I know," Matthias said, while rising to his full height. He kissed her then—hard—and something in it felt like goodbye. When he pulled away, his eyes were searching. "Whatever he saw," he said. "It has to be bad." Matthias cleared his throat. "Garian had us in the forest just outside of Ascella. Cain came to find us."

"What?" Morana's brow furrowed as Matthias ran a hand down his face, trying to smooth out the stress etched in every tick of his jaw.

"Paintball," he said, a half-smile pulling at his full lips. "Stollen from the human realm. Some bachelor idea."

Morana chuckled, but it still didn't take the dread out of her gut, the thing festering and stirring and threatening to consume her whole.

If she were to fight, would she be able to keep a tight grip on her power, or would she destroy the fae she sought to rule?

Cries sounded through the window of her room, and Morana turned abruptly at the sound, her face paling.

"We need to go," Matthias said as his hand came up to cup her face. "I love you," he whispered while leaning forward until his forehead rested against hers. "And I trust you to fight—I know you are powerful," he said. "But please, Morana." He was begging now. "Please."

Somehow, she knew what he was saying as she gripped his hand tightly. "I love you," she breathed, as the shadows wrapped around them, spitting them out onto the bloody streets below.

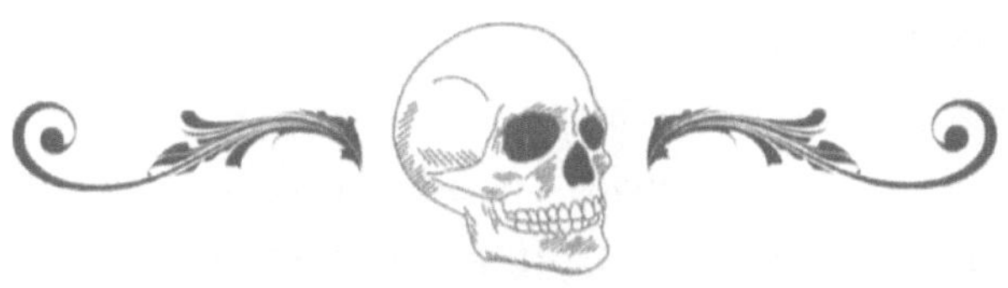

Thirty

Harpies descended on the streets of Ascella, screeching as they stretched out sharp talons and plunged them into the fae below.

Through the thick fog, Morana made out the shape of soldiers, donned in leathers and armor—prepared for a battle they hadn't known would happen.

The Light Court had appeared, ready to take the Court of Shadows from them, and Morana would be damned if she let that happen.

A light court soldier charged her, and Morana unsheathed her sword as she shoved her power outward. The intensity of it halted the soldier in his tracks before she drove the weapon through him.

Copper coated her tongue as she took in the battle waging around her. Matthias's dark power stretched out from him like a mighty wave, shoving its way into the minds of the vulnerable fae not ready for his attack.

Their screams rang in her ears as her sweat slicked skin caught fire despite the snow still coating the ground.

She was power and magic as she wove herself together—her soul—to stop the soldiers in their tracks, cutting them down one at a time.

She relied heavily on her sword—hoping that the weapon would keep her from losing control.

A harpy plunged from the sky, hastening toward her as Morana dragged her blade from the chest of a female soldier. The fae woman fell to the ground, her eyes open and her body still when Morana reached upward with the light, wrapping the creature in crackling fire until feathers and flesh burned away.

Without thinking, Morana reached for that magic, feral delight wrapping around her—her hunger increasing the more she fed the beast inside her.

It felt heady—pleasurable until she felt the edges of her limits. She could see them clearly now, and the exhaustion hit her with the ferocity of one of Callum's caged creatures.

She buckled under the pressure, the amount of power she had been using—it was more than she was used to. Morana fought from crying out as a splitting headache ripped through her skull.

Through the pain, she gained control of her magic— but at what cost?

On her knees, she looked up to see Matthias, face hardened as he slashed his own sword across the neck of a Veeden, the thick smoke rising around it.

The song rang through the air, and Morana fought to find her power again, hoping to achieve something like what she'd done at the border. Maybe without her magic waning from overexertion, she'd have more control.

Panic caught her throat when she realized that her mind was struggling to focus, her body tired and aching. It brought back memories of being in Raidan's temple—used like an animal training for battle.

She fought through it; the mist rolling out over the ground, kicking up snow and dirt in its wake. When she felt the minds of the Veeden when she twisted her power together. Morana shoved them back, commanding them to retreat, but there was another force there. Something else in their minds telling her it wasn't a mere creature she was fighting.

"Raidan," she whispered, standing from her spot on the ground.

Looking through the mist, Morana tried to block out the sounds of screaming—the smell of blood.

White hair moved in the darkness, and Morana caught a glimpse of rose-colored eyes, her anger boiling her blood.

Without thinking, she left Matthias. Her feet carried her through the carnage in the streets—the sounds of metal clashing together. As she ran for Inara, her rage intensified, her shadows hungrily stretching out before her to catch the god. But the woman was like a ghost as she disappeared and reappeared through the light and shadows flickering over the city.

Just when Morana caught sight of her again, the woman looked back, eyes lighted as she dropped into the ground. Brow furrowing, Morana mustered her courage and sprinted forward, coming up to the sewage drain on the street. Someone had removed the grate, and when she saw the flicker of light beneath, Morana didn't ask questions. She gripped her sword and plunged down into the darkness, her boots catching on each rung of the ladder with smooth precision.

The next moments stretched on as Morana chased the woman through the shallow waters of the tunnels, guided by her distant laughter echoing off the stone walls.

The dripping pulled at Morana's memory, causing her heart to gallop in her chest as her palms turned slick even where she gripped the hilt of her sword.

She swore she could hear the slick sound of scales sliding against the water, rubbing on the stone below.

Morana turned, her breath coming out in harsh pants. She called on the shadows, wrapping them around her flesh to sooth the panic rising in her chest.

Raidan had sent basilisks after her before. It was nothing she couldn't handle. Still, the memories of his abuse, the time she spent locked in the dungeon, it all flickered through her mind, making bile rise and her panic intensify.

Like mother, like daughter.

Her mother's voice echoed through the chamber, and Morana believed the words. She wanted to run.

Run from the memories of Raidan, the power she couldn't control, the realm she fought to protect.

Inara's laughter drew her out of her head as she watched the goddess disappear behind a corner. Morana shook off her fear, following her as she tried to keep her hands steady.

The phantom sounds continued to chase her through the tunnels.

She couldn't stop the fear—each sound of slick scales taunted her—threatening to steal her composure. Morana reached out with the mist, desperate to find the mind of the creature she heard. Maybe it would be like the Veeden. Maybe she could control the giant snake before it ever got the chance to get close enough to her.

Still, there was nothing.

When she turned the corner, Morana saw Inara standing there, cloak billowing out from her body. Inara held a sword of her own, the light crackling over the metal.

"There you are," the woman said, her voice cold. The feral smile on her face sent Morana's gut churning. "Queen of Darkness," she spat. "How does it feel now that you've turned part of my court against me? I should have ended you from the start." She nearly growled as she spoke, anger rippling off the goddess in waves. "Raidan wasted too much time on you."

"And where is he?" Morana asked, her tone steady despite the fear clogging her throat. "I heard he was in the city." Her grip tightened on her power as she prepared to fight.

That feral smile widened, and Inara tilted her head to the side in a mocking gesture. "He's in The Wastelands," she said, her voice too smooth—too sweet. "But I'm here," she taunted as the light cracked in the air above her. Morana fought the urge to recoil. "Ascella would be a glorious prize. Don't you think?"

"No," Morana growled, sweat trickling down her temple.

Inara tsked, a pitying look on her face. "Have you grown attached, then?" The goddess licked her lips like a beast fit to devour its prey. "Still whoring yourself out to anything powerful?" she asked. "It seems you simply *cannot* keep your legs closed."

The anger that had burned hot before cooled— simmered. It was something different—something animalistic as Morana watched the taunting goddess, her power moving quickly over the ground.

She could hear nothing else but the blood roaring in her ears—feel nothing but the desire to kill.

And this time—she wanted it—all of it.

"There's a better prize to be claimed here," Inara spoke again, her voice muffled by the rage Morana felt. "Raidan wants me to retrieve you." The goddess laughed a hollow sound. "But I think you'd be better off gone." She spat, venom and disdain laced in every word. "I can see it in your eyes." She tilted her head to the side. "You've spent too much time with Death, Queen of Darkness. Consumed by him, and yet still useless."

Inara's power lashed out, and Morana felt the slashing and burning pain penetrate her skin. The memory of a cold dungeon floor plagued her and drove her to her knees. Betrayal pierced her pounding heart just as it had the first time she'd found herself in Inara's clutches.

Morana stuttered, trying to combat the woman's magic with her own, but that same power came down on her again. It sent pain rippling down her spine, shooting out to her limbs.

When Morana reached for her magic again, it slipped through her fingers, slowly fading until she could hardly feel the flicker of it.

"Awe," Inara said, holding a small object in her hand. "Does this look familiar? It's the same thing we used to subdue Matthias." She paused. "Well, Axton used it, then. Isn't it funny that you spread your legs for him, too?"

That whip cracked out again, hitting her skin, the scar of the wound running far deeper than the flesh.

"Do you know what happens to whores in this realm?" Inara asked.

Something broke through the sounds of magic and the goddess's voice, that slick sound of scales, but she shook it off—convinced it was in her head.

"I heard from Raidan," Inara began, delight shining in her rose-colored eyes. "You made a friend in his dungeon."

Morana stood up, head whipping to the familiar skittering sounds—inching closer from around the corner.

She couldn't look at the creature—that much she knew, but would she be able to fight it the same as she had earlier? How many times could a person fight their demons before succumbing to them?

Doubt clawed at her, fighting to climb out of the hole she'd shoved it in.

A grate moved, and a figure dropped from above. Morana knew the moment she saw his thin and fragile frame.

Gold tears coated Cain's face, smeared and dripping onto the cloak he wore. The strange paint hid his freckles, making him look older and less warm than the man she had come to know. "Morana," he growled. It was then that Morana realized he held a dagger in his hand. Her heart lurched, mind catching up with the image before her. "Morana!" he shouted. "Turn around!"

She obeyed, fighting the wave of emotion that washed over her.

Inara's eyes were wide, fixed on the scribe. Her distraction gave Morana the chance to cut her sword across the goddess's wrist. The movement severed the limb and sent the small object binding her power careening across the floor and into the water of the tunnel.

Morana listened as Inara screamed, blood dripping from her wound. Power rushed back into Morana, and she fought the urge to look as she heard Cain scream, too.

Only the sound of his blade sinking through scales kept her eyes squeezed shut. Morana would know the sound anywhere.

Once she heard the body drop, she turned—horrified as Cain lay broken in a puddle of dirty water and blood. His eyes were still open, tears drying as the white color left his irises—replaced by the green color she'd come to know.

Stunned, Morana slammed her hand over her mouth, fighting the sobs that begged for release. Something in her chest broke at the odd angles, the twisted image of Cain's dead body. She could hardly breathe—hardly see the point in it.

Death had always surrounded her since the moment she'd been entwined with this realm. But no death cut as deeply as this. One part of the home she had made—a soul she cared for—taken from her. Cain had welcomed her— spent time with her in the palace. Even in his mocking, he'd genuinely cared for her.

In a realm full of doubt and lies, Cain had always been truth. Far too young to be laying in this place—light in the Court of Shadows snuffed out.

Salt leaked from her eyes as Morana turned to the sound of Inara's cackling. Pain ripped through her chest, and that same cold rage returned.

She glanced at the mangled limb Inara held, growling as her power swelled, returning with the object now safely hidden in the tunnels.

She would not be consumed by death—would not drink of its poison. Instead, she would become death—wild and dark—utterly insatiable.

Unleashing herself, Morana pinned Inara to the ground, slamming her body into the shallow water and holding her to the disgusting floors below.

Inara spat at her, but Morana could see the fear beneath. "You think you can kill a god?" she asked through an airy laugh. Blood stained the goddess's teeth, and her sword lay discarded from the force of contact with the ground.

"Considering who I am?" Morana snarled. "I don't think it will be an issue."

Inara laughed again; her cloak now soaked with the disgusting water. "And who exactly are you? A whore? Nothing but a weak mortal."

Morana smiled then, the shadows twisting and plunging them into darkness. "Oh, no," she said. "I'm far more than that." Tilting her head to the side, Morana pulled her dagger from its sheath. "Don't you know, Inara? I'm a true god." She dragged the tip of her blade from the goddess's neck and down her chest. Morana thought better of slitting her throat. Through the heart would do. Just like Inara had done to her so many times. "Nothing like the false god you've paraded around as."

With mixing power and a glowing gem in the hilt of her dagger—marbled burgundy and black—Morana plunged the weapon into the woman's chest. Shoving the light into her until her body ripped itself apart. Flames engulfed the goddess of light, eating away at her until it all but disappeared.

With only a gross sense of satisfaction fueled by death and destruction, Morana pulled the weapon from the goddess and pocketed the object.

But this time, she hadn't been consumed. She'd been set on a goal—that raging power channeled into something far greater.

Revenge.

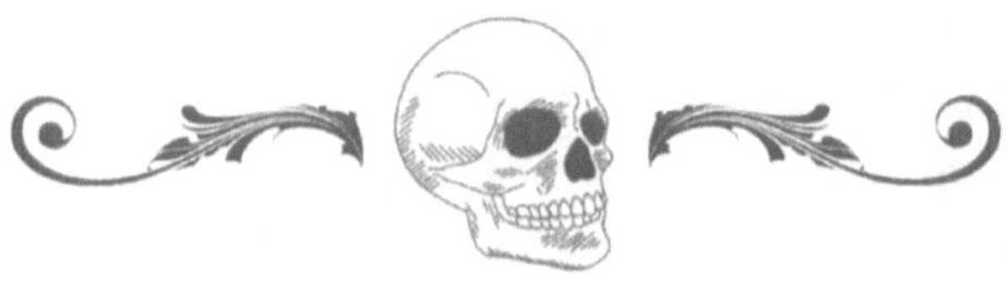

Thirty-One

Walking through the street, Morana let power ripple around her, the light backing her as mist and shadow swirled over the streets of Ascella.

The city had been painted red, bodies littering the ground, but the battle had quieted. A retreat happened soon after Morana emerged from the sewers, coated in blood and grime.

Matthias appeared in front of her, shadows parting, as he grabbed her face with his hands.

A dark strand of hair fell across his dirt-streaked brow, eyes wild and hands trembling. He searched her gaze for a hint of what happened—where she'd gone. Morana sensed barely controlled rage rippling beneath the light touch he had on her face. She latched on to it, anchoring herself to keep from going under.

"Where were you?" he asked, and she allowed the shadows to caress his mind, showing him exactly what had happened beneath the city.

She could still see Cain's mangled body—the basilisk lying dead next to him. Her heart clenched, tears working to the corners of her eyes as Matthias took in the scene—the events of the evening.

When he'd seen it all, Morana collapsed into him, wrapping her arms around his torso and breathing deeply as the tears fell. He'd come to save her.

Cain had seen what would happen—warned her in the tavern and saved her when the basilisk rounded the corner. Maybe he knew the memories it would drag up—maybe he saw how Morana would freeze.

He'd sacrificed himself for her. She didn't know why—but he had.

Matthias pulled her in, his arms wrapping around her tightly as if he could protect her from the pain of loss.

This loss was different from those she'd suffered before. When her mother had left, Morana hadn't seen death—hadn't choked down the bitter taste of it.

All her life, she had spent her time running and avoiding growing attached to the people and places around her—knowing they could be ripped from her at any moment.

However, something about the court—the realm—all of it begged her to open up. She'd let Matthias into her world, allowed herself to feel for the god and all those in his court. It was the reason she was still fighting—the reason she wanted Raidan dead.

The Court of Shadows meant something to her. *Cain* meant something to her. He was just a kid—a piece of home and the life she was building apart from the ghosts that haunted her past.

And he had been building a life of his own—coming to accept his own power—one and the same.

Wiping a tear from her eye, Morana looked to Death, his own eyes lined with sorrow.

When she reached up and brushed the dampness from his cheek, she let her chest crack open—a new pain tearing through her heart.

This one wasn't like the pain of betrayal. It wasn't like the pain of Raidan's hand across her face—Inara's magic slashing across her back.

No, this pain was laced with something sweeter, something that eased the bitter sting.

"We should head back," Matthias said, voice gentle.

"Okay." Her voice broke on the word as they stood there in the street, surrounded by blood and destruction.

Matthias gripped her hand, shadows swirling around them before he plunged them into darkness and ushered them home.

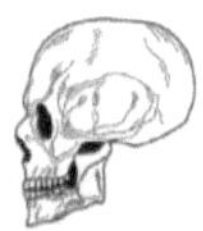

"What do we do now?" Elivira took a long drink of wine. Mud coated her hair and eyes, reflecting a tiredness they all felt.

None of them had changed since the battle, quickly returning to meet in the dining room. Matthias had passed on the war room. He knew everyone would be exhausted and desperate to settle in for the night despite the looming threat outside the palace walls.

"We take another city," Matthias supplied, eyes meeting each of the lords seated around the table.

Hames had returned from the Vulcan after he caught word of the battle. Morana noted the regret etched into his features—the discomfort of being absent when his court needed him most.

"Raidan wasn't even here," Morana added, squeezing the fork in her hand. She ground her teeth, Inara's words ringing in her ear. He was still looking for her and longing to bring her back to The Wastelands.

"I know," Matthias spoke, his tone reassuring. "We have Zora," he declared, "Ohriid, too. If we can unite the courts, we can wage war against Raidan in the hopes that it would all be enough."

Garian grunted, the first sign of his presence. "You can't expect to just claim the Court of Light for yourself," he supplied. "Inara is going to have supporters there. It is her court. You can't depend on her corruption to be enough to sway people to your side." He glanced at Morana, face stoney. "And power isn't enough to persuade them, either."

Matthias sat back; brows furrowed in thought. "You're right," he mused.

Elivira took another sip of wine, glancing at Ronan as he leaned forward, placing his elbows on the intricately carved wooden table. "So," he said. "We find someone else to rule."

"There is no one else in line for the throne," Matthias stated. "There hasn't been a sign of a god for their court since Inara, and even then, we know that wasn't a true sign."

"Conan," Morana whispered.

Elivira's scoff gave away her opinions on the idea, but Morana continued anyway. "He's aligned with our court, sure, but he's a powerful lord in the Court of Light."

"Is he going to go against the other lords?" Garian asked. "Does he have the spine for that?"

Morana took a sip of wine, allowing the flavor to coat her tongue and the alcohol to ease the memories of what had happened hours ago.

"He's a fox, Garian. Far more capable than we've given him credit for. He gleaned information about Inara and Raidan—information about Matthias far before he should have known anything." She set the wine down, glancing around the table as Matthias's hand moved to rest on her thigh, a calm reassurance.

"It's not ideal," she confessed. "But Conan has secrets none of us are truly aware of." Morana thought back to the power she'd felt. She swallowed, fighting the fear in her gut. "Besides," she said, "we don't really have another choice."

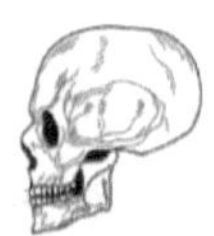

Matthias had Cain's body pulled from the sewers, placed on the pyre, and given a proper burial at the palace. The lords, Willow, Kit—they'd all attended, watching the flames and listening to the howl of the wind through the trees.

It was almost as if the winter chill sensed his death. Despite the burning, the cold seeped into their bones—carving his memory into the marrow.

Morana had stood there with tears rolling down her cheeks, staring at the flickering flames—the memories playing tricks on her eyes. She could see him there, scrawling on parchment and throwing barbs. It was as if the twisting black smoke painted the memories for her, her vision blurring on account of the moisture coating her cheeks.

After the morning, Morana had returned to her room. Matthias disappeared into the human realm to focus on responsibilities there, and his absence had given her time to think. Even so, she didn't know if time to think was what she needed.

Sitting on the floor by the fire, Morana curled her knees to her chest, resting her tear-stained cheek there as the late afternoon sun shone through the window.

The crackling in the hearth steadied her—gave her something to focus on other than the death that seemed to follow her lately. There were a thousand ways she could have saved him—a thousand ways she could have sacrificed herself.

But that wasn't what happened.

Cain was dead.

"I brought food."

Willow's gentle voice floated through her room as the woman came to sit next to Morana, straightening her dress after setting the tray down in front of them.

"Matthias is worried about you," Willow confessed, leaning forward to pluck a piece of cheese from the platter. "He's having us move your things to his room early."

"Right," Morana sighed. "I almost forgot about that."

She caught Willow's wan smile from the corner of her eye. The fae woman no longer looked at her, but stared ahead.

"Nothing like death to cast a cloud over a wedding." Willow took a bite of the cheese in her hand and fixed her gaze to the fire, losing herself in thought.

Morana shook her head. "It's not that I'm unhappy," she began, "I couldn't be happier." Her stomach twisted, guilt creating a wound she wasn't sure she'd be capable of healing. No number of shadows could stitch together the regret. "His death," she began. "It's still my fault. He came to save me."

Willow placed a gentle hand on her shoulder, her thumb rubbing small circles. "He came to save his court," she spoke, her tone steady. "And he believed you were best for it—as queen." Willow leaned in just slightly. "I believe he was right, Morana. You will make a wonderful ruler."

Her tears gathered, threatening to break free as Morana looked to the woman who'd been more of a mother than her own. "If I'm supposed to be a god," Morana began, "if I'm supposed to be this powerful, then why would some fae teenager have to come to my rescue?"

It wasn't true. Cain wasn't *some fae teenager.* He was far more than that.

The tears were falling now, and Willow took them in with grace—no judgment and no blame.

"You can't look at it like that," she started. "It's like you believe your life wasn't worth rescuing, and I assure you, Morana, it was—it is." Willow squeezed her arm gently. "You have the power to turn the tide of this war, the power to kill Raidan—but that doesn't mean you have to do everything on your own. You have a family now—an entire court."

Morana nodded, overwhelmed by the way her words soothed the pain.

"And as for needing rescued," Willow said. "Sometimes even the gods need saving."

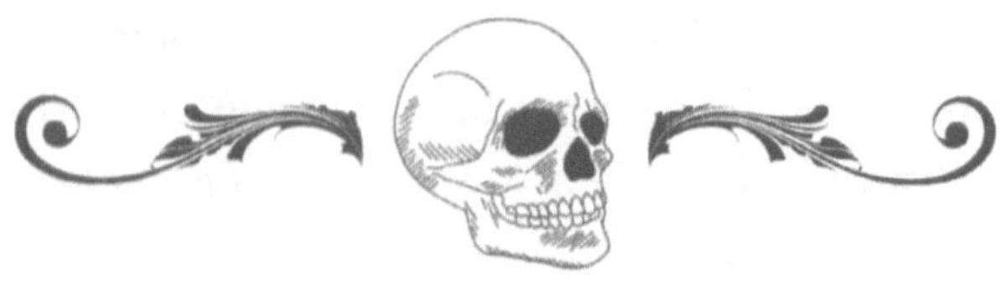

Thirty-Two

Thick darkness lingered outside the windows of her room—as if the night knew of Cain's death and longed for the sadness to darken the court as a reminder of loss.

There were no stars outside, no light from the moon, either.

Morana turned away from the window, staring at the ceiling above and wondering where Matthias was.

He'd gone into the human realm—returning to his duties as god of Death there after being so consumed with the war and politics of the courts.

Morana fingered the golden thread embroidered on her comforter. It was her last night staying in her own room. While Willow had stated Matthias wanted her in his, she knew this would be her last chance to say goodbye to the place she had called home.

That feeling of home didn't stop the fear.

Morana lifted her hand, sliding it under the pillow behind her head to check that her dagger still sat undisturbed.

Inara's death brought her some peace, but she knew Raidan would be looking for her. Especially if word of the goddess's demise traveled as far as The Wastelands. And the truth was, Morana wasn't certain she'd be ready to face him.

While she'd had enough control of her powers in the sewers, it wasn't consistent enough for her to be confident in her abilities. Doubt still wrapped its vines around her heart, squeezing until she let the pain of loss all over again. It brought with it a nagging feeling deep in her gut that told her she was missing something.
Raidan wouldn't be as easy to kill.

Closing her eyes, Morana willed herself to sleep, drifting until she heard something gently hit the floor from the window.

She shot up, grabbing her dagger as a cloaked figure prowled through the room. The smiling woman lowered her hood, her dark eyes catching the dim light leftover from in the embers in the hearth.

Morana's heart pounded as she stood quickly from the bed, her dagger in hand, and her magic pooling around her ankles and ready to be used.

One fucking night, she thought. *All I wanted was one fucking night.*

"Queen of Darkness," the fae whispered. "Raidan's looking for you."

The woman lunged, her dagger catching Morana's shoulder when she leaped over the bed—anxious to get away from another assassin. Anxious to have one fucking moment to think about she was doing before the monsters crept out of the darkness.

Pulling on her power, the white mist flicked out over the floor, coating it with a delicious fog—one that brought feelings of pleasure to Morana's bones.

The binding magic halted the assassin's advances mere inches from where Morana now stood. Her hand stilled inches from Morana's face as magic twisted in the air, making her feel more and more detached—more vicious.

"I thought Raidan didn't want to kill me," she said, grinning at the woman, now shocked in the wake of her halted movements.

Morana touched her with the shadows, trailing them over her skin and promising punishment. The taunt had a dark laugh dragging from her lips. "Look at you," she crooned. "So very afraid."

When the shadows dipped into the assassin's mind, Morana found Raidan's influence coating every inch of her thoughts. The major god to the north had armies of creatures—followers craving power—including the woman standing in the presence of the Queen of Darkness.

"What is it you want, exactly?" Morana asked, her eyes flicking to the blade inches from her throat, and the fog still wrapping around the woman's arm.
"He'll only grow more persistent," the assassin ground out.

She struggled against her restraints, wild blonde hair breaking free from his braid.

Morana took in the dirt and blood streaking the light skin of her face, the small tear in the knee of her black pants. There was no doubt about how she'd gotten into the palace. This fae woman had climbed—no shadows in her blood, then.

"After your little show the other night," she continued. "Raidan is out to find you again. He always knew you were powerful." The woman practically spat the words, fueled by bitter rage.

Stepping back, Morana fingered the tip of her own dagger, accidentally piercing the skin on her finger, and sucking the blood away. Her eyes nearly rolled back in her head, the light crackling in her chest and begging for full release.

She wouldn't allow it—not this time.

"If Raidan wants me for my power, why are you lunging with that weapon of yours."

The woman smiled. "Maybe I have my own motives." She grunted, fighting against the restraint. "There are more of us, and we will continue finding our way into your ridiculous palace."

Morana's gray eyes snapped up, her dagger pointing at her assassin. "What makes you say that?"

That vicious smile widened.

"How do you think?" she asked. "You'll keep being betrayed by those around you. And as long as he lives, you'll never escape it."

Despite herself, Morana felt the rapid pounding of her heart in her chest. The blood roared in her ears at the admission.

"Who is betraying me?" she asked, stepping forward and crowding the fae woman's space. "Who is it?" her voice had risen, taking on a commanding element she'd only heard from Matthias.

"Wouldn't you like to know?" the woman spat, and Morana shoved the dagger into her stomach, her power pumping through the blade. Morana leaned closer to whisper in the fae woman's ear.

"Fuck you," she said before watching the assassin's body slump, the woman falling to the floor to bleed out.

Morana surveyed the room, a part of her expecting another attempt at any moment. If someone in the palace had betrayed her—if someone had been allowing the assassins access to her, and was now working with Raidan, she would never know a moment of peace.

Her panic increasing, Morana looked around the room once more before exiting into the hallway.

She wound her way through the palace, her mind dizzy with worry until she plowed through Matthias's door, the guard stepping back as soon as she'd arrived.

He stood abruptly from the chair by the window, dropping the cup of tea he'd been nursing so the ceramic shattered on the floor, causing Morana to jolt.

"What is it?" he asked, his tone coated in darkness.

His shadows swelled, and he was on her in an instant, fingers prodding and poking, his eyes searching her face for any hint of what occurred.

Morana leaned into her magic and let it numb her from the inside out. She closed her eyes, feeling the way Matthias's touch became more demanding.

"Who did this?" he asked, his thumb wiping away a streak of dirt on her face.

"It's nothing," she said, taking a calming breath as she tried to convince herself to believe it. "Just another body to dispose of." She paused, opening her eyes to gauge his reaction. "And possibly a traitor within the palace walls."

Matthias's anger burned hot, his eyes blazing with the force of his power. He shoved the shadows into her mind, gleaning whatever information he could come up with.

He turned on his heel, one hand fishing in the back pocket of his pants for a small pack of cigarettes.

Morana stared at him while he lighted it, wondering how long it had been since he'd had one. It seemed stress brought out old vices.

He blew smoke from his full lips, shoulders rigid as he fought to gain control of his anger.

"I want to rip that fucker apart," he admitted, and Morana blinked, noting the ferocity of his tone.

"We can't," she said, "not yet, anyway. Is there something we can do to figure out who's betrayed us?"

Matthias rolled his shoulders, but it didn't seem to help. "We need to visit Callum," he ground out. "If we've been betrayed, whoever they are is probably afraid of being found out. We could have good use for the dream-eater."

"Would Callum give that creature up?" Morana asked.

"He will," Matthias said, his dark eyes moving to meet hers. She could see his rage there—the worry buried beneath. "I won't give him a fucking choice."

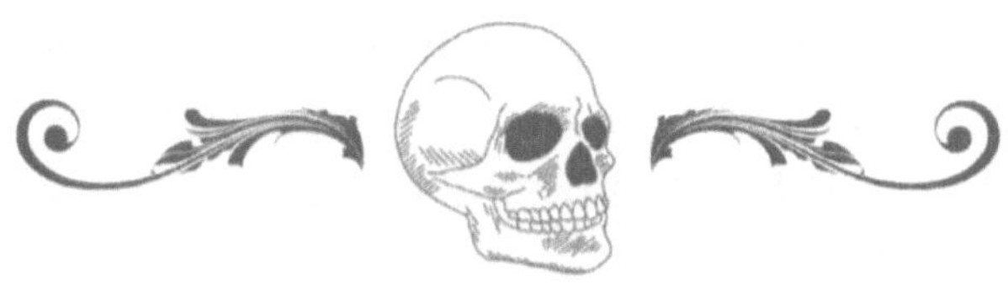

Thirty-Three

Willow ran her fingers through the gently curled strands of Morana's hair, checking over every detail of her appearance before the celebration.

With her stomach churning, Morana glanced into the floor-length mirror to find Sarnai sipping on a cup of tea on Willow's bed.

The room was larger than she'd thought it'd be—but then again—that was her own mistake. Willow was like a mother to Matthias. It made sense that her room would be fit for someone as close to Death as she was.

"How many people will be there?" Morana asked as she smoothed the black fabric of her gown in an attempt to steady the churning in her gut.

She had chosen black for her corseted gown. The sweetheart neckline, and sheer, off the shoulder sleeves, fitting for a wedding. The color spoke of death and shadows, and she assumed that was fitting.

Willow's brows rose, her eyes tracking Morana's movements as she tied off the back of the gown. "Plenty," she said. "But you needn't worry about that."

Looking to Sarnai, Morana spoke. "He's been sending assassins." Morana swallowed, remembering the dark figure entering her room from the window and feeling the way her blade cut through the woman's gut. "Raidan," she clarified.

Sarnai's eyes shot up, the goddess's umber gaze meeting Morana's in the mirror. "What do you mean?" she questioned.

"There've been multiple assassins in the palace. One came into my room last night and held a blade to my throat. Even though I was able to stop her—it still happened. It's the second time since I've returned."

Sarnai set her cup on the oak nightstand, rising from her spot on the bed with her brows stitched together. "That's impossible," Sarnai asserted. "Nobody should be able to get into the palace like that anymore—especially not from the Court of Light. Matthias had Ronan look into ancient runes after they'd gotten in before your engagement ball—way back when you were new to the fae realm."

"That's the concern," Morana supplied. "They shouldn't be able to get into the palace, but they continue to get into the palace, regardless."

"And what does Matthias say?" Sarnai was pacing, vines growing as if they'd sprouted from her skin, and twisting along her arms.

"We are going to need to test those in his court, but many of the lords are strong enough to resist his prying." She cleared her throat, glancing at her hands clasped in front of her. "He believes the dream-eater could help reveal any fears of being caught—if we can make a deal with the creature."

Willow halted, her face paling as Sarnai spun on her heal. "What are you saying?" Sarnai whispered.

"After the wedding today, we will be returning to Callum, asking for the dream eater, and testing the lords first."

"Gods," Sarnai whispered. "Do the lords know about this?"

"No, and they can't know about it," Morana pleaded. "I shouldn't have even told you."

The doors opened, bringing the scent of salty air and ocean water with the lord plowing into the room.

"Ronan?" Morana questioned, shaking off the previous conversation.

His smile was wicked, and Morana knew he had something planned. Though, when she met his shining eyes, she could hardly fathom Ronan or any of the other lords betraying her. Hames, maybe, but he was loyal to Matthias. Of that, she was certain.

"You can't be in here," Willow scolded, attempting to shoo him out of the room.

"Oh please," Ronan scoffed, his smile never wavering. "She hasn't given into any of my advances. I'm here to mourn the loss of that chance." He glanced at Willow in an attempt to charm her, no doubt. By the pinch of her brow, it didn't seem to be working. "She's about to be shackled to Matthias," he said, before returning his eyes to Morana. "All is lost. That greedy motherfucker."

Morana chuckled, nervously playing with the sleeve of her gown. "What do you want?" she asked.

"You look ravishing, by the way." Ronan took a step back. "I brought a gift."

"What is it?" Morana hadn't finished the question before the lord dipped out of the room. He returned from the hallway with a large object covered in cloth.

"Oh god," Morana breathed, her face falling. She could hear Sarnai's muffled laugh sounding behind her. "That's not what I think it is, is it?"

Ronan set it down, gathering the fabric in his hands while balancing what appeared to be a painting. "It's not the painting you did, if that's what you're asking."

"Is it—"

The cloth fell away to reveal a large painting of a naked man, dark hair and tattoos with shadows twisting in the background. For all it was worth, the painting was decent—decent enough to know it was Matthias.

Sarnai released a heinous cackle behind her as Willow quickly covered her own mouth, stifling her laughter.

Morana's gaze trailed down, following the chiseled abs, the trail of hair leading down to—

"Why is his dick so small?"

Willow snorted, barely able to contain herself as tears gathered at the corners of her eyes.

Ronan's smile widened, his eyes glistening with mischief. "Accuracy," he supplied.

"This is a wedding present?" Morana asked, the smile breaking across her lips. She watched Ronan lean the painting against the wall, his eyes flashing as he scratched at his arm.

"The very best," he said. "For my new queen. When you see this painting, I hope you think about all the much larger and more satisfying dicks you missed out on. Mine, for example."

Morana chuckled again. "Thank you," she spoke, smiling up at him.

"Okay, okay," Willow said, grabbing a small towel draped over the arm of one of her chairs. She started swatting at him, sending Ronan retreating to the door. "You've done enough," she said. "Now, get out!"

Ronan left with laughter on his lips.

When Morana turned, Sarnai had returned to the bed, picking up her cup of tea. "Is it really that small?" she asked, tilting her head toward the naked art.

Morana laughed to herself, taking one last look in the mirror and steeling her nerves. "Of course not," she answered. "He's a god, after all."

Morana didn't miss the hint of a smile working at the corner of Willow's mouth—the way she shook her head as she tidied up the room.

"Are you ready?" Sarnai asked, striding forward and offering her arm. Morana nodded. Despite it all. This felt right.

"I have been for a while."

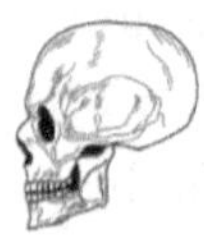

Black heels clicked against the dark floors in the palace as Morana moved toward the ballroom.

Even with the doors closed, she could hear the murmuring of the crowd—confirming Willow's previous claim that there would be many in attendance. Morana didn't know how she felt about that.

Would the court accept her? Would more assassins make their way into the palace?

She waited for Matthias, her thoughts spinning as she stared at the double doors, pondering what was to come. Despite her nerves, she kept her hands steady in front of her, willing them to still as her shadows whispered around her ankles.

Matthias appeared in a swell of darkness, his suit all black, a stray strand of dark hair kissing his forehead. When his eyes took in the sight of her, they caught fire. Morana could feel that heat as his gaze tracked down her body, pausing briefly at the swell of her breasts, moving down until he saw the magic twisting at her ankles. His own shadows moved out to meet hers, calling to her.

He stepped forward, his hand tracing along her jaw. Morana's breath caught as she looked up into darkened eyes, trying to decipher what he was feeling. Was he nervous?

"My wife," he whispered before placing a kiss to her lips. Morana melted into him, allowing his presence to ease some of her worries.

When she pulled back, she caught the smile cracking across his face, the faefires dancing in his eyes.

Home.

"No priests?" she asked, though she knew the answer. Matthias had discussed the details of the ceremony and coronation the previous night as they tried to take their minds off of Cain—the war—the assassins.

"We are getting married before the gods," he said, "but there are no priests."

"And why is that?" she asked, running a finger over his jaw and relishing the gentle scratch of stubble.

His smile widened. "Because," he began, "we are the gods, Morana."

Morana chuckled as Matthias placed a kiss to her temple. He offered her his arm as the doors opened.

She took a deep breath when she saw the crowd. Dark tablecloths, blood-red roses, and curious stares greeting them as they walked forward.

There was no telling what the court felt about her appearance as queen—what they had been told about her.

Even so, Morana tracked over the many faces in the crowd, spotting Garian, his wife, and the small child seated on her lap. She noted the smile on his face—so rare.

Her eyes moved across the room to see Elivira, Hames, Reese, and Ronan. The family that had come alongside her—believed in her. She certainly hadn't earned them, but as she walked into the room, her grip tightening on Matthias's arm, she promised herself she would earn it.

And that would start with winning the war.

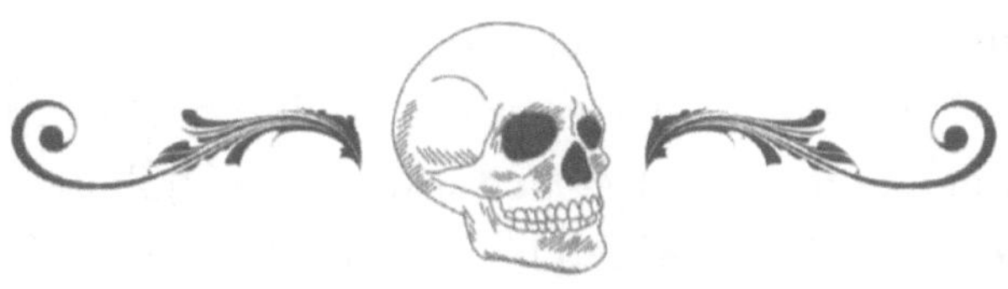

Thirty-Four

Wine, dancing, and food surrounded the ballroom as Morana sat on the throne with Matthias standing at her side. She peered out at the crowd, noting the smiling faces of the fae—her people.

The crown sat heavy on her head, obsidian and rubies set into gold and reminding her of the responsibilities she now had—as queen.

There could be no running—not from her power, and not from the war.

Tomorrow, they would travel to Callum's realm, the fauna realm. They would ask for the dream eater and hopefully test the loyalty of the fae in the room.

Starting with the lords had bile rising in her throat. If it were one of them—she didn't know how she'd press on. But still, this was the life she'd carved for herself—a life she'd made from nothing, and she saw fit to enjoy it with her husband.

"Wine?" Matthias leaned down. His warm breath on her neck sent goosebumps over her skin as she tilted her head to the side. His lips ghosted over her flesh, sending damp heat shooting down her spine and working its way back up as a flush on her cheeks.

"Of course," she answered, smiling as she turned to find a tattooed hand stretched toward her, holding a ring. The rose-gold band twisted like vines of the forest; the dark stone speckled with what looked like stars. It reminded her of the night sky—their night on the pier the first time Matthias asked her to marry him for more than mere politics.

"You are good, Matthias." Her hand found his, her thumb brushing over the tattoos inked there before she laced their fingers together. "A good king, a good god, and a beautiful mystery."

And for that moment, Matthias remembered the stars hanging above them—reminded that in even the darkest night, a different kind of light could still exist.

Morana's breath caught in her throat as her eyes met his, the smallest hint of a smile tugging at the corner of his mouth.

"I thought," Matthias began, "I promised you a ring." He knelt down next to where she sat on the throne, holding the piece of jewelry out to her as shadows twisted around them, coating them in darkness and power. "Hopefully, this one will do the job?"

Morana cleared her throat. "Is there a reason you picked this particular design?" she asked, offering her hand.

She tilted her head to the side, noting the crooked smirk on Death's face when he registered her question.

"No reason," he said, but she knew it wasn't true.

Morana glanced at the ring, making a show of inspecting the piece of jewelry. "Don't lie to me, dear husband," she said, her tone sharp. "Word is I may be more powerful than Death himself. I expect answers."

Her teasing pulled a smokey laugh from his lips, his eyes cast down as if embarrassed. "The gem may have been found in the hall of relics," he admitted before his gaze fixed to hers, she swore she saw the shadows there in his eyes, twisting as if they were a part of his very essence—residing in the deepest parts of his soul. She knew how that felt. "I must admit, it was a bit selfish. I know you say you can protect yourself, but I figured a stone of protection couldn't hurt. Especially after last night." Matthias cleared his throat, pulling nervously at the tie around his neck. "And it looks like the night sky."

Morana felt at the ring on her finger, mesmerized by the intricate details etched into the metal. She leaned forward, pressing her lips to his.

When she pulled back, she smiled. "Thank you," she whispered—though she wasn't sure what she was thanking him for.

It could have been the ring, his protection, or it could have been the home she had found within his court. The friendships she'd formed in the midst of trial.

Whatever it was, she'd meant it.

"Queen of Darkness."

Matthias stood and turned, and when Morana looked at the base of the dais, she saw a familiar face waiting. Callum wore a red suit jacket, images embroidered into the fabric depicting various creatures that Morana now knew to be real. They moved as if inspired by whatever magic Callum held in his veins.

He tilted his cleanly shaven face to the side as he took in the image of Morana perched on the throne. If he approved of the sight, she couldn't tell.

"God of Fauna," Morana greeted, her eyes peering down at the figure below.

Convenient, she thought.

"I hear you have a need for one of my creatures," he began, bowing slightly as his eyes flicked to where Death stood behind her.

Morana allowed the shadows to swell around her, reaching out to Matthias to speak mind-to-mind.

You already spoke with him? She asked, though she didn't mind if he had already. It was one less thing she'd have to think about.

Of course, Matthias said. *I wasn't willing to wait after what happened, Morana. I sent word this morning. It's probably the only reason he showed up.*

Tapping the gilded arm of the throne, Morana kept her careful mask in place. "Possibly," she said.

One of the servants brought a glass of wine to the top of the dais, and she took it gratefully, muttering her thanks before allowing herself to take a long drag from the cup.

"I must admit," Callum began, "I have some concerns regarding your request. But if you can win the beast over and convince him to do whatever it is you need him to, then I suppose he's yours."

"And what is the payment?" she asked, swirling the glass grasped between her fingers.

The last time they'd visited Callum to secure creatures for the war, the price had been steep. Morana was the one who had obtained the creature in the first place, but she couldn't imagine Callum giving it up for nothing. He was a god, after all.

"You know what I long for," Callum answered. He clasped his hands behind his backs, lifting his chin as Morana attempted to decipher his meaning.

"Sarnai" she questioned. The wine had gone to her head, allowing her the freedom to speak. "Unfortunately, you'll have to win her interest yourself, God of Fauna."

Callum didn't react. He stood stoic at the base of the dais, expression blank before he spoke again. "My payment will come when you save your court. Kill Raidan. If you can do that," he said, "it will be enough."

Morana fought the way her stomach churned with doubt. Though Raidan's death was the plan, there were still so many uncertainties. God or not, she hadn't fully grasped her power—hadn't discussed a plan for how they'd execute the assassination—a returned favor for his attempts at assassinating her she supposed.

She was cutting down Raidan's own, planning political moves, and learning to be queen—a task she still couldn't fully believe she was suited for.

"Easy," she grinned, fighting off the feelings swirling inside her.

"Easy." Callum bowed once more before turning and walking away.

Matthias's hand rested on her shoulder from where he stood, a reminder of his encouraging presence.

Her eyes cut to Ronan and Reese sitting near one another across the room. Ronan's expression was tight, and Reese's brows furrowed as she spoke. Morana considered prying into the girl's mind, using her shadows to stretch out, but it felt like an intrusion.

"What are you staring at?" Matthias asked, following her gaze across the room.

Morana lifted the wineglass to her lips, taking another sip before tilting it in their direction. "That," she answered.

Matthias chuckled. "He's been begging her for a chance," he supplied. "I've never seen Ronan so strung up on a woman before. He's usually sleeping with anything that moves, but I've noticed the stories of his adventurous evenings have all disappeared."

Morana's brow rose. "You'd think he would have won her over by now."

Matthias laughed then—truly. "You think he could?" Matthias questioned. Leaning down, he brought his lips to her ear and dropped his voice to a whisper. "Is he still competition?" Matthias asked. "Does the ring mean nothing?"

Morana chuckled, her hand rising to cover the smile dancing on her mouth. "You should see the wedding gift he gave me."

Matthias scowled, staring down at her where she sat. "Wedding gift?" he questioned.

Morana dropped her gaze lower—lower. "Very small," she stated before turning her gaze back to the other fae in the room.

Matthias's shadows stretched out, running down her arms, whispering promises of pleasure wherever they went.

That touch of magic pulled a gentle gasp from her lips as she fought to keep her expression blank as she used her own shadows to speak into Matthias's mind. *What are you doing?*

Something fun, he teased.

Morana felt the shadows dip lower, disappearing between the skirt of her gown. Matthias's grip on her mind intensified the feeling, her skin heating and heart raging.

How quiet can you be, Queen of Shadows?

Morana fought the urge to look at him, knowing what she would find there in his gaze. The shadows twisted higher, running like a phantom finger up her thigh—higher.

She gasped again when she felt him there, magic sliding over her in a way that had her tilting her hips forward—just slightly.

"What's wrong?" Matthias asked, as she turned to see the devious smirk—the heat in his dark eyes. "Uncomfortable?"

Morana swallowed as the shadows slid over her again, moving exactly where she needed them. "No," she breathed. "I'm actually very comfortable."

"Ah." Matthias stood up fully, glancing out at the crowd as if he weren't using his magic on her with their court in the room.

Morana fought the urge to moan when she felt the fullness, the way his shadows moved like his hand—knowing and gifted in their exploration.

"Are you alright, my dear?" Matthias asked again before his eyes slid in her direction. His hot gaze pinned her to the throne, watching as he continued to move his magic over her—*inside* her.

"Quite," she breathed, keeping her gaze fully fixed to his—the flames dancing there—the only indication of what they were doing.

She could feel the pleasure rise as he worked her, bringing her to the edge before easing off—only to start again.

Morana made a whimpering noise after the second round, desperate for his touch and feeling the slickness between her thighs.

"Please," she whispered.

Matthias leaned over, his nose tracing the line of her jaw. "Now who's begging?" he asked.

Morana couldn't help the way her eyes fluttered, the building sensations rising again as he moved faster—tormenting her without so much as a finger.

She could feel her release within her grasp, begging him mind-to-mind to let her have it. Her desperation pleased him as Matthias took her over the edge.

When she came crashing down, she was thankful to see all eyes turned away from them—their court too busy with the festivities of the evening.

Morana's eyes tracked across the room, finding one fae now looking at them, a brow cocked and judgment radiating off his sharp features.

"Fucking hell," Morana said, drawing her drink up to her lips to hide her discomfort. Conan watched them from where he stood, and she questioned what he'd seen—what he'd known. "He's here?" she asked, turning to look at Matthias.

"Of course," he answered. "He is an ally."

Morana grunted in dissatisfaction when she stood, setting her wine down on a passing tray, before facing Death.

"You're starting your rule off well," Matthias whispered, a satisfied look on his face. "Are you thinking about confronting him here? Letting him know about his promotion?"

"There's an idea," Morana said. "While you wait for me, ask Ronan about the painting he dropped off in my room earlier. I'm certain it would interest you."

"Oh?" Matthias lifted a dark brow.

"I find the real thing far more pleasing than paint," she said. "Or shadows."

Matthias's gaze darkened, but she turned around, leaving him atop the dais as she moved toward the lord.

Conan wove through the crowd, but Morana caught him easily enough. She grabbed his arm and allowed the shadows to take them to the hallway—a place where they could speak privately.

When the darkness faded, she noticed the shock painted on Conan's sharp features. His auburn hair hung loosely around his shoulders as he stared at her, waiting for an explanation.

"Am I now your prisoner?" Conan asked.

Morana didn't hesitate, blowing past pleasantries. "I have something to speak to you about."

Conan scoffed, folding slim arms across his chest. "You've won my court," he said. "What more could you possibly want? Our armies are only as large as they are. We simply cannot y give you more."

"It's you we want."

"Now, Morana," his smile was cutting, "I'm not interested in joining you and Matthias in whatever activities you two have been doing in secret."

Morana rolled her eyes but couldn't stop the flush of embarrassment from making its appearance.

"Inara's dead," Morana began. "The Court of Light has no one to rule it, and Matthias and I believe you would be the best fit. We've already discussed it with our court."

Conan's sharp intake of breath alerted her to the fact that she'd caught him off guard. *Good,* she thought. Surprises always bring out the truth.

"And you don't wish to conquer the court for yourself?" he asked. "You are the Queen of Darkness, after all."

"The Court of Light will not trust me or Matthias," she admitted. "We may have won over your city, but there are far too many variables to---"

"So, you wish to use me as your pawn," he interrupted.

"Of course not."

The tightness in his jaw, the way Conan prowled forward and crowded her space, sent nerves shooting down her spine. Maybe he wouldn't accept. This could have been a terrible idea.

"What makes you so sure I'd be the right fit for that?" he asked.

"There are plenty of reasons."

"Name one," he challenged.

Morana straightened, refusing to be intimidated. "How much power do you have running through your veins, Conan? You can't hide forever. I was there with you when we met The Oracle. I know what you asked."

Conan took a step back, casually smiling as he gestured to his pointed ears decorated with various rings. She saw through his attempts at feigning ignorance. "I'm fae, Morana. I cannot possibly be a god, too."

Morana's smile was icy and sharp. "And I'm mortal," she supplied. It was answer enough.

She wasn't sure if she was playing whatever game they'd found themselves in correctly. One wrong move, and her plan would crumble. They hadn't discussed what they'd do if Conan disagreed—if he'd said no to their proposition.

Morana settled on challenging him in the same way she'd challenged Acacias. Maybe her firm belief would persuade him.

It was a risk, but she took it anyway.

"Step up." Her tone had a bite to it. "Or I'll have to."

"Power hungry?" he asked, a knowing smirk dancing on his lips.

"I'm not," she said, the shadows twisting over her skin, mist rising over the floor. "I have enough power to suit me. It's just—" she allowed the mask to split, if only for a moment. Allowed vulnerability to shine in her expression. Conan had been there when she encountered her mother. She figured she could show him a bit of the truth. "I want what's best, Conan. I'm trying to do the right thing here. Make the right decisions. I think you want to do that, too."

He nodded, pondering her confession as silence stretched between them.

"Okay," he finally answered. "I'll think about it."

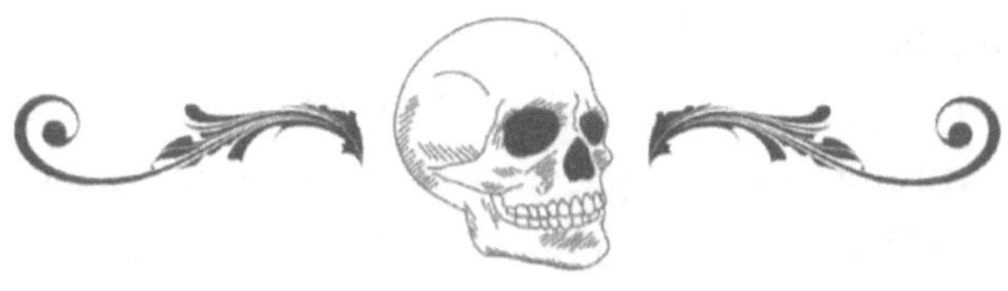

Thirty-Five

Morana sat in the center of Matthias's bed, turning the box she'd stolen from Inara over in her hands. A ball hung suspended inside the glass casing, transparent and empty as Inara's eyes when the life left her body.

It was familiar—something Morana had seen before the first time she'd descended into the Basar fountain. Axton had used whatever this was to kidnap Matthias, and she could have sworn there was black smoke twisting inside the glass when the fish had shown her the memory.

Maybe she'd be able to use the fish to figure out the box—dive into the fountain and learn how to get it to work.

Those fish held memories of Matthias's kidnapping and Axton's betrayal. Regardless of her ability to survive it, those memories still lashed out—painful and consuming.

When the door to the bedroom opened, Morana tucked the relic into the nightstand, Matthias's eyes tracking her movement as he entered.

"You're sure you don't know how to use it?" she asked, smoothing down the black fabric of her gown.

After Conan had agreed to think about her

proposition, Morana had returned to the party, set on drinking fae wine and dancing.

Despite it all, she longed to celebrate—to enjoy the life she'd built and the god now standing in the room.

"If I knew how to use that thing, don't you suppose I'd tell my *wife*?" The last word sounded sweet—like honey dripping from the lips of Death. Somehow, she knew it wouldn't harm her—maybe he'd come to save her.

"Your wife," Morana chuckled, glancing at her hands now laced in front of her.

Shadows swelled, quickly spitting Matthias out in front of her before he grabbed her wrist and used the darkness again—stopping only when they stood in his bathroom.

Morana glanced to the large tub, her breath catching when Death stepped forward, slowly running his hand down her arm and sending goosebumps rising wherever he touched.

When her eyes met his dark gaze, she noted the wicked promises still held there. He smiled, the sight devastating.

"Conan agreed." It wasn't a question, but it still sent Morana's stomach twisting.

I'll think about it.

"Not quite," she admitted as Matthias's fingers rose up her arm, demanding in their exploration—just like the shadows had been on the throne.

Her brows furrowed, insecurity taking hold. She'd just become queen of the Court of Shadows—Matthias's wife. "Do you think I've failed?" she asked, her voice barely a whisper. "Since he didn't agree. It was my idea to begin with."

Matthias leaned in, nuzzling the side of her neck as he breathed her in. That touch had desire wrapping around her again. His display on the throne hadn't been enough—she needed to feel his flesh, not his power.

"Hardly," he said, his voice a dark rumble she could feel in her bones. Matthias kissed her neck, his intentions for their wedding night clear. "In fact," he said against her skin. "I'd say you're doing quite well. First day as queen and you've already guaranteed our access to the dream eater and stole an ancient relic from the goddess of life. And now you're working toward appointing a king?"

Morana gasped when his hand gripped her waist, dragging her closer, his mouth still working beneath the shell of her ear, his voice dropping to a low whisper.

"Is there anything you can't do, Queen of Darkness?"

Gripping his shoulders, Morana fought the urge to drown in Death. What he was doing—she couldn't get enough. "I don't know," she taunted, though her voice sounded a bit breathless. "Dance?"

Matthias chuckled against her skin, that same sound embedding itself into her soul as his shadows whispered at her feet.

She was wound tight after their time in the ballroom. He hadn't actually touched her, and he had been giving far more than she had given him. It was his turn to have pleasure rippling across his skin.

"You do seem to perform better with wine in your system," he teased, nipping at her ear. "Though I'd never insult your dancing, my queen."

Morana wrapped her arms around his neck, weaving her fingers through his hair and tugging at the strands until he looked at her. His gaze heated and filled with lust.

"I think you just did," she said, watching the way his lip curled up at one corner. "I should strangle you for that."

Matthias licked his lips, his eyes dipping down to hers for the briefest moment. "I think I'd quite enjoy your hand around my throat."

Morana cocked an eyebrow, sliding one hand down the side of his neck and gently wrapping her fingers around his throat. "Like this?" she asked.

When she caught the feral look in his eyes, her body lit aflame—desire coursing through her veins—spiking her blood with intense pleasure.

"Murderous, little creature," he whispered before his fingers came up to toy with the drop-shoulder sleeves of her gown. "You're probably exhausted. Should we run a bath? Get cleaned up after the party."

Morana swallowed, glancing at the dark tub, her mind racing with ideas. "It's been a long day," she said. "I'm quite tired from my duties as queen. I may need help."

Her eyes cut to his, and Matthias wrapped a tattooed hand over the fingers still gently stretched around his throat. "Anything for you," he said.

Turning around, Morana's breath caught as his fingers skated over the laces of her corset, quickly freeing her until she stood in nothing.

Her breath came out in pants as Matthias's heated gaze traced every inch of her body. He slowly leaned to start the water in the tub, keeping his dark eyes firmly fixed to her when he worked the buttons of his dress shirt.

Morana stood, lips parted, as she traced his tattoos with her eyes. She could feel the electricity in the air as he slowly dropped his shirt to the floor, followed by the rest of his clothes.

"It wasn't enough," she breathed. "The throne—our party—it wasn't enough."

"Have I failed to please my queen?" he asked, prowling forward until his hand gently grabbed her waist, pulling her tightly to him. She could feel his hardness everywhere.

"No," she admitted, staring up at him, her gaze stripped bare. "I'm just afraid I won't live up to what you imagined for a wife."

His dark chuckle took her by surprise. Matthias pressed a gentle kiss to her lips before breaking apart. "You're very frustrating."

Morana's brows furrowed. "A little rude, considering the position we're in."

"I didn't picture having a wife before you," he admitted. "I didn't know there could be light in the darkness."

Matthias roughly pressed his lips to hers as he dragged a moan from deep in her throat. Her hands clung to his shoulders while his greedy hands skimmed up her back, down her waist, and over her ass, pulling her closer as a dark sound rumbled through his chest.

Matthias trailed his lips over her jaw, smelling like wine and shadows. "You're beautiful," he whispered. "My wife."

Morana reached down, wrapping her fingers around his length and stroking once—twice.

Matthias leaned into the touch.

"Shit," he muttered.

She kept working her hand over him, lost in the sensation as Matthias nipped at her lips, running kisses over her neck, her shoulders.

It felt as if he were touching her everywhere. When the shadows danced across her skin, intensifying the sensation, Morana leaned in, breathless and wound so tightly, she swore she would snap.

"Are we getting into the water?" she asked, her voice low—meant only for him.

Lifting her up, Matthias strode to the tub as Morana wrapped her legs around him. She could feel him there, and ground herself against his length, catching the deep groan with her mouth.

When Matthias lowered them into the tub, he sat on a lip around the edge, pulling her on top of him. His hands skated over her hips as if he were memorizing every curve of her body, every inch of skin he could get his hands on.

"This reminds me of the first time we did this," she said. "The water."

Matthias chuckled, dragging his tongue up the side of her throat before nipping at her ear. Morana felt the way her stomach curled and twisted with desire, the warmth pooling in her core.

"And I don't believe I will ever tire of it."

With that, Morana reached down, positioning him until she could feel the tip at her entrance. She sank down, gasping at the stretch as the water lapped around her chest and shoulders.

Matthias reached up, full lips parted, eyes dark and shining in the dim faefires of the bathroom. He brushed her hair back from her face as she lowered herself again—again, never breaking eye contact with Death—hoping to be lost in whatever he had to give her.

When he ran his hands up higher, grabbing her breast, tracing his thumb over her nipple, Morana came down, her release building steadily. He watched her with a predatory gaze as she climbed higher. And when Matthias ran a finger over her clit, she gasped, her movements growing harder—faster.

"*Fuck,*" he whispered, dropping his forehead to her shoulder.

The sound of his raspy voice had her moving faster. Matthias guided her hips with one hand beneath the water and used the other to stroke her until her mind was a muddy mess.

"Oh god," she breathed as every muscle in her body tightened, begging for release.

Matthias groaned into her skin, the sound tipping her over the edge—taking him along with her.

When they had both stopped moving, Matthias placed a slow kiss on her lips, savoring the taste of her. His hands ran over her slick flesh as if he still couldn't get enough—as if he never wanted to leave.

"Tomorrow will be busy." Morana's voice was soft as the thoughts started flooding her mind once more.

"It will be," Matthias answered, leaning over to grab the soap off the ledge.

Morana climbed off his lap, turning as he ran the bar over her back, clearing away the dirt and sweat from the day.

"But," he began, "we still have tonight."

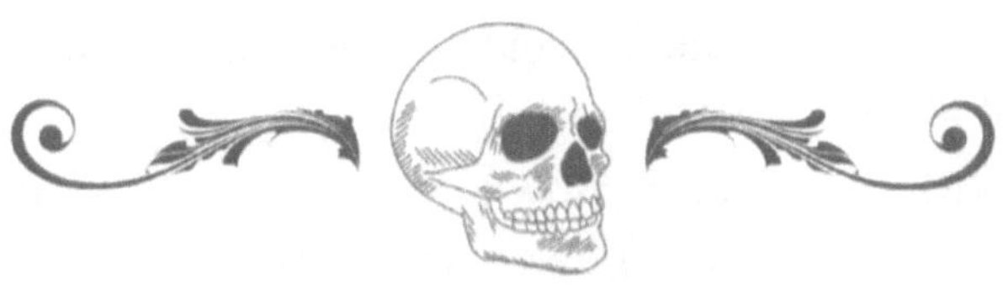

Thirty-Six

Matthias's room always reminded her of the land of the gods—the palace where Matthias had originally taken her what felt like a lifetime ago.

Morana sat on the four-poster bed, tracing the carvings etched into the dark wood. Her mind swirled with memories from the previous night. She could feel the ghost of Matthias's hands running over her body and almost feel his gaze burning as it traced over every inch of her. Her face flushed, and she willed herself to think about anything else.

There was enough to distract her mind—the box tucked in the drawer of the nightstand, the looming task of controlling the dream eater to subdue Raidan. Even the assassins and how they kept gaining access to the palace.

Morana called on her power, letting it ease some of her worries.

Unpredictable as it was, she could always rely on her magic to soothe her. She wouldn't let Raidan win—not like this.

Morana jolted as the door swung open. Her head snapped to the direction of voices, finding Sarnai striding into the room. The goddess's navy dress twisted around her long legs; the low neckline held together with delicate chains shaped like the vines of a tree.

Morana quickly noted Matthias hustling after the goddess. His hair was mussed, and frustration etched into the tense set of his features.

"You cannot let yourself into my room," he huffed, running a tattooed hand through the already wild strands of dark hair.

"Oh please," Sarnai responded, refusing to cease as she made her way closer to the bed. "That is a ridiculous rule, and you know it."

Morana stood, tugging at the hem of Matthias's black t-shirt and willing it to cover as much as it could manage.

"Marriage has made you a bore, Matthias." The goddess waving him off.

He grunted. "As if you didn't already believe that of me prior to the wedding."

Sarnai stopped a few feet from Morana, spinning in her heels, the slim skirts of her dress flowing with the movement. The goddess stared Matthias down, and Morana could hear the hint of a smile as she spoke.

"Oh, to be sure," she said. "I'm only emphasizing the point now that you're preventing me from seeing the only woman keeping me sane in your godforsaken court."

"The gods haven't forsaken this court." Matthias gestured to Sarnai. "Morana, you and I—"

Sarnai interrupted him, refusing to acknowledge his protests. "I love dealing with your palace gardens, Matthias, but plants don't talk back. Nor do they share the very explicit and entertaining details of their sexual exploits."

Morana chuckled, the sound turning toward laughter when she caught the horrified look on Matthias's face.

"You do not need to know the details of my wife's sexual exploits."

"Why?" Sarnai taunted. "Too afraid she will admit to taking that lord of yours for a ride? I was there when she painted that wonderful work of art."

Morana folded her arms across her chest, the smile now firmly plastered on her face. "He knows that's not true," she finally interrupted. "He has full access to my memories."

Sarnai rolled her eyes dramatically, finally turning toward Morana. "How romantic," she remarked. "Could you tell him I'm allowed to come in here?"

Morana rolled her tongue along her cheek, her eyes cutting to Death. "She's allowed to come in here," she parroted.

Matthias breathed out a frustrated sigh. "Ridiculous," he muttered before striding over to where Morana stood and wrapping an arm around her waist. He pulled her closer, pressing a kiss to her temple that made her face heat. It reminded her of all the other places he kissed last night.

"Did you need something?" she asked Sarnai.

The goddess's umber eyes lit up, her toned arms folding across her chest as she raised her chin. "I heard you're visiting Callum today."

"And?" Morana asked, as shadows twisted over her skin. She let Matthias into her mind easily, as if it were second nature.

Oh, here we go, he said.

Sarnai's gaze hardened, her glare cutting through Matthias like a knife. "I want to come with you," she asserted.

Morana's eyes widened before she collected herself. "I hate to break it to you, Sarnai, but Hames is coming, too. I'm certain Callum won't pay you any mind with the lord present, and I know you're desperately hoping your enmity will slowly turn to a passionate tryst."

Matthias cocked a brow, suppressing a smile.

Sarnai scoffed—loudly. "That's not what I'm hoping." She rolled her eyes and Morana couldn't stop the tug at the corner of her mouth and the amusement lighting up inside her. "If we are to go after the dream eater," Sarnai continued. "I want to see it. I'm left out of the action far too often."

Morana tilted her head in question. "You want to convince the creature to come with us?"

"God's no." Sarnai raised a hand in front of her face, and Morana watched as vines wove their way through her fingers, speaking of the goddess's power. "I want to watch," she finished with a satisfied smirk.

"Ruthless," Matthias whispered under his breath, and Morana turned to look at him. His black t-shirt, much like the one she was wearing, stretched around his bicep where the tattooed crows disappeared beneath the material. Morana remembered tracing the ink, her fingers sliding up his hot flesh, dancing down his stomach as his abs tightened beneath the contact. She swallowed, trying to shut down the memories, but caught the subtle raise of Matthias's brow.

Caught red-handed.

"Well," Morana said, clearing her throat. "I'm not sure what Matthias would have you do."

Matthias chuckled. "You are queen," he said. "It's for you to decide."

Something in her chest warmed at that and Morana's gray eyes met the umber stare of the flora goddess.

She smiled. "We would love to have you, Sarnai."

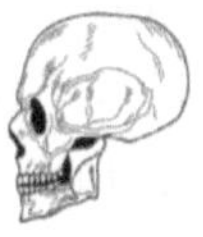

Mist floated over the gray water, lapping against the side of the small boat. The gentle rocking was enough to lull anyone to sleep. Even the creatures that lurked in Callum's realm—not the dream eater, though.

The monster feasted on nightmares.

"I don't see why Callum didn't lift the wards," Sarnai complained, picking at the black pants covering her legs. It was strange to see her in anything other than a flowing dress.

"What is he trying to do here? Wear us down so he can go back on his promise? He *would*."

Morana chuckled at the distaste evident in the goddess's voice. She glanced at Hames, who sat with a lantern at his feet, carving shapes into a stick with his dagger. By the tight line of the lord's lips, the subtle roll of his eyes, and the way he started digging deeper into the wood, Morana knew she wasn't the only one the lord didn't like.

Maybe Callum was his only friend.

Morana chuckled, drawing Matthias's attention briefly before he looked to the goddess.

"Lifting the wards is dangerous," Matthias answered. "He usually allows us to leave that way, so long as we exit quickly. If not, there's a chance any number of creatures could escape."

Sarnai scoffed. "Then he should keep a tighter leash on his monsters."

"Would you stop talking?" Hames muttered under his breath, earning a cutting look from Sarnai.

"Honestly, Hames, I bet you're fun at parties." Sarnai stretched out a hand, a vine slithering from her fingertip and wrapping around the lord's ankle. For what it was worth, Hames didn't flinch, and something about that annoyed the goddess.

"See," she remarked. "No fun."

Morana leaned into Matthias, speaking low so only he could hear. "Are they always like this?"

"Half of being queen," he started, his eyes lighted with amusement, "is dealing with the children that work to run your court."

"How have you survived so long?"

Matthias leaned in, but she didn't miss the truth of the weight of the crown flashing across his face. Even so, he kept his tone casual—teasing. "I'm a death god," he reminded her. "Maybe I've been dead the whole time."

"I married a zombie."

Matthias chuckled, staring out across the water as Morana spotted the stone dragons appearing through the mist. The caged bellies held mysterious creatures—creatures Morana hoped to never see—things she couldn't name.

They moved in near silence, only the sound of water and the creaking boat to keep them company. It was Morana who spotted the last dragon, the darkness inside the metal caging keeping the dream eater in.

She glanced at the small platform stretching out from the cage, eyes catching on the regal-looking god standing with his hands clasped behind his back. His emerald-colored vest showed off toned arms, his dark eyes swimming with excitement, as if Callum enjoyed the danger of the beasts he collected.

Something about the fauna god's delight sent Morana's heart hammering in her chest. There was no telling what it would take to subdue the creature. At the very least, she would have to walk through her nightmares once more to satiate the monster's appetite. There was no telling how Callum fed the thing—if he did.

At the worst? Morana would end up entirely consumed—broken and bloody—a failure.

For a moment, she felt the need to run. Maybe her mother had been right after all.

"What are you thinking about?" Matthias asked, his brows pinched together. As the boat creeped toward the stone platform, he placed a warm hand on her thigh, squeezing gently in encouragement.

"Death," she breathed.

The last time she'd faced the dream eater, he'd shown her the picture of her mother. The one where she had cared and then ran, claiming it was all too much.

After the time with The Oracle, Morana wondered what nightmares the beast could come up with.

Like mother, like daughter.

She hadn't run. Yet.

Matthias grimaced before leaning in to whisper to her. "If you mean your own death, I won't allow it. If you're talking about me, I'd be happy to oblige whatever wild fantasy you've crafted in your mind when we get back."

Morana swallowed down her fear, thankful for the distraction Matthias tried to provide her with. Still—it wasn't enough.

"Well," Callum spoke as Hames tied the ship to the platform, wrapping a rope around a wooden pole jutting from the stone.

Morana watched as Callum's eyes flicked to Sarnai, pausing and lingering. He seemed surprised at her presence, but aside from that, his expression was unreadable.

Sarnai's umber eyes turned to him, one brow cocking in challenge as the air crackled between them.

Matthias cleared his throat, breaking the spell and bringing Callum back to the present. "Yes?" the fauna god asked.

Gesturing to the cage, Matthias responded. "The creature."

Callum ran a hand through his dark hair, eyes flicking to the goddess once more before he turned to the cage. "Yes, of course," he said. "You saw these the first time you entered my realm." Callum strode toward the bars of the cage, running a hand over the metal. "These bars are somewhat of a relic. An ancient metal designed for keeping creatures in." When the god looked back to Morana, she caught the slight curve of his mouth. The gentle lift that indicated he thought he had them. "Do you have something to restrain the beast?"

Tugging on her magic, Morana allowed the white mist to float over the ground, rising around them in a flagrant show of power. She offered the god a cutting smile, one that mirrored the confidence he had before. Despite the rapid beating of her heart and the doubt swirling in her mind, Morana held her ground.

"Something just as strong."

Callum ran his gaze over her—assessing. "And might I ask what that is?"

Morana cocked a brow, tilting her head to the side in challenge. "It's me."

"Lovely." Callum ran a hand down the metal of the bar, green magic moving from his palm and into the surface he touched. Slowly, the bars started shifting, a door forming from iron in front of him.

He kept his eyes glued forward as he addressed her again. "You need only prove it, Queen of Darkness. I won't let you take the dream eater back to your realm unless you can prove you are in control of it. Should something happen, of course, I don't want the blame placed on me. I need to ensure you're capable."

"I've controlled the Veeden." Morana felt Matthias's hand at her back, steadying her before she stepped forward, offering herself to the fauna god and his test.

Callum scoffed, turning to face her. "The Veeden are nothing compared to this, and that is a truth you should already know."

"Don't be such an asshole, Callum."

At the sound of Sarnai's voice, Callum seemed to stumble. His casual confidence fading when his eyes caught hers for a beat too long. That same unreadable expression crossed his face—the moment of pause Morana couldn't decipher. He bowed ever so slightly, acknowledging Sarnai with respect—something the goddess hadn't offered him in return. "As you wish," he spoke—his voice softer than before.

Stepping to the door, Morana took a deep breath, calling on her magic to soothe her nerves when Callum opened the door. In a moment, she would be back in the clutches of her worst fears—desperately hoping she could bind the beast to her will.

When the door locked behind her, she stood in darkness, no trace of the metal bars, no light filtering into the space where the dream eater resided. She couldn't hear Matthias or the others—couldn't sense them either.

She was completely alone.

"She's returned."

The familiar voice seemed to come from everywhere, sending a chill down Morana's spine as she desperately awaited what the creature would do.

"So, I have," Morana responded, holding her chin high, prodding the cell with her magic, anxiously feeling for the mind of the dream eater.

"It seems you've come with new fears, Queen of Darkness." There was a subtle hiss to the voice, one that had her jaw clenched tightly and her eyes closing. It's not as if she could see the beast, anyway. "You are truly a queen now. But I will have you know. I always believed you capable. With the new title, I'm certain your fears will be most satisfying."

It felt as if she were descending into unknown depths as the dream eater took hold of her mind. Morana fought the feeling, grasping at her power and pushing it out, but still, she couldn't find the creature.

When she landed on the hard ground, she lost the breath in her lungs as she stared up at the dark ceiling above. The gold etched into the trim, the black coloring, all of it reminded her of the palace of Ascella—of *home.*

The stone beneath her back felt cool, and Morana tried to sit up, noticing the restraints holding her to the platform.

When she looked around, Matthias's court surrounded her with hungry eyes. The white robe hanging off of Matthias's figure sent her stomach twisting in her gut. Bile rose in her throat, and the image came crashing into her.

Strapped to an altar, the court stood before her. Her eyes widened as she took in Matthias, an ornamental dagger clutched in his hands.

He was too close, and Morana began thrashing on the stone tablet, desperately trying to escape.

"We give thanks to the gods for this offering," he said. "The answer to the long-sought war between the two courts." Matthias stepped forward, his eyes lit with joy as he lifted the dagger above his head, holding it over Morana's heart.

"No!" Morana screamed, pulling against the restraints as the chains cut into her skin. She could feel blood dripping down her arm where her flesh had caught it, but it didn't stop the feral thrashing—the fear that surrounded her.

"You are our sacrifice to the gods," Matthias spoke sweetly. "A sacrifice for the power we long for." A slow smile stretched across his face, and Morana felt as if the blood had exited her body, her whole world spinning on its axis. "And in case you forgot, Morana. I am a god."

The knife lowered quickly, and Morana squeezed her eyes shut, trying to get out.

"It's not real," she muttered. "Not real. Not real. Not real." She was practically chanting, her eyes still closed as she felt the magic pull in her chest. Morana called on it, her eyes snapping open when the power touched the mind of something new—a powerful creature filled with twisted memories and fear.

That fear overwhelmed her, as if she felt the emotions of everyone who had fed the dream eater. Morana screamed, her back arching off whatever cold stone she was lying on.

Fighting to catch her breath, she pressed into the magic, letting it guide her as she wrapped it around the mind of the dream eater.

The monster fought back; its mind slippery as she attempted to hold it in her grasp.

"You can't bind your own fears, Queen of Darkness."

Morana grunted, sitting up despite the burning in her muscles. It was as if she'd spent hours battling the wicked thing.

"Like hell I can't," she panted, slowly rising to stand.

With one final thrust, Morana shoved her magic into the mind of the beast, feeling the creature shutter as an ear-piercing scream released into the cage.

When she felt the firm grip around the dream eater, the beast showed its face for the second time. More terrible in the light than it had been before.

She noted the collar as the darkness faded, leaving to reveal the metal cage around them and the door waiting for their departure.

When Morana turned, tugging on whatever hold she had on the monster, she watched as Hames inched closer to the enclosure, his sword at the ready as if he were willing to defend her.

Morana's eyes caught his briefly, and she nodded once.

Bringing the beast beside her.

"Done," she said, turning to Callum, whose eyes were wide in shock.

"Can we go now?" she asked.

Matthias stood next to Hames, proud and supporting a wicked smirk.

"Yes," Callum said, glancing between the beast and the god before him. "Yes, of course."

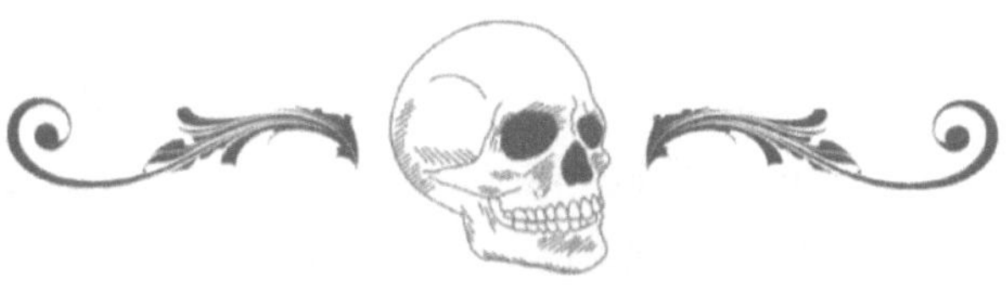

Thirty-Seven

The gray sky stretched overhead, speaking of the vastness of the world Morana hadn't known existed. Different realms, gods, fae, and magic—all of it didn't exist a year ago—not to her.

Morana glanced at the snow-covered path in the palace gardens. Many of the plants slept beneath the frost, awaiting the spring that was slowly approaching. Morana touched the crown atop her head and lifted the skirt of her black dress as she made her way to the palace doors. Guards stood along the far wall, watching for more assassins, no doubt. Morana hadn't known peace since the last woman prowled into her room.

The Basar fountain promised answers, as it normally did, but Morana had no desire to revisit the hungry fish beneath the murky water.

Still, Raidan wouldn't stop, and she was confident the box would give them answers. The relic had been enough to subdue Matthias, and it had even worked on her in the sewers beneath Ascella. There had to be a way to unlock its abilities. Whether it would work on Raidan or not, that was a different question—one she'd need the fish for.

Morana pushed the heavy door open, the orange light of the faefires flickering in the sconces lining the long hallway to the deepest parts of the palace.

Morana paused when she caught the bulky figure moving quickly down the hallway.

Hames was still dressed in leathers and furs, his hair wild and hanging to his shoulders where a sword was strapped across his back.

Rushing to catch up, Morana cursed her heels and reached out to grab the lord's arm. The contact sent him spinning. His expression hardened until he registered who had grabbed him.

That hardened expression, the way his hand flexed over the hilt of the dagger at his belt, reminded her of the way he looked outside of the dream eater's cage. The beast now resided beneath the palace, Callum coming periodically to help care for the creature.

"Can I help you?" he asked, glancing at her hand still gripping his bicep. She pulled away quickly as if the contact burned her.

"I just—" What did she intend to say? Thank you? Or maybe Morana merely wanted to take the time to learn about the lord. Win him over.

"You just?" His brow furrowed as Morana fought the nerves swirling in her gut.

"Thank you," she said. "When I went in with the dream eater, you were standing and willing to defend me.

Thank you for not letting your opinions of me color your actions."

His jaw ticked beneath his beard, but aside from that, he didn't react.

"What are you planning?" he asked, his voice gruff.

Lifting her chin, Morana felt the weight of the crown atop her head and the weight of the decisions that now rested on her shoulders. "We need the dream eater to help with something."

"I'm well aware," he ground out. "I just paid the creature a visit."

Morana's brow creased.

"I'm not the traitor," he declared. "It's been decided. Now," he eyed her again, and she fought the urge to crumble under his gaze. "What *else* could you use the dream eater for?"

"Excuse me?" she asked.

"What else?"

Morana's mind reeled. She didn't like feeling off balance in front of the lord, didn't appreciate Matthias beginning to weed through those in the palace to find out who'd let the assassins in without her. Still, she tried to grasp his meaning.

If they had the beast—along with other creatures for the war. They could use it.

If the box proved useless—

"We could get Raidan alone," she said, her mind catching up with the idea. "It would be difficult, but there's a possibility the dream eater could subdue him." Hope bloomed in her chest. "Should my other ideas fail, the beast could feed on his fears long enough to give us a fighting chance.

Hames stared at her, his expression giving away nothing. "And what makes you so sure Raidan has fears?"

Morana's stomach dropped, doubt creeping like a vine up old brick. There were no guarantees, but this plan was all she had. If they couldn't use the box—if the Basar didn't give her the information she'd needed—

She spoke with confidence, despite the feelings lurking beneath the surface. "Everyone is afraid of something, Hames."

"It might not be enough."

She knew that. Damn, did she know it.

"Yes," she whispered. Morana cleared her throat, noting that though his expression was difficult to read, there was no judgment there. "I'm going into the Basar fountain today." She paused, hoping that she wasn't over-explaining. It was hard not to. The desire to get the lord's approval ran deep. She was queen now and longed to have the same respect as her husband. "I also have hope for something else we might use aside from the beast."

Hames looked her over as if he were trying to find the crack in her façade. He nodded once again before turning to walk away.

Morana's heart plummeted. The disappointment tasting bitter on her tongue.

"You are not going to ask me what it is? Ask me about my plans?" she asked, causing Hames to pause, though he hadn't turned to face her. "You're a lord after all. I'd think you'd want to know."

Hames didn't respond.

"You will just defer to Matthias, then?" While she knew it shouldn't hurt, knew Matthias was better equipped to relay information, it still stung.

Hames finally turned, his gaze cutting through her.

"I trust you, Your Majesty."

He bowed once, his hair falling in his face before he turned to walk away, leaving Morana stunned and silent.

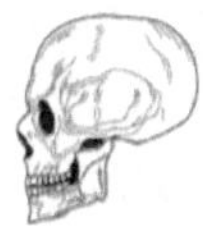

"Let me go in." Matthias tried to convince her.

Morana stood with Matthias at the edge of the fountain in the Hall of Relics. Memories of the Basar fish beneath the water's surface rose to her mind. She could feel the way they cut through skin, the way they'd tried to consume her. It was the price to pay for their knowledge.

They needed to know how to use the box—needed the Basar fish to show them something. The dream eater had tested the rest of the lords, with Matthias taking the lead on the interrogations.

They'd moved to some of the staff, but still—no luck.

This, however—

This task was something Morana could accomplish. The creatures shied away from the light, and she'd grown more comfortable using that magic. Even as her hands trembled, she knew she'd be fine.

The only thing causing her hesitance were the memories from before—the times she'd entered the fountain, so afraid of being consumed.

"That's ridiculous." Morana rolled her eyes, but Matthias kept his dark gaze pinned to her. "They won't bother me," she said. "They don't like the light."

Matthias grimaced before running a hand down his face. "Fucking hell, Morana. Let me do this."

"No. It makes very little sense, and you've been in the dungeons with the dream eater as he has his fill of our court. You watched that *thing* devour the fears of those closest to you in the attempt at solving who betrayed us. This task," she asserted, "is for me to handle."

Matthias grabbed her arm, spinning her to face him. "I did just fine with these things before."

"So, you regret marrying me?" Morana cocked an eyebrow in challenge, knowing exactly how the statement would get under his skin.

Matthias practically growled in response. "That's not what I'm saying. I don't like you diving in the fucking fountain."

Morana rolled her eyes. "Let me be queen."

"Let me be king."

She waited, letting their statements linger in the air before she huffed a laugh. "Quite the argument. We've been married for what? Days?"

Matthias wrapped his fingers around her wrist and stepped closer as he pulled her to him, his eyes boring into hers. The intensity there made her stomach dip before he placed a bruising kiss to her lips—one that spoke of his frustration with her.

"Be safe," he said, his forehead rested against hers.

Morana smiled, breathing in his scent, memorizing the feel of his fingers threaded through her hair.

"Never," she whispered.

She pulled back. Taking off her shoes, Morana hiked the skirt of her gown up and climbed to the lip of the fountain. She looked down into the depths of the water, the knowledge of what awaited her weighing her limbs down like heavy lead.

Before she could think better of it, she jumped.

When the cool water hit her skin, Morana sucked in a harsh breath. She instinctively pulled at the light crackling in her chest, swimming down until she felt a sharp sting in her arm where one fish had latched on.

Light flashed, and the fish darted away.

Morana looked around, bubbles breaking free from her lips. She had only a small amount of time, and if she wanted to see how the box could be used, she'd need to give them an offering. Locking the light inside her, she let the fish come, and if only for a moment, allowed them to pull her deeper into the abyss.

The long spiraling staircase in Raidan's temple stretched down to the depths as careful feet tested the stone before descending further. Each scuff in the darkened palace sent her heart pounding in her chest.

"You don't belong here." A cold voice sounded behind her, and she turned, looking up into the amber eyes of a demon.

"Actually," she said, straightening. "I think I do."

Raidan cocked an eyebrow, running his cold gaze along her figure as she clutched her cloak tightly.

"What makes you say that?"

"The woman you want. You want access to her, and I want her gone."

Raidan took a step closer, his black shoes scuffing over the stairs and sending sweat down her spine, but she didn't back down.

"Tell me your motive," he demanded, "and I may consider bargaining with a child."

She scoffed, hiding her fear behind false bravado. "My brother saw his death last night. The girl is to blame. If I give you access to her, you can get her out of my hair."

"You wish to save the boy?"

She stiffened, jaw clenched tight as a draft whispered through the stairwell, her red hair floating around her face.

"Does it matter?" she asked.

The monster took another step down, bringing him close enough to touch. "It most certainly does." He smiled, flashing white teeth as he reached for her wrist.

She fought the urge to flinch when he exposed her forearm, roughly shoving the fabric of her shirt upward.

"Shall we make a bargain like the fae?" Raidan asked. "So, I know you won't betray me."

"Whatever needs done."

"Very well."

Raidan swiped a finger over her flesh, the magic burning as it seeped into her bones, carving the deal she knew she had to make.

She screamed. The sound echoing through the temple—heard by no one as the brand took shape on her forearm.

"Well, Kit," Raidan said, a feral look on his face. "I hope you know the palace of Ascella well enough to complete your task. I'll bring my bride back, so long as you let my assassins in."

"Who are your assassins?" Kit asked, swallowing as an uneasy feeling twisted in her gut.

Raidan laughed, a hollow sound. "You truly believe the fae don't long for power? And where else would they find it but in an ancient god?"

Kit nodded once; her eyes fixed to his as doubt crept up her spine.

She shoved the feeling away—for Cain.

"Run along," Raidan whispered, leaning in just slightly. "Inara holds the Imelda Box, and if you play your cards right, she may give it to you. With the right runes painted in blood on the surface, magic can be captured." Raidan's hot breath sent a chill down her spine. "Wouldn't you like to hold the Queen of Darkness's power in your hands? Control her?"

"Yes," Kit breathed.

Raidan stepped back. His features hardened. "Then go."

Morana gasped, the light still lashing out like a whip around her, fighting the fish off her body as she grabbed the ledge of the fountain.

Matthias was there—warm hands wrapping around her arms as he hoisted her to safety, wrapping her dripping figure in a warm towel and pulling her to his chest.

She couldn't stop the ringing in her ears—the sting of betrayal that sliced through her chest. She wanted to vomit, to cry.

"I don't know how to use the box," she admitted, her voice low. "But I know who betrayed us."

"Who?" Matthias nearly growled as he gripped her shoulders, as if he could find the answer written somewhere in her eyes.

"She's just a kid," Morana whispered. "She wanted to save him."

The sobs broke free, soaking Death with sorrow and pain. It brought back everything she regretted about Cain's sacrifice—the pain she'd felt.

"Who was it?" he asserted, face severe as he placed a gentle thumb beneath her chin, forcing Morana to look at him. "Who did this?"

Her voice broke on the word. "Kit."

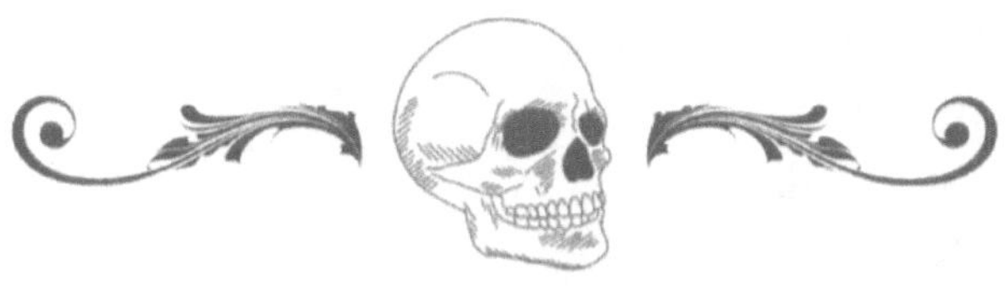

Thirty-Eight

Matthias disappeared, leaving Morana drenched and wrapped in a towel next to the Basar fountain.

"No," she whispered. "No, no, no."

She gathered her skirts, heavy with water as the shadows swallowed her whole. She had them drop her back into the palace of Ascella near the main kitchens where Kit spent most of her time.

The first thing she saw was the immense darkness.

Matthias's power filled the utterly silent kitchens. Strange considering the main kitchen was typically filled with staff providing meals for the palace.

Morana reached out with the shadows, trying to force some of his magic back. She was successful enough to make out Kit standing by the far wall, Matthias snarling in her face as she held her chin high.

The girl's sleeve had been pulled back to reveal the binding mark of her bargain—similar to the one Axton had carved into his skin so long ago.

Morana remembered that initial betrayal, the way Axton had led her into Inara's clutches—feigning ignorance about the entire realm.

She swallowed.

Kit wasn't Axton.

She wanted to save Cain.

"Matthias, stop."

Morana stood in her soaked dress, watching the shadows stutter. There was a beat before they dissolved—as if he were fighting to gain control of his own power—as if his magic might be as consuming as her own.

It gave her pause as Matthias turned to look at her, never removing his grip from the girl's arm.

Maybe he'd entered her mind during those moments because he *knew.*

Morana shook her head.

For what was worth, Kit didn't fight him. She stood ready to receive whatever punishment Death had in store. Something about that didn't sit right.

Morana saw the anger written in every line of his face, the tension in his jaw. He was going to kill her, and he didn't care.

"Matthias," she pleaded, reminded of the power the man she had married held.

He seemed to be warring with himself, but his gaze broke free, snapping back to the fae girl when she spoke.

"He lied to you," Kit said, her voice breaking. It was the first crack in her mask—a crack that revealed the sorrow painted on her soul. "The first thing he saw, his first *vision,* was his own death." Morana watched as tears gathered in her eyes, spilling slowly. "He saw himself saving you."

Morana stood, her heart breaking as the guilt of that night came crashing into her. She would have done the same thing—sold her soul for someone she cared about so deeply. Especially if it meant saving the one she loved.

Her eyes caught Matthias, who had settled more, letting go of Kit and taking a step back.

With that one moment of reprieve, Kit lunged, a dagger appearing in her hand, and her teeth clenched as she darted toward Morana.

Matthias didn't waste time. The darkness taking hold of her mind as the girl screamed, dropping to the ground, her knife hitting the floor with a loud clank.

"Say the word," Matthias said as he stared down into the girl's eyes. "Say the word, my queen."

Morana took a step forward, wrapping her hand around his bicep and feeling the anger and tension in his muscles.

He relaxed just slightly but held Kit's mind firmly within his magic. The fae girl had stopped screaming, resorting to silent tears where she knelt on the ground, gripping her stomach.

Morana's hard eyes took her in, her heart still aching from the betrayal—from Cain's death.

Could she blame her?

Cain was her only family, and now he was gone. Kit had been right about one thing. The reasoning for his death was plain. And while Willow believed the boy had made his own choices, Morana still couldn't get rid of the guilt in her chest. She didn't think she ever would.

"I don't want her to die," she whispered.

"She betrayed you," Matthias ground out, his hands trembling at his sides. "She betrayed the rulers of her court."

"She's just a kid." Heart breaking, Morana watched Kit as she lifted her eyes. The surprise was evident there.

Morana blinked back tears, remembering her father's harsh words, the pressure she'd been under to fix his problems—to save him.

And despite her deficiencies, she'd been given grace. She'd found love in this realm—peace—and she'd hoped that the scars of her past hadn't colored her in a way that was irredeemable.

Her power made her hungry for death, but in this moment—she could be something else—*choose* something else.

She longed to be a good queen.

"It's because she loved him," Morana said, certainty woven into her tone. "Send her to the dungeons. Have her watched."

Guards stepped forward, summoned by the demand and taking the girl away.

When the kitchen had cleared of the guards and the traitor, Matthias turned to her, slightly relaxed.

"Should you change your mind," he whispered low, "I have no problem seeing her put to death."

"I will let you know." Morana cleared her throat.

"You're the one she betrayed," Matthias said. "And while I long to see the light leave her eyes, I understand your reasoning." He trailed his thumb along her jaw, watching the motion with a softness to his gaze. "It is up to you," he said, "my queen."

"Matthias," she whispered, the question lingering. "Your power—" Morana grimaced, trying to formulate the words. "Is it difficult to get out of the bloodlust—once you've given in?"

He blinked. "It gets easier the longer you've had it," he admitted. "I didn't have anyone grounding me after my parents died. I wanted to make sure you didn't go through that, too."

Morana took a deep breath, closing her eyes. There were no words left—just a new understanding and a new depth to whatever connection they had. He understood. She didn't know why she hadn't realized it before.

Morana nodded once before exiting the room.

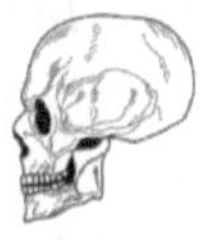

"You figured it out."

Morana spun, the temple walls surrounding her as the cold chill of The Wastelands took her breath away.

Morana looked to Raidan, recognizing the stone floor, the walls made of bone and clay. They were in one of the cells in the dungeon.

"Figured what out?" Morana asked.

She still wore the black nightgown with lace trim she'd donned before bed. When she glanced down, her brow furrowed, her mind registering that she was in a dream.

That didn't matter, though. In order for Raidan to be in her dream like this, he had to be in her mind. Just as Inara had been. And while Raidan's power didn't give him that ability, there were many relics and fae who supported him that could make it happen—especially when her guard was down.

Raidan stepped forward, amber eyes burning wherever they took in her attire. Morana's skin crawled with memories of the god's unwanted touch—the threats.

Stopping a few feet from her, he smiled, the dim lights of the dungeon casting half of his face in darkness.

"How my supporters kept getting to you, my queen."

Morana scoffed. "Your queen." She folded her arms across her chest, rolling her eyes.

"Whether you believe it or not, you belong to me."

Morana cocked a brow, the weight of the ring on her finger feeling heavy—safe. She glanced down at the stone, reminded that Matthias slept only inches away.

Fighting her mind, she tried to break free, finding herself trapped. The panic rose in her chest, her eyes snapping to Raidan's once more.

"Ah, ah," he scolded, stepping forward and running a finger over the ends of her hair. Morana recoiled, desperately wanting to escape. Her eyes were wild as Raidan

looked at her with feral delight. "You think that ring on your finger means anything to me?" he asked. "There is little you can do to stop me. The runes Matthias's lord placed around Ascella are only so strong, Morana." Anger flashed in his eyes. "I will find you. You will return to The Wastelands."

Morana's lip peeled back into a snarl. "Fuck you," she spat, taking a step backward.

Raidan's chuckle sent a chill down her spine as she broke out in a cold sweat.

"Don't insult me," Raidan said.

Thick fog rose over the cold dungeon floors, rising around them until Morana could see the Veeden break through the mist. Morana fought the dizziness in her head, the one that begged her to give in to their song.

She held her ground, reaching out with her own power, and prodding at the minds of the creatures. She hadn't had to control them since Ohriid—hadn't even seen the vile monsters since, but she was confident that she could do it again.

"Give in, Queen of Darkness."

Morana's eyes caught fire, as she felt the minds of the creatures enter her grasp. The Veeden halted.

"No." Morana's smile cut like a broken shard of glass, her tone icy.

Raidan's power rose, whispering across her skin and pulling at her strength. It took so much concentration for Morana to keep the Veeden at bay, she hardly had time to fight against him before she was firmly in Raidan's grasp.

"Kneel," he commanded.

Morana could feel the tug of power pulling her to the ground, forcing her to bow before the demon. She fought it—refused—losing some of her grip on the Veeden as they inched forward.

"Kneel," he said again, his voice rising with anger.

"No." She ground her teeth against the effort to keep herself erect. "I will only bow before my king." Morana squared her shoulders, raising her chin despite the burning in her thighs.

When Raidan's magic wrapped around her neck, Morana's magic began slipping further as that mist squeezed.

Her hands rose to her throat, desperately seeking purchase where she found none. Morana gasped, desperate for the oxygen he deprived her of.

Still, she did not bow down to him.

"Kneel!" he yelled, his magic making her knees buckle as he loosened his power on her neck.

Morana fought even as her knees came crashing to the hard floor, sending a jolt of pain through her.

She continued to fight, unable to rise under the weight of his magic. With every attempt, her legs burned more, the pain shooting through her spine and consuming her wholly.

As the Veeden continued their advance, Morana felt like a thousand knives were cutting into her flesh. She tried to rise but failed. A scream exited her lips as she fought him.

It was all too much.

Keeping the Veeden back, fighting his magic—it was all too much to manage.

Raidan had her trapped in her own mind. How, she didn't know.

"Finally," Raidan breathed. He stood so close he nearly touched her. "Now stop fighting it."

"No," Morana ground out.

Nostrils flaring, Raidan looked down at her, and somehow, she knew by the feral look in his eyes that he wouldn't relent. He would break her.

"You shouldn't be here." Darkness flooded the room with the familiar voice.

Morana longed to turn around, to catch sight of Death, but she couldn't turn. Raidan held her firmly in his grasp.

"Death," Raidan said. "Back in the dungeons for more?" he asked, cocking a brow.

The shadows swelled, and Morana found herself comforted by the darkness.

"Let go of my wife." She could hear the anger in his voice, picture the expression on his face. It was one of a king—a god.

Raidan laughed, his head tilting back as if he enjoyed the interaction. "I'll be back for her, you know."

Morana knew it to be true, and she hoped they'd be ready.

Before she could respond, his magic released her, darkness swallowing her whole.

Her eyes shot open as Morana sat up in bed. Matthias leaned over her, his hand on the side of her face and his breathing rapid.

"It's okay," she said, searching his gaze. She could tell by the look in his eyes that he didn't believe her.

"He's going to come for you." Matthias shifted closer, sweat dripping down his temple. "Kit is in the dungeons, and as far as we know, he no longer has access to the palace. He will only grow angrier."

"You're right," she responded, allowing a half smile to appear on her face. Even so, the adrenaline slowly receded. There in her mind, Morana had been afraid. "We will be ready for him. We have the dream eater—the box. Ronan is working on figuring out how to use it. We will be ready," she asserted.

Matthias nodded once; his dark eyes boring into her. "I can't lose you," he whispered.

The night lingered outside their balcony—the stars glittering above the snow-covered city. Morana swallowed, closing her eyes as the fear of losing this place—her home— rose inside her. She wouldn't let that show, though she was certain he saw it, anyway.

"You won't," she said, though she could tell it did nothing to ease their worries.

Matthias brushed his lips against hers, warm and seeking as he ran his tongue over her bottom lip.

She opened for him, gasping as he held her closer. Morana's hands rose to his chest—his shoulders—as she tried to cling to whatever she had left.

When his hand moved up her torso, thumb flicking over her hardened nipple, Morana moaned into his mouth, losing herself to the sensation.

Matthias kissed her deeply, leaning her back on the bed. And when he took her, chasing her fears to the back of her mind, she couldn't help but be reminded of all she stood to lose should she fail.

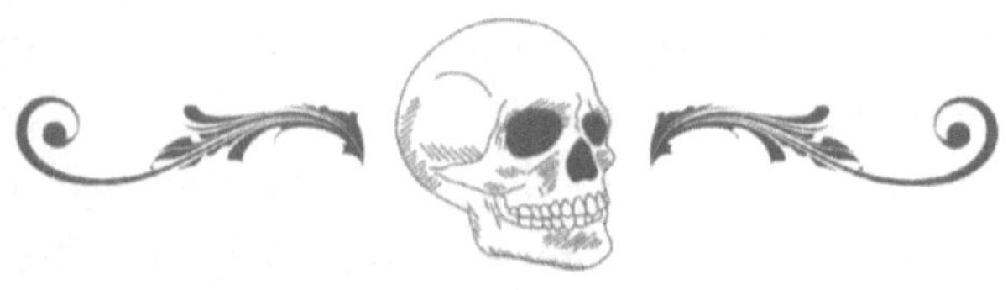

Thirty-Nine

Morana sat in the library; feet propped on the table as she stared at the box. Her eyes kept sliding to the chair across from her—empty and cold.

It had been two weeks, and they were still waiting for Ronan to track down the runes to use with the box. It was all he'd learned so far. The dream eater sat undisturbed in the dungeons with Kit to keep him company.

Morana hadn't gathered enough courage to go down and visit the girl, though she supposed time was running short. She would need to decide what they would do with her. She couldn't stay in the dungeons forever.

"Where's Matthias?"

Morana turned to see Sarnai appear through the shelves, her dress a deep purple today. The goddess offered a wan smile as her umber eyes flicked to the chair. She would know as well as anyone why Morana sat up here alone—who she was thinking about.

"The human realm," Morana answered, shoving the box into the pocket of her jacket. Pulling her feet from the table, she sat forward as Sarnai stood across the way.

The goddess looked at the chair, a million emotions flashing across her face.

"And why are you up here alone?" she asked, her voice warm. "Do you need someone to keep you company?"

Morana chuckled, squelching the sorrow in her chest. "I'm fine." She offered Sarnai a sad smile. "I am, really. Though I was thinking about visiting his sister in the dungeons."

"Are you sure that's a good idea? She tried to kill you, Morana. She could try again."

Morana cocked a brow. "You don't think I'd be able to stop her?" She pulled on her magic, weaving the mist and darkness together, allowing a crackle of light to part the shadows and fog before clearing it away.

Sarnai rolled her eyes, sitting atop the table. "What a gross show of power," she criticized. "How very like a god."

A true smile split Morana's face as she looked up at the goddess. "Like when you turned my bathroom into a forest when you learned of my engagement?"

Humor decorated her expression as Sarnai responded. "Might I remind you I too, am a god."

"Of course."

Silence stretched for a moment as Morana trailed her finger along the surface of the table.

"You're really going to go see her?" Sarnai asked.

"I need to."

"And what will you do there? Are you going to execute her? Let her go? Her bargain will remain until one of them dies. She has to remain in the dungeons until we defeat Raidan."

"There isn't a way to—"

"No." Sarnai's brows furrowed. "At least, not that I know of. We may still have a fighting chance against Raidan, though. Especially if that slut of a lord figures out what rune magic you'll need. Then we'll have both the box and the vile creature below the palace." Sarnai glanced at Morana's pocket. "Matthias told me it'll lock away some of Raidan's power."

"That's what the Basar fish showed me when I first dove into the fountain." Morana sighed, tipping her head back to look at the ceiling, the dark chandelier swaying in the dim lights. She'd spent a long time in the darkness now, found her home in it. "It would make sense," she started. "Axton used it on Matthias. Inara tried to use it on me while we were in the sewers before—" Morana swallowed against the tightening in her throat.

"Yeah." There was sorrow in Sarnai's voice, the same pain Morana had felt when she walked into this section of the library. She missed the scribe—the subtle scratch of pen on parchment—all of it.

"Well." Morana stood. Pulling her braided hair over one shoulder. "I suppose it's time to see what our prisoner is doing."

"You can count me out on that adventure," Sarnai grumbled, inspecting her nails.

"You were all too willing to come to the fauna realm with us." Morana fought the urge to chuckle. Sarnai was showing her hand all at once. The only adventure she wanted was seeing Callum, despite how she had treated him. He was clearly obsessed with the goddess.

"And that was enough adventure for me. I found myself satiated after that little excursion. Full to the point of throwing up." Sarnai refused to look up, her eyes firmly fixed on whatever was so fascinating about her fingers. "Gross god," she muttered under her breath.

"Ah," Morana said. "I see." She drew on the shadows, knowing her next comment wouldn't bode well. "Callum must be massive if he filled you up to the point of vomiting. Did you sign a waiver?"

The goddess lunged, but Morana was too quick, disappearing on a cloud of darkness before Sarnai could reach her.

As the shadows dissipated, the dungeons greeted her, illuminating her path with faefires in the sconces.

Morana heard prisoners pounding in their enclosures, begging to be let out.

She adjusted the crown on her head, stepping through the darkness until she came to the quiet cell that housed Cain's sister. She didn't dare go in, just turned and waited.

The girl appeared from the darkness, cleanly dressed and her hair tied back low on her head. She looked good—well fed, and Morana was pleased to see that she was being treated with dignity—as requested by the queen.

"You look good for a prisoner," Morana commented. Her gaze hardened. She wouldn't betray her compassion, not while a bargain still held the girl with the enemy.

"I heard someone requested the best treatment for me." Kit cleared her throat. She looked older, her features sharper, her expression less kind.

"Well," Morana offered, unsure of what else to say.

"Did our queen have anything to do with that?" Kit asked, green eyes lighted. "Shall I bow down to the woman whose life was worth the death of the only family I had?"

Morana fought the urge to flinch. She held her head high, feeling the weight of the crown atop her head.

"You needn't bow," she answered as she allowed a feral smile to stretch across her face. "Though I should remind you that my husband nearly killed you for your betrayal. It was your *queen* who spared you. It is your *queen* who keeps you clean and well fed, and it is your *queen* who will decide your fate after Raidan's death."

"You think you'll be able to kill him? Whose lives are you willing to sacrifice now, Morana? Will you kill your entire court for power?"

Morana blinked. This time, she couldn't hide the tensing of her shoulders, the way the girl's words cut through her.

Guilt crept upward, unearthed from where she had it buried in her soul. Queen or not, Morana felt helpless. Not only did she hold the weight of the crown, but the weight of all the death she'd carried since arriving in the fae realm. She'd killed—murdered. She would continue to do so to protect the home she loved.

"Enjoy your time in the dungeons," Morana said, a bite to her tone. "I'll inform you when I've made my decision."

And with that, she turned to walk away, gathering the shadows around her to pull her out of the dungeons.

"Wait."

Morana halted, turning her head slightly to listen to the girl.

"Make sure you kill him," Kit pleaded. "That bastard deserves to suffer."

There were layers to what she said—a story woven into the way she spoke the words. Morana's gut churned with the thought of what may have happened between Raidan and the girl. She knew how he was—what he could be like.

Morana nodded once, allowing the shadows to swallow her whole, spitting her back out in the hallway outside of the throne room.

There, Ronan approached her. He was breathing heavily, blue eyes shining with hope.

"I found it," he said, rushing to stop in front of her. "Matthias is on his way back. I've found the rune, but we will need to test it."

"And who are we testing it on? Me?"

Ronan shook his head. "Garian volunteered."

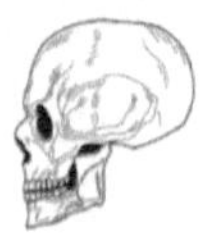

Garian stood in the center of the training room with his sword discarded on the dark mat. His stoic expression betrayed nothing as Morana and Matthias entered the room, Matthias gripping the box in his hand.

As they entered, Morana looked to see Ronan offering a casual smile. Next to him stood the blacksmith.

"I hope you don't mind," Ronan said. "She wanted to see my immense power and knowledge."

A chuckle sounded from Garian's direction, and their gazes fixed to the lord who rolled his tongue along his cheek.

"Sure," he said, voice quiet.

"You don't believe me?" Ronan asked, cocking a brow in challenge.

"Believe that you wanted to show off? I absolutely believe that." Eyes shining, Garian turned his dark gaze to Reese, a knowing look passing between the two.

Ronan turned to her, looking her over once before muttering, "traitor" and earning a laugh from her lips.

"Well," Matthias began, his deep voice calling attention. "I guess we should start."

"Right." Ronan stepped forward, a dagger in hand. He walked up to Morana, asking her for her arm. "My queen," he said, bowing low. "I promise it will only hurt for a moment."

"Why my blood?" Morana asked.

"The more powerful the blood, the more powerful the rune, of course."

"Ronan," Morana began, "are you saying that my blood is more powerful than Death's? You dare insult your king?" There was nothing serious in her voice, only a playful, teasing tone.

Matthias leaned in, his arm brushing against hers and sending warmth through her veins. "I'm not ashamed to admit you are more powerful," Matthias said, staring down at her. "Though you wouldn't know it if I hadn't showed up." He smiled at her then—beautiful and devastating.

"Not wrong," Morana answered.

"Oh gross," Ronan groaned. "Let's get on with it."

Morana offered her hand, and Ronan drew a shallow cut across her palm. She channeled the shadows, carefully stitching the wound and eradicating any pain she may have felt.

Ronan demonstrated what they should draw, a strange series of crossing lines over a circle. "Binding," Ronan said. "It's an ancient symbol for binding."

Morana nodded as Ronan came to stand behind her, wrapping one arm around her to show her how to hold the box.

"Now," he breathed, "You channel your power toward your victim, and the box will do the rest, suck in their power so they cannot access it."

"Right," Morana said, brows furrowed.

Matthias cleared his throat, standing far closer than she expected.

"Can I help you, husband?"

His lips pressed together as he looked to Ronan. "Not at all. Just making sure my sluttiest lord keeps his pelvis to himself while you're in this compromising position."

Ronan took a step back, eyes flicking warily to Reese. "I assure you," he said, "I have no interest in continuing my conquests."

"Is that so?" Morana stated, sucking on her teeth.

"Certainly."

Standing alone with the box, Morana looked to Garian, who began gathering shadows around him. They were faint, a mere whisper compared to the power that Matthias held—the power she held. But she did as Ronan told her, carefully willing the box to work.

It was painfully simple; the shadows appearing in the clear sphere at the center.

Garian looked uncomfortable, grunting once before muttering that their experiment worked.

"And now," Morana asked, "how do I give his magic back?"

Ronan smiled. "If you would like to give Garian his magic back, which is entirely up to you, you merely wipe the rune away."

Morana ran her thumb across the bloody symbol, erasing it from the glass surface as the shadows cleared.

Garian straightened, his magic returning as he appeared more settled.

The doors opened, and they all glanced at Elivira entering the room. The lord held a paper in her hand, eyes wild with delight.

"We've received a summons," she said. "The god of light has welcomed us to his court. We are to be in Ohriid by tonight."

"That sneaky fuck," Matthias whispered, and Morana looked to him, the crown on her head feeling lighter in the wake of her latest victory.

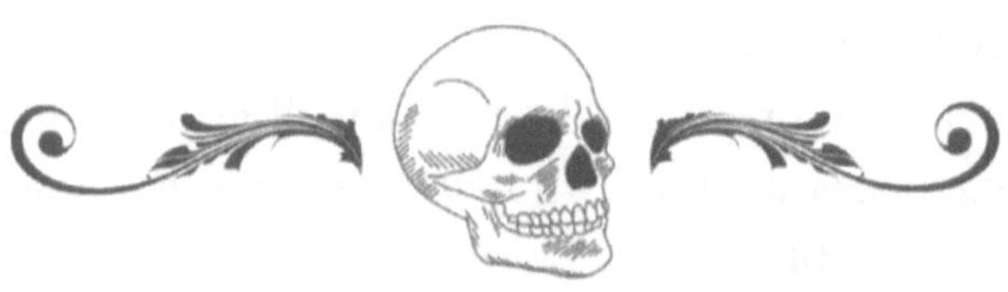

Forty

Morana stared across the long dining table stretched out before her, noting the empty chair at the end.

Matthias's warm hand resting on her thigh brought comfort, along with the lords, Garian's wife, and Sarnai in attendance.

According to Elivira, Conan had invited them to celebrate his new status as the god of life in the Court of Light. All the lords and their spouses were all invited.

Morana stared at the empty chair at the other short end of the long table where Conan should be seated. They'd been in the dining room for forty minutes—still nothing.

"You'd think he'd be here," she whispered, leaning toward Matthias.

"Maybe his status as king has inspired him to stop sneaking into rooms and taverns. Maybe he's waiting for a dramatic entrance."

Morana snorted as the doors opened behind them. Matthias turned first, a satisfied smile stretching across his face—proof of the confirmation of his theory.

When Morana glanced at Conan, she noted the crown atop his head, diamonds and yellow gems seated inside the metal. It was a direct contrast to the rubies and black stones in her own crown. The Court of Light and the Court of Shadows aligned—cordial—something that hadn't happened in centuries if her reading in the library was to be trusted.

Morana sat up, smiling as Conan walked around to his seat, dragging the wooden chair across the stone floor before seating himself. Conan casually rested his elbow on the arm of the chair, his honey-colored eyes pinned to Morana. His expression remained warm as the corners of his mouth pulled upward.

"Welcome, Queen of Shadows." Conan ran a finger along his mouth before sitting up in his seat. "Let's celebrate, shall we?'

Morana cocked a brow as Matthias's shadows stretched out to her. She let him into her mind easily enough, hearing the humor laced in his voice. *Definitely dramatic*, Matthias said, and Morana fought the urge to laugh.

Servants poured in then, carrying ornate trays filled with lamb, potatoes, carrots, and various dishes Morana couldn't recognize.

Ronan grabbed at the feast, muttering something to Garian and his wife across the table before shoveling food into his mouth.

"Congratulations," Morana finally said, loud enough to reach Conan across the table. "You'll have to tell me how events unfolded. I was quite shocked to learn of your promotion. Who could have predicted?"

Silence hung in the room as Morana and Conan stared at one another. Morana fought the smile threatening to break free. When Conan set his cup down, raising a brow before his laughter rung out in the room, she finally allowed her own grin to surface.

"You've brought your lords," Conan began. "We are in the company of friends, I should hope."

"We are," Morana confirmed. "They know."

Conan cut at the meat on his plate. "I suppose I should publicly thank you, then." He took a bite of food, looking up with warmth in his gaze. When he swallowed, he continued speaking. "If it weren't for you, I never would have—"

"What I want to know," Ronan interrupted, eyes sparkling in the light of the palace, "is not how my queen encouraged you to rule an entire court, but how you were appointed to begin with. Did you have to fight someone?"

"Always thirsty for blood," Matthias muttered.

"You're wrong," Ronan said, pointing his fork in Matthias's direction. "That's Garian. I'm always thirsty for something else, entirely."

Garian's wife, Zara, laughed, the rich sound echoing through the room. "He's not wrong."

Grimacing, Garian wrapped an arm around the back of Zara's chair, leaning in ever so slightly. "Most certainly wrong," he muttered.

Conan grabbed hold of his glass, swirling the wine before taking a sip. When he swallowed, he looked up. "No fighting," he answered. "My counselors were well aware of the power I held, and when the spot is reserved for the gods, it's difficult to argue."

"A god?" Morana cocked a brow, her tone laced with sarcasm. "What interesting and new information."

Conan chuckled as Matthias squeezed her thigh gently beneath the table. She glanced over at him, noting the light shining in his dark gaze. Her cheeks flushed, feeling his touch burning through the black dress she wore.

"We are happy to be here," Matthias finally spoke. "Happy to stand by the Court of Light's new king."

The weight of his words hung heavy in the air, their court falling silent around them.

Conan's smile fell, a serious expression shadowing his face—one that spoke of how much the compliment meant to him. It was a compliment—a damn good one considering the relations between the courts prior.

Conan swallowed once, keeping his eyes fixed to his plate. "Thank you," he said.

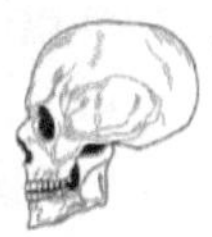

Morana smiled into her cup as Matthias leaned in to whisper in her ear, sending heat pooling at her core. His warmth washed over her as she sucked in a breath.

"I love watching you," he whispered. "Especially when you take control."

Morana swallowed the wine along with the desire clogging her throat. Everyone still sat at the table, having dined and laughed together for most of the evening. Conan's position proved beneficial when the conversation turned to the war—the box they possessed to kill Raidan.

"Careful," Morana warned. "We're still in the company of our court, husband. I don't think they'd appreciate viewing my mouth around your cock." She rolled her tongue along her cheek, feeling Matthias's gaze heat and intensify where he watched her. The laugh he released was low and dark, causing her to shift in her chair against the dampness between her thighs. If their court noticed, they didn't show it.

Matthias placed a finger under her chin, turning her head until she was looking right at him, his darkened gaze awakening the longing within her. "Why do you say that?" he asked. "I'm certainly not the only one who has noticed how pretty your mouth looks, my queen."

Morana's breath caught in her throat, the air in the room thinning as her heart picked up in her chest. Her shadows swirled around her ankles, calling to the god next to her. She wanted to leave—immediately.

"Well," she announced, clearing her throat and directing her attention toward Conan.

The god of life looked away from Ronan, a delighted smile on his lips after their conversation.

"We will need to return to our court," she said.

"Of course," Conan answered before pushing his chair back. He stood at the end of the table, ready to speak.

Something pulled in her gut, a gentle warning that drew her attention away from the God of Life.

Mist rose around them, a power familiar to her but not her own, and Morana's heart dropped. Her stomach twisting with fear as time seemed to slow around them.

The sounds of her court drowned out in the wake of her panic. She turned back, looking toward the doors as sweat beaded on her brow.

When the heavy doors flew open, Raidan's large form stalking into the room, a feral smile on his face.

"Ah, there you are," he said, his voice sending fear shooting through her veins. Morana struggled to breathe, sat frozen in the room as the monster cast amber eyes her way. "I've come for my queen."

Matthias lunged, plunging the room into darkness as magic twisted and fought for dominance.

Screams, shouts, and the sounds of metal were the only thing she heard as she tried to make her way through the fog of shadow—the lingering mist.

"How fucking dare you?" Matthias shouted.

She finally caught sight of him through the darkness, forearm pinned to Raidan's throat. The major god shoved against the wall with a smile on his face.

"I wouldn't," Raidan warmed, earning a snarl from Matthias.

"Oh," Matthias's voice was low, laced with a threat. "I fucking would."

Morana turned to catch sight of Ronan's sword drawn from its sheath at his side, plunging the weapon into a Veeden that had made its way into the room.

Conan was shouting orders, the room suddenly filled with soldiers and the sounds of battle surrounding them.

On instinct, Morana drew on the mist, felt for the minds of the creatures as she twisted her magic together. She reached out, trying to get a feel for what the demon had brought with him—the battle that had begun.

There were so many—too many.

Morana strained, forcing the Veeden back. As she bound the creatures, using all that she could, she noticed soldiers turning on one another, heard the clink of metal, and watched Garian stalk after one of the men through the halls of the palace, his wife nowhere to be seen.

Go. Matthias's voice entered her mind. *He's here for you, anyway. Go.*

She hesitated for a moment, but didn't allow the fear to linger—didn't allow anything aside from determination. She was a queen now—a god—and she would rise to the occasion.

Morana took off after Garian, finding herself in a labyrinth of hallways and corridors she didn't recognize. Her time in Ohriid had been brief, and she didn't know the palace.

A soldier lunged at her from one of the rooms, and Morana quickly drew her dagger, spinning out of the line of his blade and shoving her weapon firmly in his back.

The man's scream rang out in the hall as Morana's heart pounded. She twisted the knife, the taste of blood invading her mouth when she drew it free and shoved the lifeless soldier to the ground.

Morana looked around, trying to catch her breath—formulate a plan.

Things had just come together, but they weren't ready for this. They hadn't expected the major god here.

She hadn't brought the box with her—hadn't anticipated an attack on the palace. In fact, she was too busy enjoying their dinner. She'd hardly been ready—frozen and staring as Death pinned Raidan to the wall.

"Stupid," she muttered, heels clicking on the stone floors. Kit still resided in the dungeons; the battles still waged around her. She shouldn't have given herself so much security—shouldn't have enjoyed her time until Raidan was dead. "Fucking foolish."

Morana picked up her pace, descending a stairwell and finding a door that opened to the courtyard at the center of the palace.

Her mind spiraled as she searched for the lord she'd gone after. She tried to get a grip on what was happening, but it had all happened so quickly.

Looking at the snow-dusted ground, the cold air bit at her skin. Morana looked up, gasping as she saw harpies flying in the air above the palace courtyard. The gardens were near barren on account of the season, stretched out like a wasteland in the center of the palace. She supposed it was fitting.

When she heard a scream break through the night, Morana looked to see a harpy descending, claws firmly plunged through the back of one of the servants. Her heart clenched as she drew on her magic, feeling for the creature's mind—hoping she could stop it.

When Garian came out of nowhere, she hesitated, watching as he drew his sword. His face hardened when the lord lunched forward, the metal of his weapon broke into the harpy's back as the creature shrieked. The sound made Morana's ears ring.

When she reached out with her magic, she found more than the dying harpy. Veeden prowled through the snow-covered gardens, followed by soldiers breaking into the courtyard—no doubt looking for her.

Morana unleashed herself, magic swelling as she took as many soldiers as she could manage, plunging the light into their bodies until small fires lit the palace grounds, ominous smoke rising in the air and smelling of death and destruction. The power flooded her veins, and she relished the bloodlust. Mist floated from her body, hair whipping wildly around her face as she used it to halt the Veeden and cut down soldier after soldier.

When a soldier had crept up behind her, she felt him there, turning to plunge her dagger into his chest, the copper taste taking over her senses—her mind.

Garian was there in an instant, a warrior protecting his queen as he drove his sword forward. His weapon cut through the man, driven upward into his stomach as Garian snarled.

He grunted when he removed the metal. Slick sounds of blood and rotting flesh followed the motion, feeding Morana's hunger even more.

She lashed out with the shadows, plunging the courtyard into a darkness only she could see through. She found the minds of men, felt their fear—their determination. Morana felt the mixture of emotions—welcomed it as she shifted their sensations.

The screaming men crumpled—pain and destruction as Morana tore their minds apart just before their bodies.

When the darkness faded, only a few remained. Morana caught her breath, looking to Garian's pleased expression before he nodded toward the palace doors.

She could hear the sounds of battle echoing through the halls.

Nodding once, Morana spun, running across the blood covered ground until she re-entered the palace, greeted by a familiar face.

Kit stood in the darkened hall wearing armor, her eyes hardened and wild when they locked onto Morana, as if she'd found exactly who she was looking for.

"Queen of Shadows," Kit called, her tone mocking. "Looks like you're not much of a god after all. You couldn't even keep me locked in the palace."

Morana lunged, throwing her strength into binding the girl as Kit's eyes widened. The child had seen Morana's compassion, but she had yet to see the Queen of Darkness—a true god.

With pleasure, Morana called on her shadows, snarling and letting the darkness kiss the girl's pale skin. Kit couldn't move. Bound by magic and the ridiculous bargain she'd made with Raidan, she stood in the hallway, awaiting her demise.

Dragging her dagger from its sheath, Morana prowled forward. She could practically smell the girl's blood—longed to taste it for herself.

"Are you ready to die?" Morana asked. She got close enough to touch, but Kit could do nothing. Morana held the dagger up, slowly dragging it across Kit's cheek to release a steady drip of blood.

Watching the wound, Morana halted, her magic pausing in its consuming destruction. Her hand rose to her cheek, a reminder of death—of truth.

She'd wanted to save the girl—wanted to extend compassion—to remain as much a human as she could. And now, Kit stood before her—a traitor through and through.

"I wanted to save you," Morana admitted, her tone hard.

The girl's eyes were wild as she stood in place, a smile lifting one corner of her mouth. "Well," Kit said, her tone manic. "Some of us aren't worth saving." She spat, blood decorating the stone floors below.

Morana swallowed, tightening her grip on her weapon and trying to keep a grip on her power—her bloodlust. Matthias wasn't around to ground her—not this time, anyway.

The look in Kit's eyes—the hopelessness—reminded Morana of feelings she had had. With the mist surrounding them, Morana kept her gaze locked. Cain had died to save his queen, a sacrifice Morana wasn't sure would be worth it, but she desperately wanted to prove him right—do the right thing. "I used to believe that about myself," she admitted, "but it's not true."

Kit laughed—a hollow sound. "Well," she said. "It's too late anyhow."

Morana didn't hesitate, shoving her dagger into Kit's gut, feeling the way the girl stumbled back, her body going limp at the release of Morana's magic.

"See," Kit said, her voice now weaker than before.

Morana held her gaze, seeing so much of her own pain there. The girl had walked through the death of her only family member—the abuse. She felt alone in the world.

The reality of that cut deep. Morana had believed there was hope for her.

"I'm sorry," she whispered, dragging the dagger from her gut and letting the girl fall to the floor.

Morana turned, wiping a tear away, and headed towards the courtyard.

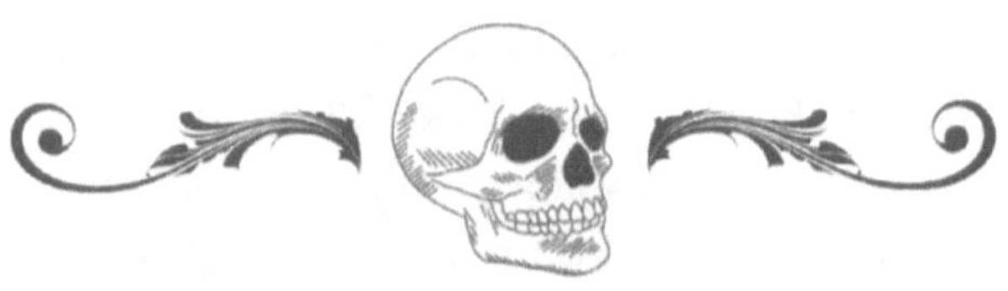

Forty-One

The air smelled of blood and death.

Morana re-entered the courtyard, looking at the red snow, stained with blood and ash. Even the sky darkened with the smoke of what she'd done.

She still needed to find Raidan—still needed to get to Matthias and figure out how to retrieve the box from their court. There were too many things to think of—too many ways they had come unprepared.

Garian stood at the far end of the garden, his wife running through the opposite doors to join him.

Breathing a sigh of relief, Morana watched as Zara broke into a sprint, throwing herself at the lord.

Garian caught her, the battle still waging just behind the walls of the palace.

They needed to go—to move.

Exhaustion weighed heavily on her bones when Morana walked to them, Zara breaking away from her husband and bowing to the queen.

Garian stepped back, offering a bow of his own.

"I killed her," Morana confessed. "Kit is gone." She gathered her emotions, hardened herself against the sorrow—if only long enough to complete their task. "We need to find Matthias. We need to—"

A shriek sounded behind her. When Morana turned, she watched as a harpy came careening from the sky above, claws stretched toward them and ready to kill.

Before she could react—draw on her power, Garian shadowed in front of her, driving his sword forward into the beast with a growl.

His dark skin was painted with blood and dirt, the remnants of a battle well-fought.

When the harpy fell to the ground, Garian turned, taking in Morana's shocked expression.

"My queen," he whispered. "Are you—"

The loud shrill of another descending harpy cut him off. The creature's claw met its target, embedding itself into Garian's back deep enough to kill.

Morana screamed, pain lashing through her chest as an anguished scream broke through the air.

The sound hadn't come from her, though.

When Morana looked behind her, she saw Garian's wife, running with tears streaking her face. Her panicked sobs were the only leftover sound in the night as Morana grabbed hold of the harpy with her magic, burning it until it was only charred ash.

Time slowed, and Morana found herself frozen, the darkness around them deepening as the smoke receded to reveal stars peeking through the mist.

Zara kneeled, hunched over her husband's body and pleading to any god that would listen to save him.

Her chest tightened, tears leaking from her eyes.

Whose lives are you willing to sacrifice now, Morana? Will you kill your entire court for power?

Zara sobbed, almost praying as Garian's blood coated her gown.

During what felt like a lifetime ago, Morana might have believed in a god who would listen.

But now, she knew the truth of gods. She knew the humanity and weight they carried—the limits to their power. She stared helplessly at the broken woman and allowed her tears to fall; the pain carving itself in her bones, scarring the marrow—a permanent mark on her soul.

"Please," Zara begged, her voice cracking. "Do something."

Morana shook her head, her own tears falling faster, blurring the vision of the desperate woman. "I can't, I—" her voice broke off—hopeless.

"Please!" she shouted. "I'm begging you, Morana. Please try."

Morana closed her eyes, the steady stream of tears tracking down her cheeks, her heart breaking in her chest.

Whose lives are you willing to sacrifice now, Morana? Will you kill your entire court for power?

The voices echoed in her mind, ripping her soul to shreds.

Like mother, like daughter.

Morana gasped, watching the broken woman as her face twisted—the hope leaving her eyes—the light winking out.

"Too much death," Morana whispered, certain that her chest would cave in.

"You saw something else, too?" she asked.

"One of the lords," he answered. "I can't tell you which one, but he was standing at the bank of a river, watching a woman wash her clothes in the water."

"What does that even mean?"

Cain shrugged, picking up his pen and placing it back on the paper. "I haven't figured it out yet."

It was all too much. Morana had watched so many die. The man at the shooting range, Axton, his grandfather. She'd watched Cain, Inara—servants she'd murdered in cold blood.

It all came back to her—the death killing her soul right along with the lord who had trained her.

He was gone—there was nothing she could do.

No.

Rage bubbled with the sadness in her chest, rising like the tide as she moved forward, calling the shadows.

She didn't know if it was possible—if she could heal something like this. She knew it would drain her power, leaving her vulnerable for whatever awaited them in the palace, but she had to try.

Morana closed her eyes, grasping Garian's hand, cold where it lay limp in the snow.

Memories flashed in her mind, every death she'd caused—every horrible thing she'd caused because of her power, her sorrow, flashed like a movie.

Dragging the shadows around them, Morana plunged them all in darkness, feeding her magic forward, trying to stitch together the wound across Garian's back.

Blood—so much blood—coated the ground, seeping through the skirts of her gown where she kneeled. She didn't know if it would work—thought it would be useless.

"Please," Zara muttered, her soft sobs breaking Morana's heart further.

Morana felt dizzy against the amount of power she drew, but she didn't stop. She pictured Garian in front of them, body whole. She pictured the slight tick of his jaw when he was amused—the way he'd pushed her in training.

When her soul felt hollow—the memories fading from her mind, Morana looked to the man still on the ground, face down in the snow—his body cold and unmoving.

She shook her head, tears still streaming down her cheeks—cold in the wake of the winter wind.

"I'm sorry," she whispered, though she knew it wasn't enough.

A sound broke from Zara's lips, the sorrow tangible in the night air.

Nobody else existed in the courtyard aside from them. The dead bodies around them, the fallen soldiers, the dead harpy Garian had slayed—none of that mattered.

"I'm sorry," Morana repeated.

A gasp sounded, and Morana looked to Zara, expecting another sob, but when she looked to the woman, her eyes were wide, staring down at her dead husband.

Morana's heart pounded in her chest. The night silent around them as she looked to Garian rolling onto his back, his mouth open, eyes staring at the night sky around them.

He looked over, his voice scratching around the edges, his wife still frozen in place. "Acting like a god there, my queen," he croaked.

Zara fell into his arms, coated in blood and dirt as he held her.

Stunned, Morana stood, her body swaying, her magic drained.

"I need to go," she whispered, her mind fixing on Raidan.

Garian nodded, his arms wrapped firmly around his wife.

Walking out of the courtyard, Morana could feel the emptiness in her chest, the lack of power—the exhaustion. It reflected the emptiness of the palace—creatures and soldiers now missing and gone.

She stumbled into the dining room, finding it empty. The table and chairs turned over and the absence of shadows.

Tripping over one of the plates, Morana found herself kneeling on the ground, her eyes heavy, her limbs weak.

She'd never used that much power before—never called on that amount of magic at once.

Footsteps sounded by the door, but she couldn't look up. She knew from the unsettled feeling in her gut who had arrived.

"Whored yourself out to Death," he said, stopping so that Morana caught sight of the black shoes in front of her. "It means nothing."

Morana slowly looked up, anger still stirring despite her exhaustion. Her lip peeled back when her eyes met his, the taunting expression on his face.

"Are you here to take me?" she asked, her voice cold.

Raidan laughed, kneeling and placing a finger under her chin. The touch made her skin crawl, dragging memories from the darkest corners of her mind.

"Oh no," he chided. "I'm here to kill you."

Morana stared him down, grinding her teeth together—her rage like a beast set free.

"I'd like to see you try."

There was no fight left in her—not truly. Once, she had feared the consuming power of her own magic. And now, she saw how depleted it could become—how weak gods could truly be—how weak she could be.

She'd given it all to save Garian—the same way Cain had given it all to save her.

It was worth it, and if she should die here on the floor of a palace that didn't belong to her—so be it.

Darkness surrounded them, Matthias storming through the shadows as he made his way toward Raidan.

"I suggest you back away from my *wife,*" he snarled.

Morana caught sight of the object he held; the box grasped firmly in his hand. White mist began to fill the sphere, and Raidan's smile fell. His face twisted as he caught sight of the object, and the runes painted in blood—blood that wasn't hers.

It was a risk—but she trusted Death despite.

"Where did you get that?" Raidan asked, panic clear in his voice.

Morana smiled, still kneeling amid the mess of the dining hall.

"You should know," she said as Raidan stumbled back, the life and magic draining from his face. "He got it from your worst enemy." Raidan fell to the ground, looking less like a monster and more like a weak man—one desperate for any kind of control.

"I got it," Matthias began, "from the Queen of Darkness."

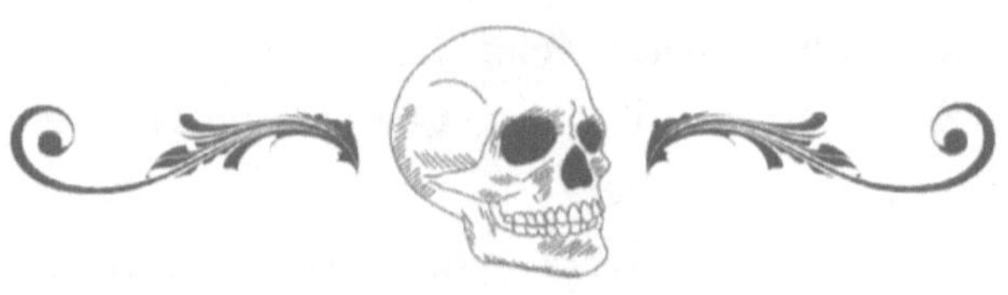

Forty-Two

Sitting atop the throne, Morana looked down at the empty room, the dark closed doors looming in the distance, awaiting their guest.

She ran a finger over her lip, pondering what would happen as nerves fluttered in her stomach.

"You look concerned," Matthias said from where he sat next to her, seated on a gilded throne of his own. He looked like a king, his shadows twisting around him, the crown placed carefully on his head. Morana glanced at the tattooed hand gripping the arm of his throne, fingers clasped painfully around the piece of furniture.

She huffed a laugh. "So do you."

He didn't deny it. Merely pulled the relic from beside the throne, holding the box up to reveal the white mist floating around the center—Raidan's power locked away tightly.

"You're sure that will hold?" Morana asked. She tried to keep her voice steady, but her nerves betrayed her.

"Ronan insists," Matthias answered. He leaned forward, resting his elbows on his knees as he inspected the box, his black button-up pulling across his back as he shifted.

When Death turned to look at her, his dark eyes softened. "You don't have to do this, you know." Matthias cleared his throat. "You've done enough already. I can handle Raidan."

"I want to," Morana interrupted. The statement rushed out of her. "Besides," she said, a small smirk forming at one corner of her mouth. "I am queen, after all. This will be my first execution."

"Second," Matthias corrected. "Though even then, the title was yours. It's only ever been yours."

Morana's throat tightened, the emotions rising as she heard the creaking of the doors overhead.

Ronan and Hames dragged the prisoner in with chains around his wrists and ankles. Raidan looked pale, his eyes dull and hair matted. It satisfied the part of her that still lingered in his dungeons. But being this close?

When his eyes met hers, Morana fought the urge to tense. Rage boiled in her chest, begging her to end the monster of The Wastelands, but she sat still.

Matthias stood next to her, slowly stepping down from the dais with his focus fixed to the demon in the room. His shadows swirled, twisting and promising retribution.

"Raidan," Matthias spoke, his tone cold.

The major god's attention fixed to the box in Matthias's tattooed hand. The growl that left his lips was pitiful.

Morana chuckled at the sound, watching as Hames and Ronan stood with a firm grip on the weak man in the room. That's all he had ever been. Raidan had spent his time seeking power beyond what he already had running through his veins.

It seemed unfair that a man like that would be given the power of a god. Then again, it seemed unfair that Morana sat upon a throne, a queen over the fae—a god in the very same realm.

"It's nice to see you," Matthias continued, stepping closer as the darkness surrounded them. "I would like this to have been much longer, but under the circumstances, we will need to make this quick."

They were plunged into the shadows, and Morana saw nothing from where she sat. She only heard the ear-piercing screams of Raidan's suffering—a sound that had a slow smile stretching across her face. It was retribution of his own.

She kept her eyes fixed ahead, awaiting her turn to deal with the god—to repay him for all the sorrow he had put her through.

When the shadows cleared, Morana watched Ronan and Hames's hardened expression—saw the bleeding and broken prisoner slumped onto the floor between them.

Matthias's back was to her, but his voice rang out loud enough for her to hear.

"If you think I'm vicious," he said, "wait until you meet my wife."

Turning on his heel, Matthias made his way back to up the dais. He sat down on the throne next to her and casting her a knowing look—one that reminded her of the plan—all they'd discussed.

Morana could feel her power buzzing in her veins— begging to be used.

"Raidan," Matthias spoke, his voice commanding as the major god looked up, utterly broken. "May I present Morana, Queen of Darkness, Ruler of the Court of Shadows." Morana felt the whisper of his magic across her cheek—a gentle caress. "My wife," he finished.

The fear in Raidan's eyes sent a thrill through her, a reminder that the suffering would end.

Too many people had died on account of the war— in the pursuit of power, and Morana was ready for it all to cease. If she did anything as queen—if she could leave a mark on the fae realm at all—it would be this. To finish the task her mother failed to complete.

Like mother, like daughter.

Or not.

Morana stood, her heels clicking on the steps, her dress twisting around her legs as she descended the dais.

Raidan snarled, thrashing against his chains as they clanked on the dark floors of the palace. Morana didn't flinch, her hands steady at her sides as she made her way to stand directly in front of him, one hand behind her back.

"Having your power locked away makes you almost human," she taunted, tilting her head to the side. "Far too easy to kill, Raidan." Morana didn't miss the fear in his amber eyes. "You kept that box so close. No one would ever think to use it against you, but I guess you were wrong. The moment Inara died at my hand; I knew I had obtained something special."

Raidan had stopped thrashing, staring up at her with his teeth bared and sweat dripping down his brow.

"I think it would be quite entertaining to see a major god killed with a human weapon," Morana said, turning briefly to look at her husband, still seated on the throne. "Don't you think, Matthias?"

"You wouldn't dare." There was a gravel to Raidan's voice—a dryness that spoke of the days he'd spent beneath the palace, locked away with the dream eater—tortured by his own fears. Morana was thankful they'd obtained the creature—were able to use it to subdue him after Raidan had been captured.

"That's where you're wrong," Morana answered, leaning down until her eyes were level with his. He fought forward, but Hames grunted and pulled him back, keeping the monster a careful distance away. "Of course, I'm going to kill you, Raidan." Morana smiled, enjoying the pain she saw flicker across his face. "I'm married to Death, after all."

Morana stepped back, pulling the gun from behind her and placing it in front of the god's head. She didn't hesitate—didn't blink as she watched Raidan's demise with a grim satisfaction.

Morana turned, leaving his dead body on the floor.

Her heels clicked as she walked up the steps, her black dress dragging behind her. She lowered herself onto the throne. This time, she watched as Ronan carried the body from the room, dragging the mangled flesh across the obsidian floors before Ronan shadowed the god away.

Morana looked to Matthias as he watched the same scene, knowing for certain she was no longer afraid of Death.

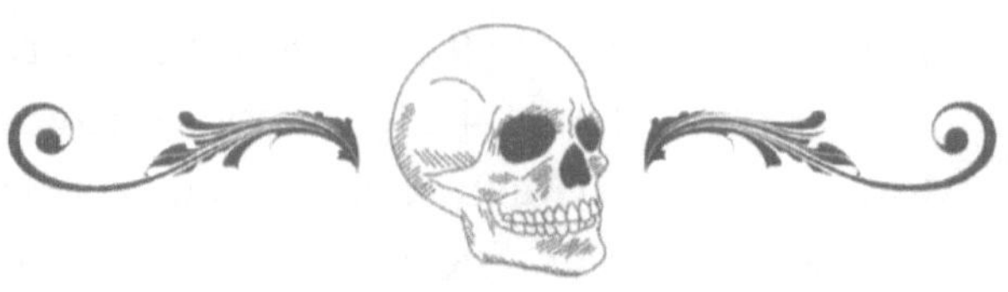

Epilogue

Elivira buried the box outside of Namid, deep in the forest, while Ronan worked to secure the object with rune magic.

Morana didn't know if it would be enough but destroying the relic hadn't worked. Hiding it in the hall of relics within Matthias's other palace wouldn't work either. Axton had gotten into that castle easily enough. At least this way, it wasn't hidden in an obvious place. They hadn't even told Conan about it.

Callum had been thankful for the dream eater's return, the monster now housed within the belly of a stone dragon decorating the entrance of the island. Sarnai had insinuated that Callum was compensating, but Morana wasn't so sure, noting the blush on the goddess's cheeks when she made the joke.

Morana sat on the throne, remembering the last time she'd perched herself in a similar position, awaiting the death of the god to the north, saving the fae realm from a monster's power.

This time, a party carried on, fae dancing and celebrating with the members of their court—of her home.

Matthias's warm hand rested on her bare shoulder, his thumb rubbing circles on her flesh and sending warmth washing over her.

He leaned down, his lips brushing her ear and causing her to shudder. In all their time since the end of the war, she hadn't grown tired of his touch—his care. Matthias had taken her through the city, brought her on rides through the forests in Namid. He'd shown her what she had been missing—the piece of happy she hadn't had before.

"You look magnificent tonight," he whispered, gently nipping at her ear.

Morana rolled her head to the side, letting out a breathy chuckle as she crossed her legs, squeezing her thighs together to relieve the pressure.

With his other hand, Matthias presented a goblet of wine in front of her. She took it, dragging a long sip of the sweet liquid. She kept her eyes forward where she caught sight of Reese standing at the far corner of the room, Ronan quickly approaching with a determined look on his face.

"Ah," Morana said, tilting her cup in their direction. "Look at that."

"Well, thank the gods you stopped getting in the way," Matthias teased.

Morana looked up, catching the wicked glint in his eye as he looked down at her, his hand still placed on her shoulder.

"That was rude," she said before rolling her tongue along her cheek, fighting the grin threatening to break free.

"It's not the only rude thing this mouth can do."

Morana cocked a brow, watching his dark eyes trail down her throat, her chest, and back.

"Is that a promise?" she asked.

Matthias leaned down again, placing a slow kiss to her mouth, pulling at her lip with his teeth before breaking away. "Most certainly."

Morana licked her lips, desperately trying to steady her breathing.

"Where's Sarnai?" she asked.

"Gone."

Her brow furrowed as she turned to look out at the crowd, scanning to find the goddess.

"She was here earlier," Morana said. "Where could she have gone to?"

Matthias's dark chuckle sounded above her. "No clue, but you'll never believe who else is missing from our party, my queen."

Morana looked out over her court, desperately trying to figure it out before the thought hit her.

"Oh gods," she whispered.

"Don't say that," Matthias scolded. "It's only making me think of other circumstances in which you would whisper those words to me."

Morana's cheeks flushed.

"And how do you feel tonight, my wife?"

Morana flicked an invisible piece of lint off her gown, keeping her eyes lowered as desire coursed through her blood. "Like we should leave our own celebration early," she said.

Matthias was close again, his hot breath ghosting over her shoulder as she fought the urge to moan. Morana tilted her head to the side, her entire body burning.

"You think?" he asked, his voice low.

"Yes." Her voice was breathless.

"Mmm." Matthias dragged his soft lips over her shoulder, his hand running down her arm. "Are you feeling anything else?" he said.

Morana thought for a moment, looking out as the fae drank and danced around them. Her eyes cut to where Ronan and Reese were spinning around the dance floor. A smile plastered to the blacksmith's face, and Ronan's blue eyes glittered in the light of the faefires.

Letting the shadows float down her arms, Morana directed the power to Matthias next to her, running that magic up his legs—higher.

"Careful," he warned.

"I suppose I'm feeling one more thing," she said, licking her lips before answering. "I'm feeling powerful."

ACKNOWLEDGMENTS

This part of the book is always difficult for me. Even so, I have some really important people to thank.

The Light Conquering has been the most difficult book I've ever written. It's taken the longest, required the most amount of care, and was written during major life changes. I found myself grappling with where I wanted the trilogy to end, and I really struggled to trust myself to write this book.

With all of that being said, there is one person who truly made all the difference in this book. My friend and editor, Kenna, never once doubted me. I could go on and on about who she is as a human being, but we simply don't have enough pages because I ordered the cover before I got a final page count.

Kenna, you believed in me, Morana, Matthias, this story. I cannot thank you enough for the hour-long phone call where I realized Matthias had the depth of a thin sheet of paper. Thank you for helping me build these characters and tell this story. I'm so glad this book is coming out on your birthday. You deserve it.

I want to thank my dear friend, Wednesday. Even though you loathe Morana with your entire chest, you still encouraged me and listened to my struggle. I'd tell you how much it meant to me, but I know you don't like feelings.

I want to thank my friend and narrator, Ali. Thank you for your encouragement, too. You were always a safe space to realize I didn't know what the fuck I was doing. You believed in me anyway.

Thank you to the ARC readers who have traveled through the entire series. Janene, Taylor, Katalyn, Mckayla,

Nicole, Cherise, Lara and anyone I may be missing (I'm panicking about forgetting people here). You all stuck with me through this story, and I cannot express how much that meant to me. (Jesus Christ, if I forget someone here, I'm going to cry. Send me hate mail if I forgot you).

Thank you, Kera and Becca, for your encouragement and absolutely amazing content on TikTok.

I want to thank my husband for his support in this dream of mine, and his inspiration for some of the best scenes in this book. The funny thing is he never reads my acknowledgments, so he will have no idea this is here, and we can all laugh at him together.

Thank you to *Florin* coffee in Columbus, Ohio for fueling the writing of this manuscript. Your caramel lattes are the best around.

I want to thank Garian for staying alive. I was hella scared there for a second. In a previous version of this book, we lost you. I'm glad we didn't.

Finally, thank you to anyone who reads this book. I couldn't do this without you.

ABOUT THE AUTHOR

Emma Steinbrecher is a New Adult Fantasy author who also writes under the name Emmie J. Holland for her New Adult Romantic Comedy books.

She lives in Ohio with her two dogs, her son, and her husband.

When she is not writing, she enjoys hiking, learning new hobbies, and reading.

If you're anxious to read any of her other works, here is a list of the books.

A Clan of Wolves Duology
A Clan of Wolves by Emma Steinbrecher (Book 1)
A House of Witches by Emma Steinbrecher (Book 2)

Romantic Comedy Stand-Alone Books
The Unbelievable Misadventures of Olive Finch by Emmie J. Holland
Pride, Pancakes, & Paris by Emmie J. Holland

The Death Hunting Trilogy
The Death Hunting by Emma Steinbrecher (Book 1)
The Raidan Awakening by Emma Steinbrecher (Book 2)
The Light Conquering by Emma Steinbrecher (Book 3)

Novellas
The Queen's Guide to Teapots and Pastries by Emma Steinbrecher

AUTHOR WEBSITE

Don't forget to check out Emma's website for signed books, exclusive content, and a newsletter that is literally so inconsistent, it won't bother you at all. You can, however, get first dibs on ARC sign-ups and other announcements through the newsletter, so it *is* worth something.

www.ingramcontent.com/pod-product-compliance
Lightning Source LLC
Chambersburg PA
CBHW022019300726

48970CB00003B/953